Born in London in 1966, Laure
at university and then worked a
other publications – the New Sta
The Observer and Lime Lizard, a much mourned indie
music magazine.

Lauren now
and, when n
novel, *Chaine*

Together v
girls-behaving
website maga
www.tartcity.

Furth

'Lauren Hend
a thoroughly e
tically sexy w
Times Metro

'Camden Tov
. . . this lady h
kind of "alte
laugh.'
Francis Fyfiel

'Sam Jones is
ness, quick re
fresh antidote
some of today
The Times

[illegible] Lauren Henderson read English [illegible] and then worked as a journalist for – among other publications – the New Statesman, Marxism Today, The [illegible] [illegible] now divides her time between Italy and London and, when not eating pasta, writes full-time. Her sixth novel, [illegible] is published by Hutchinson. [illegible] Stella Duffy [illegible] writers, Lauren has set up a writing [illegible], Tart Noir, which can be visited at [illegible].com.

[illegible] praise for Lauren Henderson and *The Strawberry Tattoo*

'Lauren Henderson's feisty sculptress heroine Sam Jones is a [illegible] engaging, totally modern sleuth [illegible] with a way [illegible] self-deprecating [illegible]'

'[illegible] Henderson [illegible] Sam Jones really strut her stuff [illegible] has the kind of style and chutzpah of the [illegible] "alternative" comedian who actually makes you laugh'

[illegible], Mail on Sunday

'[illegible] a breathless romp of charming [illegible] quick repartee and impulsive conduct, a lively and [illegible] antidote to the sometimes over-serious attitudes of [illegible] women of detection'

'Sam Jones, the funkiest detective on the block'
Daily Mail

'Henderson is the dominatrix of the crime scene, capable of provoking laughter even as she inflicts pain on her characters.'
Time Out

'Leads the pack of . . . girls behaving badly crime writers.'
Mike Ripley, *Books Magazine*

'Sam Jones shows herself to be an opinionated, sexy, courageous and delightful heroine. If there were more young crime writers of Lauren Henderson's calibre, the future of the genre would be a lot more assured than it is.'
Marcel Berlins, *The Times*

'Sam is definitely a heroine for the new millennium. Lauren Henderson's books about Sam bubble with energy and wit.'
Evening Standard

'Lauren Henderson makes acute and witty observations about New York and New Yorkers . . . the descriptions are so wonderfully vivid that you can genuinely see each one . . . All this is done with an enviable economy of words.'
Shots

By the same author

DEAD WHITE FEMALE
TOO MANY BLONDES
THE BLACK RUBBER DRESS
FREEZE MY MARGARITA
CHAINED!

the strawberry tattoo

Lauren Henderson

ARROW

Published in the United Kingdom in 2000 by
Arrow Books

5 7 9 10 8 6 4

First published in the United Kingdom in 1999 by Hutchinson

Arrow Books
The Random House Group Limited
20 Vauxhall Bridge Road, London SW1V 2SA

Random House Australia (Pty) Limited
20 Alfred Street, Milsons Point, Sydney,
New South Wales 2061, Australia

Random House New Zealand Limited
18 Poland Road, Glenfield
Auckland 10, New Zealand

Random House (Pty) Limited
Endulini, 5A Jubilee Road, Parktown 2193, South Africa

The Random House Group Limited Reg. No. 954009

www.randomhouse.co.uk

A CIP catalogue record for this book is available
from the British Library

Papers used by Random House are natural, recyclable
products made from wood grown in sustainable forests.
The manufacturing processes conform to the environmental
regulations of the country of origin

Typeset by Deltatype Ltd, Birkenhead, Merseyside
Printed and bound in Great Britain by
Bookmarque Ltd, Croydon, Surrey

ISBN 0 09 927843 X

To Manhattan. I bloody love the place.

ACKNOWLEDGEMENTS

With huge thanks to all the New York posse who so nobly kept me company on the various bar crawls, gorge-fests and clubbing required by the demands of research. Bini and Francis, the Elizabeth Taylor and Richard Burton of the Village; Aaron – Mr Connected; Katrien; Tia; Kelle; Gay, the blading queen; and everyone else who took me to parties and did their best to keep me amused. Special gratitude to Angela Westwater of Sperone Westwater, who kindly answered lots of obvious questions without sneering at me, and to Andy and Kay for putting me in touch with her. Big thanks to Adrian, who couldn't do a better job as a publicist if I paid him in hard cash rather than sun-dried tomatoes, and to Margot and Sandy for their editorial comments. Lois and Michelle, you have really lovely flats. Apartments. And thanks, on that subject, to my New York dialogue coach.

CHAPTER ONE

There was a boy in it. As so often. He was very handsome and he was staring at me with flattering concentration.

I was enjoying this immoderately.

He was dark, which in general I prefer, with big dark eyes and full, pouty lips. But mainly I noticed his eyelashes. They were very long, and he was standing so close to me that I could almost feel the gentle whisper against my skin as he lowered them. He was looking at something below my line of vision, pointing at it urgently; I bent over to see what it was, rather reluctantly, because I wanted to go on looking at him instead. But all I could see was white, a shiny white surface stretching away into the distance, and I had no idea what I was supposed to be searching for. He was speaking, but despite the fact that he was pressed up against me, I could hardly hear him. I pulled back a little and was struck again by how dark his eyes were, how wide . . . .

We were in a tiny narrow room, the walls painted a dull dirty yellow, flaking and peeling so badly I thought of something funny to say about them and then didn't. That kind of restraint is highly unusual for me, and I started to wonder if I were feeling all right. But I was promptly distracted by a more pressing problem. Literally: the room was closing in on us, exactly like that scene from *Star Wars* where Luke Skywalker, Han Solo and Princess Leia are trapped in the rubbish compactor on the Death Star. Suddenly we were braced against the walls, desperately straining every muscle to keep them from compressing us down into pulp. I looked around for the hairy one – what was his name? Chewbacca – to help, but he wasn't around.

'Quick, you call him!' I said to the boy. 'He might come for you. He's very hairy, you know.'

But he didn't know what I was talking about, and he started to bat his eyelashes, and suddenly such a gale blew up that the walls fell away and we were floating, caught helplessly by different multi-coloured whirlpools and sucked down into their hearts, our limbs flung out by the wind. It was like being dragged into the opening titles of *Charlie's Angels*. For a moment I saw us both, thrown apart, our silhouettes, black against the bright primary swirls of colour, dwindling into their centres . . . .

'Goodness,' I said. 'This has gone very Seventies all of a sudden.'

And then I woke up.

★ ★ ★

My eyes opened and I knew with absolute conviction that I had recently done something very, very bad indeed. It was one of those nebulous sensations where your brain, already clouded by heavy mists of alcohol and various chemical substances, struggles simultaneously to retrieve the information and shove it into the deepest darkest pigeonhole at the back of the skull. Unfortunately there was so much stuff in there already that this latest atrocity wouldn't quite fit.

Damn. I could still feel it hovering in skull hyperspace. I sat up slightly, propping some pillows behind me, rather surprised that I wasn't feeling suicidal with pain at the change of position. Oh, that's right. Class A drugs. Always great for cancelling out the worst symptoms of the morning after. Which was another reason I wasn't suffering too much physically: it was past two in the afternoon. People who complain about hangovers are always the ones who have to get up for work. I recommend simply cutting out the last part and sleeping through it instead. But then I can. I haven't had a proper job for so long I can't remember when.

By now the mental torment had cranked itself up several gears and was giving of its best. I was still unable to remember the precise character of the abomination against nature I had committed, and the frustration was growing unbearable. As usual, I would rather know the worst than be tortured by endless speculation. That was me all over. Open the box even if the cat's dead. At least that way you know what the score is.

Oh God, what if I didn't manage to remember what I did last night without help? I shuddered, perfectly aware that blackouts were one of the main signs of alcoholism. Like most people who drink with gusto, I had lists of these memorised from various magazines, with the ones that didn't apply to me picked out reassuringly in mental highlighter. No, I didn't have blackouts (well, not if I could remember what happened last night under my own steam, I didn't); friends of mine had never said they were worried about my intake (not being hypocrites); and, um, it didn't impair my ability to do my job. Such as it was. Somehow the lists never included vomiting in your sleep, which I found perplexing. A friend of mine from art school did this once – it was spectacular, in a perverse, Tarantino-esque kind of way – and it had always remained for me pretty much the benchmark for when you were entering I Have A Problem territory.

In any case I would rather die than ring anyone who had been present last night and pump them for information. Hah! I thought triumphantly, effortlessly accessing that file. At least I knew who I'd been out with, which was a start. An embarrassing start, because it had been a group of young British artists, or yBas, a shorthand now adopted by some of the more fashionable art critics, and one I loathed. The sooner it was cancelled off the face of the earth the better. Not to mention some of the more pretentious antics indulged in by the leading yBas themselves.

That was a thought. Could I have put theory into practice and murdered some young British artists? I perked up immediately, toying with a series of exciting possibilities. Maybe I'd sawed someone in half and pickled him in a giant fish tank – or knocked someone else over the head and videoed her in a coma for an hour – or shoved yet another into a vat of concrete and let it set, then cracked it open and removed her, leaving only the space she'd made (*deeply* significant) . . . . My own fate would be easy enough to work out: strung up on a chain like one of my own mobiles with lots of silver-sprayed ivy coming out of my mouth. Less meaningful, but then I wasn't a conceptualist. And I wasn't a young British artist except in the literal meaning of the word. I didn't compact images of myself down into a garbage bag, or paint all the names of men I'd failed to get off with over gallery walls, or make fountains of chocolate that looked like rather dribbly poo. (Though actually I'd loved the chocolate fountains.)

I was pretty damn unfashionable, actually. Which was why it had surprised me when, just after a joint exhibition I and some other not-at-all-shocking bods had done at a Kunsthalle in Germany, a very well known New York gallery owner called Carol Bergmann had asked me to take part in another group show she was organising in October. It was to be called 'Two By Four: Works by Young British Artists'. But it was in New York. For that I bowed my head and let her hang the yBa label round my neck.

Besides all the other obvious advantages of the place, my best and oldest friend – practically my adopted sister – had gone to live in New York more than ten years ago, leaving me a painting as a farewell gift. I hadn't had a word from her since. As soon as the trip had been suggested, a vision had popped into my mind of Kim's face as she turned to wave goodbye at Heathrow passport control, and a sharp pang in my gut had indicated how much I still missed her. On arrival I fully intended to hunt her down like a dog.

(One of my New Year's resolutions was to give up saying gnomically, 'If I had only known how things would turn out . . . '. So I shall bite my tongue at this point. It probably wouldn't have made that much difference in any event. People would still have died. And people die wherever I go – I'm more or less Miss Marple crossed with weedkiller – so staying at home would have made two sets of murders instead of one. Considered in that light, going to New York had been the right decision.)

Anyway, that was what I had been doing last night. I had gone out for drinks with the other three yBas who were providing two works each for the exhibition. (Two By Four. It was a pun. If this were a sample of Carol Bergmann's ready wit we were in for a non-stop laugh-fest in the States.) Most of them knew each other already to some degree, having all been at Camberwell and thus forming part of that neatly connected mafia, and I had bumped into one or two at various arty bashes: but still, a formal bonding session seemed like a good idea.

I flashed back to the pub on Curtain Road; it would be Curtain Road, wouldn't it, just as later on we had gone to the drum and bass night in Hoxton Square. It was as if we had wanted to fulfil the yBa stereotype that the Old Street roundabout was the centre of the known universe. Feature writers made it sound as if the caffs down Old Street were the Nineties equivalent of the Algonquin Round Table. It was a surprise that *Hello!* hadn't taken some photos yet for their society pages. 'Mr Damien Hirst and Miss Rachel Whiteread sharing a joke over beans on toast, shortly to be joined by Miss Gillian Wearing, who has promised to drop by for a cup of tea and a bacon butty . . . .'

Our New York contingent consisted of two boys and two girls. The other girl, Mel Safire, I knew a little, though I had to squint around the pub for a while before making her out. She had gone full-throttle for that look where you deliberately downplay your sexuality, not to mention your sex. It's easy enough to achieve. You start by dressing in the kind of utility chic – all hiking gear and walking boots and huge strap-across rucksacks with seventeen interior sealed waterproof pockets – that looks as if you're just about to set off on a trans-Arctic expedition. Then you throw on an over-large army surplus coat with big brass buttons and one of those ethnically patterned knitted hats with a floppy bit at the top where the pompom should be. Now you resemble a moujik who's managed to get hold of a mail-order catalogue from a fashionable winter-sports shop. Your eyebrows are strong, dark and unplucked, your forehead shiny and your lips spurn anything more exotic than Lypsyl Rose. If you are thin, with cheekbones sufficiently pronounced so that you can cut off most of your hair without looking pudding-faced, this look will work for you. Mel was, and it did.

She was shy. At least that was the most flattering explanation for the fact that she had a Walkman strapped to her waist and kept fiddling with the headphones as if she wanted to put them on and escape into another world. Still, she was friendly, with a surprisingly clear voice, like a single bell-note that cuts through louder conversation. We were probably too different ever to become friends, but I liked her well enough. I had heard she had a reputation for being an obsessive, but so far there was no sign of it. I didn't mind her work, either: she did huge paintings of tiny, blown-up sections of naked flesh. They qualified as sensationalist enough to make her a proper yBa because they were usually of genitals or secondary sexual organs, but so enlarged that only by reading the label next to them would you have known what they were. This was pretty cunning, allowing her both to paint well and be technically rude enough not to remain excluded from the great tidal wave of cheap, fashionable sex-violence-and-mutilation that was currently so popular.

Rob Robinson seemed quiet, too. That was a polite way of saying that he bored me. I had the impression that if he did start talking it would be about computer games or remixes of deliberately obscure records. His appearance was techno-geeky: he had entered the pub in the kind of big survivalist anorak that men nowadays collect and for which they are willing to pay violently inflated prices. This was the whole irony: that his and Mel's new brutalist outfits had probably cost six times the price of my little sweater and much-loved pewter slit skirt. Rob had then divested himself of the anorak to reveal that he was wearing head-to-toe denim, the very dark blue, new-looking kind. His jacket was snug, his jeans over-large with three-inch turn-ups and, on the back pocket, the biggest and silliest logo I had ever seen. It might look all right in *iD*, but I bet none of the editors actually wore that kind of thing out. I smirked, hearing the whoops of the fashion victim ambulance siren, and smoothed down my skirt complacently. I had never seen the point of wearing clothes that didn't fit.

And then there was Lex. He breezed into the pub as if he owned it, positively proud of being late, cocky and convinced of his own charm. I disliked him on sight. They say you always hate the people in whom you recognise yourself.

'All right?' he said cheerfully round the table. 'Mel, my darling!' He ruffled her hair. Mel looked flattered rather than annoyed. 'Rob! My man!' Lex ruffled Rob's hair too. Even this didn't seem to go amiss. By this time my lips were drawn back from my teeth. If I'd been a dog I would have been growling. I was waiting to see if his hand came anywhere near my head. Higher than my neck and I would bite.

'You must be Sam,' he said. I had narrowed my eyes mesmerically in a stare that meant don't-even-*think*-about-ruffling-my-hair, but, to my great annoyance, I felt the hostility fading as soon as we looked at each other. I heard the little click in my stomach, the one that happens as two people recognise their mutual attraction, and saw by the slight widening of his eyes that he had sensed it too. We nodded at each other by way of greeting; at this kind of moment you don't shake hands, being nervous of the electrical currents.

'I saw that article on you in the *Herald* a while back,' he said easily to me, pulling up a stool and straddling it in that male way that means 'my balls are so big I have to sit with my legs wide apart'. 'Nice photo. And you did the set for that Shakespeare down King's Cross, didn't you?'

We hopefully-up-and-coming artists all kept tabs on each other. However different our aspirations might be – Richard Serra or Louise Bourgeois, Marcel Duchamp or Paula Rego – everyone else was a kind of rival, for critical acclaim at least. Lex was being honest in acknowledging this, which I appreciated. I didn't warm to him, though. I thought he was only doing it to show how secure he was. I'd been about to use exactly the same manoeuvre myself.

'Yes, I haven't exactly had an orthodox career to date,' I said amiably. 'Not like you – Camberwell, Black Box and now Saatchi, so I hear.'

Black Box was the gallery all the young and self-consciously iconoclastic artists aspired to. It had been mean of me to mention Saatchi, though. I hadn't heard that this was a done deal and Lex would doubtless be superstitious about it being discussed too openly. But I am usually nastier to people I fancy – I like to see if they can take a bit of punishment – and Lex was a professional rival, too. He was asking for it on several fronts.

'Saatchi's interested in you?' Mel said, wide-eyed. 'That's brilliant, Lex!' I noted that she sounded impressed rather than jealous. Lex's charm had made her forget that he was the competition.

'Oi! Never say that out loud, it's bad luck,' Lex said, holding up his hands in instinctive protest. 'The S-word, I mean. That's still pretty far down in the pipeline.'

I tried not to smirk. My source of information had told me that he had been boasting about it in the Groucho a few nights ago. But there couldn't have been any other artists present.

'Change the subject, change the subject,' he continued, when it looked as if Mel was about to say something more. 'I'll get another round in, shall I? What's everyone drinking?'

'Saatchi,' Mel breathed when he was at the bar. The mere word itself was enough to conjure up a heady atmosphere of money and renown.

'Bit of a mixed blessing, though,' said Rob, who obviously considered himself the voice of reason. 'He always wants to buy up most of your stuff. Then it sits in a basement for years, where no one can see it, and if he dumps you all in one go your value drops like a stone.'

'Yeah, well, I know that,' Mel said acidly. 'But what I couldn't do with all that dosh . . . and the space is brilliant.'

'If you ever get to show in it. I mean, you might just stay in the basement for ever.'

'I wouldn't turn him down if he made me an offer, Rob. Would you?' Her tone was even more cutting.

'I dunno, actually,' he said. He had short ginger hair which contrasted with his pink face so that it was hard to see if he was blushing or not. Now he fiddled with his heavy black-framed spectacles, looking embarrassed. 'I might,' he said finally.

Mel gave a snort of disbelief. I didn't. Somehow I thought Rob meant it.

Lex returned triumphantly with all four glasses pressed tightly together between his two hands, the way amateurs or boys showing off carried them. He dumped his burden onto the table, foam splashing from his pint into Rob's Guinness. Rob flicked it off ostentatiously, but Lex ignored this by-play.

'So, how's it all going?' he said. His presence raised the energy levels of everyone round the table; there was a charge coming off him which we could not help but acknowledge. I observed his body language, the legs once more straddled across the stool as if it were as wide as a Western saddle, the way his easy gestures – reaching for his pack of cigarettes, bumming a match off Mel – took in more than his own share of space. As he lit his cigarette, ducking his head to the match, he looked up at me from under his eyelashes, his big dark eyes unashamedly flirtatious. Lex Thompson was a raging tart.

'Anyone else but me met this Carol Bergmann woman?' he was saying.

'Oh, you know her?' Mel said. Her voice changed, softened, whenever she talked directly to Lex. We were each responding to him in our different ways; when I fancy someone I tend to get tougher with them, even more sarcastic than usual, and tonight was no exception.

'Mm. Met her in New York last year,' Lex was saying. 'Great place. Went for a couple of days and stayed for a fortnight. Can't wait to go back. We should hit some clubs when we get there, hang out a bit.'

He winked at me and Mel. It was automatic for someone like Lex to flirt with every attractive woman he met, and the wink was general enough to have no meaning beyond a friendly gesture. But Mel blushed slightly and looked down at her drink.

'I was wondering about that, actually,' Rob said. 'Because they're only taking us over for a couple of days, right? For the opening, basically. But I was wondering if we could change our tickets and stay on.'

'Have to sort out your own accommodation,' Lex said knowledgeably. 'Carol's putting us up in the Gramercy Park, but she won't run to longer than she's already agreed.'

'Is that what the hotel's called?' Mel asked, her eyes still dropped.

'Mm. Great place.'

'Where exactly is it?' I said innocently, having sensed something a little vague about Lex's response. I was forming the impression that he was the kind of person who loathed not knowing more than anyone else about the subject under discussion. Especially if it was a cool, happening kind of subject.

'It's, uh, on Gramercy Park,' Lex said, as if this were the most obvious fact in the world. Still, he was avoiding my gaze.

'Is it near the gallery?'

'Oh, well, uh, it's pretty central. Cool. Carol always puts up her artists there. Can I have a light, Mel?'

Clearly the precise location of the Gramercy Park Hotel would have to wait till we arrived.

'I'm not staying there, anyway,' I announced. 'I've got a sub-let.'

All eyes turned to me.

'How come?' Rob said enviously. 'Does that mean you're staying for a while?'

'I have to get there a week or so before the exhibition opens,' I explained. 'To install the sculpture. So, with what Carol would have had to pay for a hotel, I thought I'd see if I could find a flat to rent instead. A friend of a friend lives on the Upper West Side—' (how easily I said that, without having any idea of what it signified. It might have been the equivalent of Mayfair, Brixton or Cockfosters for all I knew) '—and she's away for a month or so in October. She's letting me have it for half the rent, as long as I water her plants and forward the mail.'

'Well, fuck me,' said Lex, summing up the general mood of the meeting in a few well-chosen, if not particularly elegant, words. 'You jammy cow.'

★ ★ ★

'Bollocks! Bollocks!' This was Lex, in a near-seamless continuation of his previous ejaculation. Only by now it was many hours later, we had changed venue, and he was shouting the words over an insistently fast and thumping bassline. 'How can you possibly fucking say that my work doesn't inspire emotion? You should have seen people reacting to that piece I did at Black Box last year! They were all over the place!'

I sneered at him.

'I'm sorry,' I said, or rather shouted, as coldly as I could under the circumstances. 'I really don't see that a load of lads spitting out diluted cough syrup all over the floor counts as emotion, except perhaps in the most literal sense—'

'It wasn't just sodding cough syrup! It was syrup of figs! It took me ages to get hold of that! And there was flat beer and tea, mixed together, in the Tallisker bottle, and vodka in the water – *and*,' he added with great pride, as if this would clinch the argument, 'I left the chartreuse as it was! No one was expecting that!'

'Oh, for God's sake, Lex!' I was exasperated by now. 'Just because you lined up a load of bottles on a table with different stuff in them from what it said on the labels, and some idiot boys were fool enough to taste them—'

'It's about challenging people's perceptions of the real!' Lex insisted. 'Breaking down our standard assumptions and showing how much we depend on labels—'

'Of course we bloody depend on labels! Take all of them off the tins you've got at home and then try finding the baked beans!'

'Well, that bit was more about mass-marketing,' Lex yelled across an increasingly loud break of sound, 'how we expect certain things from a particular brand, because of advertising—'

'Then what you should have done,' I said, sighing, because it was so obvious, 'is bunged a lot of bottles of vodka, say, on the table, right from supermarket brands up to Absolut or Finlandia, to see if people could taste the difference.'

Lex's eyes went absorbed and distant for a second. 'Nah,' he said, 'that would be—'

'What?'

'That would be too practical!' he shouted. 'So, what, you're saying your stuff actually provokes emotion?' He put huge and sarcastic stress on the last two words.

I was drunk enough by now not to be embarrassed by the turn the conversation had taken.

'I dunno! I'm just saying that the emotional range you go through while swilling your mouth out to get rid of the taste of cold beer and tea mixed together and cursing the so-called artist at the same time—'

'I don't bloody call myself an artist! Well, only as a convenient shorthand—'

'ANYWAY – that kind of sensation's about as shallow as you can get. People probably experience a much more complex array of feelings watching *Babe* on video.'

'I can't hear a word you're saying! Let's go and sit on the stairs, OK?'

I nodded. Lex turned and shoved his way through the crowd of people milling around the bar. I followed the shoulders of his battered fawn suede jacket as they jostled a path for me over to the staircase on the far side of the bar. Earlier I had taken one look at the dancefloor and beat a hasty retreat. A battery chicken would have sized up the situation and returned with relief to its cage, finding it pleasantly roomy and well-ventilated by contrast. Still, it was better than the last drum and bass club I'd been to, just behind Regent Street. There no track had been longer than ninety seconds – without a tune there wasn't anything else to sustain it for longer – and every time the DJ put a new one on he stopped dead and blew a whistle several times, at which everyone screamed and waved their arms around and joggled back and forth. A basic mathematical calculation will find that in ten minutes this had happened roughly six times, which was about how long I lasted.

And there had been the added handicap that practically everyone had been wearing puffa jackets tied round their waists, even while dancing, for some quirk of fashion whose reasons were obscured in the mists of time. Maybe Goldie had turned up at a club once looking like that and everyone had copied him, not realising that after about half an hour he'd taken the jacket off and stowed it somewhere sensible. So it was almost impossible to move because of all the duvets with sleeves slung at waist height, slipping against one another, scratching at any exposed passing flesh with the teeth of their zips. And the dancers, jerking up and down like Duracell rabbits in their little white vests, were sweating heavily under the low ceiling, the sweat running down their bodies and soaking into the channels of the puffa jackets . . . .

'So, what were we saying? Whoah, I can almost hear myself when I talk normally, that's got to be an improvement.' Lex dropped down on a stair and patted the tread beside him invitingly. I joined him, chugging back some of my beer, and then had to squeeze in closer because someone was coming downstairs. 'Yeah, what were we saying?' he repeated. 'Nah, fuck it. Enough of that.'

He drank most of his whisky chaser and turned to look at me directly. My thigh was pressed up against his jean-clad one, and the contact was very pleasant. Automatically I glanced down to check his footwear and made a mental tick against Caterpillar boots, rather sloppily laced. Under his suede jacket he wore a denim one with a T-shirt under that, a look I've always approved of. His hair was dark and cut short; I had the impression that it would be curly if he let it grow. His skin was a clear pale olive, his eyes big and dark. Indeed, he looked much as I might if I'd been a boy. Only his eyelashes were much longer than mine, the bastard. When he opened them wide, as if he were protesting his innocence, they framed his eyes in great dark spikes Twiggy would have been proud of. And he knew exactly how pretty he was.

Mel and Rob had left already, the former, I thought, distinctly reluctant to leave me and Lex alone; my instinct in matters of sexual attraction has been finely tuned over the years. But she and Rob had boyfriends or girlfriends or pet gerbils waiting for them at home, and those claims must have taken precedence.

Lex's thigh was pressing ever more insistently against mine and, enjoyable though it was, in the big picture this was not a good situation. We had a show to get through together, and in principle I was firmly opposed to shitting on one's own doorstep. I decided to finish my beer and leave. Halfway down, someone else pushing past us jogged me and the beer would have gone everywhere if Lex hadn't righted the bottle in time, his fingers deliberately closing over mine for much longer than the emergency warranted.

'Whee!' I said when I'd got my breath back. We were both cackling with laughter, for some reason. Clearly we were drunker than I had realised. I cleared my throat and mentally slapped myself around the face.

'I've got to go,' I said resolutely, impressed by my own maturity.

'Oh, what? No way! Come on, Sam, don't wimp out on me.' He grinned. 'I've heard all about your staying power.'

'Is that a challenge?' I said, rising to it immediately.

'It's a fact.' He looked at his watch. 'Shit, it's only one! You can't bottle out this early!'

'I really do need to go home,' I said feebly.

'Tell you what.' Lex batted his dark silky eyelashes at me. 'Let's go do a line of charlie. That'll keep you going.'

It was the drugs and not Lex's eye-work that persuaded me to stay. I swear it on my life.

★ ★ ★

The minuscule cubicle in the women's toilets was painted a pale yellow. The walls were filthy, thickly encrusted with graffiti – some of it quite witty – and peeling like a terminal case of psoriasis. I made an amusing little crack about them having had too much AHA cream which Lex, being a boy, didn't understand. Too many scientific terms for his tiny mind. In mitigation, however, it could be argued that he had his mind fully on the wrap he had produced from one of his jacket pockets. Unfolding it, he tapped out a steady stream of white powder onto the equally white cistern. I noticed that the wrap was cut out of a football magazine. He might as well have had 'New Lad' tattooed on his forehead.

'Ladies first,' he said, gesturing to the cistern.

'All right if I go instead?' I said satirically. Bending over, I hoovered up a line. It cut sharply at the lining of my nostrils.

'A bit speedy, isn't it? Not,' I hastened to add, 'that I'm complaining.'

'Yeah, it's nice,' Lex agreed, bending over in his turn and thus providing me with the kind of view I could have watched for much longer than the sadly brief few seconds it took him to snort the other line. He ran his finger over the cistern and smeared anything left, together with most of the dirt and grime that had been there already, over his gums. New Lad, new hygiene.

'So,' he said, looking at me, 'here we are.'

And then he kissed me.

It wasn't a tentative buss; it was full-on, shove-the-girl-up-against-the-cubicle-wall, hands-all-over-the-place. PG Wodehouse would have called it the Stevedore, as opposed to the Troubadour, approach. The only word for it, frankly, was snog, and I am sorry to admit that, mainly but not entirely due to these shock tactics and my advanced state of drunkenness, I found myself responding with enthusiasm, despite the proven uncleanliness of his gums. We crashed back into the small space between the toilet and the wall, radically disarranging each other's clothes, tongues wrapping themselves around tonsils with abandon. My head knocked back against the wall. I heard the ageing plaster crumble under the pressure. Lex's hands were closing around my bottom, smoothing the shiny material around my hips enthusiastically.

'Mm, sexy,' he purred into my neck, kneading the skirt like a feeding kitten.

For some reason the way he said it struck a false note. There was something self-conscious about it, as if we were making a porn film and he was talking for the benefit of the camera. I pulled back a little and caught such a smug expression on his face that my fingers snapped back from one of his fly buttons as if it had given me a short electric shock. No one ever takes me for granted.

'Close,' I said. 'But no cigar.'

I pulled my sweater down again. With the increased vision this permitted me I was happy to see that Lex's face had wiped itself clean of anything remotely resembling smugness; for a moment it was blank – which quite suited him – and then his lips parted in disbelief. He looked very fetching when he pouted.

'What? Bollocks! Come here!' He dragged me towards him and ground himself against me. The tender romance of this caress softened neither my heart nor any other part of my anatomy.

'Sorry, gorgeous. Got to go.'

'What?' he repeated. 'Sam, you can't do this to me! Come on, baby, it was going so well—'

How Seventies of him. 'You sound like the singer in Hot Chocolate,' I said, adjusting my skirt and picking a couple of pieces of yellowing plaster out of my hair.

'What's wrong with that? Hey—' He started kissing my neck. This was very pleasant, but I ignored it womanfully. 'It needn't change anything! We can still be friends afterwards—'

I always loathe it when someone says that.

'Who says we're friends now?' I inquired, and stepped neatly past him and through the door. A couple of girls had just come in, sweaty from dancing, their eyes bright. They were both wearing the ubiquitous puffa jackets round their waists and the cladding was enough, in the small space, to cause a traffic jam of M25 proportions.

As I was squeezing past one of them said, separating out her words for emphasis:

'God, I am so fucking up for it it's not true. I could've grabbed him right there and given him what for, and I don't even fancy him that much, know what I'm saying?'

'You're on heat!' her friend bawled, giggling madly.

I had a flash of inspiration.

'Well, someone in there could do with it,' I broke in, nodding to the cubicle. 'If you don't mind finishing what I started.'

They broke into noisy and raucous laughter.

'All right, Shaz, what about it?' the first girl said as I left the toilets. She was the size of a house even without the jacket bulking her out. Lex had better get out of there quickly if he wanted to remain unmolested; once she cornered him between the toilet and the wall she'd have him bang to rights. I hadn't warned her about his hairy back. It had felt like he was wearing a mohair sweater under his T-shirt. Oh well, she'd just have to find out for herself. You opens your cubicle door and you takes your chances.

* * *

The brief amusement I felt at the way I had handled my exit faded fast, the smile on my lips spreading wide into a silent scream. I rolled over in bed whimpering and biting the pillow, and not, I stress firmly, because the memory of Lex's tongue halfway down my throat had rekindled any passion in my loins. Oh, the shame, the horror. It was worse than anything I could have imagined. I had kissed – no, Sam, look the brutal truth right in the face without flinching – I had *fumbled in the Blue Note toilets with a young British artist.* How I was going to live with myself after this I didn't know.

And what on earth was I going to tell Hugo?

CHAPTER TWO

'*Are* you going to tell Hugo?' was how Tom chose to put the question when he came round the day afterwards.

I couldn't deny that the idea of pretending the whole small sorry incident had never taken place appealed to me with near-overpowering force; but against that I had to weigh the possibility of it all coming into the open later, and how much worse it would look if it did.

'The thing is,' I said, topping up our vodka and tonics – it made me feel incredibly sophisticated and mature having a mixer to hand rather than just a bottle of hard liquor – 'The thing is that Hugo's really good at spotting when something like that's happened. Particularly if he ever sees me and Lex together. Because, knowing Lex, he'll either ignore me pointedly or try to get off with me again in a proprietorial kind of way. Either of which will be so obvious to Hugo's super-trained powers of observation that Lex and I might as well have neon signs over our heads saying: "Have Had My Tongue Round That Person's Tonsils Recently" and arrows pointing to each other.'

'Does Hugo really have super-trained powers of observation?' asked Tom jealously, going off at a tangent. Being a poet, he considered himself to have the monopoly on *mots justes*, piercing insights and an unerring perception of the subtleties of human behaviour. Sheer fantasy, of course. But he was very good at descriptions of plants in iambic pentameter.

'He is horribly sharp about anything to do with sex,' I admitted. 'And it extends into more general areas. He says it's the actor's honed eye onto the world.'

'Sammy, please. *Not* honed eye.' Tom shuddered 'Just try to imagine what that would look like.'

I did. 'Ick.'

Ever since Tom's first collection of poems had been published a few months ago (covering, fairly extensively, the flora and fauna of India, which he had visited last year, with a side order of heartbreak and despair) he had become unbearable about picking people up on their less wisely chosen metaphors.

'What I can't understand is why you're getting hot and bothered about it,' Tom complained. 'I mean, what's it matter to you? You always run a mile if the bloke you're shagging starts trying to tell you that you can't feel up other blokes in toilets. Frankly, I've always thought you considered that a basic human right, like not being tortured, or proper sewage provision.'

India had really scarred Tom on the dysentery front. He had lost two and a half stone and was now obsessed with plumbing.

'The thing is,' I said again, fiddling with the lemon slice in my vodka and tonic (lemon slice, note. Next I'd be getting a hostess trolley), 'I don't really want Hugo to be off snogging some tart of an actress in the loos of a sordid pub in Stratford.'

'Well, if he is, dump him,' Tom said blankly. 'Isn't that what you always do sooner or later, anyway? I mean, what's the problem here, Sammy? You're the Don Juanita of Holloway and Camden Town. You've probably shagged more blokes in toilets than I have girls in my entire life.' He paused. 'OK, I'm depressed now,' he continued. 'I don't want that to be true. Could we do some counting up, please?'

Eyes squinting with concentration, he started mumbling girls' names under his breath and pressing down one finger after another.

'You don't get it, Tom,' I said, exasperated. 'I like Hugo.'

He stared at me in shock, girl-tally momentarily forgotten.

'You *like* him? You mean, you *like* him?'

'Yeah, I like him, OK?' I said gruffly.

'You mean you—'

'I like him! OK! Could we just leave it there, please?' Writhing in embarrassment, I finished my drink in one go and curled up into a ball in the corner of the sofa. 'Ow,' I said, rubbing my bottom.

'You've got to get that bloody spring fixed.'

'I know.'

'So. *So*,' Tom said, pouring me some more vodka. 'You *like* him. Well, well, well. I never thought I'd see the day. Sammy actually *likes*—'

'Shut up. Fuck off. All right? Anyway,' I said, waving away the proffered tonic bottle and drinking my vodka neat – sod sophistication, sometimes you needed to dispense with anything but the bare essentials. 'Anyway, I thought you got on with him OK. I mean, you thought he was all right.'

Tom hadn't warmed hugely to Hugo, who – I was the first to admit – could be very annoying. But I had suspected that he had summed up Hugo as being able to deal with me, which was equally annoying, if true, and had given him the all clear on that account.

'Yeah, he's OK. I was going to say he's nice, but he isn't. If you know what I mean. But then, you aren't nice. At all. So it's fair enough. Actually,' Tom said reminiscently, 'we had a good crack about the footie while you were off getting the drinks in.'

'You and *Hugo* talked about *football*?' I stared at him in disbelief. The only sport I could imagine Hugo being remotely interested in was cricket; I suspected him of having modelled himself largely on Psmith. But football lacked all the qualities which Hugo would consider sufficiently aesthetic.

'Yeah. We had a good crack, I told you.'

I decided to let this one pass. Clearly Hugo had been playing one of his elaborate games of bluff with Tom and the poor naive lunkhead hadn't realised. In which case I could only do harm by pointing it out.

'How's he doing?' Tom added, having warmed to Hugo in retrospect.

'Really well up till now.' Hugo was at the Royal Shakespeare Company, down in Stratford, on a roll after a very successful Edmund in *King Lear* at the National. The RSC's rep policy meant that he was juggling several roles, and so far – Berowne in *Love's Labours Lost* and Ferdinand in *The Duchess of Malfi* – it was perfect casting: one witty intellectual and one evil sororicide. Doubtless he would be horribly sexy in both. Still, from the sound of it his nemesis had just checked in: 'But he's just started rehearsals for this new play, and he's hating it with a passion.'

'What's it called?'

'Don't remember. Something stupid. Hugo calls it W**king and F**ting. He plays a pimp who falls in love with a rent boy. Only the rent boy's so scarred he only wants sex if someone's raping him. And the rent boy's sister is in love with Hugo, who beats her up a bit to please the rent boy, who hates her because their mum abused him and not her. But what he doesn't know is that their father, besides being a drug dealer—'

'Enough. God.' Tom was holding up a hand. 'I just hope it's bloody well written. Otherwise that kind of thing's just cheap exploitation.'

'You pompous bastard. But I agree, actually.' In my recent spell as girlfriend-type-person to up-and-coming actor, I had found myself attending more plays than I had done for a very long time. Most of them were rigorously modern dramas requiring all the actors to say 'cunt' repeatedly, this being considered the worst swearword possible and therefore cast-iron proof that the author was young, rebellious and hadn't told his parents what time he'd be back that evening. I use the male pronoun because, with a couple of exceptions, the authors were all male. The women's plays, of which I had also seen a few, tended to be more subtle stuff which didn't attract the fanfares and shock value of the Angry Young Lads tendency; still, if I saw one more sensitive play about mother-daughter relationships I'd dig up my own and hold a black mass over the coffin.

What I had particularly noticed about the boys' plays was that there was usually only one girl in them, and that she would, in the course of the evening, be called upon to take her top off, dress as a stripper, or both. The would-be intellectual authors restrained themselves to informing us that the girl was wearing no knickers or had epic tits without actually causing her to produce them for display purposes. Still, this attention inevitably meant that at least half the audience would have its mind trained only on her VPL or bosom area for the rest of the evening.

In short, I had not been impressed. I said as much to Tom, who made the right disapproving shocked noises and then ruined it by inquiring, about as subtly as Jim Carrey registering surprise, which of the plays I had mentioned in my little rant actually involved full-frontal female nudity. I sneered, and was about to start bugging him about some of the more lurid flower/vulva comparisons in his book when the doorbell rang, sparing him temporarily.

'Hi, babe,' said Janey, my other best friend. She was laden with her customary huge satchel and a Marks & Spencer carrier bag, which was clinking and rustling temptingly. As she came in, I relieved her of the latter. Its contents had to be more interesting than the scripts with which the satchel was doubtless stuffed to the gills.

'You're so thin!' she exclaimed to Tom, not having seen him since he got back from India.

'Spent a lot of time in Diarrhoeabad,' Tom said. 'It's this little town in Gujurat. They have a guaranteed weight-loss programme. You have to keep drinking fluids, otherwise you die, which is the only catch, but apart from that it's better than a health farm. Cheaper, too. God! You've lost a lot of weight too! I could get my arms around you twice!' He held her by her shoulders and looked her up and down. 'What happened? Did you get dysentery as well?'

Janey smiled complacently. From being a plumply formed Rubens, she had turned into a still curvy Renoir. The extreme pallor of her skin and her fair curling hair gave her an air of fragility, emphasised by the unexpectedly fine jawline that was now much more visible.

'Oh, I've been working very hard,' she said with elaborate casualness that fooled neither of us. 'I've been too busy to eat.'

'Janey's a PRODUCER AT THE BBC,' I announced, since Janey had clearly been struck by a fit of modesty. 'She's just finished shooting her first series.'

'Oh, that's brilliant! Congratulations!' Tom enfolded Janey in an embrace. 'Is that why you've got so smart? What happened to all those hippie-ish scarves and jewellery and stuff? It's going to take a while for me to get used to you power-dressing.'

With the disrespectful familiarity of a brother, Tom plucked at the single strand of hand-beaten silver beads around her neck, rather like a gorilla toying with the idea of ripping them off to see if they would taste nice. His hands were as unwieldy as bunches of bananas. Sometimes I wondered if his opposing thumbs were fully evolved.

'Stop it, you oaf.' Janey slapped him off. Tom retired, looking hurt. 'Sam, can I have a drink? I brought some nice white wine.' This was her tactful way of indicating that she preferred not to drink any rotgut I might be storing under the sink.

'Opened it already.' I handed her a glass and ripped open the packets of Marks & Spencer's designer tortilla chips, placing the eviscerated shells on the table with their contents spilling out.

Janey stared at this prospect distastefully.

'Don't you have a bowl to put those in?'

'Ye-es. Technically speaking.'

Janey knew exactly what that meant. 'All right, I won't ask what you've been mixing in it. Mm.' She drank some more wine. 'This is very nice. So, Tom. How was India? Apart from the dysentery.'

Tom stared at her. 'You haven't read the book, have you?' he said dolefully.

Janey looked guilty. 'I'm sorry. I've been shooting on location in Wales and I haven't had time to do anything else – I'm really sorry. I'll go out and get it this afternoon.' She paused. 'What do you mean? Is the book a travelogue? I thought it was poems.'

'It is,' I said. Tom was too steeped in gloom to answer, and not because Janey hadn't purchased a copy of *So Near/Too Near* (I told him those deconstructionist backstrokes went out of fashion a decade ago, but he wouldn't listen). Chronicling in detail Tom's break-up with the girlfriend who had accompanied him to India, it served as a useful shorthand guide for people wanting to know how the trip had gone, indicating all the points of sensitivity to be avoided. In fact, after a perusal of the increasingly brutal and depressing events so faithfully described by poor Tom, the reader was fully warned that the only really safe topic of conversation would be floral. Vulva comparisons an optional extra.

'Tom and Alice,' I continued, deciding to summarise this for Janey to get Tom's pain over with as quickly as possible, 'split up in India, and the book's mostly about that—'

'She *left* me,' Tom corrected bitterly. He was slumped into the armchair, head ducked, staring dully at his shoes. His familiar old navy Arran sweater, normally padded out at the front by a small but firm beer belly, hung loose around his torso as if his body had been deflated several degrees. It was pitiful for a man who had once resembled an extra-large and cuddly version of Paddington Bear. Even his chunky Irish face looked drawn without a nice amount of flesh round his jowls.

'OK,' I went on, 'um, Alice left Tom—'

'For an *American hippie guru with a straggly beard.*'

'Tom's very savage about the beard, and in fact the guy's facial hair generally,' I informed Janey. 'It's one of the best poems in the book. You'll never be able to see a pair of sideburns again without shuddering.'

Janey refilled her glass with alacrity. 'I'm really sorry, Tom,' she said, casting around her for a way to alleviate the situation. 'Have a biscuit?'

Tom's huge head lifted, a faint ray of hope beginning to gleam through the bleakness of his expression.

'Are they chocolate?'

'Double chocolate chip,' said Janey winningly, holding the box just out of his reach as if trying to tempt him back from the brink of a precipice. There was a long pause. Then Tom leaned over and took three. Janey let out her breath in relief. Tom still looked sullen with grief, but the rate at which he was cramming in the biscuits suggested that his life was not completely without incidental pleasures.

'What about you?' he said, wiping away with his sleeve the crumbs from around his mouth.

'Oh, everything's going OK. With a few setbacks. I just came from a meeting with the composer, who's driving us mad. He keeps trying to write whole symphonies when all we've asked him to do is ten seconds of lurk.'

'Ten seconds of lurk?' I was baffled.

'Oh, you know. Music to create an atmosphere. Someone's lurking in the shadows, and the music has to sound ominous. You piece in what you need. Fifteen seconds of panic here, twenty of rural calm there . . . .'

'How weird. It's like being a haberdasher, cutting lengths off different trimmings.'

'You could say that.' I didn't think Janey was particularly amused by the comparison.

'How's Helen?' Tom asked her. 'She got a part in the new series?'

'Um, no,' Janey said in that faux-light tone you use to indicate that you're all right about a recent break-up. 'Helen and I aren't together any longer.'

Tom looked incredulous. 'Helen left you just when you started producing a series? She must be out of her mind! Or did she go off with someone more important?'

He had perked up considerably at the idea of Janey, too, being alone and bereft. This despite the fact that her ex-girlfriend Helen had made toxic waste look warm and caring.

'Tom!' I said curtly. 'Hobnailed boots alert!'

'Actually it was me who left Helen,' Janey said, coughing. 'I'm with someone else now. She's my co-producer on the series.'

'Oh, right,' Tom said, deflated. 'So I'm the only one who's been abandoned. Brilliant. That makes me feel really great.'

'His book got excellent reviews,' I offered. 'I've seen the cuttings.'

'The reviewers were the only people who read it,' Tom informed us, embittered. 'And they get it free.'

'But poetry doesn't sell, Tom,' Janey said, her tone rather too much that of a thriving BBC producer pointing out the obvious. 'You know that.'

'Well, hark at you,' Tom said resentfully. 'Calloused by success. What should I be doing, according to you, Janey? Writing TV serials with lots of gratuitous nudity and drugs and ten seconds of music to bonk to, which everyone'll forget about half an hour after they've seen them? Maybe then I could afford to live somewhere a bit better than a co-op house in Stoke Newington where we have to have meetings of the washing-machine committee every two hours.'

This is the trouble when people actually start making it in their arty career of choice. While everyone's struggling together, mutual support is constant and unquestioning: it has to be. Then someone takes their first step up the ladder and everyone else thinks you have it made. But, once you've got over the heady rush of actually standing on the sodding thing, you realise how far there is still to climb, and the friends who haven't yet made it that far are resentful when you point this out. Whereas the ones further up the ladder can't help looking down on you a little.

It was as sobering as a dash of cold water. Despite the success of my exhibitions to date and the prospects in New York, my income was still very unreliable, coming in great staggering bursts of feast punctuated by considerably larger periods of famine. And at least there was occasional money in sculpture; there was none in poetry. In one way Janey was right to point out this harsh reality. But from another perspective her doing so was an unbearably smug pronouncement which could only be made by someone safe in a much more commercial realm than mine and Tom's.

'I was just saying—' she started.

'Yeah, right.' Tom ignored this. 'We're all doing so bloody well, aren't we? I've earned about twenty pence from exploiting my heartbreak and betrayal, Sam's got an exhibition in New York and is struggling pitifully to have something approaching a normal human relationship, which would be a laugh if it weren't so painful to watch – it's like a psychopath trying to go steady and settle down – and you, Janey, have turned into a power-crazed, superior BBC megalomaniac in a tailored suit.'

'That is totally unfair!'

The combatants needed distracting before they came to blows. I decided to throw in my adventures in toilet world last night as a bone.

'Janey, don't listen to him,' I said. 'I need your advice on a matter of the heart.'

This was a cast-iron certainty to make Janey sit up and pay attention. Briefly I recounted the details, with a short character sketch of the other protagonist. Janey listened, blue eyes wide, head propped on one hand in the classic agony aunt position, taking sips from her glass. Finally she said:

'And you're sure you *need* to tell Hugo?'

'That's what I said!'

'Shut up, Tom,' we said in unison.

'After all,' she continued, 'you're going off next week. Is this Lex going to be there?'

'Not at once. He's coming over about a week later.'

'So you'll have a bit of time together before the exhibition opens. I mean, to let the situation adjust itself. Hugo's going over for the opening, isn't he?'

I nodded.

'Well, look, by the time he arrives it'll all have simmered down. By the sound of this Lex, once he realises there's no joy to be had from you he'll have forgotten all about you and be off chasing anything else with breasts and a pulse.'

'Gosh, thanks for the flattery,' I muttered.

'Everything will be over and done with when Hugo gets there,' Janey continued, ignoring this. 'Relax. It's really not going to be a problem.'

'Unless she gets pissed again and decides to make a Lex-rated night of it,' Tom said unhelpfully, still resentful at having been told to shut up.

I glared at him. 'Your puns are crap,' I said coldly. 'Always have been always will be. Men,' I added scornfully to Janey. 'Can't live with them, can't kill them except under a ridiculously narrow set of circumstances.'

'You should know,' Tom retorted. Still sensitive, he had been pushed too far and this was him snapping. Janey drew in her breath sharply. His reference would have been unforgivable if I hadn't been making major efforts in the past year or so to come to terms with my homicidal past. It still was reasonably unforgivable, though, and, going by his shocked expression, Tom had realised this as soon as the words were out of his mouth.

'I'm really sorry, Sammy,' he mumbled. 'I feel like the biggest piece of shit alive.'

'Metaphor watch is bleeping,' I said acidly. 'Last time I looked, shit was dead. Take a hint from it.'

Janey put an arm around my shoulders. 'You're redeeming yourself through art,' she said, only half-flippantly. 'And there's more to come in the Big Apple. Try not to kill anyone over there, OK?'

'Can't promise anything,' I said, picking up my glass and shooting

Tom one of my special evil glares. 'But I'll do my level best to avoid it.'

CHAPTER THREE

'Where to, lady?' the cab driver said without looking round.

'Spring Street. The Bergmann LaTouche Gallery.'

'Whatever.'

He couldn't have sounded more bored if I had offered to recite him the collected speeches of John Major. Still, I warmed to him. At last this was the fabled New York misanthropy. I had been looking forward to the combination of malign neglect and random insults to make me feel at home.

The cab pulled away with a jerk that sent my head slamming back against the seat. A voice said loudly: 'Prr! This is Eartha Kitt.'

I looked around me wildly, but I appeared to be the only person in the cab. And, going by his photograph, the driver was definitely not Eartha Kitt. So either the bump on the head had given me a light concussion, or . . .

'Cats have nine lives, grrr,' Eartha went on, 'but unfortunately you have only one. So buckle your seat belt for safety. Have a purr-rr-fect day!'

Obediently, I did up the seat belt. What Catwoman said went.

Manhattan was the least welcoming sight I had ever seen. The skyscrapers, each trying to shoulder away and outdo its neighbours, were so totally uninterested in leaving space for any human inhabitants that the choppy grey waters of the East River looked positively inviting by contrast. As we crossed them I had the sensation of a giant portcullis raised above our heads, not as a threat, but as a warning. New York's motto would definitely be something medieval and pitiless. The only thing missing was a collection of freshly severed heads spiked along the bridge.

We shot past a parked Mack truck, so huge it was like a flash from *The Terminator*, the opening sequence where the machines have taken over. A delivery man was swinging himself down from the driver's seat, mountaineering gingerly down a series of crampons set in the side of the truck to help him reach terra firma intact. He looked like a tiny, frail, partially evolved joke of nature which the truck could crunch up and spit out any time it wanted to. And the cars were enormous, too. Why was that? Maybe people in America were widening out just so they didn't feel dwarfed by their vehicles. The problem of obesity here could be solved in a stroke simply by banning everything bigger than a Nissan Micra.

Suddenly we screeched to a halt five centimetres away from another cab. I was grateful to Eartha Kitt, as her advice had stopped me fracturing my forehead against the partition. These cabs were so solid they felt bullet- and probably even bomb-proof; the driver was the real menace. We pulled away with another potentially neck-dislocating manoeuvre, jumping the light so that we (I use the pronoun figuratively) could pass the hapless driver in front and scream abuse at him. Unsurprisingly, he promptly took offence. At the next traffic light he pulled up next to us and started yelling:

'Fuck you, man! Fuck you!'

'Fuck you!' spat back my driver. I mean the spat part quite literally. Dribble ran down his mouth. He looked like Hulk Hogan's thinner, nastier younger brother, right down to the stringy fair hair and the trailing moustache.

'Fuck you!' responded the other driver at full throttle. The lights changed. We were off again. It was turning into a race out of the Dastardly and Muttley cartoon. Luckily I was jet-lagged and spacey enough to treat it with a kind of dopey, detached appreciation, rather than panic at being trapped in a speeding cab with one lunatic while another snapped at our hubcaps. My driver speeded up still further, upping the insult stakes triumphantly by yelling:

'Fuck your *mother*! Fuck your *mother*!' out of the passenger window as the other cab pulled level, accompanying it with the kind of gestures of which even a visiting Martian would have grasped the significance.

'AAAAAAH! Fuck *you*!' ululated the other driver. 'Fuck *you*!'

'Where in Spring Street didja say?' my driver asked me, swivelling his head round to stare at me while scorching rubber with the speed of our passage. His voice was relatively normal, which made the homicidal, eye-popping mask of rage on his face even more unnerving.

I gave him the number.

'OK, next block,' he said. At that moment the other cab shot up beside us on the wrong side of the street. Leaning over towards us, one hand precariously on the wheel, its driver doused mine with a great spray of water from a plastic bottle. At least I hoped, for everyone's sake, that it was water.

We did a screaming emergency stop that bucked the cab in the air like a bronco, tyres shuddering, cutting the other cab off. My driver was out so fast I wasn't sure if he'd bothered to open the door first. I squinted at the meter. Nine dollars eighty. I dropped a ten-dollar note on the front seat and jumped out the other side – prudent me. I didn't want to find myself being used as a human shield.

'AAAAAH! PIECE OF SHIT! I'M ALL WET!' my driver shouted while trying to rip the other's door off its hinges with his bare hands.

'I left the fare on your seat, OK?' I yelled.

'Right, right,' he said abstractedly, going back to his cab and reaching for something under the front seat. Over his shoulder he yelled: 'COME OUT AND DIE, YOU FUCKING WATER-SPRAYING PIECE OF SHIT!'

Making a quick check on the street numbers, I realised that Bergmann LaTouche was only a few doors away. I trotted along briskly, looking neither to right nor left. Behind me the screaming and honking was getting louder, now accompanied by what sounded like someone trying to compact down a car using only a large hammer and a lot of excess energy.

Lounging in front of Bergmann LaTouche's high, white-painted door was a man who looked like an albino gorilla with tattoos. I would never be able to compare Tom to a primate again. This guy was the real thing, right down to the low forehead and the huge, dangling arms whose knuckles nearly scraped the ground. He wore a long-sleeved thermal T-shirt under a baggy pair of dungarees.

Despite his being long-waisted, the dungarees hung so low that the crotch was at mid-thigh, the hems puddling around his work boots. This made it impossible to size up his bottom. Perhaps it was saggy, and he had adopted this style of dress to conceal it.

He said something in such a low drawl I couldn't make it out.

'Sorry?'

'What's goin' owen down there?' he said, raising his voice with what seemed like an effort. There was an entire symphony of honks going by now; the cabs were blocking the road and other drivers were protesting vehemently.

'My cab driver's beating up another cab driver.'

'They fightin' over you?' he said, as if this would be quite a normal occurrence.

'Of course not,' I said blankly.

'Goin' at it good?' He was almost coming to life now, his voice reaching a normal pitch.

I shrugged. 'Why don't you go down and have a look?' I suggested, rather repelled by his obvious enthusiasm for a fight. It was all too easy to imagine him in a zoo with a sign saying: 'Partially Evolved Hillbilly. Dangerous. Please Do Not Feed.'

'Nah. Cain't leave my post,' he said with more than a tinge of irony.

'Do you work here?' I asked.

'Yeah.' He added something I didn't catch.

'Sorry?' I said again, increasingly annoyed.

'I'm the handler. I move stuff. You English?'

'No, I'm from Brooklyn.'

'Huh? Oh.' He grinned. 'Brit sense of humour, right? Hi. I'm Dahn. You must be part of the next show.'

'Hi, Dahn.' I assumed this was Don. 'I'm Sam Jones.'

'The installation one.' Don pulled a face. 'I hate theym. Too much like hard work. No offence. This your first tahm in New York?'

'Yup.'

Down the road the cries of testosterone-charged rage had ceased, as had the panel-beating, though the klaxons were still blasting at full volume. Cutting like a knife through the din I could hear the increasingly loud whine of a siren. Clearly the drivers had heard it, too. A cab shot past us from the direction of the fight, going so fast it was a mere streak of yellow vanishing into the distance.

'It's broken up,' Don said superfluously. 'Well—' he spread his hands wide, as the second cab speeded past, it too making good time '—what can I say? Uh, I guess "Welcome to New York" would be good, right?'

CHAPTER FOUR

As soon as you walk into any serious gallery, the receptionist will size you up to see if they think you're capable of dropping a few grand – at least – on a work of art. Duggie, who runs the gallery where I show in London, trains his assistants to check out the visitors' shoes, which he swears by as the most reliable indicator of wealth. But the usual procedure is the quick, full-body, up-and-down flick with their eyes, which, if they are skilled enough, can feel rather like someone scraping a steel brush over the more sensitive parts of your anatomy. I assume that if the verdict comes out positive, the sensation is more one of being lovingly caressed by the silky hair of highly trained and enthusiastic sex slaves, but so far I haven't been in a position to confirm this theory.

The girl on the desk at Bergmann LaTouche was so beautiful that to be sized up by her was a privilege. And I appreciated the skill of the extra sideways-and-down glance to see if I was carrying a portfolio and might therefore be a trouble-causing aspirant artist.

'Hi!' she said in a bright automatic tone. Her accent was American, but she was a mix of races in which Asian had won by the shortest of heads. Her skin was smooth and the pale fawn of buffed expensive suede, her eyes wide and dark and almond-shaped. And now her smooth forehead was creasing into a frown.

'I'm sorry,' she said politely, 'but don't I know you from somewhere?'

She was wearing a pale silk shirt and charcoal gabardine trousers, her hair was scraped back into a little knot at the back of her neck, and she appeared to be wearing no make-up at all. But she looked eerily flawless, which in practice meant that she was wearing a lot more than I was, only applied with infinitely more cunning. No jewellery, no adornment, apart from the silver twist of her belt buckle, but the shirt and trousers looked as if they had been cut to fit her, and her hair was beautifully done, with a few perfectly groomed little strands emerging with artful care from the knot. New York minimalism done to perfection.

'I'm Sam Jones,' I said. 'Part of the next show.'

'Oh, of course! I must have seen your photo in the press stuff.' She looked relieved to have placed me. 'Hi, I'm Java. Nice to meet you. I'll call Carol down for you. I don't think she's in a meeting.'

'Java?' I said, after she had buzzed up to Carol Bergmann.

She gave a rueful smile. I was glad to see that her teeth were sharp and slightly irregular in a non-American, reassuringly imperfect kind of way.

'I had this hippie Dutch mother. My dad's Korean. My mom still doesn't know where she got the name from.'

'A pack of coffee?' I suggested. 'Lucky you didn't end up being called Continental Blend.'

Java's smile remained exactly in place, but her eyes froze. For a horrible moment I thought I had offended her, but then I realised that she simply hadn't understood me.

'I'm sorry?' she said, polite as ever.

'Huh!' Don said behind me, in a way that I interpreted as meaning amusement rather than disdain. He heaved himself off the door jamb and strolled over to us.

'British humour,' he informed Java. 'Really dry. Like sherry,' he added to me. I blinked, partly because he had pronounced dry as 'draaah', and it had taken me a few seconds to work it out.

'Well, *some* kinds of sherry,' I said cautiously. My head was spinning slightly, and not just from the jet lag. I was beginning to feel as though I were trapped in one of the more surreal Monty Python sketches.

Java had obviously decided not to pursue my comment, which was a wise decision.

'Sam, this is Don,' she said. 'He's the preparator.'

'My God, really? I had no idea he was so important.'

'I'm sorry?' Java went into the lovely-smile-but-what-the-hell-are-you-saying routine again. She was a very sweet girl, if, perhaps, a few maggots short of a Damien Hirst installation of a rotting cow. This was only in the British sense of humour department. In everything else she turned out to be more than competent.

'Yeah, right,' Don said to me. '*Preparator*. More like the bellhop. Anyway,' he yawned, 'I got art to shift. See ya later.'

At least, I thought that was what he said. He started well, but tailed off as he neared the end, falling back into the familiar mumble. Shambling past me, and managing not to drag his knuckles along the floor as he walked, he crossed to an open door behind Java's big white desk. Through this I could see steel lift doors framed on either side by the treads of an equally industrial-looking staircase. Don pressed the button to call the lift as a high-pitched clinking noise signalled the arrival of a woman in high heels coming swiftly down the metal staircase from the floor above.

'Don't tell me you're calling the elevator just to go down to the *basement*, Don,' she said incredulously.

'Hey, why walk unless you have to?' Don drawled.

The lift doors opened with a ping.

'Here's my ride,' he said, giving us a little wave. 'Bye, ladies.'

'He's a real character, isn't he?' Java said to me. 'Big Don. Most of our clients love him.'

'What about the rest?'

'Uh—' she grinned '—they think he's a tad disrespectful. And kind of shabby.'

'Which he is,' said Carol Bergmann, approaching me with her hand held out. 'But he's damn good at his job. Sam! Hi! You only landed a couple of hours ago, didn't you? I wasn't expecting to see you today.'

'I dumped my bags at the flat and came straight out again,' I explained, shaking her hand. 'I thought if I stayed there I'd go to sleep and mess up my time clock.'

'Probably very sensible,' she commented. I had never seen anyone who, in their way, was more stripped for action than Carol Bergmann: hair cut short and brushed firmly back from her face, black trouser suit designed for the working woman who just wanted to put it on and forget about it, no make-up at all, visible or otherwise. The only touch that could have been considered slightly frivolous was the height of her heels, and she obviously did not consider them a weapon of seduction. In fact, the noise they made as she sped along meant that, if anything, they intimidated anyone who got in her way. It was like being in the path of an express train bearing down at full throttle.

'Well, so how was the flight?' she was continuing. 'Driver pick you up OK?'

'Everything was fine, thanks.'

'Good, good. So you've met Java and Don already. Maybe the best thing is for me to give you a tour of the gallery and introduce you to everyone else who's in today. Be a good start. Did you have time to look around the exhibition?'

I had actually cast a glance round the main room as I came in. It looked like there were a couple of others leading off it to the right, but the contents of the first one had not encouraged me to explore further. It was hung with four huge and splodgy canvases daubed with a variety of unattractively murky colours. (Daub and splodge are not technical terms, by the way. I get to use them because I'm an artist.) If you stared at them hard you could finally make out a couple of banal images lurking in their depths, rather like a high art version of those Magic Eye pictures. Not trusting her viewers to work it out for themselves, the artist, someone called Barbara Bilder, had helpfully provided hints to these with the titles. Thus, the cesspit-like swill of 'Three Cypresses' turned out to contain, when squinted at in the right way, three cypress trees surrounded by a load of glop the texture and colour of a barrel-load of decaying human waste. And so on. Tact was definitely called for.

'A little, yes,' I said smoothly. 'But they're very subtle. I'd really need more time with them.'

And a frontal lobotomy. But there was no need to spell that out.

Carol Bergmann was nodding approvingly. 'That's what I've said from the beginning. Isn't it, Java?'

'Oh yes, Carol.'

'Barbara sells slowly. But the collectors who have her pieces say they just get better and better the longer they look at them.'

And the more their eyesight deteriorates with age, I thought.

'I'll show you around here briefly,' Carol said, whisking me through the open space at the side of the entrance area and into two linked rooms which seemed much smaller only because the main gallery was so vast. The walls were painted a uniform white and the floor was concrete throughout, like Java's desk, which was an unapologetically unadorned slab of the stuff.

'So this is the downstairs. The entrance is one of our big viewing areas,' Carol said, waving a hand magisterially as she clicked rapidly towards the staircase, sounding like a Morse signal in a tearing hurry. 'It's wonderful to have those high ceilings, isn't it?'

I was trotting so fast to keep up with her I hardly had breath to answer. We clattered up the steel openwork treads of the staircase and up through a narrow white lobby into a room whose floor was so shiny that I fumbled instinctively for my dark glasses. A ray of the setting sun, piercing under the translucent blinds on the huge windows, struck the pale wooden floor so brightly it looked as if it were about to burst into flame. There must have been half an inch of polish, like a single sheet of glass. You could almost have skated on it. Now if this had been an installation, I would have got the point at once.

'This floor is spectacular!' I said, hoping that Carol wouldn't notice that my tone was much more enthusiastic than it had been for Barbara Bilder's paintings.

She gave me a funny look.

'It's so shiny,' I clarified, realising that I sounded as if I were tripping.

'Well, yes. We've just had it polished,' she said kindly, as if humouring a child. 'Now, this is the other real viewing room. I think we'll be putting your installation downstairs and the other one suspended in here. We need a lot of space for your pieces.'

The space up here was much more beautiful than the concrete zone downstairs. Light poured in through the three huge windows at the far end, diffused by the blinds, which were the near-opaque misty grey of tracing paper. The shine on the floor reflected and threw up the light in a way that would flatter my mobiles immensely. On either side of the room were two white-painted pillars, a relic of the days when this had been warehouse space, but they wouldn't interfere with the viewing of the mobile. In fact, I might actually be able to use them.

'It's wonderful,' I said to Carol, who looked pleased.

'Good. Good. Now this is Suzanne.' She indicated a tall statuesque woman behind a desk directly on the right of the entrance lobby. Caught up in my appraisal of the room, I had barely noticed her presence. I blinked in shock. I must be more jet-lagged than I had realised: it was the only explanation for how I had managed to ignore a six-foot blonde built like a Varga girl and dressed like Rosalind Russell in *His Girl Friday*. Suzanne was a throwback to the age where men referred to women of her proportions as stacked, and called them dames while whistling between their teeth and tilting their hats back. I repressed the urge to whistle myself.

'Hi,' Suzanne said, with a little smile. She had more poise than the Statue of Liberty. It was impressive, if not instantly endearing. Carol was continuing:

'And that's Kate.'

The desk up here was smaller and clearly much more of a work area than the one downstairs; it held a computer, at which Suzanne was sitting, and the walls behind it were stacked to the ceiling with files. Off this little area ran a long narrow office, humming with activity, its shelves filled with art magazines and boxes of slides, a giant photocopier squatting at the far end. The woman Carol was indicating stuck her head through the open door, a stack of papers in her arms.

'Hi,' she said cheerfully. 'I'm Kate. Great to meet you.'

Her thick red hair was cornrowed tightly to her head – not plaited and pinned down, but actually cornrowed. The effect was very striking. She wore a bead choker, a tight stripy sweater and a combat-style pair of red needlecord trousers that fitted so well they had probably cost more than one would imagine.

'We're all very excited about your show,' she went on. 'Young British artists go crazy in New York.'

'That's more Lex and Rob,' I said. 'They're the real chaos and anarchy merchants.'

'That's a great accent,' Suzanne said, revealing in the process that she herself wasn't American. She sounded like a French/Dutch cross;

the accent was smooth but had a guttural edge to some of the consonants. 'I love the way the English talk,' she went on. 'They're so—'

'Refined,' said Kate. 'So kinda clipped and neat.'

She flashed me a big smile. I had taken to her at once; she looked positively human, especially next to Suzanne's daunting example of Aryan perfection.

'Well, I like your hair,' I said to Kate. 'It's fabulous.'

She touched it automatically.

'It's a royal pain in the ass.'

'Very hip, very now,' Suzanne said unexpectedly in the campest of voices. Kate cracked up.

'Sorry,' she said to me, 'that's kind of our catchphrase *du jour*. It was in this magazine of Suze's and we can't stop saying it.'

'I do need to show Sam around the gallery,' Carol cut in rather curtly. 'I have a six-o'clock appointment and we should be getting on.'

'Yeah boss!' Kate saluted Carol smartly, bringing her heels together. 'Tell you what, I'll go whip myself with the cat-o'-nine-tails so no one else has to take time off from their work to flog me.'

Carol was smiling, almost as if against her will. Suzanne slapped Kate's red corduroy bottom.

'That's enough insubordination from you,' she said firmly. She smiled at me, and this time it was much more friendly. Kate's infectious enthusiasm clearly made Suzanne loosen her corsets. As it were. 'Catch you later, Sam.'

Kate wiggled her fingers at me and disappeared back into the office.

'I'm working!' she called back. 'I'm working!'

'Kate's such a clown,' Carol said, not unaffectionately, as she led me across the expanse of polished wood and into the smaller room that led off it. 'But she has a wonderful eye. I'm going to get her to work with you on hanging your mobiles. She's a great fan.'

'I look forward to it.' And I did. Kate and I would have a blast.

Despite its lesser size, the room in which we were standing was a lovely space, almost a perfect square. The white enclosing walls, blending into the glossy floor, gave it a great sense of calm. Even

Barbara Bilder's 'More Scenes From A Sewage Farm' couldn't completely destroy the atmosphere. I wanted to stay there for a moment but Carol, Ms Moto Perpetuo, was already crossing the room. She tapped briskly on a door that I had hardly noticed was there; it was set into the far wall so smoothly that a casual glance would have swept over it without even seeing the hinges.

'Stanley? Are you in there?'

A voice called: 'Come!' from behind the door, and there was a faint buzzing sound. Carol pushed it open and gestured for me to enter first. I was in a long narrow white room lit by streams of daylight flooding through the high windows. There was a large blued steel table in the centre of the room and two extraordinary things hanging on the wall which looked like collages made by a small child who had just discovered Technicolor and egg boxes simultaneously.

Two men were sitting at the table. One, at the far side, had a bulging, extra-large Filofax, two catalogues, a file box of slides and various other bits of paper scattered in front of him. Skinny as a rake, he was pale as a corpse and wore big black-framed glasses: your classic geeky intellectual, a Jewish Jarvis Cocker without the twisted fashion sense. His hair was messy, as if he had been running his hands through it, his jacket unbuttoned and his tie askew.

The other man, leaning back in his orange leather chair, was fiddling with a small electronic organiser which didn't appear to be switched on. He, in contrast, was picture-perfect. Why not? The nerd in the suit was clearly doing all the work. A tubby little man of indeterminate age, with butter-blond hair and the plump rosy cheeks old ladies love to pinch, he jumped to his feet as Carol and I came in. What a gentleman. Immediately he took my hands in both of his and pressed them together in a tightly packed flesh sandwich. I didn't take to him, particularly as he was smarming at me with a self-conscious, I-am-a-ladykiller smirk as he squashed his palms stickily around mine. A watch that must have cost ten thousand dollars slid down his wrist to join our love-fest.

'You must be Ms Jones! I saw your photograph, but it doesn't do you justice. It's a real honour for us to have you here,' he said, his voice greasier than a plate of lard-fried eggs.

I tugged at my hands. They wouldn't come out. He had started to knead them intimately, which was revolting.

'It's the other way round. Really,' I said, pulling harder. There was something particularly frustrating about having my hands incapacitated. And his were getting damper by the minute.

'No, I assure you—'

He broke off because I had twisted my right hand round enough for one of my more knuckleduster-type rings to cut into his fingers.

'Gosh, I'm sorry,' I said, withdrawing my hands from his loosened grasp. 'Did that cut you? It's rather sharp.'

The nerd made a small sound that I interpreted as a snigger.

'Sam, this is Stanley Pinketts, a fellow director,' Carol said. 'And Laurence, his assistant.'

There was a tap on the door.

'Carol?' came Suzanne's voice. 'There's a call for you.'

Laurence leaned over to the control panel on the desk and buzzed the door open for her.

'I wouldn't disturb you,' she said apologetically, 'but it's Mrs Kaneda.'

Carol looked at me, obviously not wanting to seem rude. But I could tell it was urgent.

'Go ahead,' I said quickly, 'take the call. I mean, I just dropped in, we didn't have an appointment or anything.'

'I'll look after Sam while you're on the phone,' Laurence offered, shoving his glasses more firmly onto his beaky nose with one thin finger.

Carol hesitated a moment, then shrugged.

'Fine. Why don't you make her a coffee. You're the only one who knows how to work that thing. Sorry about this, Sam.'

I held up my hands in a no-need-to-apologise, coffee-sounds-just-fine gesture.

'Suzanne, put the call through here,' Carol said crisply. Suzanne disappeared at once. 'Stanley, would you mind staying?' she went on. 'I might need to check the figures with you.'

Laurence guided me out and shut the door behind us both.

'I'll be safe if I stay clear of your rings, right?' he said.

'More or less.'

'Good. "I might need to check the figures with Stanley",' he continued mockingly in an imitation of Carol's über-businesswoman voice. 'The only figures Stanley knows about aren't exactly fiscal. What she means is that Stanley throws a fit over every decision he's not involved in, so it's easier to keep him around when the big ones are going down.'

'Should you be talking to me like that?'

'Certainly not. But since I haven't said anything along those lines to you, it doesn't matter, does it?' He swiped his palm over my face, a few centimetres away from contact. 'All wiped clean,' he intoned. 'You will not remember any of my previous comments . . . . Would you like a coffee?'

'I *need* a coffee,' I corrected. 'I'm jet-lagged and I've never been to New York before and the taxi driver who brought me here tried to kill another one and I've just met seventeen new people.'

'So a quieter day than usual in the big city. And it's sixteen people,' Laurence corrected. 'Stanley doesn't count because he's a slug. I thought you'd worked that one out already. Nice hand-work, by the way. You cut him bad?'

'Minor lesions only.'

We were passing Suzanne's desk. Laurence waved at her but didn't stop. We crossed the lobby and paused briefly at a white door with a keypad next to it. Laurence entered a code and the door buzzed.

'We're in!' I said. 'Everything's so high-tech here . . . My God.' My voice tailed off. The Technicolor-and-egg-box artist had excelled on the far wall. I bet that it contained every single colour on the spectrum.

'Striking, no?' Laurence said. 'They're very popular. No-brainers always are. This way.'

He led me into a small kitchen and started doing things to a coffee machine with more switches than the cockpit of a 747.

'Don't you need a licence to operate that thing?' I asked, sitting down in a plastic chair of frighteningly modern construction. 'Wow, this is actually quite comfortable.' I yawned.

'Not comfortable enough to go to sleep in,' Laurence warned. 'Hang on. Caffeine coming right up. Do you want a cappuccino?'

'No, thanks. Milk dilutes the effects. Can I have a double?'

'You Europeans are so un-health-conscious. It's quite charming. I take it you don't mean decaf?'

I made the sign of the cross at him, hissing.

'Right, I get the picture.'

'Do you have any biscuits?'

He stared at me. 'You mean cookies, I take it. Are you nuts? Practically every single person here's on a diet. Anyone who tried to bring cookies into the kitchen would be stoned to death.'

'You don't exactly need to diet,' I pointed out. Laurence was as thin as a rail, his shirt sagging at the waist because his stomach was so hollow. The difference between him and Jarvis Cocker was that the latter knew how to dress his bones, while Laurence could make even the most expensive suit look like he'd bought it at a charity shop. I noticed that his fishbelly-white skin was lightly dotted with pinky-brown freckles, and that his brown eyes, behind the thick lenses, were very sharp.

'Exactly,' he said, putting the coffee cups on a small tray. 'So come through into our humble cubbyhole and have some Oreos from my private stash.'

Oreos turned out to be delicious, besides coming in a really cute tin with a picture of them stacked up inside. And the gallery assistants' cubbyhole wasn't bad either. It wasn't cosy – nothing in this place could remotely be described as cosy – but it was comparatively welcoming, perhaps because the quarters were so cramped that it could make no attempt to seem design-conscious.

As I drank my espresso, Laurence filled me in about Bergmann LaTouche. I had already decided that I liked him. He had what Don would have called a 'draah' sense of humour.

'There are three directors at BLT. You know Carol, of course, and you just met the inimitable Stanley – actually that's not true, he's very imitable, give me your hand—'

'Ugh, no, please, not again—'

'OK – then there's Jeannette, Jeannette LaTouche, but she's never here. She does the social schmoozing and brings people in, but she's not one for the nuts and bolts of running the place. It's basically Carol's show. Stanley wanted something arty to do, to impress his bimbos, so he bought in. His family has scads of money. I think Carol's regretting it now. Anyway, then there are three assistants – I'm not Stanley's assistant, by the way, I'm my own man, that was just Carol being cruel – Java, our lovely receptionist, Suzanne, who does the inventory—'

'Does the inventory? What, full-time?'

'Yeah.'

'Jesus.'

Laurence raised his eyebrows.

'Oh, just the scale of the operation—'

'Hey, you're in the big league now, little lady. OK, who else is there? The archivist – she's full-time too – book-keeper . . . oh, and Don, the handler.'

'Don't you like him?'

There had been an edge to Laurence's voice as he came to Don. Now he shrugged elaborately, adding a fresh sprinkle of dandruff to the grey shoulders of his suit.

'Don's very into his image. All that he-man stuff leaves me cold,' he said dismissively.

'Into his image?' I said incredulously. 'Dressed like that?'

'Oh, it's the boy-from-the-Virginia-backwoods thing. Country boy in the big city. He thinks it gives him this kind of hokey charm.'

'Hey, guys.' Kate stuck her head round the door. 'Laurence, get your big feet off my desk, boy. Anyone want to come to the bar? It's past six.'

The word 'bar' had me on my feet and reaching for my jacket.

'Well, talk about Pavlov's barfly,' Laurence said, swinging his legs down from Kate's desk and standing up too.

'Laurence?' Kate said, nodding at me. 'What about Carol? I mean . . .'

There was a long pause.

'Oh, Jesus, she's still on the phone,' Laurence said finally. 'She's always hours with Mrs Kaneda. And it's Sam's first night here. We can't abandon her, can we? It wouldn't be polite.'

'No, you're right.' Kate relaxed.

'So I can come?' I said hopefully, though without quite understanding the by-play.

'Sure,' Kate said. 'We just have to be careful that Carol doesn't think we're poaching you.'

I raised my eyebrows, unable to imagine a situation in my London gallery where Duggie, the owner, objected to my going for a drink with his assistants. Actually he would be amazed if I suggested it, as none of them were at all appetising, but he would scarcely mind. Maybe New York rules were different. But it still seemed strange.

'But she could be in there for another hour,' Kate was saying. 'I'll just drop in and run it by her. She'll probably be grateful to us for taking you off her hands. I know she's got a dinner appointment.'

'When doesn't she? You're in a hurry,' Laurence observed, watching me pull my gloves on as fast as if I were practising it as an Olympic sport.

'Coffee will only take a girl so far,' I explained. 'Now I need some vodka. And do they have any bar snacks at this place we're going to?'

CHAPTER FIVE

'I don't know,' Kate said to me apologetically as we settled into the booth. 'Maybe we should've taken you somewhere more hip than here. It's a real dive.'

'Oh, no,' I assured her. 'I like it. It's cosy and I'm shattered. Anything too designer tonight would have given me hives.'

'Well, if you're sure . . . . We always come here. I don't know why.'

''Cause it's not posey and the drinks are cheap?' Laurence suggested.

It was a little bar on Bleecker Street, only a five-minute walk from the gallery. I found this area much more congenial, or perhaps it would be fairer to say familiar, than my lofty perch on the Upper West Side; SoHo was generally constructed on a more human scale. The buildings were lower, the streets closer together, and we had passed a shop with the best array of fluorescent wigs I'd ever seen, music spilling out from the wide-open door in a slow insistent rhythm. It was like Camden with money.

This place was simple and basic: wooden floors, wooden booths, a glowing bar at the far end and surprisingly low lighting for six in the evening, when it was only just starting to get dark. Soon I would learn that this was one of the factors that made New York bars so fabulous. They were so dark you couldn't see how much you were drinking, they served cocktails as a matter of course, and they stayed open till very, very late. It was paradise, really.

'Oh, by the way,' Kate said to me, 'Carol asked you to come in tomorrow and she'll take you to lunch. She said about twelve-thirty.'

'Come in earlier if you like and I'll show you some of the stock,' Laurence offered. 'We've got some weird and wonderful stuff.'

'That's probably a good idea,' I said. 'Get myself out of bed and onto New York time.'

'About eleven-thirty,' he suggested. 'I find that after more than an hour of looking at art, one's eyes glaze over.'

'It's a date.'

'What can I get you?' the waitress said, coming up to our table.

New York bars even had table service. You didn't have to move if you didn't want to.

Kate ordered a margarita. I immediately seconded that.

'They have margaritas here,' I said dreamily as the waitress left us. 'I like it already.'

'They have margaritas everywhere in the city,' said Laurence pityingly. 'I didn't realise you Brits were so starved of culture.'

'Yeah, right. Like there's centuries of history in America,' I retorted.

Suzanne laughed. Laurence rounded on her at once.

'Suzanne, you're from *Belgium*. You can't talk. *I* know,' he went on gleefully, 'let's play Ten Famous Belgians! We haven't done that in at least two weeks.'

'Shit,' said Kate, 'I was going to write them down last time so I could reel it right off next time we played.'

'It's a game we invented a while back,' Laurence explained to me. 'To taunt Suzanne for being a snotty European. First one to name ten famous Belgians gets a free drink.'

'Surely she always wins?' I said, looking at Suzanne, who was lighting a cigarette. She rolled her eyes at me, but didn't comment.

'Oh, Suzanne's banned from playing, of course,' Laurence said airily.

'That's not very fair.'

'Oh, we get her a drink too. We're not total bastards.'

'Yeah, yeah,' said Suzanne witheringly. But she seemed to take the teasing with a good enough grace. And when you're tall, blonde and built along the lines of a ship's figurehead, it's easy to convey that you consider petty mockery beneath your notice.

Our margaritas arrived in big ribbed half-pint glasses, studded with ice and a hefty straw.

'God, this is good,' I said, downing half in one slurp and beaming round the table.

'So how do you like it here?' Java said.

'Do you mean here in the bar or here in New York?'

'Well, either, really. But I meant the city.'

Everyone pricked up their ears. They genuinely wanted to know. I thought this was quite sweet. Londoners wouldn't have asked the question, not giving a damn about the answer; our attitude would be that if New Yorkers didn't like it in London, they could sod off and die. And the first part was optional.

'I've only been here about ten seconds,' I said, drinking some more margarita, 'but so far it seems great. The gallery is a wonderful space. I'm really looking forward to planning out my installation. Ugh, that sounded so naff and gushing,' I apologised. 'I'm usually much nastier than this.'

'We'll make allowances for the jet lag,' Kate said kindly.

'I need to know where to go shopping,' I said with decision, as my eyes fell on her extremely nice bead choker. 'I should get started as soon as possible. I've only got a month.'

'Clothes?' she said.

'What else is there?'

'OK, I'll give you some places. Kinda downtown, funky stuff, right?'

'Where are you staying?' Laurence asked.

'I've got a sub-let on the Upper West Side.'

'Where exactly?'

I gave the address, which was on West End Avenue in the lower seventies.

'Great! We're practically neighbours!' he said cheerfully. 'I'm in the lower eighties.'

'Don't you guys need oxygen masks that far uptown?' Kate said sarcastically.

'Oh, for God's sake, Kate, it's not as if I lived in the *upper hundreds*,' Laurence retorted. 'And I don't have to pay through the nose for a skanky little East Village dump.'

'Could we cut out the eternal uptown/downtown debate?' Suzanne said a trifle wearily. 'I'm sure Sam isn't that interested.'

'I would be if I knew what it was about.' I finished my margarita. 'Shall I get in another round?' I waved at the waitress.

'My God,' Laurence said, temporarily distracted, 'I've always heard the English drank like fish, and it's so true.'

I looked round the table. Everyone else was, at most, halfway down their drinks.

'Shit,' I said. 'And I was going slowly because of the jet lag.'

'Is it true you guys all drink till you fall over?' Java wanted to know. 'I heard it's a Saturday night thing over there.'

'Not fall over,' I corrected. 'Stagger, perhaps. Another margarita, please,' I said to the waitress. 'OK, you were saying?'

'Uptown versus downtown,' Suzanne said. 'I'll do this—' she held up her hands to ward off Kate and Laurence, who were both trying to speak. 'Being a snotty European, I can see both sides of the question. Uptown has the park, river walks, the museums, bigger apartments, especially the higher you go. But there's not that much going on and everything shuts pretty early. Downtown is much more hip. But it's grungier and it costs much more so everyone lives in shoeboxes.'

She looked around the table. 'That was pretty fair, right?'

A round of nods answered her.

'Where do you live, Suzanne?'

'Midtown,' she said cheerfully. 'You must come around. I have a great place.'

'Talk about spending a fortune, though,' Laurence said. 'A thousand bucks a month just for the marble in the lobby.'

'I don't spend a fortune,' Suzanne said tranquilly. 'My flatmate does. He's a banker,' she explained to me.

'One of Suze's many rich would-be boyfriends,' Kate said. 'He thought giving her somewhere fabulous to live practically rent free would win her heart.'

'And has it?' I asked.

Suzanne gave me a beautiful smile. 'It certainly didn't hurt. But I don't believe in making decisions in a hurry.' She put one hand up to check that her hair, drawn back into a bun at the nape of her neck, was still in place.

'She's holding out for the richest Belgian in New York,' Kate said affectionately.

'Does he have to be Belgian?' I wanted to know.

'Tradition matters,' Suzanne said seriously, an effect that was rather undercut by being simultaneously carolled by Laurence and Kate. Clearly it was a familiar saying of hers.

'I should be going,' Kate said, looking at her watch.

'Meeting someone?' Java asked.

'Yeah.'

The way she said this, her voice flattening out as if she didn't really want to answer, made my ears prick up. Kate had been so ebullient up till now that this change of tone was instantly obvious. Suzanne picked up on it immediately.

'Oh shit,' she said, leaning across the table to look at Kate more closely. 'Kate, it's not Leo?'

Kate shrugged. It wasn't a confirmation or a denial, it was an evasive, don't-push-me kind of shrug. But Suzanne rode right over the signal.

'Kate! You said it was over!' she said, unable to help her rising intonation. Whoever Leo was, he had Suzanne more than worried.

'It *is* over,' Kate said. 'Relax, OK? Oh, look who's come in.' She waved at Don, who had just shambled through the door, accompanied by another guy. He raised his hand in greeting and went over to the bar.

'That was a bad attempt to distract me,' Suzanne said sternly. 'You never say hi to Don normally.'

'Yes, I do. I'm not that rude. Look, I really have to go.' She chucked a five-dollar bill on the table and stood up. 'Get them to tell you about the Don thing,' she said to me, pulling on her jacket. 'It's a good story. Are you coming in tomorrow?'

I nodded.

'OK. So when I see you I'll give you the shopping rundown. Bye, everyone.'

She waved and was gone. Suzanne stared after her.

'Something's not right,' she said crossly. 'If she's seeing Leo again . . . .'

'Old boyfriend?' I said.

'Bad news,' Java informed me.

'Kate tends to like them with problems,' Suzanne said, drawing on another cigarette. 'But Leo . . . .'

'Leo was overdoing it, even by her standards,' Laurence said.

A pall of seriousness hung for a moment over the table. Though I was curious about the nameless sins of the absent Leo, I was definitely not in the mood for *Sturm und Drang* this evening. I wanted everything to be light and bubbly and fun so it would keep me awake until at least eleven o'clock. I sensed that as soon as things got heavy my head would hit the table and stay there, snoring.

'Tell me the Don story,' I pleaded as winsomely as possible. 'Kate said it would be funny. I need funny right now.'

'*Well*,' Suzanne and Laurence said simultaneously. They paused and looked at each other.

'Go ahead,' said Laurence. 'You're the girl. It's a girl story.'

'This is *so funny*,' Java promised me.

'*Well*,' Suzanne said again, her eyes gleaming with amusement. 'This happened about a year and a half ago, just after Don joined the gallery. He's pretty much Kate's type – she likes them kind of butch.'

'Does he have problems?' I inquired.

'Just *wait*,' Suzanne said. 'But yeah, he's got kind of a druggie past, I think.'

'And it's not like his "art" is going anywhere fast,' chimed in Laurence cattily.

'Oh, he's an artist?'

Laurence burst into a fake coughing fit. '*Please* don't make me laugh! My asthma!' he pleaded through the simulated wheezes.

'Carol lets him use a room downstairs as his studio,' Java explained to me. 'It's kinda derivative, though. His work.'

'Could I just tell the story? Would that be OK with you guys?' Suzanne said pointedly. 'So we all go out for a few drinks after work, and one by one we all peel off, but Kate and Don are stuck to each other like glue by that time. I mean, it's pretty obvious. They've been sitting on the same sofa for the last hours, thighs clamped together, and she's actually been pretending she can understand what he says *and* thinks it's funny. So they go back to hers and start making out, things are getting hot and heavy, and finally they decide to go for it. Only neither of them have any condoms. Things get more and more frustrating—' she waved her hand in a large embracing circle '—and at last Don says right, that's it, he's going out to get some. There's a 24-hour drugstore on the next block. So he puts on his things, goes out, and . . .' she paused for effect, '*never comes back*.'

'No!'

'*Oh* yes,' said Suzanne, who was enjoying this tremendously. 'Just disappeared.'

Java was shaking her head in a pantomime of disbelief.

'What a wimp!' I said incredulously. 'Performance anxiety, right?'

'That's what I think,' Suzanne said. 'Scared he wouldn't be up to it. And apparently he tells the guys that he's this real stud. Hah!'

'Or it's about the size of a cocktail weenie and he didn't want her to know,' Java suggested.

'Also possible. So he's all mouth and no trousers,' I said thoughtfully, looking over at Don, who was still at the bar.

'What?' said Laurence, leaning over towards me.

'All mouth and no trousers,' I repeated. 'It means you talk a lot about how good you are in bed, but never follow through. In Don's case, of course, it would be "all mouth and no dungarees".'

'Excellent,' Laurence said, a contemplative smile on his face. 'I like these British expressions.'

'This friend of mine thought he was pretty hot,' Java added, 'until I told her that story. Now she wouldn't go near him if you paid her. I mean, who wants to be left with your engine running and nowhere to go?'

I had a big flash of missing Hugo, who would inevitably have pointed out that the latter part of the analogy wasn't exact, and that she would have done better to say 'and no one to disengage your clutch'. Or possibly 'slip it into third'. But I mustn't get maudlin about Hugo. I wasn't half drunk enough for it to be allowable.

'Did Kate ever confront him about it?' I asked instead. 'She looks like the type who would.'

'Sure,' Suzanne said, giving this a wonderfully sarcastic spin. 'She went up to him the very next day and said, "Well, what happened to you?" And he goes, "Oh, I forgot I had to ring my brother down in Virginia. It was real important." '

'What a loser,' Laurence said smugly. 'That just adds the final touch of patheticness to an already unconvincing – Oh, hi, Don!'

Don loomed up over us, the other guy hovering by his side. Laurence, whose face was temporarily hidden from Don, grimaced at me horribly.

'Did he *hear*?' he mouthed.

I raised my shoulders helplessly.

'Hey, Kevin,' Suzanne said, 'you haven't met Sam, have you? Sam Jones. She's one of the English artists. Sam, this is Kevin. He's one of the gallery assistants. We were bringing her up to speed about work stuff.'

I admired the girl's aplomb. She might look like an ice queen but she was a good operator in a sticky situation. If I were in a tight place it would be Suzanne I'd pick to watch my back. In contrast Java, sitting next to me, was stricken with embarrassment and consequently as useless in a tight spot as a would-be ladykiller with performance anxiety.

'Hi, Kevin,' I said, determined to rival Suzanne's cool. 'This lot have just been filling me in about who's who at the gallery. But they didn't get to you yet, you'll be glad to hear. Do you guys want to sit down?'

'Uh, OK,' said Kevin, sliding in next to me. He was blond and very good-looking in such a blank, unreflecting way that the gaze passed straight over him and settled straight away on something more interesting, if less regular.

'You splitting, big guy?' he said to Don.

Maybe Kevin had information we didn't; but his choice of adjective, after Java's hypothesis a few moments before, sent Laurence's eyes wide in an effort to stop laughing and caused Suzanne to reach hurriedly for a cigarette before realising that she had one already smouldering in the ashtray.

'Yeah, I'm off,' Don mumbled, shoving his hands deep into the pockets of his donkey jacket. 'Got to haul ass.' He nodded a goodbye to our cosy little group and was gone, shouldering the door open.

'Did dungarees come back in while I wasn't looking?' I wondered. 'They have to be the most unflattering garment ever designed.'

'Bubble skirts,' countered Suzanne.

'Boob tubes,' Java added.

'Oh, come on, Java, you'd look great in a boob tube,' Suzanne said firmly.

Java shook her head. 'They make me look like I haven't got anything up here at all,' she said, mournfully tapping her chest. 'The stretchy ones just flatten you out completely.'

'It's the look,' I said unsympathetically. 'You're lucky you can wear it. It'd take a steamroller to flatten me out.'

'Well, I don't like having no boobs,' Java said stubbornly. 'Even if it is the look.'

'I didn't know you hung out with Don, Kevin,' Laurence was saying.

'Oh, well, you know.' Kevin ducked his head. 'He's a great guy. Some of the stories he tells – he's really been around, man. It's pretty impressive.'

Laurence looked distinctly underawed. I could understand his basic dislike of Don; with his sharp intellect and skinny physique he might well resent a guy who, just by mumbling a few disconnected phrases and resembling a brick shithouse, managed to pull easily enough. Even if he couldn't follow through on it. But I was beginning to wonder whether Laurence had a thing for Kate, and resented Don's success with her – such as it was. It would explain why he seemed unable to let the Don-baiting go.

'Oh?' he said, overdoing the casually interested bit. 'What kind of stories? Do tell!'

'Laurence, I've got another British expression for you,' I interrupted. 'Key merchant. It means someone—' I mimed putting a key in Java's back and turning it '—who likes to wind people up.'

'I get the gist,' Laurence said aloofly. 'Thank you so much for that, Sam.'

'I haven't had a chance to look at your material yet,' Kevin said to me. It was strange how his undoubted handsomeness cancelled itself out; the more you looked at him, the more bored you were with the even, perfect features, unanimated by any saving flicker of personality. He was like a doctor in a daytime soap. 'I've been really busy with Barbara's show. But we're all looking forward to yours.'

'When does hers come down exactly?' I asked.

'End of next week,' Kevin said, and there was a slight flatness in his tone echoed by the studiedly neutral expressions of everyone else around the table.

'Is it not doing too well?' I probed, inquisitive as always.

Kevin shrugged.

'Barbara's work always moves slowly,' he said. 'But, I don't know, the timing of the opening wasn't so great. There were a lot of really big shows opening that week, and the reviews weren't so hot, which didn't exactly help. We're doing what we can.'

'I heard she's not too happy,' said Suzanne.

'Well, would you be?' Kevin said. 'She didn't like it that the Vallorani retrospective opened the same day as hers did. But what can we do? I mean, we have to plan nine months ahead! How can we know about something like that?' He gestured in what was clearly a rhetorical plea; everyone else knew the schedule as well as he did.

'Why was she cross about the Vallorani retrospective in particular?' I asked. 'I mean, there must be lots of stuff going on right now.' Autumn was always the busiest season for art dealers.

Kevin pulled a face. 'She thinks they're very similar in style,' he said. This was obviously a direct quote.

'Boy, that's some nerve she's got,' Laurence said.

'What d'you want? Artists, right?' Kevin caught my eye. 'Oh, shit. Sorry.'

'No offence taken,' I said.

'Can I get you a drink?' he said, still embarrassed.

'Duh!' I said, flashing him a big smile.

'I'm sorry?' Kevin said nervously.

'I thought that was American for "Yes, of course, stupid",' I complained. 'So much for my attempts to use the local idiom.'

★ ★ ★

Laurence and I were the last survivors of our merry little band. Kevin had peeled off after about half an hour, as soon as Java had announced her intention of leaving, in fact. He had offered to walk her to the subway.

'He's a trier, I'll say that for him,' Suzanne said drily as they left the bar.

'She's terribly pretty,' I said, being fair. 'Anyone would want to have a go.'

'Talking of which, I have to go too,' Suzanne said. 'I just didn't say it before because I didn't want to get in Kevin's way.'

'She's so nice,' Laurence said to me.

'I'm so nice,' she agreed. 'Sam, will you be OK for getting home?'

'Don't go yet!' I pleaded. 'It's only eight-thirty, and I need to stay up till eleven! If I go home now I'll pass out, and I haven't had anything to eat yet . . . .'

'Don't worry, I'll look after Little Orphan Annie,' Laurence said to Suzanne.

'You're so nice,' she said.

'I'm so nice. Do you like Mexican?' he asked me.

'If they look like Antonio Banderas.'

'That's a really bad joke. And he's not Mexican, he's Spanish.'

'Isabel Allende had a fantasy about wrapping him up in a tortilla and eating him,' I countered to confuse the issue.

'She's Chilean.'

'Well, we're getting closer to Mexico, aren't we?' I said unanswerably.

'Bye!' Suzanne was halfway out the door. 'See you tomorrow!'

'You have to realise that people here work hard and get up early,' Laurence lectured me once we had moved to a little Mexican hole-in-the-wall on the next block. 'You can't expect to be able to drag important gallery assistants out drinking with you every night till the small hours.'

'It's not nine yet, and you're hardly drinking,' I said reproachfully. 'Not to mention that you ordered a tofu burrito, which I find pretty sad and not remotely Mexican, frankly.'

'I have asthma and food allergies and lots of neuroses,' Laurence said, unabashed, 'which I think make me a fascinating person.'

However, my black bean grilled vegetable burrito with extra sour cream and guacamole was infinitely nicer than his dairy-free, spinach, brown rice and organic pinto bean one, which naturally made me smug. I pointed this out.

'Being a fascinating person doesn't come easy, you know,' Laurence said. 'You have to work at it. Sometimes you even have to suffer for it.'

'Whereas Kevin has completely given up the struggle,' I said bitchily.

'Kevin is a straight, straight arrow,' Laurence sighed. 'The kind of guy that says what he means and does what he says and thinks irony is the adjective that goes with the thing you use to press your shirts.'

'Nice to have a couple of those people around,' I commented. 'It's a cheap way of feeling superior.'

We spent the rest of the meal ripping to pieces as many people as we could think of, and by the time we walked out into the night streets we were in near-perfect harmony.

'Hey, TAXI!' Laurence yelled suddenly, breaking into a sprint. If nothing else, it shattered the moment. I stared after him in shock. As we got into the cab, I commented that this was a sign of a real New Yorker; nobody here, no matter how cool and laid-back their image, had the slightest hesitation or embarrassment about bellowing across the street, fighting for a cab or giving the driver clear and constant instructions about the best way to get where they were going.

'Well, what d'you do in London?' Laurence said blankly. 'Just raise your hand a little and go, "Oh, cabbie, if you wouldn't mind stopping it would be awfully nice"?'

I giggled. 'Not quite. But if you yelled like you just did in London everyone would turn round to look at you. Here they don't give a damn.'

'"Oh, look at that awe-fully vulgar American,"' Laurence said gleefully. '"How terribly loud they are, my deah!" Hey,' he said to the driver, leaning forward, 'I said West End first. We want to take a right here, OK?'

The driver executed a squealing turn to put us in our place. As he cut the corner at a precise ninety-degree angle, this ended up being practically on top of each other.

'Whoah, there goes my burrito,' I said, sitting up straight again. 'I can feel it all squashed up against my right stomach wall . . . . There's something about burritos that makes me think they reassemble back into that shape and size as soon as all the pieces hit your stomach.'

'One great lump of carbo,' Laurence agreed. 'Of course us dairy-free mavens have it a tad lighter.'

'Right,' I said a few beats later, when I'd caught up with his meaning. Several margaritas and jet lag didn't help with Americans using dialect at high speed.

As the taxi shot up Tenth Avenue, braking and accelerating with abandon – sometimes simultaneously – I found myself clasping my stomach with both hands as if to cushion the burrito against the impact. I should have side roll bars installed.

'So, are you seeing someone?' Laurence said casually.

I thought this was a good way of putting it. If he'd asked if I had a boyfriend my toes would have started to curl; but seeing someone seemed pleasantly light and airy.

'Yes, I suppose I am.'

'You don't sound too keen on him.'

'No, I am. It's just that I'm not used to, um, actually *seeing* someone.'

'So are you guys going steady?'

'Well, we're seeing each other,' I said cautiously, baffled by this new query. 'Does that count?'

'I don't know,' Laurence said with the air of a professional relationship assessor. 'Are you dating him?'

'Laurence, I haven't the faintest idea what the fuck you're talking about. Oh, whoops—'

The taxi made a left that sent the burrito dangerously high up my oesophagus. I tried to massage it down again.

'I'm going to have to explain the dating thing to you,' Laurence said. 'It's important and it will take some time. Remind me to set aside an afternoon in the days to come, OK?'

'Sure.'

'Which number West End did you say?'

I fumbled in my pocket and produced the crumpled memo to myself I had prudently made.

'Next block,' he said to the cabbie. 'On the right.'

We squealed to a halt. I tried to give Laurence some money but he wouldn't hear of it.

'First ride is free,' he said. 'Welcome to the city.'

'Well, thanks. I'll see you tomorrow, OK? Thanks for looking after me.'

'Any time.'

The taxi screeched away. I turned towards my building to find the doorman already holding the door open for me. By now all my various New York experiences were blurring together – crazed taxi drivers, the castellated Manhattan skyline, downtown bars. I could hardly remember where I had dumped my bags; this afternoon felt like days ago. The green awning which stretched out grandly from the façade of the apartment block, almost to the street, came as something of a shock. It was so posh. So was the doorman, in his gold-braided uniform and cute little peaked cap. He was smiling at me politely.

'4H, right?' he said. 'You're staying in Ms Bishop's apartment? Ramon – the day guy – told me you got in this afternoon. Hope you have a pleasant stay.'

'Thanks,' I muttered. He had recognised me with frightening ease. Doubtless Ramon had described me as a typical dissolute scruffy British chick who was sure to fall out of her taxi, drunk and disorderly and full of Mexican food, within eight hours of arrival. And Ramon had been absolutely right.

The entrance hall, floored with marble and shiny with gilt, had me blinking as if someone were shining a torch in my face. The lighting in here felt like a hundred watts and it gleamed off the huge polished armoires on either side of the foyer as if they were glass-fronted. I made straight for the lift, which was panelled, mirrored and carpeted as elaborately as one of Louis XIV's retiring rooms. If the doorman hadn't already told me which apartment I was staying in I would have forgotten, which would have been embarrassing. I should have tipped him just for that.

It was definitely strange coming back to someone else's place rather than a hotel room. Not only were hotels neutral, but it was immediately reassuring to see your possessions strewn over every available surface. As soon as I put something down in Nancy Bishop's apartment, however, it disappeared seamlessly into the clutter of throws, knick-knacks, piles of magazines and *objets d'art* arranged carefully on every table, sofa, bookcase and whatnot. I was beginning to suspect that she was not, in fact, absent doing a play in San Diego, as I had been told, but running a stall at a series of antique fairs. If she didn't sell more than she bought the apartment would burst.

There was such a strong sense of her own life and personality here that I felt rather squashed out. Besides, I was used to the great, draughty, open spaces of my studio. Cosy it was not. Apartment 4H, by contrast, was on a mission to boldly go further than cosy had ever been before. The frilly pelmets and seventeen embroidered cushions on the white-painted four-poster bed were the final touch. My head was still spinning and even the sight of my gutted suitcase spilling the contents of its stomach all over the bed, like something out of a Patricia Cornwell novel, didn't help much with my self-orientation.

Suddenly I remembered that I hadn't made a start yet on hunting Kim down like a dog. I'd meant to look her up in the phone book as soon as I arrived. The prospect seemed scarier than I'd anticipated in London. What if she'd gone native, like Natalie Wood becoming a squaw in *The Searchers*, and didn't want to see me? A wave of margarita-induced self-doubt swept over me. I needed to talk to someone sympathetic. Why this brought Hugo into my head I have no idea, but there it was. I grabbed the phone, threw myself on the part of the bed not already occupied by my carefully planned capsule New York autumn wardrobe, and dialled his number in Stratford.

He answered after five rings, sounding sleepy and bewildered. It was so unusual for Hugo not to be in full possession of his faculties that I felt a warm rush of affection flooding through me.

'Hello! It's me!' I yodelled.

'Sam? *Sam*?' He still sounded fuddled. 'Do you know what time it is?'

'Um, hang on.' There was a digital display clock on the far wall. I squinted over. 'It's jus' past eleven,' I announced.

'No, you fool! Here!'

'Oh, you mean in England? Aren't you—' I made a heroic effort to do my maths. 'You're five hours behind, so it's, um, it's six o'clock—'

'We're five hours *ahead*.'

'Oh, OK, so it's – um, it's – *oh*.' I cleared my throat. 'Sorry! Did I wake you up?'

Hugo snarled at me.

'But I want you,' I whined. 'I have a four-poster bed with no one to tie up to it . . . .' My native cunning was kicking in now.

'Oh, darling,' Hugo said sarcastically, 'you are so fucking romantic. I'm really touched.' But I could hear his tone was softening.

'And the men here all wear really baggy jeans,' I complained, 'so you can't see anyone's bottom properly.'

'Poor baby! What sensory deprivation you must be suffering! Who have you been out drinking with? Or did you manage to get into this state all by yourself?'

'I went out with some people from the gallery. There's this one guy you'd like, he's very dry and funny.'

'Attractive?' Hugo inquired.

'Not at all.'

'Oh good, so you'll just be having intellectual sex with him. That cheers me up tremendously.'

'Sod off, Hugo, you're surrounded by all these gorgeous actresses . . .'

'Sorry, my sweet, what was that noun again?'

'Uh.' I had to think about that one. 'Actresses?' I offered finally.

'Exactly. No, you're pretty safe. I don't know why you should be preferable to a whole slew of actresses – you have an ego the size of a house yourself – but somehow you are.'

'Oh, that's so nishe . . .' I said sentimentally.

'You're drunk and maudlin,' Hugo said firmly. 'Go to sleep.'

'You're rude and bossy,' I muttered, offended. 'You go to sleep.'

'We'll both go to sleep.'

'OK, tha's a good idea. Goo' night, Hugo.'

'Good night, darling. I'll ring you soon.'

'Tha's nishe.' I was fading fast.

'At four o'clock in the morning, your time, of course,' Hugo said, and hung up before I could retaliate.

Perhaps it was for the best. I wouldn't have made a particularly snappy comeback. I just about managed to pull my clothes off before I crawled under the covers and started snoring like a pig.

CHAPTER SIX

The gallery door was locked. I pushed it harder to check, but I could hear the sound of wood coming to a stop against metal. Feeling like an idiot, I tried pulling it towards me, just in case that would work. It didn't. And the huge ground-floor windows had their white shutters firmly closed. I took a few steps back and looked up at the first-floor windows. The blinds were down and I couldn't see anyone moving behind them.

Damn. And I had been doing so well. Up bright and early, unpacking and settling into the apartment, getting used to the constant noise from the street – brakes squealing, the hydraulic whoosh of bus doors opening and closing, periodic shouts and clanks of janitors shifting huge garbage bins in the yard at the back of the building, and a cacophony of honking cars trailing music behind them so loudly you could almost see it, like aeroplanes dragging banners across the sky. One minute it would be a swirl of big band music, the next hip-hop, and after that drum and bass, as if I were twisting the frequency dial on a radio. The sound systems were loud enough for the bass to pound and shake at the scaffolding on the building opposite mine. Certainly in New York you couldn't forget there was a world outside your window; it was demanding enough to come up and rattle the glass with both hands if you didn't pay it enough attention.

The locked door was my first setback of the day. I tried the buzzer. Even if the gallery were closed in the morning, everyone would still be here, working. And I had an appointment, for Christ's sake. They should be expecting me.

After a long wait, a voice said through the intercom:

'Who is it?'

'Sam Jones,' I said, as 'Jones. *Sam* Jones,' to my great disappointment, never sounded quite right.

'Oh,' said the voice with a kind of flat surprise. 'OK. Hold on.'

I raised my eyebrows and waited. I heard footsteps and then the door swung slowly open. Behind it was Java, her prettiness blurred and distorted behind the swollen red rims of her eyes and the bright pink tip of her nose.

'Java!' I said, shutting the door behind me. 'What is it?'

'Did you lock it?' she said at once. 'Only we're not letting anyone in but the cops.'

My eyes widened. 'What the hell is going on? Are you OK?'

It was a stupid question and I regretted it as soon as I saw the tears welling up in her eyes. She gulped them down as best she could and shook her head dumbly, turning back towards her desk. I followed her. But I had only taken a few steps into the gallery when I froze in my tracks. Blood was smeared all over the white walls, dripping down onto the floor, scrawled into curses like something out of a horror film. The only thing lacking was meat hooks dangling from the ceiling; then it would have been a dead ringer for an abattoir.

My body was rooted to the spot but my brain was racing, trying to work out what had happened here and how long ago, whether I needed to grab Java and run for the door. And where was the body? Or the bodies, considering how much blood there was? I had a nasty vision of the rest of the gallery staff lying in a heap of gutted corpses somewhere close. Not to mention that whoever had disembowelled them and daubed their contents over the walls might still be here . . . .

But something didn't make sense: the blood was bright red, so red it should still be dripping, and it wasn't. Though it looked as fresh as paint – as paint – I took a few paces closer to the nearest set of stains to confirm my second guess, and felt myself relaxing slightly.

OK, no mass slaughter for today. Still, the hate on display here had been violent enough. Whole canfuls of paint had been thrown all over the walls and the paintings. I swivelled slowly round, my jaw dropping as I read more and more foul words splashed over the canvasses: 'Whore', 'Bitch', 'Slut' and 'Filth' were the most frequent, personal enough to make me draw the conclusion that this went beyond mere art criticism, even in a radical form. Trails of drips cascaded down from the graffiti and stained the concrete floor, frozen into waves.

'Jesus Christ,' I said in disbelief. 'When did this happen?'

The paint was dry already. And there wasn't a trace of it on Java. It was why, even in my mad speculation earlier, I had never considered her as a homicidal assassin.

And then I heard the familiar sound of a pair of high heels coming down the metal stairs from the first floor, moving so fast they sounded motorised.

'Sam! We've been trying to call you,' Carol said as the rest of her came into view. 'As soon as we remembered you were coming in, Laurence started trying your number. You must have left early . . . God, I wish we'd thought of it before . . . .'

Her voice tailed off. The skin of her face was drawn tightly back from her bones, testimony to the stress she was under. I could see the shape of the skull beneath, as clearly delineated as a death's-head. For the first time since I had known her, she looked uncomfortable, not fully in control of the situation. What kind of advertisement was it for a gallery that one of its newest artists should walk in to find the current exhibition defaced, maybe even ruined?

Carol Bergmann was obviously wishing with all her heart that she could make me disappear in a puff of smoke, magically rematerialising only when the graffiti was cleared away and the gallery was once more as pristine and white as a new fall of snow, its floors sheets of glass. But I was here now, and I could see the wheels spinning behind her eyes. To send me away would be an irrevocable mistake. If I walked out the door now, my head whirling with speculations perhaps even more lurid than the truth, I would spread stories of uncontrolled mayhem to all the other British artists. No, it was better to draw me in and try to enlist me on their side, make me a part of what was happening, protective of the gallery's interests . . . .

And she was absolutely right.

'Why don't you come upstairs, Sam?' she said finally, adding, in a tone that said that this was a bad scenario, but the best solution possible:

'You're here now.' Suddenly she looked utterly weary. 'The least we can do is give you a coffee.'

* * *

I never got the coffee, which annoyed me considerably.

Everyone was gathered in Stanley's office, the one where I had met him and Laurence yesterday. It was the largest, with enough room to collect all the gallery staff round the table. Most of the faces I recognised: Stanley, Suzanne, Laurence, Kevin, Don. There were three others to whom Carol, always punctilious, introduced me briefly, but I forgot the names as soon as she had pronounced them. Chairs were found for both me and Java, with Carol, naturally, at the head of the table.

My eyes met Laurence's briefly as I pulled up my chair. He looked terrible. Any colour in his face had drained away, and the freckles stood out hectically against their dead-white background. His hands couldn't keep still; placed on the table in front of him, as if to ground them, they kept fidgeting with each other as if he were picking at a scab. He seemed quite unconscious of what he was doing, oblivious to the irritated glances other people cast at him.

'We have to take stock of the situation,' Carol was saying. 'Frankly, I can't wait to start clearing up this—' she gestured to the door of the room, meaning to indicate the whole gallery beyond '—this *crap* on the walls. And floor.'

I thought of the crimson stains of paint splashed over the beautiful wooden parquet outside.

'But we can't, not till the cops get here.'

'The cops?' Laurence said blankly. Clearly not everyone had known that they were on their way.

'I rang Barbara at once. I had to.' Carol spread her hands wide. 'If it had just been paint on the walls we could have got away with it. But the paintings will need major cleaning work. There was no way I couldn't tell her. And she wanted me to call the cops.'

'You can't blame her, I suppose,' Suzanne said.

Carol gave a sharp little shrug.

'Cops mean publicity,' she said succinctly. 'I can't believe she hasn't thought that one through. Though it'll be much worse for us than her.'

Stanley cleared his throat, as if asking why.

'For anyone who doesn't yet know,' Carol said, her voice cold, 'the gallery was not broken into. That is, someone used keys to get in and knew how the security system worked. Can I just check now, formally, that everyone here has their keys and has not told anyone who doesn't work here about the ins and outs of the alarm system?'

Everyone shook their heads. Suzanne said:

'But, technically, someone might have copied our keys and put them back. I mean, it's really unlikely, but we can't rule it out.'

'What about the security code for the alarm?' I asked.

'There isn't one,' Carol said. 'There's another key you turn in a hidden panel. We're not—' she looked uncomfortable at having to say this in front of me, but ploughed on '—we don't really have to worry too much about security. We're not dealing in old masters that have an established market value. A large part of the price of a piece here comes from the cachet of the fact that we – Bergmann LaTouche – are selling it. I mean, there's no underground market in this kind of modern art. It has no street value. So we're not at much risk of a break-in.'

'I agree,' I said, to reassure her. 'A burglar's much more likely to go for the computers here than for the art.'

Carol looked relieved. 'I'm glad you understand.' She looked round the group of people. 'By the way,' she said, 'where's Kate? I haven't seen her this morning.'

'She rang and said she'd be a little late,' Suzanne said after a pause. 'She was checking out that new frame guy.'

Carol checked her watch and frowned slightly.

'How long can that take? I'll have a word with her when she comes in.'

Even in the midst of chaos, nothing escaped Carol. I was impressed.

A sharp burst of white noise issued from the intercom by the door.

'That'll be the cops,' Carol said, getting up to buzz them in. 'Hello?' she said, no more loudly than usual; but somehow it echoed all round the silent room. 'Hello?' More white noise followed. '*Barbara*?' Carol said, her voice increasingly tense. 'Is that you?'

There was a collective, stifled groan of disbelief.

'Hang on,' she said finally. 'We'll be down straight away.'

'Jesus,' she said, taking her finger off the talk button. 'I tried to put her off coming in . . . I didn't want her to have to see the state we're in.'

'I guess she wants to see the full nightmare,' Laurence said ghoulishly. 'Bet she doesn't close her eyes at the scary bits in horror films.'

Carol shot him a killing look.

'Stanley,' she pronounced, the tone of voice making it an order, 'I think you should take Kevin and get down there right now to smooth things over.'

I didn't like Stanley, but I felt a wave of sympathy for him all the same.

'But Carol—' Stanley looked horrified, his eyes wide as saucers. 'Why me?' he pleaded desperately. 'I mean, you're the senior partner! It should be you!'

'Barbara,' Carol said firmly, 'is a man's woman, and you're the charmer here, Stanley. Go down and work the old Pinketts fascination. And Kevin won't hurt either. Off you go. She's waiting.'

It was like a call to battle. Pushing back his chair, Stanley stood up with the air of an aristocrat facing the tumbrel. Wanting to look his best for the execution, he smoothed back his already slick yellow hair with the palms of his hands and adjusted his tie.

'Right,' he said, tweaking at the silk handkerchief in his breast pocket. 'Kevin?'

Kevin was on his feet, swallowing hard. He followed Stanley in silence from the room. No one said a word. We sat and listened to their footsteps crossing the parquet, descending the stairs, and, more faintly now but still discernible in the hush, treading over the concrete floor towards the door. The lock clicked and the heavy door slid back, creaking a little as it went. There was a murmur of voices, one more high-pitched than the others. The door closed again. Such a long and terrible silence then ensued that by the end of it I felt like a helpless spectator at a slasher film, waiting for the psychopath to jump out from behind a cupboard and start stabbing away. All it needed was some slow John Carpenter music building gradually to the inevitable nerve-gutting shock. When Barbara Bilder let out a scream, I think we were all grateful for the catharsis.

It didn't last too long, just enough time for us to have recovered from the initial jump out of our seats. To do her justice it sounded as if she had shrieked in protest and disbelief rather than self-pity; there was an edge to her voice which made me even more grateful than I had been before that I wasn't the one down there dealing with the situation.

Glances of sympathy for the absent sacrificial lambs were exchanged.

'Maybe Barbara'll spatter some real blood on the walls,' Laurence muttered. 'I wouldn't put it past her.'

Now the voices downstairs were going at full blast. Barbara Bilder didn't seem to be pausing for breath; maybe she could do that flute-player's trick of simultaneously inhaling through her nostrils while keeping a continuous flow of air issuing from her lips. The feet were coming up the stairs now, but she kept on talking. Her wind must be pretty good. There was another horrible pause as they entered the upstairs gallery, this time succeeded by a long-drawn-out wail of grief. But the whole routine was speeded up by now, and shortly afterwards all the chatter resumed, the volume increasing with alarming speed. They were coming right for us.

Laurence looked as if he wanted to hide under the table. Carol steadied herself and stood up, facing the door with her jaw set, like the captain refusing to move from the bridge while all the rats are looking around desperately for escape hatches. The only way out was the window, and it would have been more than a little undignified.

The voices were right outside the door now. A moment later and Stanley was holding it open.

'Barbara,' he said solicitously. 'After you.'

I heard a series of glottal stops as everyone swallowed hard and composed themselves. Laurence's hands were working at each other so hard that Suzanne, unable to bear it, reached over and slapped at them. He looked up at her, shocked, then down at his fingers, stilling them, obviously unaware of what he had been doing.

Barbara Bilder came through the door and paused just on the threshold. Behind her were Kevin and an older man who was presumably with Barbara. Every face swivelled towards her. We must have looked like a classroom of the Lower Fourth which has behaved so badly that the headmistress has been called in to reprove both them and the teacher.

'Three years' work,' she said in a small, choked voice. 'Three years' work!'

Wordlessly, Kevin scuttled round her and retrieved a chair from the side of the room, holding it out to her as if it would console her. Slowly she sank into it.

'Three years' work,' she repeated. 'I just can't believe it.' She looked round us. 'When I catch the person who did this,' she said furiously, 'I'm going to strangle them with my bare hands!'

And she sounded like she meant it.

CHAPTER SEVEN

Barbara Bilder was one of those rare people whose charisma is powerful enough to make you disregard the lack of distinction in their appearance. Technically she was a nonentity: small, dumpy, forgettably dressed in a big shapeless sweater and trailing skirt, her hair scraped back from her face into a tight little bun, she could have been an Eastern European housewife who spent most of her life complaining about the rising cost of potatoes. But there was something about her that drew your attention and kept it, even before she had fixed you near-hypnotically with her big, shiny brown eyes. Her voice, too, had a strange fascination. It was both high and smooth, almost like a chant, oddly enthralling.

'I'm just in *shock*,' she was saying now. Though her words were totally banal, we were all leaning forward to catch them just as if they had been vital for our salvation. 'I don't know what to say. I'm *poleaxed* . . . .'

Trailing off, she looked up at Stanley, who was hovering beside her. 'You will find out who did this, won't you, Stan? Promise me you will!'

'We'll do everything we can,' Stanley promised.

'I know I can rely on you,' Barbara said gratefully, still gazing up at him. I saw exactly what Carol had meant about Barbara being a man's woman; there was something eternally girlish about her calculated to appeal to the male protective instincts. She trod the line perfectly; she didn't breathe her words, or bat her lashes, or behave too kittenishly. Very sensible. Such manoeuvres would be grotesque for anyone over sixteen and particularly for a woman who was as physically attractive as a babushka. And yet she projected her brand of appeal so powerfully that Stanley was busy patting her hand and saying 'There, there' so reassuringly that he must have been restraining himself from adding that she wasn't to worry her pretty little head about anything.

'Can we get you anything, Barbara?' Carol said sympathetically. 'A glass of water, coffee . . . ?'

I perked up when coffee was mentioned. If Barbara was getting some I was putting in my own order. But the wretched woman knocked it on the head.

'No, really, I'm fine,' she said. 'But thank you, Carol. You're so kind. I just need time to take this in.'

I subsided gloomily, beginning to nurse a grudge against her.

'Sure.' Carol pulled up her chair and sat down. 'Barbara, if you're OK to talk about this, we're having a council of war right now, as you can see. We're expecting the cops at any moment. Can I—'

'The cops?' Barbara stared at her. 'Oh dear Lord, that was me, wasn't it? I was so upset when you told me, I didn't think! But—' she put one hand up to her mouth '—the publicity! Oh, why didn't I just say to keep it quiet?'

The man who had come in with her was standing behind her chair, resting his hands on its back. He put them on her shoulders now, squeezing reassuringly.

'You know that's what I suggested, darling,' he said. 'Let Carol deal with it. She's more than capable.'

She reached up and took one of his hands briefly, giving him a brave smile. They both wore wedding rings, I noticed. I could safely assume that this was Mr Barbara Bilder.

'Oh, Jon,' she sighed. 'Why didn't I listen to you? Why am I such a silly thing?'

'There, there, honey. Try not to get too upset,' he said comfortingly. Though overlaid with a patina of American, I could tell that his accent was English, and I found myself looking at him curiously. It was ludicrous, this interest in other Brits abroad: so often they were people you wouldn't give the time of day to at home. Some deeply rooted atavistic instinct, no doubt. But there was something very familiar about this one. It was niggling at me. He was tall and grey-haired with a long pleasant face, wearing a corduroy jacket and check shirt that looked as if he had had them for the past thirty years. I almost felt as if I recognised them. And when Barbara had called him 'Jon' another piece of the puzzle had clicked into place. I knew him from somewhere, I was sure of it. Still, I was equally positive that I had never seen Barbara before. She was not the kind of person you forgot.

'Listen, Barbara.' Carol was biting the bullet. 'The trouble is – our trouble, I mean, Bergmann LaTouche's trouble – is that the gallery wasn't broken into. Someone used the keys and knew how to deactivate the alarm.'

Jon, who had been bending over Barbara, now straightened up and stared at Carol almost accusatorially. She squared her shoulders and lifted her jaw, meeting him straight in the eyes.

'But that means—' he said. 'One of you guys here—'

'I'm fully aware of that, Jon,' she said. 'It's about the worst situation imaginable.'

Most people were staring resolutely at the surface of the table. To look round at the rest of the group now would inevitably be interpreted as an attempt to decide which person present might be the graffiti artist. No one said anything for quite a while. Barbara Bilder had stiffened in her chair. Carol was biting her lip. Even she was looking down, unwilling to catch anyone's eye.

And then Stanley decided to try to raise the tone of the conversation.

'Well, this is all very gloomy, isn't it?' he said, over-brightly, as if he were about to be put on the rack and was attempting to confuse his torturers into offering him a cup of tea instead. 'Let's try for a happier note. Barbara, Jon, I think I should introduce you to the newest artist to show at Bergmann LaTouche! She just arrived in the city yesterday. I'm sure she'll love to meet you.'

I wondered whether I was supposed to stand up and do a twirl. Stanley crossed the room to stand behind my chair, pressing my shoulders as Jon was doing to Barbara.

'This is Sam Jones,' he said, sounding as enthusiastic as if he had just blanked out the content and implications of the whole preceding conversation. 'Sam, I want you to meet Barbara Bilder and Jon Tallboy. Barbara is one of our most respected artists.'

He beamed over at her.

Having reached the point where tragedy shaded into surrealism, the situation had, lemming-like, taken a leap right over the edge. Laurence was staring at Stanley as if he had lost control of himself and were running round the room screaming hysterically: 'Help me! Help me! I can't go on!' while tearing off his clothes. And, in a sense, he had. This retreat into some bizarre kind of polite ritual was an impassioned cry for help.

The trouble was that everything was about to complicate itself still further. It wasn't simply that Barbara and I, like two marionettes under the control of an increasingly deranged puppeteer who had decided to segue into a drawing-room comedy halfway through a rendering of *Psycho*, found ourselves impelled to stand up and go through the motions of shaking hands while murmuring greetings to each other; no, it was even weirder. Because as soon as Stanley had pronounced the surname of Barbara's husband, I had known at once why his face seemed so familiar to me.

'You're Kim's father!' I said to Jon Tallboy as I shook his hand, with the relief of someone who has finally solved a particularly nagging riddle. 'Do you remember me? Kim and I were at sixth-form college together, and then art school – no, hang on, you went off to New York when we went to art school, and then Kim went over to see you and never came back. Is she still here?'

My voice was triumphant. Poor Jon Tallboy, however, still reeling under all the appalling revelations of this visit to the gallery, looked as if this strange coincidence were the final straw.

'I'm sorry,' he said, his voice dazed, 'I don't quite—'

Beside me Stanley was practically gibbering. His nice social impulse had comprehensively derailed itself, taking him with it. I felt rather sorry for him; in a way it hadn't been too much to ask that we all say hello and pleased to meet you, providing him with a brief shining moment of sanity in a world gone mad. Instead Jon Tallboy looked as if I had just sandbagged him in slow motion.

'I'm Sam Jones,' I said helpfully, spelling it out for him more slowly. It seemed better to get the recognition part over with straight away. 'I was a friend of Kim's. I used to hang out at your house all the time.'

He was still staring at me wildly.

'OK, I had green hair,' I said with resignation, realising that I was going to have to embarrass myself. In for a penny and all that. 'And a dog collar. You always used to make a joke about it.'

He had meant well, though. That was why I didn't mind reminding him. My punk phase hadn't lasted long, but it had been full-on at the time. Jon's brow cleared.

'*Sam*? *Sam*! My God! How are you?' he said, recognition dawning. He hugged me, then drew back to look me up and down. 'Well, I can see for myself. All grown up and comparatively respectable! I remember that green hair as if it was yesterday . . . . Didn't you and Kimmy once dye hers red in the bathroom sink? Her mother was furious with you.'

I winced. Maybe I had made a mistake initiating this whole old-school reunion thing with the entire staff of Bergmann LaTouche listening in, their ears flapping, pathetically grateful for the tiniest distraction. I was just glad Hugo wasn't there. He would have bombarded Jon Tallboy for humiliating pieces of information about me and employed them for his own amusement at my most vulnerable moments.

'I should have known straight away,' I apologised. 'I was staring at you for ages, sure I knew you from somewhere.'

'It's been a long time,' Jon said, waving away this apology. 'And I didn't recognise you either . . . . My God!' he said fondly. 'To see you all grown up – the last time I saw you, you looked like Return of the Living Dead.'

I thought it best to interrupt these reminiscences before they became terminally embarrassing.

'How's Kim?' I asked.

'Oh, good, good. She's got this trendy downtown life, working as a waitress in some restaurant in the East Village – that's where she lives. You should get in touch with her.'

'I'd love to. I was meaning to look her up.'

At least something had gone more easily than I expected today.

'So you're showing here? That's wonderful!' Jon Tallboy was looking positively cheerful. Nice to have someone actually perk up when they remembered me, rather than holding up a crucifix and starting to babble the Lord's Prayer. Or maybe at this unpropitious moment he was simply milking any piece of good news for all it was worth. I could scarcely blame him.

'It's a group show,' I said self-deprecatingly, not wanting him to think I was elevated above my station. Maybe in twenty years, if I were lucky, I too could have my own one-woman show here. Why, perhaps someone would even break in and daub 'Whore' and 'Slut' all over my pieces. I brightened up at the prospect. At least that would imply that I was still enjoying an eventful sex life at nearly fifty.

Unfortunately Jon Tallboy had followed me a short way along the track of my mental processes and stopped dead at the point where we reached the connection between the one-woman show and people trashing it. His face fell. This wasn't just a metaphor; his skin sagged visibly as his smile drooped and faded.

'This is such strange timing,' he said, looking helplessly over at his wife. 'I don't know what to say.'

I too looked at Barbara Bilder, and was taken aback. Up until now, despite her distress, she had basically been projecting friendliness, as if she felt that through all this trouble she was at least surrounded by people who meant well. Now, for the first time, I had a hint of what she could be like when a situation did not please her. The shiny brown eyes had become as flat and cold as if she were trying to bounce me off her stare, away from her and her husband. It wasn't that she disliked younger artists; she had been perfectly nice, if disoriented by Stanley's bizarre timing, when we had shaken hands. I decided that she must be jealous of Jon.

The impression that she was physically repelling me was so strong that I nearly took a step back. I had thought she was charismatic when she entered the room, but that was nothing to the effect she was projecting now. I got the message. Jon Tallboy was completely off-limits.

It was a blow, considering my well-known weakness for grey-haired corduroy-wearing father figures. I would just have to bear up bravely and try to forget him.

★ ★ ★

'Today is like riding a roller-coaster,' I said to Laurence a short while later. 'Just when you think you've finally oriented yourself the ground drops away and you're screaming all over again.'

'Tell me about it.' He still looked terrible. 'I still can't get over Stanley. "*Let's try for a happier note,*" ' he repeated, incredulous. 'It was frightening. I've never realised before what people mean when they say someone came apart at the seams. You could practically see him unravelling before your eyes.'

'Is he OK?'

Laurence shrugged indifferently. 'Who's OK? Carol sent him to his office and he's probably on the phone to his shrink right now, popping Prozac like breath-fresheners.'

We were following Barbara, Jon and Carol as they toured the gallery, examining the damage to the paintings at close range. I was tagging on because my usual morbid fascination with disaster and destruction wouldn't let me leave until I had sucked the situation dry and spat out its bones.

'I would take another antidepressant, too,' Laurence said seriously, 'but it wouldn't do anything. I'm too wound up. Besides, I'm trying to cut back.'

'God.' I was finding this hard to believe. 'And you guys call me an alcoholic when I have an extra margarita. What a bunch of drug snobs you are.'

'Look, Barbara,' Carol was saying as she indicated a particularly disfiguring streak of paint over one of the canvases. 'It's not wonderful, OK? This is oil-based. That means trouble getting it off. There's some hope, because of that fixative you always use. But I don't want to be too optimistic. It's not really my field.'

'If they'd only used water-based paint!' Barbara said plaintively. 'The difference it would have made!'

'No point expecting this scum to be considerate,' Jon Tallboy said, stooping to clasp his arm still tighter around his much smaller wife. 'We can just thank God it wasn't an aerosol spray.'

Barbara shivered. 'I can't even think about that,' she whispered.

'I wonder why it wasn't,' I said *sotto voce* to Laurence. 'Much easier to use.'

'Yeah, but these splashes make much more of a *statement*,' he said, with a partial resumption of his mocking tone of yesterday. 'I mean, you can just throw this stuff around as crazily as you want. It looks much *angrier*.'

'It certainly does.'

'No, I see exactly why they chose this medium.' Laurence was getting into his stride. 'It says rage to me, it says uncontrolled, it says blood on the walls—'

His voice was rising dangerously high. Carol swivelled her head and shot him a furious glance. Meekly he subsided as she turned back and said reassuringly to Barbara:

'I'll be calling in a specialist restorer right away. I know just the person. Maybe she can even drop by this afternoon and give us a first opinion.'

'That would be wonderful,' Barbara said sincerely. 'Please let me know straight away what she says. I'll be sitting by the phone.'

'Of course. Barbara, I want to assure you that we will do everything we can to track down the person responsible. Even if it is a member of my own staff.'

'I'm sure you will, Carol. I have complete faith in you.'

Barbara was being surprising docile. No, on reflection I wasn't that surprised. She was a sensible woman; throwing a tantrum now wouldn't have helped, apart from giving her and everyone else a headache. This way she was surrounded by people reassuring her, ready to attend to her every need. Much more pleasant.

The small phalanx – Queen Barbara, her consort, chief advisers and courtiers – proceeded downstairs to survey the situation there. I swallowed hard. It was definitely worse down here. The vandal had obviously started on the ground floor, which had received the whole first flush of energy and enthusiasm for the task at hand. Upstairs, for all its crimson paint splashes, did not look like a slaughterhouse. This did.

The door buzzer sounded. Carol, probably relieved to have something concrete to do, went over to the intercom by the door herself instead of despatching Laurence. After a brief colloquy she unbolted the door and drew it open.

'Come in, officers,' she said politely.

A man and a woman strolled in as slowly as if they had all the time in the world. As Carol closed and locked the door behind them, they paused and looked around, sizing up the scene. I stared at them with great interest, never having seen plain-clothes American police officers before. I was already garnering details to report to Hawkins, a friend of mine who's a DI on the Flying Squad.

They seemed to know exactly how far they could push the concept of plain clothes without actually abandoning all the rules completely, like schoolkids modifying their uniforms by unbuttoning their shirts or hiking up the skirts while still being able to protest, with an air of injured virtue, that they were conforming to all known regulations. Both of them were big and chunky, the woman's hair caught back so tightly from her head it accentuated the squareness of her face, which was so marked I could have plotted the ninety-degree angles at each corner with a protractor.

They wore their down-at-heel clothes and apparent lack of physical fitness with such nonchalance that it made their presence more impressive than if they had been smart and super-energetic. Briefly they shot glances around the gallery, checking out their surroundings as comprehensively as if they were shooting photos of the crime scene. The woman said in a flat, uninflected voice:

'Hi. I'm Detective Thurber, and this is Detective Frank. You must be Ms Bergmann.'

'That's right.' Carol drew a long breath. 'I'd better introduce you around.'

'Please,' Thurber said.

A woman of few words was somehow more impressive than an equally taciturn man. Carol seemed unusually rattled.

'This is Barbara Bilder,' she said, indicating her. 'She's the artist currently showing here. Her husband, Jon Tallboy. And this is Laurence Debray, one of our assistants, and Sam Jones, who's about to take part in our next group show.'

'Pleased to meet you,' said Detective Frank, nodding generally to us all. 'I gotta say, ma'am,' he continued with increasing animation, addressing Barbara, 'this is some show you got here. Usually I don't go so much for modern art, but this is pretty powerful stuff. Really makes a statement you can't ignore. I guess you'd call this deconstruction, right? Where you do the paintings and then trash them yourself?'

Barbara stared at him, unable to speak. There was a long pause, which Frank finally broke.

'Well, congratulations,' he continued. 'I've never seen anything like this. Sort of the art and the critical response at the same time, right? They say it's getting harder and harder to be original, but you certainly managed it, Ms Bilder. I'm real impressed.'

Another silence fell. The detectives by now were looking a little puzzled; from their point of view, Frank had made a pleasant opening. Why we were doing frighteningly realistic impressions of Lot's wife in return – we might lack the salt but we had the frozen-into-pillars part down perfectly – was a mystery to them. At last Laurence, his voice high and shaky, sounding as nervous as a pubescent, broke in:

'The show has been *vandalised*. It's not supposed to be like this. The red paint is *graffiti*. Someone trashed the show last night. That's why you guys are *here*, OK? We called you in.'

Thurber had remained impassive all through Frank's praise of the show, and her expression didn't change a whit as she assimilated this new information. Frank's eyebrows rose slightly, but that was all. It was true about New York cops being battle-hardened. If I'd just committed a *faux pas* like that I would have run screaming from the room.

'I see,' said Frank, adjusting with praiseworthy ease to this new perspective. I wondered whether, in the car afterwards, he would bang his head repeatedly against the dashboard, muttering 'Shit! Shit!', or whether he just took this kind of thing in his stride.

'Well, that's very interesting,' he said. 'Though we don't know anything about a call?' He looked at Thurber to double-check this. She shook her head slowly. 'I guess that means I have a few questions to ask you, Ms Bilder.' He nodded at the nearest word on the wall, which happened to be 'Whore'. It recurred with unnerving frequency. 'Who would you say really doesn't like you? Enough to do this to your show? Or maybe I should say, is there someone who doesn't like you – and really, *really* didn't like Kate Jacobson?'

He looked round our blank faces. 'That's why we're here,' he explained. 'We're from Homicide. Manhattan South. Investigating the murder of Kate Jacobson.'

There was total silence. Then Carol said angrily:

'The *what*? Don't be ridiculous!'

'We've been informed that she was an assistant here,' Thurber said, her flat lifeless voice as uninterested as if she had been reading the shipping forecast. 'She was killed last night. Her body was found this morning in Central Park.' She looked up to see the effect this information had on us. Her eyes flickered from one face to the other, while her expression remained as deadpan as ever.

'She'd been strangled. Well,' she added precisely, 'garrotted. In Strawberry Fields.'

CHAPTER EIGHT

Half an hour later I was pacing the downstairs gallery, back and forth, back and forth across the concrete floor, feeling like a criminal in an over-generous cell. As much of my fist as would fit was stuffed into my mouth, and I was biting down hard on the knuckles. If Laurence had offered me an antidepressant, despite my recent bold words, I'd have grabbed at it. As a second best, however, the sensation of gnawing at my own flesh was strangely relaxing. At least, as the New Agers said, it concentrated one in the moment.

Shock had never taken me quite this way before. But then I was jet-lagged, in a strange country, marking out with my feet the territory in which I was supposed to be having a big career break in a week's time. It was no wonder that I felt disoriented. Add to that the factor of not really knowing any of these people, and it was like being thrown onstage, and expected to act in an unfamiliar, constantly shifting mix of farce and tragedy. The effort had put a severe strain on my usually solid nerves: it was either start to cannibalise myself or burst into psychotic high-pitched laughter.

Carol had asked me if I wanted to sit with Barbara and Jon in her office while the three of us were waiting to be interviewed by the police. I couldn't fault her professional hospitality. It was just that I preferred to chew my fist in decent privacy. And I didn't much fancy being left alone with Barbara and Jon, trying to make conversation while the former shot dagger-glances at me every time the talk shaded around my previous acquaintance with the latter.

Thurber and Frank had commandeered Stanley's office and were taking statements from everyone in the gallery, one by one. (It was impossible not to notice, as a sideline to the main action, how easy it was to take over Stanley's office. A strong-minded child of six could probably have strolled in here and demanded it.) The cops who had been called about the vandalism had eventually turned up and been promply dispatched again by Thurber. It was a homicide investigation now.

Carol was in there with them now, having naturally gone first, and the rest of the staff had retreated to their own offices in various states of shock. Laurence had been very badly hit by the news of Kate's death; or maybe I noticed his reaction more because I had been with him when he had heard. I had thought he was going to faint. If I'd known him better I would have slapped him round the face. As it was I had to help him to his office and hope he would get a grip before the summons came from Thurber and Frank. He was shaking like a sapling in a hurricane and I doubted that the two Valium he had popped – so much for trying to cut back – would help with his lucidity.

I was just working up a nice rhythm – teeth into knuckles echoing the tread of my feet – when Jon Tallboy came hurrying down the stairs. On his bottom half he was wearing old chinos which hung in over-loose folds around his stork-like legs. With the corduroy jacket and tattersall shirt, he looked like an absent-minded professor. All he needed was a pipe.

'Just getting my coat,' he called over his shoulder. 'I think I left it down here.'

Removing my fist reluctantly from my mouth, I dried it on my sweater.

'Sam!' Jon Tallboy said hurriedly, advancing towards me. 'I just wanted to snatch a word with you—' He shot a rather hunted glance over his shoulder. 'Here you go.'

He pulled a wallet from his jacket and extracted a card, scribbling something on the back of it.

'Kim's number,' he explained. 'And there are my and Barbara's details as well.'

'Thanks.' I took the card. 'Do you mind my asking why this is such a coat-and-dagger operation?'

Haha, how very amusing I was. I needed to get that fist back into play, or very soon the psychotic laughter would be rearing its crazy head again.

'Barbara is a wonderful woman,' Jon Tallboy said devoutly. 'But she's just a little jealous. Maybe that's putting it too strongly—'

I didn't think so.

'She just – you know, of course, that I left Kim's mother for Barbara,' he said. 'That's why I came to the States. And Barbara – well, it's not exactly – I don't want to give you the wrong idea – it's just when Kimmy came over to visit me, I think Barbara was a little reminded of, you know, my life before meeting her. Kimmy's quite like her mother – so – anyway, she's obviously very upset at the moment – Barbara, I mean – and I didn't see any point making it worse by talking about – she finds it difficult sometimes – but I'm *sure*,' he continued with more aplomb, finding himself on safer ground, 'that Kim would love to see you. You must give her a ring. And maybe we could meet up. You, me and Barbara, I mean. She loves to meet younger artists, give them a helping hand. She's so generous,' he finished, with nary a hint of irony.

'*Right*,' I said carefully, thinking that Jon Tallboy was just like Humpty Dumpty: when he used a word it meant only what he wanted it to mean.

'I must be going,' Jon said hurriedly. 'I don't want to leave Barbara waiting by herself. So we'll be in touch?'

He smiled at me, a warm, friendly smile marred only by the fact that his eyes didn't focus on me for more than an instant, darting away nervously to the direction of the staircase. I didn't remember him being so weak. Or maybe Barbara brought it out in him. The next moment he was retrieving his coat from Java's desk and hurrying back upstairs, the leather soles of his shoes flapping on the metal staircase in his haste to rejoin his wife.

I looked down at his card. It announced that he was a critic for *ArtView*. I knew it, vaguely. One of those unbelievably glossy magazines, heavier than most coffee-table books, which only American money and advertising can afford to produce. Back in the UK he had been an art teacher at the local comprehensive. Marrying Barbara had certainly taken him upmarket. Perhaps he considered free will had been a small price to pay for it.

I shoved the card into my pocket and debated what to do next. I had to be on hand to talk to the police, but they would be working their way through the entire staff, so there was no great urgency. I would doubtless come bottom of the list. Plus, as they said over here, I was starving. I looked at my watch. It was two o'clock. No wonder. I'd picked up a very indifferent bagel for breakfast before I caught the bus, but that felt like aeons ago now. And as soon as I realised I was hungry my stomach started turning over like a combine harvester getting ready to sink its teeth into some wheat.

There must be somewhere close by I could get a sandwich. And at that thought my stomach went into roaring overdrive. It would start to eat my intestines if I didn't feed it now. In a second my hand was on the door latch. I turned it, half-expecting alarm bells to burst out as I did so, and opened the door.

Outside it was as bright and sunny as it had been a few hours ago. I had noticed before that when a murder happens an incidental effect – once you've had time to take in the news – is surprise that the world is still going about its business: the rain hasn't started bucketing down in empathy, and people aren't rending their clothes in mourning on the streets.

I stood for a moment on the pavement, orienting myself, a rush of relief spinning through me at my temporary escape. SoHo seemed like a trendier Bond Street: warehouse-sized galleries interspersed with expensively artistic designer clothes shops which I Must Not Enter At Any Cost. Across the street was what looked like yet another gallery. But, as I watched, a couple of people emerged from its dark façade carrying enormous polystyrene cups, tiny trails of steam emerging from the hole pierced in the top of each one. The black clothes they were wearing were a perfect backdrop for the fragile little curls of steam. It was a pretty effect. I headed over the road and went up the steps.

Inside it was like a Covent Garden café – the Café Casbah in its glory days – stretched out into hyperspace. There were the same black-framed tables, the same aspirant artworks on the walls, the same pretty but ineffective waiting staff, the same blackboard with tasty-yet-healthy-sounding specials chalked up in swirly handwriting, the same cards on the noticeboard for macrobiotic Jungian workshops and colour therapy flatshares. There was even the same marble counter stacked with layers of tempting baked goods. A Covent Garden eaterie would not label almost everything either fat-, dairy- or egg-free, however, nor would it offer seventeen different kinds of coffee, some of which probably took longer to order than they did to consume.

Still, it was with an odd sense of familiarity that I had to repeat my simple order – a mocha coffee and a large piece of carrot cake – three times to the young man behind the marble counter, who was twirling his dreadlocks and staring dreamily at his admittedly charming reflection in the framed poster on the far wall. Dimwit would-be models-slash-actors were the same all over the world.

Dreadlock Boy finally managed to fiddle boyishly with the terrifying complications of the coffee machine, producing my mocha with an air of shy triumph. The tip of his tongue protruded between his lips with concentration as he cut my cake. Bless. I looked around to see if there was a table available. I thought I could see someone waving from the far corner, and headed in that direction. If they weren't hailing me I would look an idiot, but in a strange town that never worries me too much.

Suzanne and Don, an unlikely combination, were sitting together. So much for my furtive escape from the gallery. Suzanne was staring at the glassy brown surface of a cappuccino whose foam had melted a long time ago, completely untouched. And indeed Suzanne looked incapable of consuming anything. As far as I knew she hadn't cried at the news of Kate's death. Instead it seemed that she had retreated far into herself. She moved like a puppet whose strings were being pulled from high above, and her gaze was infinitely detached, registering everything but hardly reacting to it, as if storing it up for processing later.

It was Don who had been waving at me. There were two empty plates stacked in front of him, but he still fixed his stare on my carrot cake as I put it down with the single-minded attention of an ape eyeing the last fairy cake at the chimpanzees' tea party. He seemed determined to be cheerful; perhaps I was being unfair to attribute this to a wish to prove his toughness in the face of sudden, violent death. But I didn't think so.

'Hi,' I said, sitting down. I was unsure of what to say, confronted by two people in such different states of reaction. 'I thought you guys were still in the gallery.'

'You mean the morgue,' Don corrected sarcastically. 'Nothin' for me to do, anyway. Cain't start cleanin' up theyt shit on the walls till everyone's good 'n' done with lookin' at it for clues.'

'You talk to the police yet?'

Don shook his head. 'Cain't say I'm in much of a hurry to, either. Wait till they pull my record.'

'Oh, you too?' I said in an access of chumminess. It was not the right response. Suzanne's head lifted from the contemplation of the coffee and fixed on me instead with what would have been horror if she hadn't been near-catatonic with shock. 'What did they get you for?' I asked matily.

'Oh, punched out a couple of sheriffs, did a few nights in jail here and there for bad attitude . . . .' Don lit a cigarette. Doubtless whatever he would admit to was the tip of an iceberg proportionately bigger than the one that sank the *Titanic*. 'Hick stuff. And you?'

'No convictions. No charges even pressed,' I said, shrugging and wishing I hadn't started this conversation. No sooner said than changed. 'Anyway, guess what just happened?'

I told them about my encounter with Jon Tallboy. I didn't see why I should cover up for his inadequacies. And I was curious to hear their reaction.

'Shee-it, that guy sure is pussy-whipped,' Don drawled, slapping the table to emphasise his point.

Suzanne glared at him. 'Hey, watch it. You know damn well how sexist that is.'

Her voice seemed to come from a long distance away, not quite connecting with the sense of the words; but the automatic reaction showed traces of the old Suzanne. I was grateful that she was coming back. Don shrugged.

'OK,' he said, hiking up his accent for extra emphasis, 'I could whup his dumb candyass with both hands tied behind mah back and mah legs in a vice. How's thet fer size, little lady?'

He leered at her. Suzanne ignored him completely. I looked at him with disfavour myself. Trying to wind up Suzanne was fairly pathetic, considering how upset she was. I wasn't warming to Don.

'Man can't say anythin' here without being jumped on,' he muttered. His head was ducked but I caught a flash of blue as he looked up under his lashes to see what effect this further provocation was having. I was beginning to agree with Laurence; Don's dumb country boy act was all a front to see how much he could get away with.

'You know, I don't remember asking you to sit with me,' Suzanne snapped, getting stronger by the moment.

'Hey, cool it!' Don said amiably, shoving back his chair. He held up his hands as if to ward her off. 'Let's not fight, OK? I'm off to the little boys' room. Give you ladies a chance to talk amongst yoursaylves.'

'Are you OK?' I said to her as Don shambled off.

She gave me a long, unnervingly detached stare. I was glad when her eyes dropped to her pack of cigarettes on the table.

'God, he bugs me sometimes,' she finally said, lighting one. 'Ever since he came over I've been sitting here waiting for him to say one word about Kate, and has he? No way. He just ate like a hog and burped a lot.'

'What do you think happened to her?' I asked. Hearing her talk like her normal self somehow liberated me to dig into my carrot cake, which was calorie-counting-free and all the better for it. I felt it was in bad taste to be eating at a time like this, particularly after Suzanne's disparaging remark about Don, but I was uncontrollably hungry by now. And it seemed somehow less offensive to be stuffing down a snack than an actual meal.

'I have no idea,' Suzanne said simply. 'I thought she was going off to meet Leo last night. And she let us think that, didn't she? I mean, if she was meeting someone else, she didn't say. And she knows how much I'd hate the thought of her seeing him again. So it must have been something pretty secret if she'd just go ahead and let me assume it was him.' She took a long drag on her cigarette. 'I tried to ring Leo,' she went on. 'This morning, when I heard. But he wasn't in. Or he hadn't got out of bed yet,' she added nastily. 'I left a message.

But I'll tell the cops that's where we thought she was going last night. I've got no reason to protect him.'

I nodded slowly. 'What's this problem of his?'

Suzanne sighed. 'You don't look like you'd be shocked,' she said. 'He's a junkie. Does most stuff he can get his hands on. Crystal meth, special K, but mainly H. Only every now and then – or at least that's what he told Kate. But still.'

'H? You mean heroin?'

She nodded. 'It's so easy to get in this city. I don't know if you've heard, but it's got really fashionable over the last few years. Just go down to Tompkins Square Park, there's hundreds of dealers ready to pop you a dime bag.'

'Dime bag . . . .'

'Oh, ten bucks a bag. Enough to get you high, anyway.'

'You seem to know a bit about it,' I said cautiously.

She gave me a tired smile. 'When Kate started seeing Leo, I asked around. He's like a friend of a friend of mine. I found out more than I wanted to know. Not that I see her any more,' she added. 'That friend, I mean. That's New York for you. You go through people and jobs like you do paychecks.'

'How cynical.'

'Oh, New York . . .' Suzanne said, dismissing this. 'You've got to be tough here. Everyone has their own agenda, you know?'

I left a little pause, then said: 'Can I ask you something? Why did you tell Carol Kate had rung in and said she'd be late?'

There was no need for me to spell out the fact that Kate would have been long dead by the time Suzanne had said she'd rung the gallery.

'Oh, that.' Suzanne looked less fazed than I would have expected. 'When Kate didn't show for work I just thought she was running late, you know? I'm used to covering for her. Time-keeping isn't exactly her priority.'

She didn't even seem to realise that she had slipped into the present tense. And before she could catch up to it, a cup of coffee plopped down on the table in front of us. I hadn't even seen Don coming back. He sat down, mumbling something, pushing back his chair so he could sprawl out his legs. Suzanne stared at the cup pointedly.

'You didn't think to ask us if we wanted a coffee?' she asked him.

Don broke into a shit-eating grin. He looked like a little boy who's deliberately done something naughty to provoke his mother.

'Knew you'd get mad at me for not getting you one,' he said, as if confessing.

'Right, that's it. I'm getting back to work.' Suzanne shoved back her chair and stood up. 'And you'd better, too. You know? Work? Remember that?'

'Hey, ain't nothin' for me to do over there yet.'

'Apart from talking the cops through all your convictions for manslaughter,' Suzanne said caustically. I winced. She turned to me. 'Coming, Sam?'

I was caught between a rock and a hard place. My sympathies were with Suzanne, but I didn't want to get on Don's wrong side; never piss off the guy who's going to be installing your exhibits. I paused for a moment. Don was still grinning at me.

'Don't stay on my account,' he said affably. 'I don't take things personal.'

'OK,' I said, but now I was annoyed that Don had acted as if I needed his permission to leave. Maybe I was reading too much into it, but I didn't think so. Don was a master winder-up. I stood up as nonchalantly as I could. 'Catch you later.'

'Sure,' Don said smugly, and started slurping his coffee like a pig at a trough in a deliberate effort to set our teeth on edge.

'I wish it'd been him,' Suzanne said viciously as we crossed over to the gallery.

'Sorry?' But I knew what she meant.

'If someone had to get killed. I wish it'd been him. Or Barbara – I don't like her and I think her paintings suck. But no, it had to be Katie who died. There is a God, right?'

We had reached the door of the gallery. Suzanne had let off steam in the open air, where no one could overhear us; and now, as she unlocked the door and let me in, she wouldn't look at me again. Avoiding my eye, she headed upstairs. I followed more slowly. I was thinking hard.

★ ★ ★

'Well, that all seems pretty straightforward, Ms Jones,' said Detective Frank. 'We'll hafta run your story by the doorman at your building, of course.'

'Oh God.' For some reason this prospect hadn't occurred to me. 'Do you have to? I only just got there yesterday. I was hoping to build up to notorious gradually, not just explode it on them all at once.'

Frank leaned back in his chair, exchanging a glance with Thurber.

'Well, what if we say you reported the theft of a camera?' he suggested. 'You think you left it in the cab and we're checking to see what time exactly that would be.'

'It's better than nothing,' I agreed. 'It might even work, if the doorman's as thick as a plank.'

Frank gave me an understanding smile. 'We'll do our best,' he assured me. 'It's not part of our job to go harassing visitors to New York.'

I was suspicious of everything this pair said; they were being far too nice to be true. Still, I had to pretend to take them at face value.

'That's a relief,' I said. 'So if the doorman backs me up, that would let me out?'

'If he confirms there's no way you could have got out of the building again. Kate Jacobson was killed around midnight. If you got back at eleven and stayed there, you should be OK. And with your flight landing yesterday afternoon I don't imagine you had much time to scope out secret exits from the building, right?'

'It wasn't my first priority,' I said, wondering why he had told me the time of death. Maybe there was mandated disclosure of that kind of information over here. Or maybe he was trying to catch me out.

'Though she was killed pretty near where you're staying,' Thurber chipped in. The robotic flatness of her voice was always a shock after she hadn't spoken for a while.

'Where was that?' I asked.

They both stared at me.

'No one told you yet?' Frank said, surprised. 'Strawberry Fields. Thought you'd know that, being British and all.'

And now I did remember him saying that Kate had been found in Strawberry Fields. But coming as it had just after his terrible *faux pas* about Barbara's paintings, not to mention the news of Kate being strangled, the oddity had somehow passed me by.

'I'm sorry,' I said. 'I don't know what you're talking about. Would that be halfway down Abbey Road? Next to Lucy in the sky with diamonds?'

They were both looking at me in honest bewilderment. I treasured the moment. It's not often you can claim to have perplexed two New York cops.

'Strawberry Fields,' said Thurber, the voice as dead as the computer program from a Radiohead album, 'is just opposite the Dakota building.'

'Right,' I said encouragingly. But she seemed to have stopped. They were staring at me again, and now it wasn't so friendly.

'Where John Lennon was shot!' Frank said incredulously. 'They made this garden opposite in Central Park into a kinda shrine. Memorial, you know? Kids hang out there all day, playing guitar. That's why it's called Strawberry Fields.'

I shuddered. 'It sounds foul,' I said candidly. 'Endless versions of 'Woman' and 'Imagine' sung out of tune by teenagers in flared paisley trousers. Thanks for warning me.'

Frank didn't think I was funny at all. He was glaring at me as if he'd found out I once killed someone – in self-defence. But under suspicious circumstances.

'I always liked the Monkees better,' I said lamely, deciding I had gone too far. 'If they were all singing "Daydream Believer" I'd much prefer it. They were cuter, too.'

'Davy Jones,' said Thurber unexpectedly, a gleam of something approaching humanity in her blank-wall eyes.

'Mickey Dolenz,' I responded. 'Each to their own, eh?'

Frank harrumphed in disgust. I was grateful we didn't fancy the same Monkee. No way I wanted to get into a catfight with Thurber.

That wound up the interview. I didn't think they suspected me. But they kept their cards very close to their chests. I had asked them whether Kate's gallery keys had been found on her body, and when Frank had told me that they hadn't it was clear that this was a piece of information they were happy to release for reasons of their own. I emerged from their company feeling that they had got everything they wanted from me and given me only what they chose to in return. Sucked dry and thrown away like a worn-out glove on the garbage heap. It wasn't a pleasant feeling. My investigative pride was wounded and my metaphors were slipping like a bar of soap in a shower.

Still, it was nearly cocktail time.

CHAPTER NINE

It took me a while to locate a working payphone. Practically every handset in a half-mile radius round the gallery had been yanked out of its fittings and was dangling to the ground in an admittedly striking mess of tangled wires. Finally I found one which, despite being as bruised and battered as if it had gone ten rounds with Mike Tyson – there was even a large chunk of the earpiece missing, though no teeth marks through it – produced a dial tone on request and even accepted my money without spitting it back contemptuously. The booth was just a strut of metal and a pitiful little square foot of cover under which I huddled for protection. Standing in what was practically the middle of the pavement, people shoving past me, forced to shout my business into every set of half-curious ears, was like using a mobile phone without even the implication that you had a bit of money. Sod modern art, this was a real engagement with the harsher side of life.

I stuffed the box with quarters till it burped and pleaded for mercy, then dialled Kim's number. She picked up after only two rings, sounding as if she were in a hurry.

'Yeah?'

It was so strange to hear her voice, which was Kim's and not-Kim's at the same time, overlaid with an American accent and an unmistakably adult helping of stress.

'Kim?' I said half-incredulously.

There was a pause.

'Who is this?' she said, puzzled.

'OK, this is a blast from the past. Sit down and take deep breaths. It's me, Sam. Sam Jones.'

'*Sam*? Omigod! Sam, is it really you? Where the hell are you?'

'I'm in SoHo. I mean,' I added, unsure about the pronunciation, 'not Soho London, SoHo! New York.'

'You're in SoHo,' Kim repeated, not really taking it in. 'I don't believe it. I'm in shock. My God, how long's it been? No, don't tell me.'

'Shall we meet up?'

'Well, sure! You want to come to a class with me right now?'

'A class?'

'The gym,' Kim said rather impatiently, as if this had been so obvious only a fool could have failed to realise. 'Cardio and crunch. You wanna come?'

'What, now?'

'Sure! I was just leaving.'

'But I don't have any stuff. I mean, it's back at my flat. Apartment.'

'I'll bring you some. We could always share clothes. What's your shoe size again?'

'Five.'

'Five English . . . . Shit, a six . . . . Well, I'll bring you an extra pair of socks to stuff in the sneakers. Shit, I don't believe this! OK, meet me at Abs Central. It's on Sixth and Twelfth, east side of the street.'

I boggled, both at the name of the gym and the casual way she gave the address. 'I'll get a cab.'

'You're not that far,' she said disapprovingly. 'You could walk it.'

'Give me a break, Kim, I only got here yesterday.'

'Yesterday! Shit! OK, I'm out of here. Meet you just inside the doors in half an hour.'

She was gone. I hung up and stared at the phone, which promptly evacuated its bowels of excess quarters, farting noisily. The anticipatory excitement of meeting Kim again – the kindred spirit of my late-teenage years, my equally evil twin, the nearest thing I'd ever had to a sister – was submerged temporarily under the implications of the words 'cardio and crunch'. They sounded ominous. And what was even more unnerving had been the matter-of-fact way Kim had pronounced them, as one to whom they held no terrors. Actually, I was reasonably fit at the moment; Hugo kept himself so ruthlessly in shape that it shamed me into reasonably regular bursts of fat-burning activity. Still, I had the feeling that American definitions of fitness might be considerably more rigid than British ones.

I sneaked a quick look at my bus map, keeping it partially concealed by the booth from any passers-by who might mock me as a tourist. Kim was right. Sixth and Twelfth wasn't far at all. Still, it wasn't just round the corner either. I decided to get a cab. Something told me I would need to hoard my energy.

* * *

I didn't recognise her. If there was one thing I would never have predicted could happen, it was that I wouldn't recognise Kim, after however many years had passed. I was remembering the tomboy I had hung out with, big and confident, and then the skinny girl, shocked into unprecedented self-doubt by her father's precipitate flight to America in the arms of Barbara Bilder. The last time I had seen Kim had been at Heathrow, about to board the plane for New York and a confrontation with her father. A shadow of her former self, she hadn't eaten properly for months, and her jeans were hanging off her, held up by one of his old belts. She was wearing a sweater of his, too. She'd have dressed in his clothes from head to toe if they had fitted her.

Her hair hung lank round her face, the skin pasty and badly nourished. I had tried to look after her, but she hadn't really wanted my help. All she wanted was her father back, and now the mountain was going to Mohammed. She was determined to impress on Jon that he owed her a place to stay in New York and help with getting into art school. It had been more than ten years since she got on that plane. I wondered how much use he had been. She had sounded pretty good on the phone – confident, together . . . .

I looked around me. A seemingly endless series of frighteningly fit and toned women in cropped sweaters and low-slung trousers were swinging past and heading through the gym doors. When one of them, her short dark hair slicing back from her face in the latest gamine cut, her navel studded with a tiny silver star, detached herself from the procession and threw herself on me, I found myself backing away, thinking she'd mistaken me for her girlfriend.

'Sam!' the vision cried into my ear, hugging me so tight I saw a hundred clones of the star in her bellybutton flashing before my eyes. 'It's me! God, you look *just* the same! I'd have known you anywhere!'

The shocks were certainly coming thick and fast today. Natalie Wood had gone native with a vengeance: this was the New York equivalent of fringed buckskins and a long plait.

'Kim?' I said feebly. I could just about hear her London accent under the American patina. It was practically the only clue. 'I would never have recognised you,' I confessed. 'I feel terrible.'

Kim, sensibly, took this as a compliment.

'Shit, I'm not the same person,' she said, shepherding me through the doors and past the signing-in procedures with a slick efficiency that was alien to any memory I had of her. 'I'm kinda *glad* you didn't know it was me.'

'You look so – so New York. Streamlined and superfit.'

She beamed. 'God knows I work hard enough for it. Remember how porky I used to be?' she said ruefully.

'Kim, you were *not* porky. Ever.'

She ignored this completely. By now she was leading me into the changing room and handing me some items of clothing which looked as if she'd bought them from a designer version of Mothercare: matt black and so small they would have been tight on a twelve-year-old.

'How am I expected to wear this?' I said, holding up the crop top in disbelief. 'What happened to your breasts?'

What happened to *you*? I wanted to say. It was true that, up till her father left, Kim had always been a little on the chubby side. Now she was half a stone underweight and her stomach was as flat – well, not as a pancake, which always strikes me as a silly comparison. Often pancakes aren't flat at all; they have those bulging pockets of air which, translated into flesh terms, would be buboes. Kim's stomach was as flat as one of the lightly rippled sheets of Perspex we used to mess around with at art college. She looked amazing, though the skin on her face was stretched a little too tight. I was aware what an effort it must have been for her to lose the weight and keep it off; though now she was a thin size ten, her bones were still a twelve.

I struggled pitifully into Kim's restrainer bra – thank God she'd brought me one, Kim was always thoughtful – and the rest of the exercise gear. For the second time that day I thanked God I was in a strange city. If anyone I knew, apart from my oldest friend, caught me in a too-tight bra which corseted my bosoms together into the scanty neckline of a leotard with a G-string back, I would have had to kill them.

I turned round and squinted at myself in the mirror over my shoulder. At least the cycling shorts kept me relatively decent. Still, it was yet another shock.

'My God.'

'You don't look so bad,' Kim said generously. 'You're really in shape.'

'The *clothes* are in shape,' I corrected. 'That's what's holding me in. Wait till the seams start to burst.'

'Oh no,' Kim reassured me. 'They're double-stitched.'

'Well, that's a relief.' I tugged at the G-string of the leotard, which was outlining my private parts rather more explicitly than I usually preferred outside the privacy of my own boudoir.

'Come on,' Kim said impatiently. She was already jogging on the spot.

'Hang on, I'm just sorting out my lip definition.'

The bloody thing wouldn't move. I felt like a lap dancer about to go to work. Incredible to believe that women had operations to enhance that sort of thing.

Kim giggled, but it came a beat later than it would have in the old days, and lacked its usual full wattage. We had snapped straight away into our automatic, sisterly familiarity – impossible not to, we had practically lived together for our formative years – but the Kim I knew seemed to have been taken over, at least partially, by a New York Superwoman clone. I hoped that if I started digging I could excavate some shards of my old dirty-minded friend down in the depths of her soul.

My instinct about the ominous title of the class had been bang-on.

Cardio and crunch turned out to be an hour-long extra-strength aerobics class – on bendy boards that made you work double-hard because you couldn't go slow pretending you were worried about joint injury – followed immediately by half an hour of abdominal exercises. I had never heard of anything that bad. I couldn't believe Kim hadn't warned me; once the first sixty minutes were up I turned to her saying with relief: 'Thank God *that's* over,' only to hear the teacher yell:

'Right! Here comes the part you've all been waiting for! Everyone hit the deck! We're gonna work those abs till they beg for mercy!'

This was what the adulterers had to do in the seventh circle of hell. Dante had probably concealed it from us because he felt the news was so brutal it would fatally unbalance the rest of the poem. Alas, since we were still, technically at least, on earth, all the participants seemed to be off-duty aerobics teachers doing this for light relaxation. I staggered out after the full ninety minutes, hitting the showers without a word. It took me five minutes standing speechless as the kind water sluiced me down to remember what my name was and what I did for a living.

'Way to go!' Kim said, joining me in the opposite shower. 'You're in good shape.' She said this with as much approval as if she were telling me she liked my sculptures. Over here it was obviously considered the same level of achievement.

'I used to teach weights,' I said, soaping myself, 'but not for a couple of years now.'

'Right,' Kim said sagely, 'that explains your arm definition. How come you stopped?'

'Oh, my sculptures started selling. Very slowly. I'd probably have gone on teaching, but someone got killed at the gym I worked at and by the end the atmosphere was so terrible – everyone had been suspecting everyone else – that I didn't want to go back.'

'Oh my God. Did they catch the person who did it?'

'*I* caught the person who did it. That's partly why I stayed away.'

'Wow.' Kim was staring at me now. I stepped out of the shower, very reluctantly, and started towelling myself down.

'That must have been hard to deal with,' she said respectfully. She wasn't shocked, I noticed. New Yorkers, even adopted ones, made a point of not being shocked easily. They had a lot invested in being tough.

I shrugged. 'It wasn't so hot. The person who did it—' I couldn't say the name, even now, I noticed with detachment '—was acquitted and went back to work at the gym. Some people left and others just pretended it had never happened.'

'In denial,' Kim said wisely. 'I know all about that.'

'Look,' I said, 'do you have to be somewhere now?'

'Not till ten. That's when my shift starts.'

'Well, let's go for a drink and something to eat and catch up on everything, OK?'

'Well, sure. I can take you down to where I work. You'll really like it.'

By the time we left the gym, evening had fallen on the Avenue of the Americas. I liked that name, even though Kim told me sternly not to use it. Locals always said Sixth Avenue. I shot a glance back through the brightly lit floor-to-ceiling windows of the ground-floor gym. Despite the warm golden lighting, there was nothing cosy about the scene inside. A whole new set of enthusiasts were going for the burn. We didn't call it that any longer, but that was what they wanted and everyone knew it.

'How often do you work out?' I asked Kim.

'About four times a week. I should do more, really. I'm putting on weight.'

'Where?' I said incredulously. 'On your eyebrows? Kim, you're a shadow of your former self.'

'Oh, there's always room for improvement,' she said seriously. 'OK, let's head down this way. We can catch the 8 over to Avenue A. Show you a bit of the East Village.'

'That's where you live, right?'

'Yeah. You'll go for it.' She grinned at me. I saw a flash of the old Kim. 'It's right up your street.'

'Dirty and druggy?' I suggested.

'Exactly. Lots of people with green hair and piercings. You'll feel right at home.'

'Oi, watch it. I remember when you went fuchsia. Anyway, that green hair wasn't so terrible.'

'I used to really envy you, not having anyone to shout at you when you did something like that,' Kim said reminiscently as we waited for the bus. 'Mum was so angry with me, do you remember?'

'That was mainly because we stained the sink and it never came off,' I pointed out. 'She quite liked you fuchsia.'

'Mum was always so hung up about it being a council flat,' Kim said. 'She could never get over it. That's why she wanted everything perfect.'

'It was really nice, your house,' I said.

'But it Backed Onto The Estate,' Kim said in such an accurate imitation of her mother's voice that I started laughing. 'Mum was always like, I grew up on a sink estate like that one and now I'm right back where I started. That's why marrying Dad was such a big deal. He'd been to uni and everything. And he was a teacher. It was really marrying up in her eyes. God, it's funny to think of it. You know who she's with now? A cabbie. And she's much happier.'

'Good. Your mum was always great to me.'

'She went to pieces after Dad left,' Kim said, her voice hardening. The bus pulled up and we climbed on. I liked the New York buses; they were like liners, with their smooth motion and whooshing doors. London buses stank of dirty diesel fumes badly enough to give you a thumping headache if you sat too close to the ventilation panels. And the trails of black smoke they left were so filthy and reeking they would have furnished Dickens with ample material for a whole page of masterfully-paced invective.

'I can't believe you're here,' Kim said for the hundredth time as we sat down in the bar she had chosen. The East Village was full of people wearing those over-long pull-on woolly hats. The girls' sweaters were too small and the boys' were too big. Boys here, as I had already lamented to Hugo, seemed to wear all their clothes too big. I wondered if it were so no one thought they were gay. This was a very regressive theory, but the only one I had so far.

'It's really bright in here,' I complained, resisting the impulse to shield my eyes with my hand as I peered at the drinks menu hung over the bar. There was something odd about it, but I hadn't worked it out yet. I was too busy wondering why a supposedly fashionable hangout had hired the same designers McDonald's used to make their sitting areas so unwelcoming that people would bolt their food in twenty seconds and make for the door. Someone could make a fortune selling antacids just outside to ward off the subsequent indigestion pangs.

I didn't mean to imply, however, that this bar was done up in brown plastic wood with red and yellow seats slanting at an angle which a coma victim would have found uncomfortable. It was bright pink instead, and the white lighting made everyone look as if they had just been artificially revived.

'I thought New York bars were dark and cavernous,' I continued petulantly.

'Not juice bars,' Kim said brightly.

'Juice bars,' I repeated slowly.

'Well, sure! Want an energy shot? Everything's non-fat, by the way. It's the policy. I love this place.'

I put my head down on the table. So that was what was wrong with the picture. Spot what's missing: anything more than one degree proof.

'Kim,' I said through my arms, 'I love you, you're like a sister to me, but when I say, "Let's get a drink," I mean alcohol unless I deliberately specify otherwise, OK? I take it if I ask them for a vodka and tonic here they'll stone me to death with capsules of multivitamins.'

'Do you really need a drink?' Kim said, deep concern in her voice. She put a hand on one of mine. 'Is it a problem? You wanna talk about it?'

'I don't *need* a drink,' I said crossly. 'I *want* a drink. Oh, never mind. We'll stay here and I'll have some health-food sludge with barley extract just to prove to you that I can go without.'

'Are you going to be OK?'

'I'm not going to have DTs, if that's what you mean . . . You're teetotal, aren't you?' I said belatedly. 'How long has this been going on?'

'About five years now. And I've never felt better.' She beamed at me. 'You should try cutting it out, Sam. Just for a while.'

'There are lots of things I haven't tried yet,' I said evasively. Then I wondered if that were still true. 'I'll put it on the list, right under wheatgrass shots and operating on myself without anaesthetic.' I looked up at the menu again. Once I came to terms with the lack of my favourite ingredient, I had to admit that many of the concoctions didn't sound so bad. Avoiding anything that would have been improved by the addition of vodka, so that I didn't get wistful, I finally went for a Blue Apple (blueberries, apple juice, non-fat yoghurt and banana), which was perfectly nice. Kim, alas, had her regular, which was wheatgrass and carrot with bee pollen and ginseng. I tried, for the sake of old friendship, not to say aloud what this concoction looked like but when she offered me some I jumped back, jibbering and shaking my head like Quasimodo on an off day.

I was missing the old Kim with a powerful sense of loss, as I had never done before meeting her again. I had always known she was out there; I even had the painting she had given me on permanent display in my kitchen, reminding me of her. With my usual laziness I had assumed that we would meet up again one day and things would be just as they were, only we would be ten years older and maybe even able to afford the things we had shoplifted before. And probably we would have moved on from drinking lager and black; we'd catch up over vodka and tonics, get blasted together and do some speed in the loos for old times' sake before cruising out to harass boys and lig our way into a club where we would pretend to dance around our handbags and drive DJs crazy by asking them if they had any Abba. Small pleasures, but our own. The Kim I had before me now probably eschewed dairy products, let alone tabs of acid.

I looked at her again, familiarising myself with the bone structure that had been hidden beneath the chubby cheeks and rounded contours of her teenage years.

'Kim,' I said, it having just occurred to me, 'how come you got to stay here? I mean, isn't it really difficult to get a green card?'

'Oh, I married this guy,' she said blithely. 'He was gay and wanted to go live in England, so it worked out great. Well, for me anyway. We lived together for a couple of years and then the irony was he got this great job offer in LA and ended up moving there instead. So much for wanting to go to London. He was always a bit of a flake.'

'Did you stay with your dad when you got here?'

'Not for long.' Kim's jaw tightened. 'That bitch Barbara made it pretty clear she didn't want me around. I mean, I didn't know anyone, it was all new to me, I was just finding my feet, and after I'd been there barely a week, you know what she says to me? With a nice smile, like she's pretending she doesn't know what she's doing?'

I shook my head.

' "You know, Kim, my family's always had this old saying," ' Kim repeated, mimicking Barbara's wispy little voice. ' "Guests are like fish, they start to smell after three days." '

'My God.'

'Right. I'm seventeen, I don't know anyone, it's a pretty scary city, and she's basically telling me to get out of her house and go fend for myself. Of course Dad wasn't around when she said it, but you know what? Even if he had been, he wouldn't have heard it. I mean, he wouldn't have, like, processed it. He's so blind to how jealous she is of me. Any time he sees me, she's got to come too. And then it's not about him and me any more, it's about her. As soon as she's there, she dominates everything. Plus he's not real when he's with her. I mean, he's not my dad any more, he's her husband. No way she'll let him be both at once. If she could wipe me off the face of the earth, she'd have done it the moment I showed up here.'

If I hadn't been a recipient of one of Barbara Bilder's powerful warning-off stares, or seen the way Jon had tiptoed round her back to give me Kim's phone number, I would have thought Kim was verging on paranoia. As it was, none of this surprised me. There was a bitterness in Kim's rant for which I couldn't blame her. Though she sounded resigned as well. This wasn't a fresh complaint.

'I've pretty much come to terms with it,' she said, echoing my thoughts. 'Though it was really hard at first. I felt so rejected. You know how close we all were at home. I felt he owed me for breaking that up, and he just wasn't accepting his responsibility. Of course I've got beyond that now.'

She sipped some more green muck. Some of it had stuck on her teeth, but it didn't seem the time to tell her.

'That's why I never wrote back to you,' she said. 'I'm sorry about that.'

'Look, I don't remember sending you loads of information about my life either,' I said, wanting to make her feel better. 'Knowing me, it couldn't have been more than a couple of postcards.'

'They were funny, though. It made me really happy to get them, but then I got so sad. I couldn't write back and tell you how unhappy I was. I had to be strong, focused, you know? Or I'd just have fallen to pieces. Anyway, I got lucky. I answered this ad in the *Voice*, this guy looking for an English wife, and we really hit it off. I moved into his apartment right away, and he sorta looked after me. Him and his boyfriend took me under their wing. I was so fucking lucky,' she said thankfully. 'Everyone's got their coming-to-New-York story and mine's always the happiest.' A couple of people, leaving the bar, squeezed her shoulder in greeting as they went past. She waved back at them.

'See that girl who just left? When she first moved here, she went to stay with a guy who picked her up on the subway, an older guy, right, and he gave her her own room and everything, so she thought he was OK, and the first night she wakes up early and he's got all these lights set up around her and he's photographing her while she's asleep. The next morning she wakes up feeling something itching her, and he's got a cotton swab with Sea Breeze on it and he's cleaning her face. He says he can't understand why she gets upset, because all he was doing was cleansing her because her face was a little oily. Then she finds a notebook with all the good and bad things about her written down, he's been observing all her movements around the apartment and he says at the end that on balance she only gets five out of ten as a substitute daughter.'

'Jesus.'

'Yeah, she got out of there. Went to stay in a women's hotel and then couch-surfed for a while. Still.'

Kim pulled a face at me. I tapped at my front tooth and, understanding automatically, she wiped at her own, removing the grass. 'All gone? There are some real crazies out there,' she went on. 'I could tell you some stuff . . . .'

She was flashing a smile at me, about to embark on an even stranger anecdote. But her casual remark had made me remember

Kate, who was dead, strangled only last night by a crazy person. I couldn't grin back at Kim.

She picked up on my change of mood at once.

'Sam? What is it?'

I looked at her, realising that Jon couldn't have rung her yet. Though she was Barbara's stepdaughter, Kim still knew nothing about what had happened at the gallery. I had the feeling that I was diving in and out of different people's lives in a series of scratchy cuts on a speeded-up film. My head was spinning, and not because of the multivitamins in my Blue Apple. I took a deep breath, feeling a wave of post-exercise-class, travel-induced tiredness sweeping over me, intensified by the bad news I was about to relate.

'Look, Kim, there's some stuff I have to tell you.'

Briefly I filled her in on the events that had happened earlier that day. Kim's eyes became wider and wider as I ran through them. I finished with the story of Detective Frank thinking that the graffiti on Barbara's paintings was some kind of installation, knowing that would amuse her. It did, but not for long.

'I don't *believe* it,' she said when I was done. 'And *Kate*. Strangled. I especially can't believe that.'

'You knew her?'

'She lived around here,' Kim said casually. 'Everyone knows everyone else, at least by sight. It's a village. Literally. But she broke up with this guy she used to be dating and since then I haven't seen her in the usual places. I guess she needed a change.'

'Do you mean Leo? The guy she was dating?'

'You know him? How come?' There was an edge to Kim's voice that made me curious.

'I just heard about him from Laurence and Suzanne. And Java. Do you know them? They all work at the gallery.'

'Java? Really pretty half-Korean girl?'

I nodded.

'I've seen her around. I remember the name, anyway.' She let out her breath on a long sigh, and glanced at her watch. 'I gotta go to work,' she said.

'I don't even know where you work,' I said.

'This bar called Hookah. You'd like it. Want to come along?'

I shook my head, pleading tiredness. Also I was starving. Too many sensations were flooding in on me. Kim and I had ten years to catch up on, and the weight of all that pressed down on my shoulders as if I were fathoms deep. She looked as if she were feeling the same way. Talking to me about her father and Barbara had probably opened wounds she had thought safely scarred over long ago. We walked out onto the street in silence, hugging each other goodbye. I gave her my phone number and she promised to ring me the next day before she disappeared up the street. I found a café and got a huge sandwich to go before hailing a cab. Already my building felt like home. I greeted the doorman with such enthusiasm he looked taken aback.

My limbs ached and my stomach felt as if Xena, Warrior Princess had been using it as a punchball. I crawled into bed and turned on the TV. Nancy had cable, and I found something called the Comedy Channel: I ate my sandwich and washed it down with a beer I had found in the fridge to the accompaniment of *The Daily Show*, a spoof news programme. Its presenter, besides being very easy on the eye, was blessed with a sly sense of humour, and his catchphrase was 'Too much information!', which he used to great effect.

I knew exactly how he felt.

CHAPTER TEN

Hugo woke me up at four in the morning. I had fallen asleep at ten, which is the crack of dawn for me. So when the phone rang I was in the Twilight Zone of semi-consciousness, body and brain deeply confused.

'Who? What? Where?' I croaked, bewildered, into the receiver.

'What's the time?' Hugo was asking in a pointed way.

I located the clock. 'Four,' I said automatically. 'Oh, right. Ha ha.'

'You're not pissed off with me for waking you up.' Hugo was immediately suspicious. 'Why aren't you pissed off? What have you been doing? Is there someone there with you?'

I was so hazy I actually lifted the covers next to me to check there wasn't a sleeping body under them.

'Apparently not,' I reported. 'Unless he's deflated in the night. What time is it over there?' I said, trying to make my brain work. It was like starting a reluctant car on a frosty morning; it kept making turning-over noises and then giving up the struggle. I watched it from a distant perspective, as if I were having an out-of-body experience, floating up to sit on a cloud and looking down on myself through the mists of vapour. I was often like this when untimely ripped from sleep.

'Nine,' Hugo said reluctantly.

This did the trick. I howled with laughter. 'You got up at nine in the morning to ring me! You sad bastard!'

To Hugo and me, nine in the morning was much, much worse than four. Four might at least mean that you'd been up all night being decadent and corrupt, while nine was undeniably, teeth-flossingly respectable.

'I had an early call,' Hugo said coldly. 'I was up anyway.'

'Liar liar pants on fire,' I retorted.

'Try to restrain your acid wit, my love,' Hugo said in even colder tones. 'You know how piercing it can be. I have to go now. I have to take my clothes off and rape a teenage prostitute.'

'Will you manage to fit that in before going to rehearsal?'

'Not funny.' He sounded more bitter than angostura. 'Doing Pinter is nothing to this. You should see the foulness of the boy. He has poorly bleached hair and no projection. Thank God we're doing it in the studio. The director only cast him because he wanted to get into his pantyhose.'

'And has he?'

'Oh, the first day. The first *minute*. The young thing makes Jack Nicholson look like a blushing violet. Much, much faster than shagging one of those boys from the arcade at Cambridge Circus. That's always preceded by about thirty seconds of financial negotiations. This little tart just drops to his knees before you've said hello. Probably *is* his way of saying hello.'

'Poor Hugo,' I said sympathetically, reading between the lines. 'Director completely ignoring you?'

Hugo sighed assent. 'Not that it matters. The play is so non-existent anyway that discussion of my character would be laughable. It's just a series of increasingly Goya-esque tableaux with spatterings of fake blood from a different orifice each time.'

'Ick.'

'At least I'm not getting the worst of it,' Hugo said, cheering up a little. 'That poor cow who plays the girl is completely *persona non grata*. I may be too old for our esteemed director's tastes, but I'm still male, and I wear tight trousers to please him. She's getting the silent treatment. Thank God she's on Prozac already, it's the only thing holding her together. Every time she has to take her clothes off he just gives her this look of contempt for having a vulva. I can't describe how awful it must be.'

'Does she take her clothes off a lot?' I found myself asking with rather more emphasis than I liked.

'Sweetie,' Hugo reassured me, 'I like my women to look like

women. If I want a boy I've already got one in an hour and a half. We're doing the frottage scene.'

He sighed again. It was a deeply poignant moment.

'How's everything else going?'

'Ooh, very, very well,' Hugo said with instant complacency. 'A riot. I'm plumbing new depths of evil with Ferdinand. It's terribly easy, I just pretend that the Duchess is being played by that shocking little tart and I come over all fiendish without even having to work myself up. And my costume's too pervy for words.'

That was actors all over; the same attention paid to their outfits as to the role. Hugo always said when challenged that the clothes made the man.

I yawned again, the kind of long slow yawn that feels as if it's turning your tonsils inside out.

'Go back to sleep,' Hugo said, sounding guilty. 'I shouldn't have revenged myself this way. Doing Jacobean tragedy has warped my moral values.'

'Oh, it's OK . . .' I mumbled.

'Go back to sleep,' he said with increasing emphasis. 'You're not yourself. Ring me when you are.'

'OK. Good luck with the frottage.'

'Thank you *so* much, darling.'

The yawn had been well timed. I had sensed that he was about to ask me how things were here, and I didn't want to inform him that someone had been killed the evening of my arrival. Although he would never dream of telling me as much, I knew he'd start fretting about me, which wouldn't do either of us any good. I had learned the hard way that men need plenty of protection from the harsh realities of life.

* * *

Don rang me at eleven. Because of his accent I thought he was Hugo again, this time putting on a silly voice, and we had to battle through this initial misunderstanding before he could inform me that my sculptures had just arrived.

'Shippers don't seem to have fucked 'em up any,' he said. 'Which is pretty good goin', I can tell you. Carol wants to know when you're comin' down to look 'em over.'

'How's this afternoon?'

'Fine by me. Any time's fine by me. Be a nice change from cleanin' the floor.' His drawl gave 'floor' at least three syllables.

'How's things there?' I asked.

'I've seen better. Still, the restorer lady thinks she can get thet paint offa Ms Bilder's masterpieces. So we're all as happy as sandboys.'

Did no one like Barbara Bilder? I wondered as I put down the phone. Or was it simply sour grapes on Don's part? Working in a gallery was the worst job for an aspirant artist. It would embitter even a Buddhist on their last life before nirvana.

'Hey!' the doorman said as I emerged from the lift. He was the one who had been on duty when I had arrived, a tall, well set-up Hispanic guy, whose nice-looking face was unfortunately marred by the tiny pocks of old acne scars. They gave his skin the texture of an obscure and expensive kind of leather that, made into a handbag, would cost a fortune on Fifth Avenue. As human face covering it was distinctly less valuable. Context is all.

'You're Ms Jones, right?' he was saying. 'They find your camera?'

Merciful providence ensured that, just in time, I remembered Detective Frank's cover story.

'Not yet,' I said. 'They haven't let me know, anyway.'

He grimaced. 'I wouldn't hold out much hope. You leave something in a taxi here – well, forget the next passenger. Driver'll boost anything that's not tied down.'

'You think that's what happened?'

He shrugged. 'More than likely. They track down the driver?'

Under this well-intentioned barrage of questions, I decided that my best course was to imitate Manuel in *Fawlty Towers*.

'I know nothing,' I said regretfully, restraining myself by a hair's breadth from doing the accent too. He might think I was taking the piss out of his.

'Shame. Your first night in New York and something like this happens.'

'Well, it was insured,' I said airily. 'Look on the bright side, eh?

Oh, I wanted to ask you something. How do I get to Strawberry Fields?' I was half-expecting him to say: 'Second star on the right and straight on till morning.'

'Oh, that's easy!' he said cheerfully. 'Just turn right on 72nd Street and keep going till you hit the park. It's straight in front of you, you can't miss it.'

He looked at me more closely. 'Might want to give it a few days, though,' he advised. 'You hear what happened there? Girl got killed. Real nasty. Strangled, they say. It was on the news. Pretty girl, too. They showed a photograph. Oh, and we had a hold-up on 71st two nights ago. Couple kids with handguns. You might not want to walk down there at night.'

'God, it's like living in an episode of *Homicide*,' I commented.

'No, no,' he said quickly. 'The city's much safer now since all the Giuliani reforms. Really. You'll be perfectly OK, Ms Jones.'

That would be a first.

Today the first block of 72nd Street was as dead as a recent Martin Amis novel. It was Saturday, the Jewish Sabbath, and everything kosher – the Italian restaurant, the bookstore, the Glatt Mexican takeaway – was shuttered up tighter than a bad face-lift. I crossed the great teeming intersection where Broadway and Amsterdam merged, throwing up islands in their wake. The flood of traffic surged past like fast-moving boats, people jumping back from the sidewalks as if frightened to get their feet splashed when the liner buses swept perilously close cutting a corner. The motorbike couriers were the jetskis, dashing between the buses with the insistent buzz of giant bumblebees. Huge Mack trucks ploughed straight down the centre of the road, the great furrows of their passage buffeting cyclists off-balance as they struggled to hold their own against the cross-currents of wind. How the bladers managed I had no idea. With their black helmets and the pads buckled to knees and elbows, they looked like urban warriors, heads down, legs moving fast and rhythmically, weaving along the streams of cars, pushing themselves off ones that came too close with the metal protectors strapped round their palms.

Crossing New York's busiest avenues felt as if an invisible Moses were holding back the roaring torrents for a tiny space of time; if we didn't make it across fast the Red Sea would surge in, drowning stragglers and Egyptians. It added the thrill of danger to a cross-town walk which Giuliani's city reforms had apparently removed from most other areas of possibility. Between Amsterdam and Columbus was Hispanic territory, and I was besieged by horny would-be studs.

'Yo, baby,' they called. 'Nice lady . . . .' And 'Whoah!' when something particularly nice went by. Or they hissed between clenched teeth in a long slow Sssssss of approval, like the evil snake Prince John in the Disney *Robin Hood*. 'Nasty,' another one said to me with appreciation. He was sitting on a fold-up stool in the middle of the sidewalk and handing out leaflets.

Ahead of me I could see the green glow of Central Park. The last block was almost all residential, with perfectly spaced, well-maintained trees lining the sidewalk, casting elegant shadows onto the long awnings that reached nearly to the kerbs. I crossed the last intersection and found myself at the open mouth of a tangle of little paths, like tributaries running together into a river. They dipped and turned away, thickly hedged, their surfaces glimmering in the sunlight. The grass shone, each blade glittering with light like tiny green slivers of mirror, and the chaos of cars on Central Park West, just behind me, faded into a background hum which hardly disturbed the clear fresh air.

* * *

I loved London's parks, but this was something special. Even Regent's Park, with its boating lake and swans and bandstand, its wide open stretches of football and rugby fields with tantalising glimpses of the poor zoo animals, is flat. Only Hampstead Heath provides hills and wildness and mystery, not to mention the raucous man-to-man sexual encounters of Golders Hill Park, and that's scarcely in central London. Highwaymen hung out there only a century and a half ago. Whereas this, bang in the middle of New York, was a forest.

Strawberry Fields turned out to be practically in front of me, a little section of grassy knolls and an inlaid 'Imagine' mosaic, so much less spectacular than I had envisaged that I walked round it a couple of times before realising that I was in the correct spot. I was put right by the arrival of a tour group of Japanese who immediately gathered round the mosaic and started taking pictures. There was no police tape closing off any particular area, and no one there on duty.

'You hear about that chick who got killed here?' a kid behind me said. He plopped himself down on a bench and gestured to his companion to join him. 'Right where you're sitting, man. Got her from behind and – *chhkk*.'

He drew a line across his throat. 'Came up behind her with a wire. Nothing she could do. No matter how you struggle, once that wire gets you – *chhkk* – it's all over. Only takes a few seconds. That's what the Gestapo used.'

'The who?' said Kid B.

'You know,' Kid A said impatiently. 'The Nazis. Like, in the films.'

'Oh yeah.'

Kid B's assent did not quite convince me. I had the feeling that he was just agreeing for the sake of an easy life. I turned to glance at them and then wished I hadn't. Their heads looked as if they had been shaved with a grass-cutter, there were little billy-goat tufts of beards on their chins, and they were wearing the regulation huge, bottom-concealing trousers. On their top halves were baggy long-sleeved T-shirts, and over these were pulled much tighter ones, short-sleeved and shiny with logos. They looked ridiculous. At least neither of them had any beauty to ruin.

'So how come you know all this? About the chick that got done?' he asked, curiosity winning out over squeamishness.

'Saw it on the news,' Kid A said with relish. 'They found her in the morning, sitting where you are, like she was just sleeping or something. Nasty, huh? Tell you what, she was a babe. I saw her photo. Hot stuff.'

'So maybe it was a boyfriend,' suggested Kid B. 'Guy was jealous, right?'

'Nah,' said Kid A, worldly-wise. 'She wasn't, like, interfered with.'

'Oh.' Kid B was convinced by this sharp-witted piece of deductive reasoning. 'So who did it, then?'

'Hey, man, you asking me? I don't know! Maybe there's, like, a maniac at large in Central Park.' He lowered his voice on the last few words, trying to induce the requisite spooky atmosphere.

'There are hundreds of fucking maniacs at large in Central Park, man,' retorted Kid B, unimpressed. '*You're* a fucking maniac at large right now.'

'Well, hey! Maybe it was me! You better watch out – one dark night I'll come sneaking up behind you—'

'Hey, man, if you think I'm dumb enough to let *you* come up behind me, you fucking pervert cocksucker—'

Kid A flung a friendly punch at Kid B, who responded in kind. They scuffled around for a while under the disapproving gaze of the Japanese tour group, practically falling off the bench in an ecstasy of what in 1910 would have been called ragging – though I had the feeling that to claim victory in that particular sport you had to shove your opponent's head into the wastepaper basket.

The sun poured down on our heads, the sky a clear duck-egg blue. I stared at the bench, trying to imagine Kate sitting there at midnight. There was a thick hedge behind it. No one could have come through that without ripping themselves to pieces and making such a racket in the process that their chances of taking her unawares would have been as high as William Hague's of getting off with Eva Herzigova.

Had it been someone she knew, someone who had come here with her, who, as they talked, had strolled behind the bench and whipped the wire round her neck? It wasn't easy to imagine. Wouldn't she have turned to look at them as they walked behind her? Instead, testing out Kid A's theory, I pictured a boyfriend offering to rub her shoulders. Standing behind her, he would be in the perfect position to take her off guard; you didn't look round at someone who was giving you a massage, you closed your eyes and made appreciative noises. This was the best theory so far. But Central Park at midnight was not to me the ideal place for a back rub, not in October with the nights increasingly chilly.

I looked at the hedge again, wondering if someone could have been waiting there, crouched down so they were hidden in the shadows, still and patient till Kate arrived to keep the appointment. And then, as she sat down, standing up behind her in one swift movement and swinging the wire round her neck before she even had a chance to turn round and see who it was, before she could scream out . . . .

The kids had stopped shoving each other and were staring at me rather nervously.

'Hey, are you OK?' Kid B said.

I snapped back to the present. 'What?' I said blankly.

'Oh, nothing.' He fumbled his feet. Kid A gave him another little shove, muttering: 'Dumbass!' at him. He cleared his throat.

'It was just, you know, the way you were staring. Like, I dunno. You were looking like you saw a ghost.'

'Maybe she saw the ghost of that girl, man!' Kid A said in hushed tones. 'She's right here! Whoah! I felt, like, a cold touch on my neck—'

'Hey, fuck *you*!' said Kid B, losing it completely and giving Kid A such a shove that he fell right off the bench. Kid B was on top of him at once, pounding his head against the grass.

The Japanese looked on in appalled silence. Even the guide was mute. And then the most daring one took a photograph. The little click hung in the air for a moment. A few people raised their own cameras and exchanged glances, upon which a fury of snapping broke out, the shutters rattling away like a single crazed piece of machinery. Through it all their faces remained impassive, like hardened photo-journalists trained to report on the most terrible atrocities without flinching or showing emotion. Depraved American Youth Desecrates The Memory Of John Lennon's Message Of Peace. Kid A by now had Kid B's head trapped under the bench. Kid B flailed up with his legs and caught Kid A square on the bottom with his work boots. Kid A howled and tried to shove Kid B's chin into his nose. It was all good bracing stuff.

New York was certainly providing me with a series of surreal tableaux. Whether they were in any way edifying was another matter. I strolled away, hearing the caterwauls of rage and pain, accompanied by the barrage of clicks, fade gradually away. I could see how people went crazy in this town; the emotional temperature was turned up several degrees above the norm.

As I emerged from the maze of Strawberry Fields onto a wide

avenue, my eyes alighted on someone a short distance away. I only noticed him because he had stopped dead and looked as if he were trying to blend into the scenery. Which was difficult, as he wasn't doing a Birnham Wood comes to Dunsinane imitation in head-to-foot Astroturf.

I gaped at him in disbelief. I knew that man. Even if I had only met him once, you don't easily forget someone you have wrestled with in a toilet. Or I don't, anyway. I have very good manners.

'Lex?' I said, or rather called over the fifteen feet still separating us. 'What the hell are *you* doing here?'

CHAPTER ELEVEN

There was at least one positive aspect to our meeting like this. Any initial embarrassment completely vanished, or rather was hidden on Lex's side under a considerably greater embarrassment. I couldn't imagine that he was squirming like this simply because of the poignant memories of our last encounter. In fact I would have expected him to have been swaggering away and laying on the charm in an effort to show me what a crazy impulsive fool I had been to turn him down.

So why he was looking as if he wished the ground would open up and swallow him was a mystery. Part of the solution might lie in the fact that – as far as I knew – he wasn't supposed to be anywhere near the States yet. I had thought that all the other yBas were due to arrive at the end of next week, just before the opening. Hence my snappy start to the conversation.

'Hi, Sam,' he said eventually, shifting from foot to foot in a nervy, Mum-I-need-the-bathroom kind of way. 'Well, um, what are *you* doing here?'

This was feeble, and I shot it down with the contempt it deserved.

'What do you mean?' I retorted. 'I'm staying just down the road.' I pointed behind me to the imposing structure of the Dakota building, looming through the trees. 'Back there a few blocks. *You're* the one that's not supposed to be over here yet.'

That dealt with him. He shuffled around a bit more. 'Well, I got this really cheap standby deal,' he said at last. 'So I thought I'd come over early.'

I frowned at him. 'Well, fair enough.' So why, I wondered, was he behaving as if I'd just caught him out in some major piece of mischief-making? 'But does Carol know you're here? She didn't say anything about it to me.'

He flinched. 'Nah,' he muttered. 'I thought I'd ring her in a couple of days. Whatever. I'm just chilling out right now.'

The mystery was deepening.

'Where are you staying?' I said casually.

'Oh, with a friend. Roughing it. Then I've got three nights in the hotel at the end. Bit of luxury, right? Can't wait.'

'So are you staying round here?' I probed.

'Nah. I'm down in the East Village. Nothing this posh.'

His eyes were darting from side to side, as if looking for an excuse to escape. I was enjoying torturing him like this, I had to admit. He was so pretty, and I was making him suffer. What a lovely day this was turning out to be.

'Where were you off to?' I said as innocently as I could. It was a fair enough question. There wasn't a great deal on the Upper West Side to interest a tourist, not compared with all the museums on the other side of the park. A brief study of Nancy's notes had determined me to explore Riverside Park and the local delicatessens, which apparently were a cornucopia of free tastings, but neither of these prospects could hold a candle to everything the Upper East Side offered to a practising artist: the Metropolitan Museum, the Whitney, the Frick, the Guggenheim . . . . Either Lex was headed in this direction to meet someone, or to check out the promised delights of Zabar's Food Hall, or – Option C beckoned, as tempting as a wild card. It was probably crazy of me, but Lex was looking *so* furtive.

To be honest, I couldn't resist saying it.

'Are you going to Strawberry Fields?' I suggested.

His reaction was all I could have hoped for.

'*What*? How—' His eyes fixed on mine, huge now, liquid and dark as rich black coffee. I have mentioned before that Lex looked charming when he pouted, but it suited him even better to be in shock: his lips parted, he paled slightly, his cheekbones seemed to stand out even further. He was heart-tremblingly vulnerable. If he'd been a girl Mike Hammer would have thrown him against the nearest tree and kissed him with brutal force. I can't say that the thought didn't occur to me too, but I am not Mike Hammer. Sometimes I regret this.

'Sam—' he stammered. 'How did you know? I mean, I didn't tell you I knew Kate!'

A warm smug feeling infused my bloodstream. I loved to bluff. It was one of my favourite games. I was already betting myself that I could use my near-worthless cards to broker something much more considerable. Trying a gambit, I said:

'What I don't understand is why she didn't mention to me that you were in New York.'

'Oh, that wasn't anything really,' Lex said more easily. Drawing a packet of cigarettes from his pocket, he automatically offered it to me. I shook my head. He lit one with unsteady fingers. 'She was worried about Carol knowing we were mates,' he said. 'Apparently Carol had this assistant a while back who left to be a partner in another gallery and took loads of people with her. So she's got this real thing about her sidekicks getting too chummy with the artists.'

I remembered that brief interchange between Kate and Laurence, about checking with Carol before taking me out for a drink. It had struck me as a little unnecessary at the time, but I had been too keen to get myself round a couple of cocktails to analyse what it meant. Now it rang true. Lex was doing fine so far.

'But what's that got to do with not telling anyone you were here?' I said, diving straight into the weak part of his story. 'I don't get it – oh, hang on. You're staying in the East Village?' That was where Kate had lived. Laurence had mentioned it that same night. 'I bet you were crashing at Kate's, right? That's why she didn't want Carol to know.'

Lex dropped his cigarette. Then he jumped back in case it caught his Caterpillars and burnt the laces.

'No!' he said at once. 'I mean – no, I haven't been – I don't know what you're talking about—'

He caught his breath.

'Sam?' he said pleadingly, accompanying it with his best winning smile. He even brought the eyelashes into play. It was an impressive performance. For a moment I thought he was going to duck his head and look up at me through them in approved Princess Diana style.

'You won't tell anyone, will you? I mean, it's got sod all to do with me. I really liked Kate, but, you know, it's not like I knew her well or anything. I was just bedding down at hers. Now I'm in deep, deep shit if anyone finds out, and, I know this sounds crazy, but I've got this weird feeling that someone's watching me. Like the cops or something. I must be getting paranoid . . . .'

Unpeeling all of this slowly and thoroughly was going to take a while. And, unfortunately, I didn't have the time right now.

'Look,' I said, trying to sound sympathetic, which is always an uphill struggle for me, 'I'm on my way to Bergmann LaTouche for an action meeting about installing my stuff. They're expecting me, so I haven't got a lot of time now. What're you doing later on?'

He shrugged. 'Oh, just hanging out on Avenue A, you know. The usual.'

I had to admire the nonchalance with which he said this, as if he'd been here for a year instead of a week.

'I'm crashing just round the corner,' he added airily.

'Who with?'

'Oh, a friend of Kate's. Leo. Couch-surfing, they call it here. Only he doesn't have much of a couch.'

My eyebrows rose at this mention of Leo. He was certainly ubiquitous.

'Well, I'll come down to Avenue A and hang with you,' I said firmly, reserving other questions for later. 'Where shall we meet?'

'The Ludlow?' he suggested.

'Where's that?'

'Down on the Lower East Side. On Ludlow Street, just off East Houston.'

'I'll find it. OK, shall we say there at seven?'

'Yeah, fine.'

I didn't really think that he wouldn't show up. But I wanted to make absolutely sure.

'Great,' I said warmly. 'I can't wait to talk about all of this. And I won't say a word to anyone at the gallery.'

He looked stricken, understanding perfectly the threat I was hanging over his head.

'You won't. Will you?'

'Not now I know we're meeting up later,' I said, smooth as vinyl. I looked at my watch. 'Shit, I should be going.' I gave him a big grin. It was supposed to be reassuring; I hoped it didn't come out too synthetic. 'Seven. At the Ludlow. Don't be late.'

'I'll be there,' he said as seriously as if he were swearing on a rosary.

With a brief wave, I headed past him. After a few steps I turned and looked back. He was staring after me.

'Strawberry Fields is that way,' I called, pointing. 'Just follow the path round.'

'Oh, yeah. Right.'

If you don't know already, I thought to myself as I watched him walk away.

* * *

Don was almost too laid-back to live. I found myself wondering whether he actually had a pulse; he reminded me today of a hibernating bear. It was an appropriate comparison on many levels. I wouldn't have been at all surprised if he turned out to live in a cave: I'd heard there were some capacious ones in Central Park. It would have to be roomy. Don was about as big as a grizzly.

I couldn't decide whether his temperament was similar. Grizzlies were supposed to turn nasty if you messed around with them (well, so did I, for that matter). Still, they weren't known for garrotting their victims. They just broke your neck with one casual backhand swipe. Looking at Don, it seemed to me that this would be his preferred method of approach. I couldn't see him bothering to find a piece of wire and attach toggles at either end to make a garrotte.

There was a catch in this piece of deduction, though. Don was no fool. We had worked out a way to rig one of my mobiles so it seemed half-crashed into the uprights in the first-floor gallery, and, when he chose to be, he was completely on the ball. By the end of our conversation I was full of excitement about how it would look. He had a very sharp tactical mind. Which would mean that he was more than capable of deciding to garrotte someone precisely because anybody looking at him would assume that it was the last thing in the world he would do – just as I had. With hands like Don's, who needed a piece of wire?

I found it hard to fit Kate's name into this picture. I kept calling her 'someone'. It helped to keep my head clear. I thought of her, walking out of the bar that night, flashing a smile back at us, her orange-red hair clashing so brightly with her knitted scarf and scarlet trousers, and something grabbed my heart, squeezing it tightly. I had hardly known her, but she had been so alive, so vital, that you felt you could warm your hands at her as if she were a fire. I wondered again who she had been going to meet that evening.

'Sam? You OK?' Don ambled over. We were standing in the upstairs gallery, its floors now restored to shiny glossed perfection, its walls mercifully clean and white and empty. Don still couldn't talk about it without swearing, though. I sympathised. It couldn't have been much fun cleaning all that up.

I snapped back to the present. 'Fine. Just imagining how it'll look, hanging there.'

'Real nice,' Don said with satisfaction. 'Well. Cigarette time. You wanna come back down, get a coffee or somethin'? It really bugs me to be up here right now. I keep seeing those fuckin' paint streaks all over the fuckin' floor.'

'OK.'

We clattered back down the stairs, all the way to the basement and through its meticulously organised storage rooms to the big space at the back which was Don's territory. It opened out onto a small yard. Since he could smoke with impunity here, this was prime real estate and he guarded it well, repulsing any attempts by co-workers to nip down for a quick fag. Apart from a large quantity of half-opened packing crates, containing the latest instalments of yBa meisterworks, and quite a few canvases stacked with their faces to the wall which I assumed were Don's own oeuvre, the room was luxuriously furnished with no less than three broken-down and battered loungers of various types, the kind specifically designed for men to slump in while watching sports on TV. Some even had springs sticking out, which gave me a nostalgia rush for my own sofa. I felt more at home here than I did in Nancy's pretty little flat, which was a sad observation on my home-making skills.

'You don't mind the smoke, right?' Don said, rolling himself a cigarette and slumping his huge frame onto the largest of the Eaze-E-Boys. It creaked but held.

I shook my head.

'Some good things about you Brits,' he observed.

'Don't tell me,' I said, 'you're going to say the beer now.'

'Not that flat stuff.'

'Bitter,' I corrected.

'Yeah, it is. No, I like Belgian beer.'

'Blonde?' I suggested, naming the main type of beer.

He gave me a shit-eating smile.

'Those too.'

'There's always Suzanne,' I pointed out, deliberately stirring. 'One Belgian blonde, to order.'

Don's grin faded. 'Yeah, right. Whatever.'

'You guys don't get on?' I stirred my coffee.

'Yeah, you could say that. She's smart, though. I'll give her that,' he said grudgingly. 'No dumb blonde. Too fuckin' bad.' He tapped down the tobacco and lit the roll-up in one swift, habitual movement. Then he didn't say anything for a while. I was getting the hang of this, but it was tough going. Don, as Tom would have said in one of his drunker cod-Irish moments, was a terrible man for the pauses.

'She been talkin' to you?' he said finally.

I blinked. 'Well, we don't semaphore each other, if that's what you mean,' I said carefully.

'You know. I mean, sayin' stuff about me.'

'Don, I only got here two days ago and since then Kate's been killed,' I emphasised. 'There hasn't exactly been much time for idle gossip.'

I was pleased with this evasion. I was honing my ability to tell the truth without answering the question.

'Yeah, that's one big goddamn mystery,' Don observed. 'Kate whacked and some creep throwin' paint all over the place. Damned if I know what it's all about.'

I didn't like the fake-casual way he said this. My eyes narrowed.

'You don't seem to care much about what happened to her,' I said, drinking more coffee. 'I thought you guys had a thing once.'

'See?' Don observed. 'I knew people 'ud been talkin'. Jesus. Women. You ever try keepin' your mouths shut just to see what it'd feel like?'

'Bollocks.' I couldn't be bothered with this. 'Don't give me that shit. You know perfectly well that men gossip just as much as we do. You're just jealous because women tell each other all the juicy details. And anyway,' I said, stretching a point to annoy him further, 'it was Laurence who told me.'

'*Laurence*,' Don snorted. 'Laurence wanted to get into her panties himself. That's why he cain't even give me the time of day.'

He grinned at me slyly. I was dying to point out that Don had, as he would doubtless put it, pussied out of getting into Kate's panties; but discretion won out.

'I like Laurence,' I said rather feebly instead, feeling somehow that he needed defending.

'Oh, he's OK. For a geek. Smart boy, though,' Don said casually. 'He's goin' places.'

He fell silent again, and I waited with him, sensing there was more to come.

'Kate was cool,' he said finally. Talking to Don was like having a TV in the room which fizzed into life only in fits and spurts. I would lose transmission for a while and then, just as I was thinking the signal was gone for good, it would click back on to issue another laconic statement.

'No BS about Kate,' he reflected. 'What you see is what you get.' He looked down at his fingers, their motion on the Rizla paper ceasing as if by their own will. 'I mean,' he corrected himself slowly, 'what you saw was what you got.'

He looked shaken. Sometimes the reminder that you have to use the past tense will do that; it's the moment the news sinks in for good. I pressed hard on this opportunity.

'Suzanne thought she was going to meet her ex-boyfriend that evening,' I said. 'Someone called Leo.'

'*Leo*,' Don said very drily. For a moment I thought this was going to be his only comment; then he added: 'Man, that guy is not good news. Take it from me.'

'You know him?'

Don shrugged. 'He's around the neighbourhood, y'know? Yeah, I know him. He's a piece of work.' Don took a drag of his roll-up, looked at me assessingly, decided I wasn't likely to be too shocked, and mimed rolling up his sleeve and injecting into the crook of his arm.

'He's a smackhead, right? I knew that. Suzanne told me already.' I hadn't reckoned on the two-countries-divided-by-a-common-language thing. His stare became bewildered.

'He does heroin,' I corrected myself.

'The big H. Not a good idea, man. Don't say I haven't had my moments. But still.'

He fell silent again, and instinct told me not to break it. Don issued his communiqués up to a point and no further. He was the type of guy who loves gossip but prefers to sit in a group of people who are catching up on the latest information, giving little away himself but storing up everything for future use. To talk too much himself would be to compromise the macho image. So I concentrated on my coffee, making a mental note to ask Kim about Leo. She had been cagey on the subject before, but now I was armed with this piece of information, I might be able to use it as a lever to prise up a little more.

It's complete nonsense about curiosity killing the cat. I'm positively blooming with health.

I decided to give Kim a ring this afternoon. Maybe we could meet up later on, after I had seen Lex. She and I had barely scratched the surface of all the catching up we had to do, and I sensed it would take a good deal of time for us to readjust to each other – or rather the new, improved, nearly-thirty-years-old versions of ourselves. The mixture in Kim of what she had been, all that we had in common, and what the years and living in New York had made of her, went very deep; it wasn't just a fragile layer of sophistication through which I could break, like a thin sheet of glass, to find my friend again, perfectly preserved as she had been the last time I had seen her. Doubtless she was feeling something similar about me.

I realised I hadn't said anything for a long while; but then neither had Don. He seemed quite content, however, lying back in his lounger blowing smoke rings at the ceiling. Well, he had earned his leisure time: apparently he had been up till nearly midnight cleaning the paint off the floors and walls. I had to admit that he was restful company when silent. It was just on opening his mouth that the problems started. Well, he wasn't the first man I'd met with that particular fatal flaw.

'So,' he said at last. 'You seeing someone?'

Everyone seemed to ask this question over here. It was that famous New York directness. They thought beating around the bush was some kind of S&M practice.

'Yeah. He's an actor. He's coming over for the opening.'

'That's not till the end of next week,' Don observed. 'Gives you a bit of time to fool around.'

'Right. I hadn't thought of that,' I said coldly. 'How silly of me not to have started already.'

I was scarcely a diehard romantic, but the hardbitten cynicism with which Don had said this was not appealing. Every time I was feeling at ease with him, he would throw in something that set my teeth on edge.

'I'm going to go and say hi to everyone upstairs,' I announced, standing up and putting down my mug. 'Thanks for the coffee. So we're sorted for the installation?'

'For now, sure. You're gonna be here when we take 'em up, right?' he said, nodding at the opened crates in which my mobiles lay, looking like huge ball bearings with skin eruptions.

'Of course.'

'Don't look surprised,' Don said. 'Lots of artists cain't be bothered.'

'What about Barbara?' I asked.

'Oh, she'll be here when they come back all right.' He pulled a face. 'And I bet she's over at the restorer's right now, buggin' her to hurry up. Even though there's only a week left to go.'

'With the exhibition? They're going back up, the paintings?'

'Sure thing. Haven't you seen the newspapers? Splashed all over the arts section. She's got more publicity than she can handle.'

'Apparently it's been on the TV news a lot as well,' I said slowly, thinking of the kids in the park.

'You kiddin' me? It's got everything. Pretty girl like Kate, strangled in *Strawberry Fields*, no less – and then the gallery trashed – shee-it, if that's not news I don't know what is. We had people swarming all over here yesterday afternoon when the news got out. Journos. Carol had to do interviews all evening.'

He grinned at me. 'We're in the eye of the storm,' he said, drawling out 'eye' into a long lazy 'aaah'. I had to admit I liked his accent.

'Why is it particularly special that she was found in Strawberry Fields?' I asked. Everyone seemed to be making such a big deal out of this.

Don looked at me. 'Well, shee-yit,' he said, spreading his arms wide. 'John Lennon – peace, love and understanding, man, all that – and then some chick gets herself killed in there. It's kind of ironic, right?'

There was a sly expression on his face, however, which indicated he wasn't saying everything he knew. His blue eyes were wide and somehow mocking as they fixed their gaze on me.

'There's something else, isn't there?' I said, staring right back at him.

'I don't know what you mean.'

'Oh yes you do.'

There was no point going carefully with Don. Subtlety he would ignore, if he chose to, with sublime unconcern. Now his grin widened still further.

'Well, OK,' he said, lying back on the Eaze-E-Boy. 'Since you bullied it outta me. Kate had a tattoo. Just here.' With a smirk, he tapped what looked like the hollow of his right hip, just inside the bone; I couldn't tell exactly through the folds of the dungarees, but it was near enough.

'So?' I said.

'It was a strawberry. A little strawberry tattoo with one bite taken out. Now ain't that funny? Killed in Strawberry Fields . . . with a strawberry tattoo right next to her pussy . . . ' Don's grin was of shit-eating dimensions now. 'Wait till the newspapers get ahold of *that*.'

CHAPTER TWELVE

I went upstairs, on the prowl for fresh company. And with perfect timing Laurence came out of the security door that led to the offices just as I reached the first-floor landing. Laurence was the opposite of Don in every conceivable way. No lying around on an Eaze-E-Boy for him, perfecting his smoke-ring technique and letting the world go by. He looked as if he had the world settled firmly on his shoulders. The big, heavy, black-framed glasses made the face behind them seem fragile, the thin beak of a nose hardly able to support them. Even his head was ducked forwards as if pulled down by their weight. There were dark circles under his eyes and a snowstorm of dandruff on the shoulders of his suit.

'Hey!' he said, brightening up somewhat on seeing me. I approved of this reaction.

'I was coming to see if you were around,' I said. 'I've just been talking to Don about the installation.'

'Oh, right. How's it going?' This was more perfunctory than it should have been, but I let it pass.

'Very well. He seems to know his stuff.'

Laurence snorted. He disliked Don so much that he couldn't admit to any of his merits.

'Look,' he said, 'I've got to go have a word with Stanley. Then do you want to go out and grab a coffee?'

'Sure. Won't Carol mind, though?'

Laurence shot me a sharpish look. But: 'She's off in DC for the rest of the day,' was all he said on the subject.

'I'll go and say hi to Suzanne while you find Stanley.'

'OK.'

We crossed through into the gallery. Laurence headed off towards Stanley's office at the far end; I wandered round the desk to see if Suzanne was in the workroom behind it. There was no one there. Idly I sat down in front of her computer and started leafing through an issue of *ArtFinder* which boasted a long and, naturally – it was its house style – incomprehensible article on Barbara Bilder's oeuvre. Tiring rapidly of this, I turned to a copy of the *New York Times* magazine, neatly stacked underneath it, which offered a long interview with the artist at home. I had clearly stumbled on Barbara's latest collection of press cuttings.

I skimmed the second article. It was recent, dating back only three weeks, obviously to coincide with the opening of the exhibition, and the tone was politely respectful. Barbara was photographed with Jon, his arm around her. The article was titled 'Domestic Pleasures' and concentrated on Barbara's love-life rather than her work. I was not surprised, somehow, to learn of the affair she had had, while at art school, with an eminent artist twice her age, whose marriage had never recovered from the blow; nor of the long-term liaison she had then had with the gallery owner who had made her name by showing her work when she was a young unknown.

Five years ago the gallery owner had died of a heart attack. His wife, in an act of revenge, had promptly sold all his Bilders at a rock-bottom price in an attempt to bring down the market. It had worked. Barbara's career had been in limbo for a while, out of the current fashion. Then she had met Jeannette LaTouche – the article implied that Barbara had carefully planned the encounter – who had promptly signed her up at Bergmann LaTouche. Now she was selling steadily, and certainly the list of her paintings in various museums and private collections was impressive.

All this took a good three pages to relate. It finished on a high note: Barbara's whirlwind romance with Jon Tallboy. I was amused to read that the latter had mysteriously transmogrified, with his crossing of the Atlantic, from the deputy head of the art department at a sixth-form college into a noted British art critic and sought-after teacher. Also, according to the article, she and Jon had met at the home of mutual art-loving friends, when I happened to know that he had been bringing a group of kids to the gallery where she was showing and bumped into her in the coffee shop. Anyway, it had been love at first sight. Barbara was quoted as saying that they had been two magnets snapping together. They had left their respective spouses almost immediately and Jon had come to New York. 'No regrets,' he had apparently told the reporter. 'My life only really started when I met Barbara.'

Kim's existence was not even mentioned. One assumed that Jon had not told the reporter that he had a daughter. And judging by Barbara's behaviour on the matter to date, she would scarcely have brought the subject up herself. I found myself hoping that Kim hadn't seen this article.

'Hey!' Suzanne said from behind me. 'You want to do some data entry for me?'

I swivelled round on the chair, taking her in. Only Suzanne could carry off a tweed two-piece suit without looking like a pudding in a sack. She was carrying a big box file, shiny and new, which she dropped on the desk next to me.

'Updating Barbara's cuttings,' she said in explanation. 'I had to do it anyway, but there's so much coming in now I'm getting swamped.'

'Oh really?' This recurring press motif was becoming ever more insistent, like a snatch of melody heard for a fleeting moment in the first movement which, by the third, had turned into the theme. 'I forgot to get the *New York Times* this morning.'

'Be my guest.' Suzanne retrieved it from the bookshelves behind her and let it fall heavily in front of me.

'Jesus.' It was nearly the same size as the UK *Sunday Times*. 'This is just the normal weekday edition, right?'

She looked surprised.

'Yeah.'

'It's just so huge.'

'It's all ad space,' she said dismissively, extracting one of the many sections with the ease of long practice and handing it to me. 'There you go, page three.'

' "Imagine: Death in Strawberry Fields",' I read. 'God, what a headline.'

'The *Post* has "Who Killed the Redhead?",' Suzanne said grimly.

'Enough to make you want to do some strangling on your own account.'

I dropped the paper for a moment and stared at her.

'Suzanne, who do you think killed her?' I said, unable to stop myself from asking.

Her face hardly changed. Laurence's reaction to the news of Kate's death had been to go to pieces, but Suzanne was made of the opposite material. She was as groomed as ever, the blonde hair pulled back into a smooth pleat, her nails perfectly French manicured. Now she looked me straight in the eyes, her own clear and focused.

'I don't know,' she said finally. 'But I will.'

'Do you mean—'

But just then a door opened and closed, and footsteps could be heard on the parquet floor. Laurence came out of the back part of the gallery. On his heels was Stanley, and looking at him I was irresistibly reminded of the dupe in a Ray Clooney farce, the one who, unaware that his wife is cheating on him with the vicar and the village policeman simultaneously, is forced by her to hide in cupboards, jump out of windows and dress up as his own sister visiting from Australia under a series of increasingly bizarre excuses. He had exactly the same dazed expression.

'Oh, Sam!' he said, catching sight of me. 'Nice to see you! Glad to see you haven't been – what I mean is, that you still feel comfortable coming in here – well, that sounds strange – that is, you're quite safe here, you know.'

Laurence and Suzanne stared at him as incredulously as if he had just been beamed down from Planet Gaffe. I had a good deal of difficulty keeping my own face straight.

'Thank you, Stanley,' I said demurely. 'So you don't think I need to get a handgun?'

Stanley looked horrified. 'Oh *no*, absolutely not. No need. An isolated incident. The park is still very rough in places.'

'What about the graffiti in here?' Laurence said coldly. 'Are Sam's sculptures going to be as safe as she is?'

'We're stepping up security. You know that, Laurence,' Stanley said firmly. Beaming at me reassuringly, he smoothed back his hair with both hands. They came away shining slightly with grease, making its resemblance to butter still more pronounced. His silk tie was dotted with a bright pattern of tiny paintbrushes which stood out prettily against the dull charcoal of his suit, and the polished shoes on his small feet shone as black and glossy as a pair of beetles. Next to his impeccable tailoring, Laurence looked like he had been sleeping rough for days. I noticed that the latter's eyes were rimmed with red.

'Well, I must get on,' Stanley said. 'So much to do. *Au revoir.*' He flashed me a smile, showing perfectly capped teeth, and bustled away towards the staircase. Laurence's expression was sardonic.

'*Au revoir,*' he mimicked. 'That's about a third of the entire French Stanley knows.'

'What's the rest?'

'*Bonjour, mais oui* and *encore du vin,*' Laurence snapped, taking his glasses off to polish them.

'That's a pretty good French accent,' I approved.

'Went to school in Paris for my formative years. Dad's a diplomat,' he said shortly. 'You still want to get some coffee?'

'Just let me have a look at this first.' I skimmed the article about Kate. It was padded out with statistics about the success of the famous zero-tolerance policy: Central Park was much safer now; New York's murder rate had fallen drastically in the past few years. It managed to reduce Kate to a mere blip in the figures. A quote from Carol informed us that it was a shocking tragedy and that Kate had been a wonderful person and valued employee. A large picture of this paragon, her hair falling in a torrent of curls around her face, looked out at me from the centre of the page, her smile candid and confident. Police were pursuing their investigations. The graffiti attack at the gallery was alluded to, but rather obliquely. Maybe they were worried about Bergmann LaTouche filing a lawsuit.

'They don't mention Kate's tattoo,' I said, handing the paper back to Suzanne.

There was a crash beside me. Laurence had dropped his glasses.

'How did you know about the tattoo?' Suzanne demanded as Laurence stooped as clumsily as a stork to pick them up. Without them his face looked as exposed and defenceless as a perplexed child's, his eyes blinking fast without the glasses to shield them.

'Don told me.'

Suzanne's grunt of disgust was covered by Laurence, who exclaimed, straightening up:

'The tattoo! Shit! Don't you see, Suze? It was a strawberry!'

'So what?'

'Strawberry Fields!' Laurence said impatiently.

'My God.' She stared at him. 'You think it was deliberate? I mean, killing her there?'

'Who knew about the tattoo?' I asked.

Suzanne looked at me. 'Practically everyone at the gallery,' she said. 'Well, maybe not Carol and Stanley. But she showed most of us when she got it done. And Don would have known, obviously, because of . . .' Her voice tailed off. 'Please God, let no one who knew her leak that to the papers,' she said finally.

'Fuck someone who knew her, what about the autopsy?' Laurence was inexorable.

'Oh *God* . . . .'

'And Don told you?' Laurence said to me. 'People tell you things, don't they?'

'Mother confessor,' I said lightly.

'Yeah, right.'

'Or maybe you just ask the right questions.'

I shrugged, feeling uncomfortable. Looking up, I realised why. I didn't like the way Suzanne was staring at me.

'You ask a lot of questions,' she said. It wasn't a statement; there was something interrogative about the way she said it which indicated clearly that an answer was required.

'Do I?' I said rather feebly, hoping to stall her.

'Yes,' she snapped back.

I shrugged. 'I'm just trying to get a fix on things here,' I said, determined not to let it sound like an excuse. 'Wouldn't you, in my place?'

Now it was she who shrugged, and I had to admit she did it a lot better, that Gallic background paying off big-time.

'Whatever,' she said, turning away. It was a dismissal, and not a friendly one. Apparently I had trodden on Suzanne's toes. Well, if that were the case I couldn't blame her for getting cross. Those snakeskin courts must have cost a fortune.

★ ★ ★

'I feel buffeted by life,' I said to Laurence. He had taken me a couple of streets along from the gallery, to a little coffee shop where we perched on high stools at a bar running along the window, watching a series of eccentrically dressed people go by. I was working my way through a mini banana cheesecake which was one of the best things I had eaten in my life, accompanied by a hot cider toddy which was just as good. Laurence seemed to consider this place nothing out of the ordinary. New Yorkers were spoiled as trustafarians when it came to eating out.

'Me too,' he agreed dourly. Every so often he would take off his glasses and rub his eyes violently with the backs of his hands till they were red and sore. It wasn't the best method for releasing tension. 'What did you say a couple of days ago? It's like being on a roller-coaster. Just as I'm feeling really down, Stanley or someone'll come out with a blasting piece of idiocy. I don't know whether to laugh or cry.'

'Yesterday,' I corrected. 'It was yesterday I said that.'

'Sweet Jesus. Is that all? It feels like a lifetime. The phones won't stop ringing, Carol's going nuts trying to cope with everything – and she's had to go off to DC today . . . .'

'Should you be here?'

'No way,' he said frankly. 'But I needed a break.'

He sighed. I liked Laurence a lot.

'You must think you've stumbled into a barrel of nutcases,' he said. 'I guess I could have put that better, but I'm too tired to think straight. And don't worry about Suzanne. Of course you're asking questions. I mean, Jesus, I'd probably be suing by now for mental distress.'

I shrugged. 'It's fine. I'm used to nutcases,' I said lightly.

'I haven't been sleeping,' he said in parentheses. 'And now this tattoo thing! Talk about terrible coincidences! Or maybe it isn't. I can't decide if that makes it better or worse. Well, no, it's obviously worse, because that means it was someone who knew Kate, instead of a random maniac – or is that better? I mean, which would she have preferred?'

'Laurence, if you keep rubbing your eyes like that they're going to come out the back of your head,' I informed him.

He looked at me blearily through the knuckles crammed into his eye sockets.

'They're pretty sore,' he conceded, lowering his hands reluctantly.

'Shit, I'm not surprised. You should see how bloodshot they are. You look like an Alsatian with a stinking hangover.'

Laurence grimaced, picking up his glasses. 'I'm blind without these,' he said, pushing them back on his nose. 'Mind you, it's kind of nice not to be able to see anything right now. Everything's this big fuzzy cloud.'

'Is that what your antidepressants do? Put you on a big fuzzy cloud?'

'No, I couldn't work if they did that. Actually they kind of sharpen everything up, but you don't care about it so much.'

'Nice one,' I said rather ironically.

'Yeah, it's pretty good,' he agreed. My sarcasm had gone right over his head; proof, if any were needed, of how exhausted he was. 'Let's not talk about the gallery right now, OK?' he said unexpectedly. 'I could do with some distracting.'

'Just don't say "Tell me about yourself",' I requested. 'I hate that like the plague.'

He smiled. It was a weak effort, but we were moving in the right direction.

'I know!' I said suddenly. 'You were going to tell me about the difference between seeing someone and dating.'

'I was?'

'Well, is there a difference?'

'Sure,' Laurence said easily. 'Seeing someone means it's not exclusive. Dating is more serious.'

I blinked. 'Could you run that by me again?'

'God, you Brits,' Laurence said, baffled. 'Don't you know anything?'

'Obviously not.'

'OK.' Laurence put his glasses back on, pushing them up the bridge of his nose with one bony finger. All around us, thronging the coffee shop, hurrying past on the streets outside, black-clad

SoHoites pushed and clamoured, overheard snatches of conversation alien and yet familiar flooding past my head. One of those washes of disconnection swept over me, where people are speaking the same language and yet have such a different set of values they might as well have come from a parallel universe.

'Seeing someone isn't too serious, OK?' he said as seriously as if he were giving a lecture on Jane Austen's subtextual critique of social mores. 'Like, say I meet this girl and she's seeing someone, I could still ask her out. I mean, I would consider her single, for all intents and purposes.'

'But she's seeing someone!' I was baffled. 'I mean, obviously she isn't single.'

'Uh-uh. If she's seeing someone, she can see other people too. But if she tells me she's dating someone, then I would back off. Look, I know it seems crazy. When I came back to college in the States I kept fucking up, OK? It took me two years to work it out. Everyone else knew it already from high school.'

'Work *what* out?'

'The dating rules,' he explained impatiently. 'There are all these rules you have to follow. Otherwise the dating machine spits you out like a faulty piece of crap. So, OK. Let's imagine I'm seeing someone.'

'Which means you can see other people too? I mean, it works both ways?'

'Oh sure. Absolutely.'

'But do you know the other person is seeing someone else?'

'No way!' Laurence was shocked. 'That would never happen! You never, never talk about what you've been doing in too much detail at first. It's basically don't ask, don't tell.'

He sighed. 'It's really hard to make people understand. And you know what? Americans don't talk about this. I don't know whether they're embarrassed at how stupid it is, or they take it for granted, or what. But when I came back from Paris, I tell you, I was drowning. And no one helped. The first girl I was dating here – I really liked her, she was very tough and together, which is what I go for —' He looked momentarily wistful. 'So we meet up to go see a movie – on Saturday night, right, this is good – and I asked her casually as I was buying the tickets what she'd been doing the night before. She nearly bit my head off. How dare I ask her what she'd been doing, was I trying to snoop around her private life, etc etc.'

I stared at him, the last bite of banana cheesecake frozen halfway to my mouth.

'Laurence,' I said, 'can I ask, how, um, intimate were you with this chick? I mean, had you, you know, shagged or what?'

Laurence rolled his eyes. 'And over here we have this image of the English as refined and beautifully spoken . . . . No, we hadn't got it on, but we'd done plenty and I thought I was in with a pretty sure chance that evening, OK? So I get all confused, and I blurt out in the middle of the cinema, "But I thought you were seeing me! I mean, I didn't think you were seeing anyone else!" And she says, "Hey, buddy, we haven't had that conversation yet." '

'My *God*. What conversation?' I finished the cheesecake.

'The conversation,' Laurence said, adjusting his glasses, 'where after you've been seeing each other for a while you decide together that you're going to take it to the next stage. That is, you're going to see each other exclusively. But you know,' he said with great seriousness, 'the whole thing is really about power. It's all codified. It's a big topic of conversation here – how long it should take you to ring someone, how many days you wait after the first date before getting in touch again. I know guys who swear by a week at least. The aim is to make the point that the other person likes you more than you like them. And there's always this high tension because no one wants to put all their eggs in one basket, it isn't safe. This city eats up relationships and spits them out. People play major head games,' he said rather sadly. 'That's why I'm single right now. I'm always too keen. If I like someone I don't want to fool around. Which really fucks you up in New York. You show them you like them and they walk all over you.'

I clicked my tongue in sympathy. 'It's not so complicated in London,' I said. 'I mean, we have all the usual neuroses, but once you're seeing someone you're seeing them. Then if you cheat on them you're a bitch. I mean, I couldn't turn round and use the excuse that we'd never said we were going to be exclusive.'

'How did you meet your boyfriend?' Laurence asked wistfully.

I winced at the word. 'Um, he was in this play I did some mobiles for. Actually I thought he was gay at first. He's pretty camp. He likes to present himself as a sort of effeminate Oscar Wilde type.'

'And you find that attractive,' Laurence said blankly.

I grinned. 'Yeah.'

I saw no reason to add that Hugo's effeminacy went only so far and no further; it pleased me to be thought eccentric. Besides, if I told people how good he was in bed everyone would want a piece. As they said over here.

Suddenly I remembered that I ought to be ringing Kim. I looked around me for a payphone.

'What is it?' Laurence inquired. 'You're jittering as if you had DTs.'

'Oi, keep your tongue off my alcohol consumption, Prozac Boy,' I retorted. It was nice to see Laurence back to his normal bantering self. 'I was looking for a phone. I need to ring a friend.'

'I'm sorry, I didn't realise I was boring you that much,' Laurence said courteously. 'There's one on the corner.'

'OK.' I fixed my gaze on him meditatively. It had occurred to me that this might be a good opportunity to score some Barbara 'n' Jon gossip, were there any going. 'Guess what? Do you remember that I used to know Jon Tallboy from London? He was the father of my best friend.'

'Still is, presumably. And of course. How couldn't I recall such a touching reconciliation scene? Poor Stanley went into a catalepsy. "On a happier note . . . ."' Laurence said reminiscently. 'And Barbara shooting more arrows at you than they let off at Saint Sebastian. You must have been picking them out for the rest of the day.'

'That's exactly the point. Jon had to make up an excuse and sneak away from her to give me Kim's number. I think he was frightened I'd ask for it in front of her and provoke a major quarrel.'

'The Bilders ought to have one of those medieval mottos, like "What I Have I Hold", or "Touch Us Not Lest We Cut Your Hand Off At The Wrist", Laurence said. 'It would fit Barbara perfectly. She's pretty hot on property rights.'

'And Jon's her property?'

He shrugged. 'She bought him, didn't she? Paid for him and shipped him over here? No one had ever heard of him till Barbara married him, and suddenly he was this big art critic. She's got a lot of strings. And she's a great puppeteer. God knows if he had any idea of the kind of Faustian pact he was making . . . sell his soul to Barbara in return for being set up in a nice little berth, a couple of consultant editorships on magazines, she's even wangled him a part-time job editing art books . . . and now that the merchandise has some independent value, thanks to her careful investments, she's keeping an eye out that no one poaches it from her.'

'Would anyone try?' I said blankly.

'Well,' Laurence said with the profound cynicism which I liked so much in him, 'she hasn't made the mistake of getting him a teaching gig. Students are the big danger. Plenty of young, fresh meat sitting in the front row, crossing its legs and flicking its hair and purring "Oh, Professor Tallboy, I just *luurve* that British accent!" No, Barbara's too sensible for that. Still, you never know. There's supposed to be this big shortage of attractive single straight men in Manhattan. Though frankly, I don't know what they're talking about. I'm still available.'

I grinned at him. 'But she's even jealous of his daughter,' I said, refusing to be distracted. 'It's crazy.'

'Some people who buy property want to feel that not only do they have the full title,' Laurence said, 'but that they're the first ones to set foot in it. They want virgin territory. They rip out everything the previous owners did and start again from scratch. Then they boast to all their friends about what a wreck the place was when they bought it and how you wouldn't recognise it now. The last thing they'd want would be someone showing photos of what it looked like before.'

'Let alone its children popping up.'

'Yes, my metaphor takes us only so far,' Laurence agreed. 'But still, you see what I mean?'

I nodded. Laurence was quite right. Barbara Bilder's attitude to Jon could only be described as proprietorial. I saw the Bilder family crest in a more country-and-western vein, however. Hands Off My Man. Don't You Go Messin' With What's Mine. You Can Look But You Cain't Touch (You Slut).

I got up and went to phone Kim. I was starting to get stupid. The only thing for it was a change of scene.

CHAPTER THIRTEEN

I found the Ludlow without difficulty; it was barely ten minutes' walk away, straight down West Houston. With the aid of my trusty subway and bus maps I was navigating smoothly around New York, or I would have been if there hadn't been so many distracting shops on the way. I even went into Warehouse. It seemed ridiculous to cross the Atlantic simply to shop at Warehouse, but everyone had told me how much lower the prices were over here and I thought I might as well check out whether there was any truth in that. There was. The only thing that kept me under any sort of control was the knowledge that I was heading out for the evening and didn't want to be lugging seventeen bulky carrier bags around with me during an East Village bar crawl. I made the rule that I could only buy what would fit in my rucksack.

This still left me much too much leeway. By the time I reached the Ludlow I was wearing one of the woolly pull-on hats everyone had this year. Only mine was a soft charcoal with dark-blue velvet ribbon edging, definitely a cut above the average. While in my rucksack were a jar of iridescent body glitter, four packets of fake tattoos, a shocking green lace miniskirt, a silver choker which on first sight was very similar to all my other silver chokers but, looked at closely, had tiny little diamanté chips set into it, which clearly made it different and worth buying, a silk dalmatian-print scarf and two sex toys which were Hugo's present from New York.

In other words, I was glutted with shopping. I felt like a lion which has stalked, chased and successfully brought down a large and tasty gazelle. There comes a point, however, when even the most predatory lioness lifts her head from the carcass, decides she's had enough for the time being and rises with feline poise to drag the prey into the shelter of a convenient bush. Then she strolls a few paces from the corpse and stretches herself out indolently. That was me. Only I was thinking more of a bar with comfortable armchairs (into which I could lower myself with the smooth lazy grace of a giant cat) and an imaginative cocktail menu.

The Ludlow looked as if it was exactly that sort of place. It was practically a walk-in living room. The only catch was that the comfortable armchairs were already overflowing with people. Someone extricated himself from the depths of one as I walked in, thus ruining the delicate eco-balance of body distribution; the two people who had been sitting on either arm of the chair caved in on each other as soon as he removed himself. Two other people immediately perched on the small part of either arm that was thus exposed to the air.

The boy who had been in the armchair was wearing pyjamas, faded tartan ones with a Snoopy on the right breast. He ambled through the crowds in the direction of the bar. On his feet were unlaced trainers and his hair stuck straight up at strange angles, as if he had just got out of bed. Maybe he had. And now I looked around, he wasn't the only one in nightwear.

I caught sight of Lex leaning against the far wall, a bottle of beer in his hand, and waved till he saw me. Chugging down the rest of his beer, he pushed himself off the wall and started the long slow-motion process of cutting a path through the crowd. The air was redolent with the sweet, rich, acrid smell of pot. I couldn't imagine anything so overt in the equivalent London trendy bar. But then, people didn't wear pyjamas out in London either. Shame, really.

'Shall we head off?' Lex said as he reached me. 'It's packed in here.'

We left the Ludlow rather reluctantly. The warm, overheated reek of pot and smoke and people had been welcoming, and outside it was getting cold and dark. I pulled my hat down over my ears.

'Hey, like the hat,' Lex said, noticing it. He fingered the edging. 'Buy it here?'

'Just now. On Broadway.'

'Really nice. Makes you look cute.'

Resisting the impulse to pull off my hat, throw it to the ground and stamp on it, I limited myself to throwing him a cutting glance and setting a fast pace up towards East Houston.

'There's Max Fish,' Lex was saying, 'but it'll be jammed too. Let's try 3A. It's right up here, over East Houston.'

Lex had certainly got to know his way around the East Village, at least since our meeting in London. I wondered if he had found out the location of Gramercy Park by now so he could pretend that he'd known where it was all along.

East Houston was wide as most European rivers and lit with flaring streetlights which made it seem still wider. The cars roared past, fast as a film shot of speeded-up traffic, two strings of flooding lights running beside one another, pulling in different directions: white up, red down, a tug of bright geometric modern beauty, its edges softened as the lights blurred together. Running with the bulls at Pamplona would be a piece of cake after a few weeks crossing streets in New York. They ought to charter planes for Manhattan natives to do the festival en masse.

'That's the deli where they filmed the orgasm scene in *When Harry Met Sally*,' Lex informed me patronisingly.

I bet someone had told him that just last week, and now he was passing it on with as much casual assurance as if he'd been present while they were filming it. I shrugged. What did I care about some professionally ditzy blonde faking it in public? The point about Meg Ryan was that she made her living out of trying as hard as she could not to be scary. If it had been Ellen Barkin or Sharon Stone doing it, now that would have been interesting.

'Thursday's the best evening to go out,' he was saying as we made it to safety on the other side of East Houston. 'Friday and Saturday all the B&T'ers flood in for the weekend.'

Lex was hoping I would ask him what B&T stood for: but I already knew it meant Bridge and Tunnel, shorthand for the two main ways to reach the island of Manhattan and thus the disparaging term locals used for people who lived on the mainland. Frustrated by my silence, he added casually:

'New Jersey and Brooklyn really pollute the city, you know.'

'Oh, come off it, Lex' I said, provoked beyond endurance. 'How long have you been here, five minutes? What do you know about it?'

'Hey, man, it's what everyone says, OK?' Lex remained unabashed. 'Here we are.'

He pushed open the heavy door of a bar as dark inside as a black hole, seeming to suck in all the light only to extinguish it in the gloom. Just inside the door a bouncer was sitting on a high stool which in proportion to him looked like a child's toy. He nodded us in with a smile that for a normal person would have been reasonably friendly and for a tattoo-covered, black-shrouded bouncer was practically a kiss on either cheek and an affectionate pinch on the bottom. In some ways New Yorkers actually had less attitude than Londoners. Maybe they felt that a person who could survive in Manhattan had nothing to prove to the rest of the world.

He should have issued us with dark glasses for the first ten minutes we were here, to help our eyes acclimatise. I stood, blinking, trying to adjust to the sensation of having walked into somewhere even more tenebrous than the street outside. Not that I was complaining.

Lex was forging over to the bar. It was less crowded in here, and when we secured our drinks and went upstairs we had little difficulty finding a corner of a black leather sofa on which to perch. It was the ideal kind of sofa, sagging just the right amount without lowering you so far down to the floor that you needed a winch to get you out again. The only catch was the noise it made whenever you shifted around. The leather was stiff enough to respond to every little movement and its range of sounds was as wide as if it had a small zoo trapped under the upholstery.

'Cheers,' Lex said, clinking his vodka and tonic with mine. We took a long pull at our drinks, and I smacked my lips appreciatively. Here when you asked for a vodka and tonic they gave you a triple vodka and just showed the tonic bottle to the glass fleetingly, as if to remind it of the latter's existence.

'I do like it here,' I said, sounding maudlin already.

'What, here here? Or New York?'

'Both. But I meant New York.'

'Yeah, it's great, isn't it? I never want to leave. If I didn't have my nice little council flat in London . . . but still, I could always rent it out to someone.'

'Dodgy. I mean, it'd have to be someone you could trust.'

'Yeah, I know.'

'Where are you exactly?'

'Bermondsey. You should come down, it's really cool. It's this big block right on the river.'

'Nice.'

'Yeah, sweet.'

'Better than some junkie's floor in the East Village,' I said, cutting to the chase with what I prided myself was a deft touch.

Lex looked slightly stunned. 'You what? Oh, you mean Leo? Why'd you call him a – who's been talking about him?'

I shrugged. 'Everyone seems to know everyone else in this neck of the woods.'

'Yeah, that's true enough. Specially round these parts. It's like Notting Hill.'

'So,' I said in an intimate tone designed to elicit confidences, 'tell me what's been happening.'

Lex shifted uncomfortably, rooting himself further into the sofa, which produced in response the honks, squeaks and flaps of a group of playful sea lions. Then he lit up a cigarette, and we sat for a while as he smoked it. But I bit my tongue and didn't say a word, following the Don method, and finally my silence forced him into speech.

'Man,' he said eventually, 'this has been such a fuck-up I can't tell you. One minute I'm having a really good time, just hanging out, making friends, doing Manhattan, you know? And I really liked Kate. She was cool. I like American girls. When they're together they're really together, you know? Kate was so sussed it wasn't true.'

'I heard she liked guys with drug problems,' I said. 'That's not so together.'

'Leo? He's not so bad. Well—' Lex faltered a little here '—OK, he's not in the best of shape right now. But they were just friends. I mean, they hadn't been going out for a while. He was totally cool about my staying with Kate. So it was him I rang up when I heard what had happened.'

I noticed with a flicker of amused detachment how Americanised Lex's speech had become since coming to the States. And he was dressing more like the boys here, too. The jeans he was wearing right now looked suspiciously large.

'How did you hear?' I asked.

'Kate always asked me not to answer the phone,' he said, ducking his head. The dark lashes stood out against his pale olive skin as if they had been painted on with a fine brush. He splayed his legs and propped his elbows on them. I bent forward a little to catch what he was saying.

'I was supposed to let the answering machine pick up and see who it was,' he started. 'In case it was someone from work, right? So that morning, I mean, I knew she hadn't got back. I was sleeping on this blow-up mattress on her floor and the flat's so small she had to walk practically over me to get to the bed. I just thought, OK, she's pulled, or stayed over somewhere. I mean, it wasn't any of my business. The phone went at dawn. I was all blurry and I nearly answered it. But just as I was about to pick it up – thinking it was Kate, right – I hear this voice going: "This is Detective Thurber calling from Manhattan South, Homicide. I have some news about Kate Jacobson. Would anyone there please pick up." ' Something like that. I tell you I jumped off that fucking bed like it was a trampoline. I stood there, staring at the phone like it was a bomb about to go off.'

'What did you think had happened?'

'Fuck knows. But she said Homicide, yeah? So, I dunno, I panicked. The only thing I could think of was that I wasn't supposed to be there. It was like—' he raised his head and looked at me imploringly '—I know it sounds stupid, but I was still half-asleep, and it felt like someone had dumped me into the middle of a film. Or *NYPD Blue*. I thought: I'm staying in the flat, so I'm suspect number one.'

'And you jumped to the conclusion that Kate had been killed?'

We were speaking quietly; there were other people at the end of the sofa and on the others surrounding the big smeared glass coffee table, though it was so dark it was easy to forget their presence. I looked around me, checking that nobody was listening in, my gaze sweeping over our surroundings. The walls were a dirty dark orange and God only knew what colour the carpet had been originally. Even the faded pink neon sign over the toilet door was askew and missing one of its letters. I quite liked the word 'Oilet'. It sounded like the technical term for a tiny but vital screw-part.

At the far end of the room was another, smaller bar, its bottles and glasses gleaming dully in the white lights set behind its mirrored shelves. People came and went here like bulky ghosts in a strange dark limbo of lost but not unhappy souls, no one seeming the slightest bit interested in what we were saying. Still, I realised I had just lowered my voice even further.

Lex looked violently uncomfortable by now.

'Well, yeah,' he said helplessly. 'What else was I supposed to think? I just panicked, you know. Like I said, it was this nightmare situation. All I could think was, "Shit, I've got to leg it!" I grabbed my stuff and I wiped my fingerprints off everything I could think of I might have touched, and I got out of there as fast as I could. I wasn't thinking straight.'

I stared at him in disbelief. 'You've really cocked up,' I said. 'That's the most suspicious thing you could have done.'

'I know!' he wailed in a semi-strangled voice. 'I was such a prat! But I'd been out late the night before and I was still pretty much out of it, you know? My head wasn't right yet. I'd been hanging out, smoking a lot of gear – really strong skunk, and there's this puff they've got here called kindbud – have you tried that? It's bright green – and hydro, that's another kind . . . .' His enthusiasm faded as he reconnected to the subject under discussion. 'Anyway, I was gone, you know? Fucking gone. I think I must have been a bit paranoid when I woke up.'

'I'd say so,' I commented drily. His whole story was stupid enough to have the authentic ring of truth. And it made psychological sense. I hadn't known Lex that long, but already I could see that his cool-dude image was as thin as the fondant coating on a chocolate. Take one bite and your teeth sank into a marshmallow-soft centre.

'What am I going to do, Sam?' he said, leaning towards me so our knees were touching. 'I'm really fucked, aren't I?'

I couldn't reassure him. 'They'll know there was someone staying at Kate's,' I said. 'No way if you were in that sort of condition you managed to remove all traces of yourself. They'll be looking for the mystery man right now.'

Then I knew exactly how a seal clubber would feel when he had only stunned his victim and had to come in again for the final stroke. Lex was staring up at me piteously, his brown eyes wide and pleading, as if imploring me to finish him off, not to leave him any longer in this terrible pain. All he needed was some white silky fur and a cute pair of flippers and the resemblance would have been complete.

'Shit, Lex, don't look at me like that,' I said, finishing my drink. 'You're upsetting me. It's like torturing a puppy.'

'Well, if you're upset, how do you think *I* feel?' he said unanswerably. 'What am I going to do, Sam?'

I speak from experience when I say that it is near-irresistibly seductive to have a pretty boy throw himself, metaphorically speaking, at your feet, begging for your protection. Now I was feeling more like Sam Spade. Or Mike Hammer again. The setting helped: this was the right kind of scuzzy dive on the perfect mean street. Though I should be sitting at the bar, drinking neat bourbon, to make the picture complete. And the woolly hat would have to go.

With an effort I dragged my thoughts back to the present. Lex was looking ever more helpless, clearly sensing that this was the way to appeal to my better side. He was taking a calculated gamble that I had one.

'First I need another drink,' I said. 'Same again?'

He nodded dumbly. I went to the bar and got in another round.

'Look,' I said, setting the glasses on the table and sitting down, 'who exactly knows you're here?'

He stared at me. 'Well, I told Leo I was going out, but he doesn't know where exactly. I said we'd probably be hanging on Avenue A.'

I felt my eyes rolling. I didn't remember Sam Spade having to cope with this kind of moron.

'Here in New York, idiot,' I specified.

'Oh, right! Well, Leo, of course. And his mates. But, I mean, they're not going to go to the cops, are they?'

'Anyone from the gallery?'

Lex shook his head. 'Kate really didn't think Carol would go for it,' he said. 'I don't think she told anyone.'

'So how come you were staying at hers?' I asked curiously.

'Oh.' He shrugged. 'It was just one of those things. I got this impulse to come over early and I rang the gallery to see if Carol knew anywhere I could stay. But Carol wasn't there and I got Kate on the phone instead. I met her when I was over before, so we sort of knew each other, and she said I could bunk down at hers as long as I didn't tell anyone. Nice of her, right? I mean, she was taking a risk. She said Carol'd have sacked her if she found out.'

It was bizarre that Kate would have risked so much for someone she didn't even know; it didn't make sense. But I put this one aside to puzzle out for later, not wanting to distract Lex too much from the main subject under discussion.

'Was she meeting you that evening? The evening she died?'

Lex started, as much as he could; the depth of the leather sofa stifled sudden movements at birth.

'No way! I swear to God!' He looked crestfallen, turning to face me full on. This manoeuvre caused the sofa to squeak excitedly under his weight like a flood of rats in a panic. 'But I can't prove it. I didn't see anyone I knew. I just went to a film at the Angelika – that one with Demi Moore as the deaf-and-dumb nun – and then I went up to St Mark's and scored some blow, and then I went for a couple of drinks. I must have got back to Kate's about midnight, but I don't remember anything, you know? I was well out of it.'

'Do you know where she was going?' I asked.

'I've really tried to think,' he said, creasing his forehead as if to mime the tortuous nature of his thought processes. 'I mean, if I knew anything then obviously I'd go to the cops. But all I remember is she said she had a heavy night ahead and she might be back late. And she pulled a face when she said it. I mean, she didn't act like she was meeting up with a guy. It was more like—' he sat up straighter, grabbing one of my knees excitedly, the sofa sounding like a baby pig being slaughtered '—like it was a work thing that she couldn't get out of. But not a work thing because she would have said.'

I stared at him. 'Did she seem excited at all?' I asked slowly.

He thought about this. 'More on edge. Worked up about it.'

It was that quality Suzanne had noticed when Kate said goodbye to us, which had made her assume that Kate was seeing Leo again; a heightened sense of tension about her, as if she had something tricky to face. Would she have looked like that before going off to trash the gallery she worked for? But that had been too early. Everyone agreed that the graffiti at the gallery could not have been done till at least midnight and probably later. Until then there were simply too many people still in SoHo for whoever had done it to be sure of being able to enter and leave without being seen. And Kate had been dead by midnight.

'Did you hear about what happened at Bergmann LaTouche?' I said.

Lex nodded. 'Not till today, though. I got the papers.'

'And did you know that the gallery wasn't actually broken into?' I said. 'They came in with the keys and they knew where the burglar alarm was and how to switch it off.'

Lex was staring at me with acute concentration.

'You mean *Kate*—' he said. 'No, that's crazy. She wouldn't do that. Shit!' he suddenly exclaimed. 'I heard something! I know I heard something! Kate was talking to someone on the phone, about keys. Oh shit, I can't remember. Something like: "yeah, sure I've got the keys" – and there was something else, but I can't remember it.'

I proffered his glass. 'Have a drink,' I said. I always found that helped.

He gulped down some vodka and tonic.

'Shit,' he said. 'I'll probably wake up in the middle of the night and remember it. I was just coming out of the bathroom and I only caught the end of the conversation. I don't think she wanted me to hear it.'

He stared at me imploringly. 'It could be really important, couldn't it?'

'You didn't hear the name of the person she was talking to?'

He shook his head. I grimaced.

'But there was *something*,' he insisted doggedly. 'Sam?' The puppy-eyes were back. 'What am I going to do?'

I sighed. This damsel-in-distress thing was actually quite wearying.

'Well, from the purely selfish point of view, you could just keep your head down,' I suggested. 'You haven't got anything to tell the police. Yet. You could always hang on till you remember whatever it was that Kate said. Then you'd actually have something to tell them, rather than some lame story about panicking because you were still tripping on the finest puff New York has to offer.'

'What if I don't?'

I shrugged.

'And you won't tell anyone I'm here?'

I shouldn't have promised. I knew it was a mistake. But he was giving me that pleading look up from under his eyelashes and his lower lip was trembling. From this angle he strongly resembled the dark and luscious Adrian Pasdar, the star of a vampire film called *Near Dark* made by Kathryn Bigelow before she got big budgets and went out of control; Adrian, as a country boy called Caleb who was seduced by a beautiful vampire, was definitely on my top-ten-of-all-time list. The flesh is weak and mine was no exception.

'All right,' I muttered gracelessly.

Lex promptly hugged me.

'Thanks, Sam,' he mumbled into my shoulder. 'I *knew* you wouldn't let me down. Sam? Please can I stay at yours tonight? I'm scared. And if I come back to yours no one will know where I am. Please, Sam?'

'Absolutely not.'

'Oh, *please*? Go on! I'll be really quiet, you'll hardly know I'm there . . . .'

I doubted that profoundly. But he was batting his eyelashes again.

'All right,' I said finally. 'But just for tonight.'

And that was another great, whopping, cosmic-sized mistake. I would have to watch myself. Lex was a serious danger to my good judgement.

* * *

It seemed very late when we left the bar, and it was an effort to drag ourselves away. Outside, the orange flashes of streetlights were like streaks of graffiti sprayed across the dingy, sodium-lightened charcoal sky. The New York night, colourless and murky, gave a strangely unhealthy tinge to everyone who passed; it made them into weirdly lit and shadowed caricatures, the occasional flare of neon light across their faces giving an artificial and distinctly unflattering wash of lurid pink or green. No wonder that people kept their heads down and walked fast. I had noticed before that though you might see people in bars dressed with great extravagance, in the street everyone was covered in long overcoats and woolly hats. Display was something kept strictly for the ambience of one's choice.

I was amazed to realise that it was only nine-thirty. Already I felt tired and ready for bed. The bar had been a black hole in more ways than one, sucking in all my energy and providing me with a mere handful of vodka and tonics in return. But I had promised Kim that I would drop by the bar where she worked, if only briefly, and now I had Lex coming back to the flat with me, too. I felt irritated and scratchy, as if people were forcing their presence on me; all I wanted right now was to jump in a taxi and head for my temporary home, curling up in Nancy's four-poster with the Comedy Channel on TV, some popcorn, and a bottle of beer.

'Where are we headed?' Lex said passively. The Mr Cool About Town pose had been abdicated for the time being, not to mention the Randy Seducer. Clearly he had decided that Little Boy Lost was more effective.

'To see this friend of mine. She's working at a bar near here,' I said. 'Second Avenue and Fifth.'

'What's it called?'

'The Hookah,' I said. 'Good name, eh?'

'Bit obvious,' Lex said dismissively.

'No, hookah A H, not hooker E R,' I said.

'Yeah, that's pretty clever,' he admitted, once he'd worked this out. It took him a little while. I wasn't going to admit that I'd made the same mistake myself. 'They must get a lot of people confused, though.'

'It's the way you say it.' I experimented with a Laurence-esque British accent, thinking of the way he'd said 'my deaah'. 'Hookaaah. Hookaaaaaaaah.'

'Didn't the caterpillar in *Alice in Wonderland* smoke a hookah?'

'Yeah, that's right!' I remembered it now. 'Sitting on the mushroom with his pipe.'

'That guy Lewis Carroll was so on drugs,' Lex said profoundly. 'He must have been stoned from morning to night.'

'When he wasn't photographing little girls dressing up as hookers.'

'You what?' Lex said blankly.

'Hook-ERS, not hook-AAAAHS.' I was beginning to feel that we were doing a slacker comedy set-piece. Only we should be sitting in a diner. And I would be played by . . . um, Jennifer Tilly.

'Who would you want to play you in a film?' I said.

Lex thought hard for a while, quite unfazed by my sudden change of subject. 'That guy who plays Joey in *Friends*,' he said finally. 'I always think he pretends to be more stupid than he is, to get away with stuff.'

I was impressed by this. I'd expected him to propose Johnny Depp or Leonardo DiCaprio, someone blindingly obvious. And Lex did resemble Matt LeBlanc, when the latter wasn't too pudgy.

'Good one, eh?' he added smugly. 'Bet you thought I was going to say Johnny Depp.'

'Not at all,' I lied.

'What about you?'

'Oh, Jennifer Tilly. With dark hair.'

'God, I really fancied her in *Bound*.'

'She was playing a lesbian,' I pointed out. 'You'd have fancied Princess Anne if she'd been doing some hot girl-on-girl action.'

'Not totally true. Not outside the bounds of possibility, but not totally true. What about the silly voice, though? And I don't mean Princess Anne. Though she's up there with the best of them on that one.'

'I know,' I said, grimacing. 'Jennifer'd have to promise to talk normally.'

'Who said anything about *Jennifer*'s silly voice?'

I shoved him and he shoved me back. We found ourselves scuffling around in a friendly way for a while, letting off a little steam from the tensions of the situation: God knew there were plenty of those. Lex was a fugitive from justice; I was sheltering him; someone we both knew had recently been garrotted; and we hadn't really dealt with what had happened between us in the Hoxton Square toilets. As an American would put it, we had issues.

'Oh look,' I said, fending off a push from Lex which would have taken me into the street, 'this is Second Avenue already. It should be somewhere round here.'

'You know what,' Lex said reflectively, 'this bar sounds familiar.'

'Oh yeah,' I said, losing sympathy with him once more after our brief bout of sibling-type bonding. 'You've been here too, have you? You've been bloody everywhere. What d'you do, split yourself down the middle so you can hang out at two places at once?'

'Don't get all sarky with me,' Lex said, hurt. 'I haven't been here, as it happens. I just said it sounded familiar, all right?'

He had dropped the Americanisms for the time being, which was a relief. I was too busy looking for the bar to express my gratitude. There was no one to ask; hardly anyone else was out on the street but ourselves, and the few souls around were hurrying as if a bombing raid were about to start and they needed to get to the shelter fast. That was the East Village for you. As I swivelled round, a girl went past quickly, wearing a camouflage-patterned balaclava pulled down over her face and the regulation army surplus overcoat. I stared after her in disbelief, momentarily distracted by the balaclava. Talk about urban paranoia. Or maybe she was just suffering from a bad outbreak of acne.

The bar took a while to spot. In this neck of the woods, the more fashionable the bars, the more they concealed their frontages behind the blankest, most unwelcoming stretches of sheer brick wall. They were well soundproofed, too, so that the only hint of their presence was the surreal sight of a small stool propped on the pavement next to a chrome pole with a hook at the top. This was to show where the queue began. Even bars here had this we're-a-club-with-a-dress-policy attitude.

Some very cool hip-hop streamed out as as we opened the door, adding a brief touch of class, not to mention life, to the deserted street. A bouncer, leaning against the wall by the door, gave us his stock behave-yourselves look. It had as much menace behind it as the glassy eye of a stuffed animal. Inside the darkness was rich and sumptuous, as if we'd shrunk down like Alice in Wonderland so we could enter a jewellery box, padded and upholstered in red and gold brocade. Scarlet Oriental lights hung from the ceiling like chandeliers and there were swathes of crimson velvet curtaining the alcoves. The gleaming bottles behind the bar seemed suffused with golden light. It was something of a disappointment that Kim wasn't wearing a heavily embroidered ruby satin cheongsam. Her black denim cut-off top was pretty enough in its way, but I felt she could have made more of an effort to co-ordinate with the décor.

'It's like all those films with Shanghai in the title,' I said, sitting down at the bar and looking around me approvingly. Kim was getting drinks for some yuppie types down the other end of the bar, and I waved at her. She pulled a face and nodded at the people she was serving.

'*Shanghai Express*,' Lex offered. 'With Marlene Dietrich.'

'And *The Shanghai Gesture*, with Victor Mature and Gene Tierney. All those scenes in the casino.'

Kim came up to us, smiling. 'Hey, Sam. I'm really glad you made it in,' she said.

'I love this place,' I said enthusiastically. 'It's like a Forties Hollywood version of an opium den.'

'Cool, isn't it?' she agreed. 'It's not a bad place to work, either. It was better when there was dancing, though.'

'What happened?'

'Rudolph Giuliani happened. The mayor,' she explained, seeing my blank expression. 'He did this huge crackdown on street crime and stuff, which was OK up to a point, but then he started taking away all the dance licences from the lounges and bars. So now if, like, one person starts dancing in here they could close us down. That's what the bouncer's for, really.'

'You mean he has to go round and stop people boogying?' I said incredulously.

Kim giggled. 'Basically. It can get a bit embarrassing. But, you know, everyone knows they shouldn't do it. Look.' She gestured to the wall behind her, where a sign hung saying 'NO DANCING' in gold Oriental lettering on a red background.

'What if you just wiggle without moving your feet?' I suggested.

'That's borderline. We let people sway and rock, but wiggling would be a judgement call.'

We were both giggling by now.

'I missed you,' I said wistfully. 'I missed being stupid with you.'

'Yeah, me too.'

I cleared my throat. I could only do sentimental for fifteen seconds, and then I started coming out in hives. 'Right, that's enough soppy stuff. Who do I have to shag to get a drink around here?'

'You're such a boy, Sam,' Kim said affectionately. 'You should have scratched your crotch when you said that and lowered your voice.'

'Oh, look, you have a DJ!' I had just spotted a mixing desk by the far wall with a girl behind it who would have made Cameron Diaz seem dowdy and plain by comparison. When girls were pretty over here they really went for it; no hiding their lights under a bushel. Instead they got them out and arranged reflectors all around them to up the wattage.

'Everywhere has a DJ,' Kim said casually. 'There's a sushi restaurant around the corner that has a DJ. That doesn't mean it's a club. So, you want a drink?'

'Is the Pope a Tarmac-kisser?'

'What'll it be?'

'Singapore Sling,' I said. 'Goes with the décor.'

'Good call.'

'Can I get one, too?' Lex piped up.

Kim's attention switched to him. We had been so focused on each other, slipping back into our old happy banter, that I hadn't thought to introduce Lex, and clearly Kim hadn't realised I'd come in with someone.

'Kim, this is Lex,' I said belatedly. 'He's one of the artists in the show with me.'

That was an easy and discreet introduction, I thought. No mention of stranglings or Lex's status as Suspect Number One in a murder inquiry. So why were they staring at each other like that?

'You're that friend of Leo's!' Kim said to Lex. 'I knew I'd seen you somewhere!'

Lex looked as if he wanted the ground to open up and swallow him.

'Hey, small world,' he managed eventually.

Kim was shaking her head slightly from side to side. It was a gesture so familiar to me that the recognition filled the pit of my stomach with a warm flow of nostalgia. It meant that she was puzzling something out, putting the pieces together in her head.

'You're the one who's in some kind of trouble, right?' she said finally. 'Leo told me you were on the run or something. Shit, it's about Kate getting killed! I remember now! You're hiding from the cops!'

Her voice hadn't risen, but the way she had stiffened meant that people were looking over at us curiously. I stifled the urge to bury my head in my hands.

'Sam!' Kim turned to me. 'What's going on? What are you doing hanging out with this guy? He could be the one who killed Kate!'

'Sam's letting me stay with her,' Lex blurted out. '*She* doesn't think I had anything to do with it!'

So much for keeping that a secret. I felt like braining him with the bar stool.

'You're letting him stay with you? You must be nuts! The guy could do you in your sleep!' Kim had turned back to me. 'You should turn him in right now!'

I looked from one to the other, sighed deeply and put my head down on the bar. It wasn't really enough. I could still feel them both staring at me. I started banging it lightly against the wood surface. To my surprise, this was strangely comforting.

CHAPTER FOURTEEN

I stopped banging my head before it was permanently marked. We did finally get the Singapore Slings, though, and damn fine they were too.

'She thinks I killed Kate!' Lex said dismally, as Kim removed herself. She shot him a watchful glance over her shoulder as she moved away, warning him that she would be on the lookout in case he extracted a garrotte from his pocket and started toying with it while staring speculatively at my neck.

'Well, so do the police, probably,' I pointed out. 'I mean, you can't blame her. She's being protective of me.'

'Why don't *you*?' Lex said suddenly. 'I mean, why don't you think it was me that killed Kate?'

I sighed. 'I'm just not getting those killer vibes from you, Lex. I don't know. I've met quite a few murderers in my time – I've lived a rich, full life – and you don't strike me as the type. Though, of course—' I drank some more of my cocktail '—I could be completely wrong. You could be a crazed strangler with an urge to atone for John Lennon's murder by contributing a beautiful corpse to Strawberry Fields every October. Like sending him a handmaiden in the afterlife. Very Egyptian.'

Lex was staring at me anxiously. If it had been possible to back away while sitting on a bar stool, he would definitely have tried it.

'See what I mean?' I gave him a friendly smile. 'You're much more spooked by me than I am by you.'

'I don't know how you can talk about it so – casually,' he muttered. 'I mean, Kate's dead. Someone killed her. It wasn't me,

OK? But there's someone out there who strangled her. We might even know them. You just sound so fucking unconcerned.'

'I'm not unconcerned.'

'OK, then you sound like you don't care that we could be in danger.'

I shrugged. 'We're always in danger, Lex. We're probably in more danger of getting run over between here and my flat, or being involved in a four-car pile-up because of a crazed psychotic taxi driver than we are of being garrotted by the Strawberry Fields Strangler.'

'Well, I'm scared. I don't mind telling you.' He finished his drink in a long pull at the glass. 'Do you think your mate'd get me another of these, or will she bite my head off if I ask her?'

His hand trembled slightly as he put the glass down.

'Look,' I said, reaching over and patting his hand, 'it'll be OK. Don't worry.'

But Lex wasn't a fool.

'How can you say that?' he snapped back. 'How do you know what's going to happen?'

'I don't. I was just trying to cheer you up.'

'Yeah, well, don't. It makes me nervous. Hi, Kim?' he said tentatively, as she strode towards us, a martial glint in her eye.

'Everything all right, Sam?' she said to me, pointedly ignoring Lex.

'It's fine. Really. Could we get another two Singapore Slings?'

'Are you sure you should be drinking around him?' she said warningly. 'You don't want him to catch you off guard.'

'For fuck's sake,' Lex interrupted. 'Sam could probably drink me under the table and give me a good kicking when she'd got me down there, OK? She's as hard as – I dunno, industrial cement. It's me you should be worried about.'

Kim looked at me, momentarily taken aback.

'He's right, you know,' I said.

'Nothing's changed, has it?' Kim grinned at me. 'OK. Two Singapore Slings coming up.'

'Am I off the hook, then?' Lex said to her.

'For the time being. But watch your step.'

'Yes ma'am!' He saluted. 'She's really pretty, your mate,' he said to me as Kim moved away. 'Is she seeing anyone, d'you know?'

He was a trier. I had to give him that.

* * *

'Hi, this is Joan Rivers. Listen, can we talk? Buckle up your seat belt – by the way, you look great! That colour is you!'

'Whoah,' Lex said, as the taxi hurtled up Third Avenue as if fired from a rocket launcher.

'You know what?' I said, leaning forward when it was safer and addressing the diver through the partition. 'We're not in this much of a hurry.'

'Yeah, well, *I'm* in a hurry,' said the driver, catching my eye in the rear-view mirror. 'I really need to go. You know what I'm saying? I gotta *go*.'

I turned to Lex, confused.

'He needs the loo, idiot,' he hissed.

'Oh, *right*.'

We were screaming cross-town like a jumbo jet about to take off. It was a race against time. Would we make it to West End and 72nd before the driver lost control of himself? And why did this kind of bizarre taxi experience keep happening to me?

'I can't do it!' the driver suddenly exclaimed. Lex and I exchanged frantic glances. Then he stamped on the brakes and everything went dark, because I was being half-throttled by the seat belt. When my sight returned, I realised that we were stationary outside a Chinese restaurant and the driver was halfway out of the cab.

'Back soon, OK?' he called back at us. 'Just hang on. Don't worry about the meter.' And with that he was gone, running down the street as fast as he could considering that he was doubled over.

'Sur*real*,' Lex commented.

'Ccchhh.' I finally got my neck free. This was a hazard of being on the short side and having bosoms: seat belts tended to ride up over them and strangle you. I looked over at Lex.

'Shall we wait?'

He shrugged. 'If it's a free ride . . . he said not to worry about the meter.'

'At least it'll be cheap.'

'Did you see where he was going?'

'Nope. I just hope he makes it there in time, for everyone's sake.'

Lex was staring thoughtfully at the frontage of the Chinese restaurant.

'Look,' he said, 'they even have an e-mail address.' He pointed to the sign.

'What is it, www.typhoid.com?' I said.

Lex acknowledged my wit with scarcely a flicker of his eyelids. He was thinking about something more serious.

'I wonder if they do takeaway?' he said tentatively.

Our eyes met. There was a brief pause.

'Spring rolls, fried rice and spicy prawn something,' I said. 'I'll wait here in case our free ride leaves without us.'

The restaurant was faster than the taxi driver. When he finally returned, with the air of someone who has discharged a heavy burden, we were settled happily in the back of the cab, busily engaged on a comparison between English and American takeaway Chinese.

'I love these containers,' I was saying enthusiastically through a spring roll as the driver settled back into his seat. We stowed the food quickly to avoid a series of Jackson Pollock splashes on our clothes as the cab pulled away.

'Everything OK, mate?' Lex said to him.

'Yeah. Sorry about that. You know how it is. When you gotta go, you gotta go.'

'Right,' Lex said empathetically, and launched into an anecdote about being caught short in a pub with a long queue for the toilets. The driver gave little grunts of recognition every now and then. They were getting on so well that when the driver announced: 'That'll be fifteen bucks,' as we pulled up outside my building, I was momentarily taken aback by his sheer cheek. What jolted me out of it was the knowledge that Lex would pay him if I didn't say something, and then whinge about it afterwards. Men are pathetic about that kind of thing.

'No way,' I said firmly, recovering fast. 'You made us wait for at least ten minutes and that's much too much even if we hadn't stopped. Three bucks.'

'Three bucks! No way! Twelve.'

'Four.'

'Ten.'

'Five, and that's my final offer. Otherwise my friend here will empty our takeaway all over the back of your cab.'

The driver muttered something that sounded suspiciously like 'Fucking bitch', and hit a switch. The meter printed a receipt and over its clicking came:

'Hi, this is Joan again, reminding you to take your belongings and to get a receipt from the driver. Could you let me know when we get to Grant's tomb? I have a date with him!'

'That is so not funny,' I said, handing the driver the money. He pulled away while Lex was still getting out of the cab. The Chinese food nearly went flying. I caught it just in time. We had the last laugh, though. The cab was speeding away with its back door still open.

'Prat,' Lex said crossly, embarrassed at having done a two-step stumble over the pavement before he could catch his balance.

'I wonder if he's going to stop to close that,' I said, looking after the cab as it U-turned and headed back downtown. Maybe the driver had been calculating that the speed of the manoeuvre would whip the door closed. If so he had turned the wrong way; it had had the opposite effect.

'Jesus,' Lex said.

'I know. One more cab-driving psycho to add to my list.'

But Lex wasn't staring after the cab. He had just seen the doorman through the glass entrance doors, waiting, his hand on the brass handle, cap straight and jacket buttons shining, to let us into the building.

I smirked. 'Welcome to my world,' I said, gesturing above us. 'Look, I have an awning.' I headed for the entrance door. 'You're not in the East Village now, my boy.'

* * *

'Aaaaah! Aaaaah! *Shit!*' Lex slammed into the railings like a cartoon character about to flatten itself.

'God, Lex,' I said disapprovingly, 'pull yourself together. It was just a little turn – ooops – *whoah* . . .'

I grabbed at the railings to steady myself as a small dog yapped and snarled around my ankles. Fortunately they were protected by so much moulded plastic it would have snapped its teeth off if it tried to bite me. I truly hoped it would. But the pet rat yipped one last time, and trotted off, tinkling a miniature bell as it went. I glared after it. The Upper West Side was full of dogs like this, spoilt, petted fluffs of fur with raspberry sorbet tongues, clicketing along on tiny, sharp bird claws, being walked by women wearing coats which looked as if they were made out of all their previous chihuahuas.

'Um, hi?' Kim was saying. She floated up and swung in a generous circle in front of us, arms wide. 'You guys just going to cling to that thing all day?'

'I was doing fine,' I said with hauteur, detaching myself from the railing and pushing off again. I stalled almost at once. 'Ah, bugger. It's the getting started that's so tricky.'

'My boots're pinching,' Lex whined.

'Come on, Lex,' Kim said with the pity a woman displays to a man who is making a feeble excuse, 'you said they were too big in the shop. Here, catch onto me.'

Kim pivoted round and extended a hand to him, making everything look so easy that she encouraged me immeasurably by example; as if she had created a whole new way to move, effortless and fluid as the flow of water.

'You look wonderful,' I said to her enviously.

She skimmed forward, bringing Lex with her; he was hardly moving his feet, just letting her pull him along, beaming with enjoyment.

'You have to think of it differently,' she said seriously, swinging to a halt. 'You OK?' she said to Lex. He nodded. 'Look,' she went on, letting him go. 'Most people, when they're blading, make the mistake of closing themselves up too much. Because they're nervous. But that's the way you end up falling. Instead you should keep your hips open, and your shoulders back. Look.'

She swept away from us in a few long easy strokes, then turned, legs wide, like a bird riding on a current of wind.

'See where my arms are?' she called. They swung out from her body like wings, dipping and rising again. 'Now look what happens when I hold them in.' She mimicked me and Lex, our elbows hunched to our sides. 'You're tying yourself up in knots. You gotta let go.' Again she pivoted around, her arms flying out with the speed of the turn, graceful as a figure skater. 'They give you balance.'

I pushed myself off, getting more of a start this time, and bladed off towards her, letting my arms go out.

'That's it! Keep 'em working!' Kim called.

I went right down to the statue of Eleanor Roosevelt, halting neatly just before I hit the cobbled surround. I'd picked up braking pretty quickly; it was just a question of cocking one foot at the right angle to engage the lever on the back of the boot. Then I pushed off again, haltingly at first – I was going to have to practise that – and headed towards them again. Kim had both Lex's hands in hers, and was blading around him, pulling him in looping ellipses. Their arms were outstretched, and they looked as if they were dancing, swinging each other in figures of eight. Country dancing on rollerblades. There was probably somewhere in New York you could do that. It would be a snap for a town that had an S&M restaurant and one where all the waiters and waitresses were twins.

I flopped down onto a bench to catch my breath and watched them, Lex stumbling a little but gradually picking up confidence. Kim wore black leggings and a short black padded jacket which finished just above her waist: stripped for action. She had the body of a professional athlete, lean and strong with a beautiful economy of movement. Lex, with his droopy jeans and layered T-shirts, looked like a bag person next to her. I marvelled once again at how she had changed. Gradually this new Kim was layering her image over the remembered one, like a palimpsest; traces of her as she had been ten years ago still slipped through, but they were fleeting now, and confined to tricks of expression, a particular way she had of turning her head, or her laugh.

We were on Riverside Drive at the end of 72nd Street, a tree-lined promenade which stretched away into the distance uptown. In front of me rolling banks of grass dipped gently down to the Hudson River. It was a lovely day, crisp and clear, sunlight glinting on the rich green grass and striking sparks from the grey stone paths. Further away, just visible over the brow of the little slope that dipped down to the shore, the river dazzled my eyes, every little wave and ripple reflecting the sun in an endless series of glass shards. Down by the statue a workman was setting up a couple of amplifiers and a microphone.

'Why don't we try going down to the river?' Kim suggested. 'You can handle that slope, can't you, Sam?'

'I think so,' I said, looking at the long sweep of grey stone that curved down and away from us into a short underpass.

'Lex, I'll take you down,' Kim said. 'Just remember, if you bring your foot up enough there's no way you're not going to stop.'

Lex's faith in Kim was strong. She had managed to relax him enough to make him nod now, swallowing hard, and follow her as she pulled him gently towards the start of the slope. Once I had worked out how much pressure to apply to the brakes, I skimmed down it.

'Wow!' I said, as I came through the underpass. On the other side was a further slope, stretching down to the river path, and I pushed on down, revelling in my ability to glide downhill. Kim said this was the most difficult thing to do. I turned at the last bend in the path and the river was in front of me, so wide that I could only dimly see New Jersey across the water. Tiny boats danced on the waves, glittering in the sun. It was idyllic. The contrast could not have been stronger between this and the roaring filthy traffic behind us shooting up onto the myriad lanes of the Henry Hudson Parkway. Ahead some sailboats, moored in the boat basin, were bobbing lightly in the clear balmy October breeze. The sky was the faded blue-white of bleached denim, as suffused with light as a giant pearl.

An almighty crash roused me from my moment of serene contemplation. I swung round ungracefully to see Lex in a crumpled heap halfway down the last stretch of pathway, Kim sprawled over him.

'Jesus. Are you all right?' I skated over to them.

She was giggling. Lex looked slightly dazed, but was already sitting up, rubbing his head.

'Did you see it?' Kim said to me from her prone position. 'Lex did this spin, he braked too hard—'

'I did a handbrake turn,' Lex informed me.

'—and he just went shooting around, I couldn't stop him—'

'I'm sorry I took you with me,' Lex apologised, 'I just couldn't let go of your hand, it was like a lifebelt—'

'I probably slowed you down some,' Kim said fairly. 'Stopped you shooting off into the river.'

'Anyway, you had a soft landing.' Lex prodded his stomach. 'On my beer belly.'

'Nothing a few crunches at the gym wouldn't fix,' Kim said. 'I'll take you along sometime.'

'Uh, hello?' I said. They were so absorbed they had forgotten my presence. I noticed that Kim seemed in no hurry to get up. Clearly, in the space of time it had taken us, this afternoon, to have a coffee and go to the blade shop, she had decided that Lex wasn't the Strawberry Fields Strangler after all. Or perhaps it had been his boyish charm. Well, plenty of girls had made that mistake with Ted Bundy.

I was miffed. Kim was supposed to be my friend; I hadn't seen her in ten years, and here she was practically ignoring me in favour of knocking down and falling on a young man who, merely last night, she had suspected of having evil designs on my windpipe. I admitted that Lex stood up well to the harsh test of being seen in natural light. Still, there were limits.

'Hey, Kim,' I said in a louder voice, 'do you need a hand up or are you going to stay down there for the rest of the day?'

To do her justice, she did look a touch embarrassed.

'Right, off we go,' she said, rising lightly to her feet.

'Lex,' I inquired, 'can you feel all your limbs? If not, I'm sure Kim would be happy to do it for you.'

Kim shot me a filthy glance.

'In her role as instructor, of course,' I said smoothly. 'Come on, up, up, up. I want to go and see the sailboats.'

Some kind of festival was taking place at the boat basin. Two lines of pumpkins were arranged along the moorings, their bright orange gleaming against the blond wood like little fires, and a small crowd of people was gathered on the far end of the jetty. We took our blades off and hung them over our shoulders so we could walk onto the jetty and see what was happening. A big sailboat was moored at the end, its deck piled high with pumpkins. White sails beat above them like wings in the wind. The fittings on the boat were painted dark blue, and the hairy coils of rope curled on the boards were sunbleached to the neutral shade of sand. The orange of the pumpkins burnt against their background, the only touch of bright colour, flaring up into the sunlight. One by one we went up the plank and stood on the boat, which rocked softly under our feet. Suddenly I found myself appreciating the attraction of messing about on the water.

'It's owned by this local charity,' Kim said, reading the information off a leaflet someone had handed her. 'For underprivileged kids. They take them out and teach them how to sail.'

'That'll be useful in later life,' I commented.

Kim cuffed the back of my head. 'And I thought *I* was cynical. Jesus.'

'You ladies want to buy a pumpkin?' said one of the boat's crew. He was tall and tanned and superfit, with short fair hair and those fine silvery sailor's lines running in crow's-feet out from the corners of his blue, blue eyes. I blinked in appreciation.

'No thanks,' Kim said, her tone full of regret.

'Hallowe'en's coming up!' he persisted charmingly. 'You'll need one then!'

'It's all we can do to stay on these things as it is,' I explained, pointing to my blades. 'A pumpkin would crucially unbalance us.'

He spread his hands wide. 'Hey, come back on foot,' he suggested. 'We'll be here.'

'Sure thing.' We flashed him besotted smiles. And I gave him a little wave as we crossed the gangplank onto terra firma.

'What a poser,' Lex said sulkily once we were out of earshot.

'Just because he was good-looking,' I said. 'You guys are always so down on a handsome man.'

'No, I thought he was a wanker,' Lex insisted. 'And pushy.'

'Oh, for God's sake, Lex, get a *grip*.'

'Did you see how blue his eyes were?' Kim said to me dreamily.

Lex made a snorting sound and skated off. To everyone's surprise, including his own, the impetus took him on a few good strides.

'Look at me!' he yelled over his shoulder. We clapped. He executed a turn and swung round to face us, doing a little bow.

'We obviously need to piss you off more often,' Kim said.

'I skate better when angry,' Lex said. 'Hey, look up there.'

My hippy-scenting antenna started twitching frantically as soon as I caught sight of the group of people up on a grassy knoll above the boat basin. A large hand-lettered sign pinned to a tree behind them said:

'Free Soup! Made only from Natural Organic Ingredients. Taste it and See. Absolutely Free!'

'This is really sad of me,' I said to the others, 'but that makes me deeply suspicious.'

'I know,' Kim said at once. 'It's interesting, isn't it? How to pick out all the mistrustful urban cynics.'

'Free soup!' Lex said cheerfully, unaffected by this cultural analysis. 'I'm going to get some!'

He bladed off in the direction of the hill.

'He's so sweet and unaffected, isn't he,' I said sarcastically. 'Like a little child.'

'I'm really getting to like him,' Kim agreed, missing the irony. 'After all these New York guys just wanting a piece of ass. And then they just hide out on you, the guys here don't want to get serious. But Lex seems really open. You know, at ease with women.'

'That's because he wants a piece of ass and he's worked out the best way to get it,' I pointed out.

Kim sighed. 'Still, I like him,' she said.

'What happened to your dark suspicions?' I asked evilly.

'I just don't see him as a mad strangler, do you?' she said.

'I never did.'

'Kim! Help!'

Lex had stalled halfway up the hill and was gripping onto a tree to avoid sliding down again. His legs were splaying out behind him and he was scrabbling desperately to keep his balance. Kim shot off to the rescue. I took a deep breath, remembering that Kim had said earlier that uphill was much less difficult than down, and set off up the slope. I found that I had to work my limbs like a skater in a race, elbows thrusting out, legs pumping; but once I had realised that it was comparatively easy. I reached the free soup canteen well before Lex, half under his own steam, half shoved from behind by Kim – copping a feel of his derrière in the process, I noticed – joined me, panting and exhilarated.

The group of people round the soup burner were definitely nouveaux hippies. They reminded me of Tom's ex-girlfriend Alice, the one who had abandoned him in India for the American with the facial hair problem. Only Alice, being a social worker, had always had a slight frown, being weighed down by the cares of the world, while this lot couldn't have looked more serene and at peace if they'd been on a cocktail of Prozac and Temazepam. They wore shapeless trousers with drawstrings at the waist and big baggy sweaters hand-knit from dog hair, and apparently they considered shampoo and conditioner to be decadent twentieth-century inventions.

We queued up for soup. I was still having a lot of difficulty with the concept of someone just giving you something for free. The guy ladling it gave me a tolerant smile as he threw back his dreadlocks in order to see where the saucepan was.

'It's all organic vegetables,' he said. 'We grow them ourselves.'

'Oh, are you selling them?' I said enthusiastically, thinking I had found an angle.

'Nope. We just make the soup.'

Another understanding smile. It was very frustrating.

'This is what you should be doing for your show, Lex,' I said, joining him and Kim where they stood at a remove under a tree, leaning against it and sipping from the recyclable paper cups. 'Give stuff away in the gallery. It would send everybody crazy.'

Lex looked meditative.

'Hard to sell.'

'Oh, just video it and flog them at $5,000 a time,' I said impatiently. 'I mean, there's that girl now who sells videos of her friends dressed up in silly clothes. You can sell anything. Artist's shit in a can.'

'Shit in a can?' Lex said excitedly.

'Been done, you ignoramus. Years ago.'

'Anyway, those videos are in slow motion, those ones you're on about. And at 360 degrees.'

'Oh, right, so that makes them art. I knew there had to be something.'

'This soup is great,' Kim observed. She was looking a little disappointed.

'Were you expecting it to be crap?' I asked.

'Oh no, it's not that. No. I guess I was sort of expecting you two to be really into all this new wave of British stuff. I mean, that's what you do, right?'

'Lex does,' I corrected her. 'He's fashionable. I'm not. I actually make things.'

Lex bristled. 'Look, you're talking about some of my best friends!' he objected.

'That's the point, isn't it? You're all mates, so you've got this pact that no one's going to mention the Emperor's New Clothes.'

'I liked the shark,' Kim said quickly. 'The one in formaldehyde.'

'It has a certain primitive attraction for the first five minutes,' I admitted. 'Then it's just a dead shark.'

'Who *do* you like?' Lex said crossly.

'Marc Quinn,' I said at once. 'The blood head. Have you seen that?' I asked Kim. 'He drained off his own blood, gradually, till he had enough to fill a cast of his head. Then he froze it, put it in a clear glass refrigerated box and took off the cast. It has this crust on it from the freezing, which is paler, and underneath it you can see the blood cracking through – very beautiful and spooky.'

'Trust you to like something like that,' Kim said, grinning at me. 'Once a Goth, always a Goth.'

'You should know,' I said pointedly. I sipped my soup. 'Mm, this is delicious! I hate them! How dare they give away something like this! It's messing with my whole concept of human existence.'

'Maybe hippies really are happier,' Kim said maliciously.

'Bite your tongue,' I warned. 'Or I'll bite it for you.'

By the expression on her face, Kim seemed to be following instructions. Only she was staring away from me, down towards the river path, and so was Lex. He raised one hand in greeting. The man he was hailing saw the gesture and waved back, clambering up the grassy bank to join us.

'What's *he* doing here?' Kim said in a furious undertone to Lex.

'I rang him before,' he said easily. 'Told him what we were up to. He said he might come and find us.'

The man had nearly reached us by now. He was of medium height, so thin he was nearly skin and bone, with a sharp jaw and nose, accentuated by the fact that his hair was caught back in a ponytail at the nape of his neck. Big workman's trousers, with several deep pockets at knee height and a loop at the back to hold a hammer, hung off his narrow hips, and his T-shirt was stained and worn thin with use. From his waist hung a long silver wallet chain looping down to his right knee and back up again. He was almost ugly, his features too narrow and close together, but he had a powerful charisma. A friend of mine who had a neat way of putting these things would have said unhesitatingly that this guy looked like he was a really dirty fuck.

Kim was silent, and out of the corner of my eye I saw that she had gone very still. I was powerfully curious; and the stranger seemed wary, aware that the situation would be a tricky one to handle. Lex was the only one of us who was happy and relaxed. That little child motif again.

'Leo! Hey man, great to see you! How's it going?' he exclaimed.

I stared even harder at the new arrival. So this was the notorious Leo. Drug abuser, possessor of a ridiculous knee-length chain, and perhaps even a dirty fuck into the bargain. What a lot of strings this young man had to his bow.

I found myself wondering whether Kim had succumbed to Leo's down-at-heel charm. It would explain the iciness of her demeanour. She was sending out vibes as cold and unwelcoming as the chilled section at the supermarket. One young British artist with the over-enthusiasm of an imperfectly trained puppy; one dissolute junkie; one life-size freezer cabinet; and me. What fun the next few minutes were going to be.

CHAPTER FIFTEEN

'Hey, guys,' Leo finally said. His voice was a light tenor which too many cigarettes had rasped into a cracked lower register. Like the rest of him, it was ugly but oddly compelling. 'Shit, I feel like a midget with all of you on blades. Lex, my man!'

They exchanged a complicated handshake, their thumbs sticking out at weird angles and their wrists rotating back and forth. Doubtless it was copied from LA gangs, as seen on TV. I bet even the LA gangs copied their handshakes from ones seen on TV.

'Sam,' Lex said, turning to me, 'this is Leo.'

'Yo,' Leo said to me with something of a swagger. This annoyed me. I mean, 'Yo'? It reminded me of Notting Hill trustafarians trying to sound black.

'Hi, Leo,' I said politely. 'I've heard a lot about you. Nice to finally meet you in the flesh.'

I didn't think Leo would like my saying that I'd heard about him already, and so it proved. His eyes, already screwed up against the sun, narrowed still further, and his head tilted to one side as if he were assessing me. Well, better men than him had tried and failed.

'Oh yeah?' he said unpleasantly. 'What exactly have they been saying?'

'Oh, don't worry,' I said cheerfully. 'It was all bad.' And I gave him my best limpid smile.

No one knew whether I was joking. Least of all Leo. We stared each other out for what could only have been a few seconds, but felt much longer. The moment was broken by Lex, which was probably a relief for both myself and Leo. Neither of us were the kind of people to back down from what we'd started.

'Hey man,' Lex said, his bright tone attempting to ignore the by-play, 'guess what? Free soup!' He waved his cup in the air. 'Cool or what?'

'Free soup?' Leo said mistrustfully. 'What's the catch?'

'That's exactly what Sam's been saying,' Kim commented, breaking her silence. 'She doesn't trust people who give stuff away.'

'Yeah, well, neither do I. Maybe they've put mushrooms in it or something,' Leo suggested. 'You guys tripping already?' He was squinting into our eyeballs with the air of an expert. 'You giggling much? Seeing little green monsters?'

'Hey, man, I know what happens when I drink mushy tea, and it's not. Happening, I mean,' Lex said firmly. 'Besides,' he added, 'it'd be too early. We only just had it now.'

'You never know,' Leo said profoundly. 'Still, if it's free . . . .' He loped off towards the soup stand. Lex followed him.

'You OK?' I said to Kim.

'I can't believe Lex didn't tell me he was coming!' she said furiously. 'Shit, of all the people I really didn't want to see—'

'Did you guys have a thing?' I inquired.

Kim shrugged. 'Sort of. As much as you can with Leo.'

She closed her lips tightly. Leo and Lex, both carrying cups of soup, were coming back. They were an ill-assorted pair: Lex, walking on the blades as clumpily as Frankenstein's monster, and Leo, moving like a tango dancer, knees a little bent, eyes fixed on me and Kim. He walked well, I had to give him that.

'Do you actually keep your wallet on that chain?' I asked him. I could never get over how stupid they looked.

Leo stuck his hand into one of his trouser pockets and produced a battered old wallet to which the chain was attached through a hole punched in the corner.

'Sure,' he said. 'It's OK here, but in LA they're not wearing them any more. Too many guys on motorbikes getting their kicks grabbing at chains, pulling people along the street. Not so funny. Mm, this soup's good.'

'I might go for some more,' I said. 'Get some vitamins down me while I can.'

'I'll come with you,' Kim said at once. We clunked off. Walking with blades on a grassy surface required you to hold your feet at something of an angle to avoid toppling over. It was about as graceful as Harpo Marx dancing flamenco.

The same guy served us seconds of soup with as generous a smile as before. Maybe they were recruiting for a cult. The thought cheered me tremendously.

'Know what they're called over here, guys like that?' Kim said when we were out of earshot. 'Crusties. You know, the ones who have their dogs on strings.'

I looked at her pityingly. 'You've been away too long. That started in England, years and years ago. And they're called crusties because they don't wash much.' I mimed scratching off a layer of dirt.

We blew on our soup to cool it down, in no hurry to get back to the boys. 'Kim,' I said tentatively, 'are you still painting?' I had been waiting for the right moment to ask her this question.

Her face fell. 'Not for years.'

'That's terrible! You were so good! I still have that painting you did of all the fruit in weird colours. It's hanging in my kitchen.'

'I liked that painting.' Kim was wistful. 'I just – oh, when I first came here I had all these grand ambitions. I was determined to make Dad help me out, and he would have done. It was Barbara. She didn't actually tell me I was crap in so many words, but she was incredibly discouraging – kept going on about how hard it was to make it as an artist. And gradually she just got Dad around to her way of thinking, that I'd better give up. I dunno, it kind of beat me down. I started waitressing, and I was still trying to paint, but it was so expensive, and I didn't have any space . . . and then I started going to the gym, and really got into that. I'm studying for my personal trainer qualification,' she said more enthusiastically. 'And I've got a whole lot of clients lined up already, as soon as I get it.'

'That's a great idea,' I said encouragingly. 'I just think it's a shame you're not still painting as well.'

She sighed. 'I know. When I look at what you've done . . . .'

'I've been really lucky,' I said firmly. 'I'm riding a wave that isn't my own. I've got nothing to do with Lex's lot, you know. They're all self-obsessed conceptualists.'

'Whereas you're a self-obsessed sculptor,' Kim teased me. 'By the way, I've been meaning to say – you shouldn't call yourself a sculptress, it's really out of date. I heard you say it the other day.'

'What do I say, sculptor?'

'Right. Like now there's only waiters and actors. No -esses.'

'Heading for the twenty-first century.'

'Right on!'

Kim had recovered her good spirits. 'We better join the boys,' she said resignedly. 'Or they'll think we're bitching about them.'

'So what?' I said flippantly. 'Aren't we?'

Kim shot me a warning look.

'You don't want to get on the wrong side of Leo,' she said.

'Or?' My hackles rose at once. 'What's he going to do to me?'

'Oh, shit. I should have known you'd take that as a challenge.'

'*He* shouldn't want to get on the wrong side of *me*,' I said with hauteur. I balled up the empty soup cup and threw it neatly into the refuse bin.

'Nice,' Kim said. 'You could always throw straight.'

'It's come in useful before now,' I said. 'Mm.' I rubbed my tummy. 'That soup was really good.'

One of the crusties, walking by, heard this last comment.

'Hey, come back next Saturday!' she said cheerfully. 'We're always here, and it's always free!'

Kim grabbed my arm. 'Calm down,' she said urgently. I was already grinding my teeth so hard they'd be flour in a few more minutes.

'I can't *bear* it!' I wailed, as Kim guided me towards the boys.

'Sam's still freaked by the free soup,' she explained.

'Man, I know what you're saying,' Leo said, eyeing me with something approaching fellow-feeling. 'It's doing my head in too. Look, you're near here, yeah? Why don't we go back to yours and get stoned?'

Lex looked at me hopefully, willing me to agree. I didn't take much persuading. After all, it was Saturday afternoon, and I was on holiday. Besides, I was wondering if I could get Leo talking once the spliffs had been circulating for a while.

'Why not?' I said affably.

My motives were not entirely disinterested, quite apart from any purposes of investigation. I'd never been one for smoking puff; but Leo had the authentic air of someone from whom drugs which were more up my street could easily be obtained. If he didn't know how to get hold of some speed or some coke, I would eat my new woolly hat, ribbon trim and all. And I had been thinking for a few days now that a touch of one or the other was just what I needed to make my Saturday night complete.

* * *

We were playing Animal Snap on the living-room floor, and the phone had been ringing for quite a while before I registered the sound. Though that might have been denial. I was in no state to deal with the outside world.

'EEEeecha! EEEecha!' Lex was yelling at Kim, who was too convulsed with laughter to be able to honk like a pig back at him.

'No, man, that's wrong. That's clearly wrong . . . .' Leo was cracking up too.

'Hey, she's a mynah bird, yeah?' Lex turned to me for confirmation.

'Is anyone making a ringing noise?' I said, very confused.

Kim, ignoring me completely, collected her scattered wits and managed to produce something that sounded enough like a grunt to qualify her as having won. Triumphantly she leaned over and collected the pile of Lex's cards which were face up on the carpet.

'I did the mynah bird!' Lex protested. 'I should have won!'

'I'm not a mynah bird, you dumbass,' Kim corrected. 'I'm an alligator.'

Lex slapped his head. 'Swish, swish!' he shouted. 'Swish, swish!'

'Isn't that the phone?' Leo asked no one in particular.

'The phone!' I scrambled across the room, removed the receiver from its cradle, and sat looking at it for a moment. Something was coming out of it. Hesitantly I put one end to my mouth. Then I tried the other way, which seemed to work better.

'Sam?' The voice was agitated. Too agitated. I didn't like it. It gave me a bad feeling.

'What is it? Who is it?' I said warily.

'Are you OK?' the phone asked. It sounded concerned.

I took a deep breath, which wasn't a particularly good idea, as it made me start giggling when I let all the air out again. From the dark, saner recesses of my mind came a cold little voice telling me firmly to get a grip. I straightened up, slapped myself on the cheek, adjusted the phone to my ear and said clearly:

'Yes, I'm fine, thanks. Who is this, please?'

Leo, Lex and Kim, who were listening to my side of the conversation, all dissolved into helpless laughter, Kim repeating: 'Who is this, please?' in an efficient-secretary English accent which cracked the boys up still further. Glowering at them, I concentrated on the response.

'It's Laurence,' said the voice, still not very reassured. 'Are you *sure* you're OK?'

'Laurence! Hi! How are you?' I said over-effusively.

'Not so hot. I'm at work – well, I imagine you'd assume that.'

'Oh, absolutely,' I said with what was intended to be an easy confidence and sent the trio into roars of laughter once again. It was contagious. I had to slap my other cheek to stop myself joining in.

'It's a real crisis. Carol had three sets of people in to see Barbara's paintings. The publicity this whole business has got means that she's really in demand. There's always a silver lining, as Stanley says. But Don didn't show up for work. So we've been hauling the paintings up and downstairs ourselves, it's a total waste of my and Kevin's time. I mean, that's what Don's *for*, to move stuff. I wondered if he'd called you at all.'

'*Don*?' I said, baffled. 'Why should he ring me?' I put my hand over the receiver for a moment and turned to the others. 'Did Don ring me?' I asked.

They stared back at me, wide-eyed, temporarily laughed out.

'Don,' Lex said experimentally. 'Don, *Don*, *Don*. DON.'

I unclasped my hand from the phone. 'No, I don't think so.'

'Are you stoned?' Laurence said wearily.

'That's a rather personal question,' I said reprovingly. 'Anyway, who should Don ring me? I mean—' I recovered fast '—*why* should he ring me?'

'Boy,' Laurence said wryly. 'I'd really like to be where you are right now. And I don't have the faintest idea why he should call you. I've tried everyone else. To be honest, I just wanted an excuse to talk to you. Hear a touch of sanity coming down the phone lines. So much for that. You sound pretty out of it.'

The others had given up listening; they were slumped on the floor, and Kim had a couple of playing cards which she was holding up above her face, turning them round and round with the absorption of someone halfway through a trip.

'Look,' she said to Lex. 'The jack's the same both ways up. Isn't that amazing?'

'If you're not the mynah bird,' Lex answered after a while, 'who is?'

'Personally I think Don's taken off for the Virginia hills,' Laurence was saying. 'He goes into fugue every so often. I rang his roommate and he was furious. Says Don owes him a ton of money for rent and he figures he took off to score some.'

'How?' I said, baffled.

'Hell, I'm sure Don has his ways and means. But his roommate hinted at all sorts of dark possibilities. Maybe he's peddling his ass at Port Authority.' He sighed. 'I wish everything was completely different. That's not too much to ask, is it?'

'What's the time?' I said, trying to concentrate on the bare essentials.

'Five-thirty. We'll be here for ever at this rate. We've got someone from Minneapolis due in an hour and then everything to get back afterwards.'

'OK. I've got to go now.' I knew this sounded abrupt, but I was safer with simple statements.

'Right,' Laurence said, disappointment and fatigue etched into his voice. He had expected much more from me than this. 'Look, call me sometime, OK? Maybe we could do brunch tomorrow or something.'

'Sam?' Kim said dozily as I hung up. 'Did you know that the jack looks just the same, up or down? Isn't that cool?'

'Leo?' I said, ignoring her. 'How long before this stuff wears off?'

'You only had a quarter, right?'

'Right.' No way I was doing more than a quarter of a tab of unknown acid from an alleged junkie with a poor reputation. I prided myself on my common sense.

'Uh.' Leo stalled for a moment. He had dropped a whole one, as had Lex. It was no surprise that every so often he closed down. Kim, who had been reluctant to do any at all, had consented to share a half with me. We knew from old times together that we were pretty susceptible.

'Uh,' he said at last, pulling himself together and speaking in a professional tone, 'maybe – uh – say another hour or so.'

I needed to do something to chill out. Resuming Animal Snap would just overexcite me. I decided I needed to be alone.

'I'm going to lie down,' I announced, padding through into the bedroom and lying down on the four-poster bed. As soon as I closed my eyes, however, detailed and confusing hallucinations started to swirl before my eyes. I saw Kate, floating down a river, her red hair trailing out behind her like exotic seaweed, scarlet as the paint splattered over Barbara Bilder's paintings. Kate was a painting, too, something very pre-Raphaelite – Ophelia, that was it – and now she was turning into the original pre-Raphaelite model, Lizzie Siddal herself. Eyes closed, lying in her coffin, the body decaying but the hair still growing, spilling everywhere. Round her neck was a thin red line which widened as I watched it, separating her head still further from her body . . . .

I opened my eyes, my heart beating fast, and lay for a moment staring up at the ceiling through the gauzy muslin draped over the top of the bed. Then I started to see shapes in that, too: ghosts trailing long scarves behind them like Cyd Charisse in *Singin' In The Rain*. Only the ghosts in their white chiffon dresses were all Kate, hundreds of Kates, and each of them had a single strand of their long red hair caught by the wind machine and blown to wrap around their necks in a thin crimson line—

This wasn't working. I rolled myself off the bed and headed back to the living room. Lex was sitting propped against the wall, curled up on himself foetally, moaning softly into his knees.

'What's wrong with him?' I asked.

'He got real upset when I said I was the mynah,' Leo answered.

On hearing this, Lex started sobbing.

'Lex?' Kim leaned over and put her arm around his shoulders. 'Cheer up, OK? It's not that bad.'

Lex raised his head and looked at her through his tears.

'I want *you* to be the mynah,' he said at last.

'OK. I am. All right now?'

Slowly he nodded. A couple of large tears were running slowly down his cheeks.

'Whee, look at that, two little mermaids,' Kim said, losing it slightly. She shoved her face right up to Lex's, staring at him intently. 'Look at their little tails! That's so pretty!'

'Does anyone want to watch some TV?' I said, fumbling with the remote. By some miracle I found a repeat of *Absolutely Fabulous*; when you're tripping and you want to come down, it's always a good idea to watch people behaving more outrageously than yourself. It restores a sense of proportion. After two episodes, I felt revived enough to contemplate leaving the flat. Leo, totally spaced out, was lying on the sofa, mumbling quietly to himself. Kim and Lex were twined in some sort of embrace. The young in one another's arms and all that. I was still spacy enough to beam on them fondly before going through into the bedroom to change into something decent enough for gallery visiting.

* * *

Half an hour later I emerged from my building. Being outside was something of a shock: I had a brief rush of paranoia, suddenly convinced that someone was watching me. Sternly I told myself to sober up. I was still dazed with the effort of concentration it had required to assemble a suitable outfit and do my make-up. I had the theory that the smarter I looked, the more appropriately I would behave. So I was wearing my chocolate leather jeans, a violet button-through sweater and a dark brown leopard-skin print scarf knotted around my neck. It was a Fifties French starlet kind of look. I would have to hike up my vivacity quotient to carry it off.

The doorman called a taxi for me. The drive was relatively uneventful, apart from the recorded message, in which Judd Hirsch spoke so warmly and intimately that I became convinced that he was a long-lost friend. By the time we reached SoHo, however, I had got a grip on myself, and hardly jumped at all when the second part of the message came on.

There were still lights on in the gallery. I had left things pretty late: it was already seven-thirty and the door was locked. I rang the bell and after a short while Laurence opened it. Half his hair was sticking up and there was a cobweb on his shoulder. He looked distinctly frazzled.

'Still busy?' I asked.

His pale freckled face broke into a beaming smile.

'Sam! Just what the doctor ordered! You, uh, feeling better?' he added more discreetly.

'I think so,' I said cautiously.

'Well, come in!' He threw the door wide open. 'It's party central in here.'

'You two still heaving the paintings around?'

Laurence pulled a face. 'Yep. The latest bunch of suckers want something to hang in an alcove in their second main reception room. You want to come up and watch the deliberations?'

'Sure.'

The group gathered in the upstairs gallery included the artist herself, which surprised me. She was there with the faithful Jon, who hovered behind her shoulders like a shadow executed by someone with only the most minimal ideas of perspective and proportion. In addition there were Carol, Stanley, Kevin and a couple who at first sight looked extraordinarily youthful. Then I started noticing the amount of tucks, liposucks and implants that contributed to this impression. I was willing to bet, too, that they had had Botox injections to freeze the facial muscles and avoid the formation of lines. Their expressions were as blank as the mannequins in the windows of Bloomingdale's. Doubtless they would have been flattered by the comparison.

'Sam!' Carol looked pleased to see me, which was a relief. I hadn't been sure if this would be considered barging in. She came towards me, hands outstretched. 'Taylor, Courtney,' she said, towing me over to the couple, 'this is Sam Jones, one of our newest artists. She's showing next week with some other young Brits.'

'Oh yes, I have the invite,' said the husband, shaking my hand in a manly kind of way. 'Good to meet you. I'm Courtney Challis.'

The wife followed suit. I noticed that neither of them smiled, beyond a twitch of their lips. Still, it looked as if they were trying to; there was a little tic at the corner of each eye, as if the muscles hadn't yet forgotten what they were for.

'I don't want to be a distraction,' I said firmly, already sensing that Barbara wasn't jumping up and down and screaming for joy at my intrusion. I looked over at her. She gave me a fixed smile, scarcely larger than Taylor or Courtney's had been. But she didn't have the injections as an excuse.

'Not at all,' Stanley oozed at me. 'Not at all!'

But it was a subdued flicker of his habitual smarminess. He looked as if he would jump out of his skin if you sneaked up behind him and whispered 'Boo!' in his ear.

'We were just finishing up,' Carol said, flicking a glance at her watch. 'We have a table booked for eight-fifteen.'

'I guess it's up to us, honey,' Taylor said to Courtney. Or it might have been the other way round. They were dressed identically in dark blue blazers, pressed jeans and white shirts. Their shiny blond hair was cut the same and they both smelt of Ralph Lauren cologne. It would be hard to tell them apart if you were in a hurry.

'I guess so!' Courtney agreed. 'It's just so damn difficult to choose. Excuse my language.'

I bit my tongue to avoid saying: 'That's OK, you can't help being American,' and turned to survey the pictures. Indeterminate shapes shoved themselves sulkily through the general messy murk which characterised Barbara's painting style. She had confined herself to her usual palette of dingy greys and mud browns, with here and there streaks of feverish orange or a splodge of stuff the colour and shape of offal. It was like a series of paintings of the First World War trenches, seen through distorting glasses with a pounding headache.

'What do you think?' Jon Tallboy said to me enthusiastically.

'Very evocative,' I said. 'And powerful.' Such useful words.

They did the trick. Barbara relaxed, giving me a smile that was more welcoming than anything I had seen to date. It softened her features pleasantly. She was wearing an ankle-length dark red embroidered skirt and a vaguely ethnic sweater and with her hair wound around her head she looked like a Russian doll, face painted and calm, stocky and strong despite her diminutive size. I felt I could reach out and push her and, just like the dolls, she would rock back and forth on her plump little feet before regaining her balance.

In a huddle a few paces from us, Courtney, Taylor and Carol Bergmann were coming to a hard-won decision. I half-expected them to jump up in the air like American football players when they had finished. No one had bothered to include Stanley in the group and he hung around its fringes, a schoolboy hoping the others would finally ask him to join their game.

'OK!' Taylor finally said. 'Boy, that was a tough one, wasn't it, honey?'

'Sure was, sweetie,' Courtney agreed. They smiled at each other fondly. I was reminded of John and Mary, the couple on *Father Ted*, who fought bitterly in private and snapped into an extreme parody of marital bliss every time the priest passed by. I could just see Courtney and Taylor going at it hammer and tongs as soon as their audience was removed.

' "Memories of Spring"?' Carol asked, indicating the one which looked like a rubbish dump with more than its fair quantity of mud, not to mention fungus.

They both nodded. 'Whew!' Courtney added. 'Nice to have got there at last!'

'It's one of my personal favourites,' Barbara said, swishing forward to applaud the purchasers. She behaved as if it were they who ought to be congratulated for having made the right decision. They didn't seem to feel patronised, however.

'Oh, that's so great!' said Taylor, clapping her hands together girlishly. 'It's such an honour to have had you here while we were choosing.'

Barbara smiled graciously.

'It truly has been an honour, Ms Bilder,' said Courtney gravely.

'Well,' Carol cut in brightly, 'we should be getting ourselves together and heading out.'

'Reservations wait for no man,' Stanley said, happy to have found a subject on which he could pronounce with confidence.

'We had to fax the restaurant with our credit card number, and sign a form promising to be there or pay a penalty, before they'd take the booking!' Taylor informed everyone. 'Can you believe it? I don't know what New York is coming to.'

This was the cue for an outpouring of New York nightmare restaurant stories, all recounted with mock horror and, underlying that, a repressed triumph that the speakers were doing well enough to afford them. Laurence and Kevin exchanged a glance and started carrying the rejected paintings over to the lift. Once they were inside, Laurence remained there to hold them steady while Kevin and I took the stairs. Although not quite as dishevelled as Laurence, Kevin's bland face was shiny with physical effort and his hair was not as neat as it had doubtless been when he left the house that morning.

'You guys aren't going to the dinner, are you?' I asked.

'You must be kidding,' Kevin said bitterly. 'We're kind of lowly anyway, and today we're just the art handlers. Goddamn Don, when I catch up with him I'm gonna kick his ass. We've had a shit-awful day and it's not over yet.'

The elevator was already at the basement when we got there. Laurence had blocked the doors open and started heaving out the first Bilder. While the boys started slotting the paintings back into place in the complicated sliding storage apparatus – rather like an IKEA-designed CD stand, only on a much larger scale – I wandered through into the room beyond, Don's territory, with its broken-down loungers and odour of cigarettes and beer. This evening I could smell whisky, too, or maybe it was bourbon. I bet Don liked his bourbon, a country boy like him.

The ashtray on the arm of one of the loungers was brimming with cigarette stubs, and a glass half full with beer stood on the floor by its side, a fly buzzing around its rim. Don might just have stepped out for a moment. It was very still in the room, the strip lighting casting weird shadows over the grey walls. I felt a rush of claustrophobia. For some reason I remembered the dream I had had in London, the part where the walls were closing in on me, and in a brief fit of paranoia from the acid couldn't help turning my head to check that they were where they should be. In the next room I could hear Laurence and Kevin shifting paintings and swearing to each other. The sounds were strangely muffled; they seemed to come from very far away, as if heard through water.

One of Don's paintings was turned to face the room, propped against a filing cabinet, glue jars and paint pots in a muddle next to it. I gave it a cursory glance but I was all stared out of art at the moment. Besides, it was of a huge naked woman with a bit of red paper stuck next to her, pointing to her private parts. Just what I would have expected from Don. In front of me were the sliding glass doors which led out onto the small concreted space outside, as cramped and nasty as the exercise yard of a prison. There was another strip light outside, garishly lighting up the yard's far wall. It turned the doors into dark mirrors, reflecting the contents of the room back at me.

The reflection did not allow me to see beyond the doors. Moving closer, I pressed my face nearly up to the smeared and dirty glass and stared out. There was hardly anything in the yard besides a bicycle rack sheltered by a lean-to. A single bike stood inside it, chained by its frame to the rack. Beyond it was a pile of rubbish. No, it couldn't be rubbish. I could scarcely imagine Carol Bergmann allowing people to use the yard as a dump. But it was covered in black plastic, and had the authentic lumpiness of an unevenly filled garbage bag.

I looked at it for what felt like a long time, fighting back the idiotic urge to giggle. The acid was trying to make a brief comeback. When I had myself under control, I took a deep breath and walked back into the storage room. The boys were dusting themselves off resentfully.

'Look,' I said, 'would you two come through here a moment?'

Oddly, it was as if Kevin knew at once what I suspected. His handsome features flattened as if smeared across his face like dough, artificially blank. It was Laurence who said, wearily but quite naturally:

'What is it, Sam? I can't think much beyond a beer at this point.'

'Just come through a second,' I insisted, leading them into Don's room. I noticed for the first time that the sink in the far corner was dripping, very slowly, the drops plinking down like water torture.

'Shit, this place is a dump,' Laurence said absently.

'He could at least empty his fucking ashtray,' Kevin agreed. 'He always keep it like this? I hardly ever come down here.'

'Look out there in the yard.' I pointed to the lean-to.

Kevin didn't say anything. He had shoved his hands into his pockets, and stood like a statue, his face unmoving. Laurence leaned forward.

'You mean the bike? It's mine. Don't tell me you want to borrow it.'

'Did you bike in this morning?'

'No, I haven't used it in a couple of days. What is this, a fitness quiz?'

He turned away. Kevin still hadn't moved or spoken.

'Beyond the lean-to,' I persisted. 'What's that?'

Laurence sighed a long, slow, humour-the-woman sigh, and swivelled back, poised on the ball of one foot, wanting just to answer me and be gone.

'Refuse. Junk. I don't know. Bottom line is, it shouldn't be there. But I'm too tired to deal with it right now.'

'It looks pretty big, don't you think?'

'I don't give a shit how big it is . . . .' Laurence's voice, which had been edgy with annoyance at being kept back from his beer, tailed off. Our eyes met in the reflection on the glass doors. We stared at each other, the shadows behind and before us stretching away into the half-illuminated night. There was a long, unpleasant pause, broken by Kevin's feet shifting on the concrete floor.

'Well,' I said. 'I think we should go out there and take a look.'

The key was in the door. We all focused on it.

'What about fingerprints?' Laurence said presciently.

I shrugged. 'What can we do? We have to check.'

Laurence found a filthy rag by the sink and used that to turn the key, trying to hold it by its edges. The doors slid back. The night air was scarcely less cold than that of the basement, but damper. The yard was clammy and we shivered as we crossed it.

There wasn't room for all of us to gather round the refuse sack. I knelt down and prodded it as gently as I could.

'It's just garbage or something,' Kevin said, his voice loud. 'Dumped here till someone got around to throwing it out.'

More than one bag had been used, and only the uppermost one was actually pulled over the mass it contained. The rest were draped over the larger part of it, which had been pulled as far behind the lean-to as it would go. I took hold of the one nearest to me and dragged the bag off, taking care not to shift anything more than I had to.

'Oh, *shit*,' Laurence said. 'Oh *shit*.'

It was as fair a response as any. Don's face, livid under the strip lighting, lolled back on his neck, looking up at us. Kevin was the furthest away, but he took a few quick steps back. Golden light projected down in long slanting rectangles from the windows on the first floor, casting an inappropriately benevolent glow over the scene. As the plastic bag came away it looked for a moment as if Don were wearing a choker, a thin strip of leather cutting tightly into the skin of his neck. But once I had laid his head gently down on the concrete, I could see clearly that it was a long narrow bruise indenting the skin, dark and strong enough to have been traced with a marker pen. In my hallucinations earlier today I had seen something like this. Reality was contradicting me: the line wasn't red. It was black with dying blood.

'Oh, shit,' Laurence said softly once again.

And from behind him came the sound of retching. Kevin was being sick in the corner of the yard.

CHAPTER SIXTEEN

'Pretty perspicacious of you, Ms Jones.' Detective Frank leaned back in his chair and smiled at me. It was a nice enough smile, but the effect was undercut both by the floor-to-ceiling chicken wire which covered the window just behind him and the gory posters, one of a drug addict, one of a gunshot victim, which bracketed it. Nor was the view I could dimly glimpse through the chicken wire anything to mention on a postcard home. Sipping some brown hot water which tasted as if it had been made by hand-wringing coffee filters into a rusty bucket, I said 'Thank you' as meekly as I could.

'And you kept your head, right? Got some witnesses together and went into the yard to check out just what was in that bag. Didn't puke, either, not you. Not like that other guy.'

'Regular Miss Marple,' said Thurber. With horror, I suddenly realised that her deep dead voice was exactly the same as Marvin the paranoid android's from *The Hitchhiker's Guide to the Galaxy*. No wonder I'd thought of Radiohead before. Giggles bubbled up inside me and some, despite my best efforts, made a break for freedom. Quickly I slurped down some more brown hot water and pretended to have a little coughing fit to cover the outburst. I didn't think any further response would be required.

'Maybe that's because it isn't the first time this's happened to you, right?' Thurber continued, her voice still eerily lacking affect.

'I usually do keep my head,' I said, looking her in the eye. 'And this stuff at the gallery is nothing to do with me.'

It didn't distract her. She lowered her gaze once again to the stack of paper on the desk in front of her.

'Broke a guy's neck for him, didn't you, a few years back?' she said mildly. 'I tell you that, Ray?'

'Yeah, I think you did mention it,' Frank confirmed, tilting his chair back till it hit the chicken wire. 'Pretty impressive, huh?' he said to me.

'If you think that's impressive. I don't. And it was self-defence. It didn't even go to trial.'

'Sure, sure. And it's not like you strangled him or anything,' Frank agreed, as cheerful as ever. 'Now that would get us wondering a little bit.'

'So where are we on this?' Thurber said, as if she were asking me a question. I bit my tongue. One of the hardest things about police interrogations is telling yourself to shut up.

She shuffled some more paper round on her desk. Mixed in with a series of forms were some large black-and-white photographs. I couldn't see them closely but I assumed they were of Don's dead body.

'We have a multiple murder inquiry going on here,' Thurber went on, 'and you're not helping much.'

'I found the second body,' I said politely. 'Doesn't that count?'

Thurber shot me a glance which indicated that our bonding moment over the Monkees had been at least temporarily forgotten.

'Where were you last night?' she said.

The Q-and-A hadn't been underway for long. They would ask me this at least twice more before they let me go and my story had better be the same every time. I took a deep breath.

'At home in my apartment. I had a friend staying with me.'

'He or she?'

'He.'

'He stay over?'

I blinked. 'He stayed all night, if that's what you mean. But he's just a friend.' I didn't want any rumours getting around. 'He's one of the artists who's doing the show with me at Bergmann LaTouche. We know each other from London.'

Thurber picked up her pen. 'What's this guy's full name, and how can we get in touch with him?' she asked.

I gave her Lex's name. 'I don't know where he is right now,' I said, not wanting to ring my apartment in case everyone was still there. For all I knew they might have topped up their dose and be in the kind of state in which a Thurber/Frank double-pronged interrogation would send them over the edge into screaming insanity.

'Why don't we just try your number?' Thurber suggested, too clever not to sense that there was something I wasn't telling. To my great relief, when she dialled it, the answering machine picked up. She hung up and looked at me. 'Any idea where he could be?'

'I'm sure he'll get in touch,' I said easily. 'He's a bit of a free spirit. I think he's been couch-surfing up till now.'

'And you don't know any of his friends?'

This was bringing me into dangerous waters.

'He just rang me yesterday and said he needed somewhere to stay for the night,' I said, avoiding the question.

'How'd he know where you were?'

'I gave him my number in London.'

'He tell you then who he was staying with?'

'I didn't even know he was planning to come over earlier.'

Thurber looked at me narrowly. It was terrifying. 'You think he'll be back with you tonight?'

'Lex is pretty unpredictable,' I said. 'Maybe, yeah. I'll tell him to get in touch with you as soon as I see him.'

'You do that,' she said. 'So where was he sleeping last night?' There was nothing prurient about her question.

'In the living room on the pull-out bed.'

'How's the apartment laid out?'

'It's all open-plan, more or less, apart from the bathroom and bedroom.'

'So if you got up and went out in the night, would he know if you'd gone? Would you be stepping over him or anything?' Frank said.

'Well, maybe he'd hear the front door. The locks make a lot of noise. Though the sofa-bed's round the L-shape of the living room, so he might not even notice. But are we really talking about the middle of the night?' I countered. 'When was Don killed?'

Thurber's eyes, already drawn into slits, sharpened as if her stare were honing down to twin points of concentration.

'Were you with this guy all evening?' she snapped back.

'We met at about seven and we were together all evening.'

'So whaddaya want to know?' Thurber said as sharply as if she were attacking me.

I spread my hands. 'I'm curious. As much as you'll tell me.'

Out of the corner of my eye, I saw Frank shoot a glance at Thurber. It was clear that she led when they danced.

'We're looking for the same perp, if that's what you mean,' Thurber said to me. 'The guy you found was strangled with the same garrotte that did Kate Jacobson. As far as we can tell.'

'It wouldn't have been so easy to take him by surprise,' I said. 'He was the size of a house. Was he drunk?'

'Don't tell me,' Thurber said, in an almost friendly way. 'You smelled the bourbon on him when you took the plastic bag off.'

'That's right.' I returned her gaze. It was impossible to tell what game she was playing.

'Probably drugged, too,' Thurber said. 'We haven't had the results back yet for sure. But I'm willing to bet there was something in the bourbon. Knock him out a bit.'

'He was drinking beer,' I said, remembering the glass by the lounger. 'He must have been offered something better. I know he used to stay late to work on his own stuff.'

'Yeah, did that quite a lot, they say,' Thurber said. She gave me a very straight look. 'We need to talk to this Lex Thompson,' she said. 'And you need us to talk to him, too. If what you're saying's true, he's your alibi. Right?'

'Right.'

'Plus the doorman,' Frank volunteered.

'Oh no,' I said gloomily. 'You're going to have to talk to him again, aren't you?'

''Fraid so,' Frank confirmed, sounding about as apologetic as a bus conductor announcing that all the passengers would have to get off and wait for the one twenty minutes behind.

Thurber was unbuttoning her jacket. It swung open, and as she reached for something inside her pocket I saw the gun clipped to her belt.

'Here you go,' she said, handing me a card with her name and various phone numbers printed on it. 'He should call us as soon as possible. It's in your interest as well as his.'

'I know,' I said. 'I'll tell him just as soon as he shows up.'

'You do that,' Frank said. 'You do that thing.'

A ghost of a smile drifted across Thurber's near-expressionless face.

'It's a Glock. Porcelain,' she said, patting the gun. I realised I had been looking at it. 'Point nine mill. Bet you don't see many of those on the cops where you come from, right?'

'They don't carry pieces over there,' Frank chimed in.

'*Jesus*.' Thurber stared at me as incredulously as if I came from a place where the wheel was cutting-edge technology. 'That right?' she asked, her voice almost coming alive with disbelief.

'Yes, ma'am,' I responded. I didn't know why I said that: it just came out.

Thurber's face cracked once again into a fleeting smile. I decided that she was the scariest person I had ever met in my life. Not because of the Glock, either. It was that smile.

* * *

We went over my version of events a couple more times before they let me go. I had been interrogated by police in Britain often enough, but Thurber and Frank were something else. Maybe it was helped by the interview taking place in the middle of a crowded squad room, with people milling around us, computers buzzing, printers chattering away. It made the talk feel more informal; when a particularly noisy suspect started yelling across the room, the three of us had exchanged what-a-bore glances and huddled conspiratorially closer together so we could hear what the others were saying. In England we would probably have been in a small interview room with one bright white light overhead and the recorder on the Formica table between us tying everyone's tongues into spools of audio tape.

But the bottom line was that they were very, very good at their job. I had never felt so on my guard. Perhaps I too was being conditioned by the cop shows, but I had the instinct that Thurber and Frank really had seen almost everything already and by now could predict with a fair certainty when it would happen again. They were more world-weary than A E Housman on an off day. Or, to draw a more modern analogy, Portishead covering Joy Division.

The squad room was positively teeming with people, most of them carrying Styrofoam cups of brown hot water as carefully as if they actually cared about losing the contents. Americans were bizarre about their coffee. Either they drank this stuff, which tasted like the dirty water that lived inside an espresso machine, or they went to a coffee boutique and bought the violently expensive couture version. A column I had read the other day had described this almost perfectly as a lengthy and complex process involving approximately one coffee bean, three quarts of dairy products and what appeared to be a small nuclear reactor. Only it didn't mention the optional strawberry syrup.

I squeezed past a group of cops – now I was sensitised to their presence, I was noticing the guns everywhere – and finally reached the fence on the far side of the room. Frank, who had been escorting me, opened the gate and indicated I was to go through.

'We'll be in touch,' he said drily, clicking it shut behind me. On a bench against the wall sat Barbara Bilder and Jon Tallboy. To my surprise, they stood up when they saw me and came towards me, looking anxious.

'Sam!' said Barbara, hugging me. Taken aback, my instinct was to push her away, but I fought it nobly. She was wearing a Body Shop perfume, which smelt light and airy, like freshly starched linen. It clashed with her Tibetan tribeswoman look. 'Are you OK?' she was saying. 'You poor girl, you must be in total shock.'

'Absolutely. And hungry, too,' Jon said.

I found this baffling at first; then I was insulted. It took me a moment to realise that he was projecting.

'Why don't you come back to ours and have something to eat?' Barbara suggested. 'We were waiting for you. Carol said you're staying on the Upper West Side.'

'That's right,' I said feebly.

'Well, great!' she said. 'We're in the west nineties. It'll be easy for you to get home afterwards.'

They seemed to have everything planned out already. Barbara was that kind of woman.

The Bilders – technically they should be the Tallboys, but it just didn't sound right – lived in a brownstone on a cross-street between Broadway and Amsterdam, lined with trees on one side and, on the other, flights of stone stairs leading to impossibly high ground floors. Despite its apparent smartness, the hall smelt of boiled cabbage, the drugget on the stairs was faded and worn, and some of the mailboxes were hanging crooked. It reminded me of run-down boarding houses in South Kensington. Until Barbara opened the apartment door, I couldn't decide if this was shabby chic to fool the burglars or if the place really was run-down.

It was the former. Plenty of money had gone into furnishing Casa Bilder, and in a way I hadn't anticipated. Barbara's flowing skirts and Jon's battered old corduroy jacket had led me to expect something resembling Nancy Bishop's apartment, cosy and cluttered with old-fashioned furniture. But this was elegantly expensive minimalism, the kind of place I would have imagined Carol Bergmann living, with its shiny wood floors, white walls bare apart from the occasional painting, glass coffee tables and chairs made of strips of leather slung daringly across chrome frames. Barbara went straight through into a tiny slate-tiled kitchen and started opening drawers. It made me aware that I was hungry. Jon had been right after all. Well, I hadn't had anything to eat since the free soup.

'What would you like, Sam?' she called through to me hospitably.

'Oh, whatever's easiest,' I said.

'No, really. What would you like? Just let me know.'

Her high, fluting voice made her sound like a Fifties housewife from a TV sitcom rather than an internationally known artist. Jon was nodding at me. I was tempted to request lobster mornay with gratin dauphinoise and triple chocolate mousse to follow, then throw a scene when told that this was off the menu.

'Uh—' I stalled, wimping out of the request for lobster.

'Chinese, Italian, Mexican, Thai, Vietnamese, Ethiopian, Japanese—'

Barbara came out of the kitchen with a stack of takeaway menus in her hand.

'Here we go,' she said. 'What about Chinese? Everyone likes Chinese, don't they?'

'Lovely, thanks,' I said with relief.

'No one cooks in New York,' Jon said to me. 'There's such great takeout it isn't worth it.'

'My kind of town.'

'We love it, don't we, honey?' Jon smiled uxoriously at Barbara.

'We sure do,' she said fondly back. 'Jon, why don't you pour Sam some wine and show her the apartment while I order in some dinner?'

Showing me the apartment was a euphemism for giving me a guided tour of all Barbara's paintings. There was no other work hanging on the walls. I wore my jaw out making appreciative mn-ing noises as Jon pontificated about Barbara's vision and Barbara's saleability, often in the same breath. In England people were more discreet: but Jon had been here long enough to have no embarrassment talking about how good her sales were and how solid her client base. I almost expected him to inform me that her name had been trademarked to avoid imitation.

'Just keeps doing better and better, that's my Barbie,' he said happily. 'Steady as a rock.'

I was getting rather tired of this love-fest, and since we were in their office, out of Barbara's earshot, I saw no reason why I shouldn't throw some cold water on it.

'I've seen Kim a couple of times already,' I said firmly. 'Thanks for giving me the number. She looks wonderful.'

Jon looked flustered. 'Does she? That's good. I mean, I haven't seen her – we haven't seen each other – in a while now. She's probably very busy.'

He pulled a long face and jerked his head in the direction of the door.

'Difficult, you know?' he said, lowering his voice. 'Tricky. Of course Barbara's fond of Kim. But still. Women can be like that, you know. Difficult.'

'I didn't know you were allowed to say that kind of thing in

America nowadays, Jon,' I said affably. 'I'm sure there's some Unreconstructed Male Attitudes hotline number I could report you to. Or maybe that's just me being – well, difficult.'

Jon's whole body sagged with embarrassment. Sam looked on her work and saw that it was good.

'What about when Kim first got here?' I said, rallying my troops and attacking from a different angle. 'Did you help her get into art school?'

'It's very tough here, you know,' Jon said feebly. 'So many young artists trying to make it—'

Barbara put her head round the door. 'Dinner's on its way,' she said. 'What's all this about young artists?'

'It's very *difficult*,' Jon said helplessly, clinging to this word as if it were a lifebelt. 'Young artists – getting started . . . .'

'God, yes. You don't have to tell me about that . . . . Why don't we go back into the living room? And Sam, you must tell us all about how you're finding it here. Is this your first time in New York?'

'Yes,' I said, following her back through the door and sitting down on the armchair she indicated. 'And I thought the murder rate was supposed to have fallen. So much for what they say in the newspapers.'

There was a momentary silence. Then Barbara nodded to Jon, and on this unspoken command he folded his long body into another armchair, like a hinged ruler closing up on itself. Barbara perched on a lounger opposite me, spreading out the folds of her skirt. I was struck anew by her magnetism. Sitting there so neatly, her brown eyes fixed on me, she held the room as a star actress might a scene. Finally she spoke:

'You know, I'd almost forgotten for a moment? Isn't that crazy! Isn't that crazy, honey?' she asked Jon, who nodded gloomily. 'So terrible for this to happen as soon as you get here,' she said sympathetically. 'New York's really a safe place to live nowadays, though. Much better, anyway.'

'Unless you work for Bergmann LaTouche,' I said. 'Or have a show there.'

Another uncomfortable pause followed.

'I'm so glad the restorer managed to clean up your paintings,' I said. 'Don said they came up as good as new.'

Whoops, I had mentioned Don. Barbara flinched. Jon said gamely:

'Not quite, alas. But pretty good.'

'So, Sam, tell me about your work,' Barbara said, smiling at me. 'We didn't really have overnight successes at your age, not in my day. Well, now the publicity machines and the marketing get going much faster. You just have to make sure you build your career steadily. It's so easy to be a flash in the pan.'

Often with Barbara Bilder I found it hard to decide whether she was being bitchy or simply ingenuous. Still, I was coming down on the side of bitchy. Barbara seemed to me about as ingenuous as Peter Mandelson caught in the middle of a nice piece of top-spin.

'I've scarcely been an overnight success,' I said modestly. 'This is one of my first big breaks.'

'And then this has to happen! So unfortunate, these murders!' Barbara lamented. 'And my show being vandalised like that. I wish I could think they'd catch whoever was responsible. It must have been a very jealous person, don't you think? With an axe to grind?'

She shot me a look I could not decipher.

'The very night you got in, wasn't it?' she said. 'Such terrible timing!'

This was a motif she kept repeating. I found myself staring at her. Just then the buzzer went and Barbara nodded at Jon, who jumped up to open the door to the delivery man. She kept an eye on him, I noticed, to make sure he didn't over-tip. But this was an observation I made with the shallowest part of my brain. Another thought was whirling round the rest of the space, and the more I turned it over, the more it fitted. Had Barbara decided to invite me for dinner because she suspected me of having trashed her exhibition? The mind boggled. Did she think I was jealous of her success, or wanted to get even for her treatment of Kim? Was that why she was needling me, to see if I would give something away?

And if she thought I had done that, then she must suspect me, too, of having strangled both Kate and Don. Or at least wonder about the possibility. In which case, it had been brave of her to invite me back to her home.

Jon was laying out the food on plates in front of me.

'Just help yourself,' Barbara said. 'I ordered their mixed dinner for three.'

'Mmm, thanks,' I said politely. 'It looks lovely.'

Actually by London standards it was pretty average. Nice to find at least one thing that we did better. I glanced over to see Jon cutting up his spring roll into three slices before spearing one of them with his fork, and couldn't help laughing.

'You always used to do that!' I exclaimed. Jon looked up, the fork part way to his mouth, and a gleam of recognition flooded his face. 'Do you remember? We used to get that takeaway from the Hung Fu, round the corner from the estate, and we'd always wait for you to start eating your spring roll like that. It was like a family joke,' I said to Barbara before I realised the gaffe I'd made. 'He even ate paratha with a fork,' I said feebly. 'He couldn't bear touching greasy food with his hands.'

Barbara had stiffened so visibly that it was like watching concrete set before your eyes. Jon shot a glance at her and his nostalgic smile faded as if she had wiped it off with a J-cloth coated in cream cleanser.

'I'm perfectly aware that Jon is very fastidious,' Barbara said coldly. 'He doesn't like getting his hands dirty. It's one of the things I admire about him.'

Raising my eyes for a second, I saw that Barbara's brown eyes were still fixed on me. She looked wary, almost jittery, and her voice had wavered a little as she delivered her snub. I couldn't blame her for being nervy. I would be too if I thought I had a killer in the house. Perhaps later on I could rack up the tension by improvising a masterclass on making one's own garrotte. They were probably waiting eagerly for the benefit of my expert opinion on the much-debated choice between guitar or piano wire.

I had never, as far as I knew, been invited to dinner by someone I disliked who suspected me of being a murderess – sorry, that ending was very retrograde of me, apparently – murder*er*. It was a terrible temptation to behave badly. And, frankly, I doubted whether I would be able to resist.

CHAPTER SEVENTEEN

'Tell me at least that you didn't start toying with pieces of wire in a threatening way.'

'There wasn't anything suitable,' I said regretfully. 'Don't think I didn't keep my eyes open. But I put my feet up on the sofa and talked about Murders I Have Known, which kept the conversation flowing nicely.'

Hugo snorted. 'I'm sure you made huge play of the time you saved my life,' he said sarcastically. 'Sam to the rescue, all guns blazing . . . .'

'Of course I didn't,' I said impatiently, 'don't be stupid. I was painting myself as a homicidal maniac who so far has been able to pin her foul crimes onto innocent people – why would I go and bollock that up by mentioning actually having saved someone?'

'You're right, my love. Do forgive my naiveté. I'm sure they double-bolted all the doors and windows and lay awake all night, clinging to each other and starting at every tiny sound.'

'Oh, do you really think so?' I was pleased. 'You say the nicest things.'

'If I thought you were after me, I'd do more than just double-bolt the window,' Hugo assured me. 'My God, I'd buy my own island and train up the local sharks specially.'

'How's it going there?' I asked. He was being so obliging that the least I could do was inquire about his work.

'No need to be polite,' Hugo said. 'I'm actually hoping that this monstrosity of a play will be so terrible that it'll end the fashion for working-class homosexual drug-addled sex-abusing mindless swearing shallow pieces of garbage.'

'Of course you're most of those yourself,' I pointed out.

'I,' said Hugo haughtily, 'am neither mindless nor shallow. And I can assure you that having to rape Slut Boy twice a day and four on matinées is burning out a substantial part of the homosexual impulses which remain to me.'

'Aversion therapy. Very *Maurice*.'

'Absolutely. But everything else is going swimmingly,' he said, sounding more cheerful. 'And I've been asked to read for something really exciting. Which I'm not going to tell you about in case it doesn't happen.'

'That's very mature of you, Hugo,' I said nervously. I couldn't bear it if Hugo grew up.

'Don't worry. It's a brief spasm and will swiftly pass. So, tell me more about your murders. Let me live vicariously.'

With two people dead, I had had to tell Hugo what was going on over here. But one of the things I loved most about him was that he never, ever told me to be careful.

'It's all very strange,' I said slowly. 'It has to be someone at the gallery, or very closely connected with it. But I can't get a handle on the motive. At first I thought that Kate had been killed to get her keys to the gallery.'

'But then it wouldn't have been anyone who worked there,' Hugo objected. 'I mean, to kill her solely as a double bluff seems very tortuous.'

'Exactly. So maybe whoever did it actually wanted to kill Kate, and trashed the gallery as a way of distracting everyone from that.'

'No, that's too complicated as well. Think of the risk of being caught in the act. Whoever did it must have really wanted to ruin the exhibition.'

'Or embarrass the gallery.'

'A disgruntled employee?' Hugo suggested.

'Yeah, but who?' This was a rhetorical question. 'You know, the only person I could halfway see doing that would have been Don.'

'The one whose body you found?'

'Mm. I could imagine him doing it as a twisted kind of practical joke. He was very – knowing, as if he were laughing up his sleeve at everyone. He would have loved to see the rest of them twisting themselves in knots over what had happened. But he was the one who had to clean it all up, so that doesn't make sense.'

'Well, maybe *that* was a double bluff.' Hugo was inventing happily. 'Maybe he was strangled because the murderer found out it was him.'

'And that doesn't make sense either. I mean, Don having let someone get close enough to strangle him. He was built like a gorilla and he wasn't a fool. He acted like he could handle anything or anyone.'

'Only he was wrong,' Hugo commented.

'Yes. He must have underestimated the murderer.'

'Well,' Hugo suggested, 'maybe the murderer is the kind of person who everyone underestimates.'

For some reason, Kevin popped into my mind. Bland, good-looking Kevin who Laurence had described as the straightest of arrows. He was just the kind of person Don would sneer at.

'Brrr,' I said, shivering.

'I beg your pardon?'

'A goose just walked over my grave.'

'I'm sure that isn't right,' Hugo said. 'Don't you mean ghost?'

'Would you feel a ghost, though? I mean, they don't walk.'

'In haunted houses when they tell the story of the nun who was walled up alive, they always finish by saying chillingly: "And her ghost still walks the battlements, wailing for her demon lover."'

'Yeah, but they mean floating. And you wouldn't say a ghost floated over my grave. It's not so evocative.'

'Evocative,' Hugo mocked. 'That's a big word, my sweet. Have you been hanging out with an intellectual?'

'Piss off,' I said intellectually. 'Oh, look, I've got some blonde jokes for you. Kim gave me a book of them. Why did the blonde stare for two hours at a can of frozen orange juice?' I paused for effect. 'Because the label said "concentrate".'

Hugo sniggered.

'Why shouldn't blondes have coffee breaks?' I continued, getting into my stride. 'It takes too long to retrain them. Why do blondes have "TGIF" written on their shoes? Toes Go In First.'

'Enough! I look forward to telling those to Slut Boy tomorrow,'

Hugo said gleefully. 'He probably won't get them, but everyone else will. Look, darling, I should be going. I'm due at the gym soon. Try not to kill anyone today.'

'God,' I complained, 'you are so *demanding*.'

* * *

I came out of the subway feeling as if I'd just been for a swim. It was a warm day, and down below street level heat rose off the freshly mopped floors, swimming with bleach that smelt strongly of chlorine. The hot air blew down the tunnels like air vents outside a swimming baths, making my clothes stick to me as if I'd put them on before drying off completely. It was odd that the New York subway, less deep than the London underground, should be so much hotter. And it was October. I could see why people complained about summers in the city: in August it must be like a steam bath down here. Pores Opened In Five Minutes Or Your Money Back.

Laurence's apartment was just a block up from the subway stop. He buzzed me in.

'I'm not used to having to walk up stairs,' I announced with hauteur as I arrived at his front door. 'In my building we have lifts.'

'Deal with it, sweetie,' Laurence retorted, standing back to let me in.

The front door opened into the middle of the tiny kitchen, halving the floor space as it did so, which would have been a nuisance if anyone arrived while you were cooking. But Laurence must be at one with the Bilders on the subject of takeaway food; the burners on the small gas stove were covered with a piece of dusty chipboard on which he had piled art magazines. I peered into the main room. It looked light, and the ceilings were high. That was about all I could make out through the stacks of books which teetered at waist height, like a Carl Andre installation which had started breeding amongst itself.

'Nice, isn't it?' said Laurence with an air of pride. 'It's pretty good for this neighbourhood. Hold on, I'll just get my jacket.'

While he picked his way through the book towers, I went to the bathroom. Its condition would have disgraced a run-down NHS hospital: chipped and peeling, with the kind of stains that go beyond mere dirt. The water in the sink ran brown and smelt of chlorine. The swimming-pool motif again. After a while the water ran yellow instead. I assumed this was an improvement. Scattered everywhere on the floor were flat black pieces of plastic, the size of squashed matchboxes. Laurence explained that they were roach motels.

'They check in, but they never check out. Until you empty them, of course. A guy comes around once a month to spray the place. Bangs on the door at eight in the morning shouting: "Exterminator! Open up!" The first time it happened I nearly had a heart attack.'

New Yorkers tell you this kind of thing proudly; they like to feel that they're living in near-Third World conditions, struggling against the violence and filth of the big city. Both Don and Leo had complained to me about the Giuliani/Braxton clean-up.

'Used to be you couldn't walk in the East Village at night without being real careful,' Don had said regretfully. 'They'd mug you or shoot you as soon as look at you. People knew you lived in Manhattan, you'd get all the respect you could handle. Now no one gives a shee-yit. It's for pussies and tourists.'

'Do you think anyone's missing Don?' I found myself asking Laurence as we clattered down the steps to the subway. We were going down to the Village, where we had a brunch appointment.

'That's a weird question. But no, I don't. I mean, *I* certainly don't.'

Practically opposite the restaurant was one of those basketball courts so beloved of the movies, concrete-paved and surrounded by a steel mesh almost as high as the buildings around it. A group of young men in layers of cut-off clothing and high-laced trainers were jumping around inside, bouncing balls and shouting manfully at each other. They seemed quite unselfconscious about playing inside what was to all intents and purposes a giant goldfish bowl. It was like Laurence having no embarrassment about shouting 'Taxi!' at the top of his voice, or the couples who quarrelled loudly in the street about their most intimate details. Even the would-be cool kids hanging out on street corners, pretending to be in a Larry Clark film, their anomie so advanced they were practically comatose, always had an eye out for the effect they were having. This town was naturally theatrical.

The brunch rendezvous itself was a small place with the most luridly carved and painted chairs I had ever seen in my life, and without question the best Mexican food. The chilli sauces were rich and subtle as a good Thai curry, the tastes delicate and strong. I had eggs poached in tomatillo sauce on fried courgette sticks and a side order of cornbread; we each got orange juice and coffee, and the whole thing cost a mere ten bucks each, or would have done if I hadn't ordered a margarita. It was nearly one o'clock, after all.

Halfway through my eggs, Suzanne came in. This was, Laurence had explained, the brunch ritual: you staked out a big table and your friends dropped in whenever they made it out of bed.

'Hey,' she said listlessly, plopping down next to me. She waved away the menu the waitress proffered her. 'Huevos rancheros and fries, please,' she said. 'Orange juice and camomile tea. So.' She looked at me. 'Let's cut to the chase. We're all in deep shit now, right?'

'Are we?' I said through a melting mouthful of egg, taken aback. Suzanne was behaving as if we were tycoons discussing an international takeover at a power breakfast. This was not what I had signed up for. I looked to Laurence to deal with it.

Suzanne shrugged. Off-duty she wore a big sloppy chenille sweater over jeans, her hair pulled back, mascara and a little powder her only make-up. She looked more approachable but just as competent.

'All of us that didn't get along with Don,' she said. 'Which is all of us. The cops say whoever did him killed Kate too.'

Just then Java came in, followed by Kevin. They waved at us and stopped by the bar to order something from the waitress.

'God, Mr J Crew poster model. He looks like a bond trader on dressing-down Friday. Why'd she bring *him*?' Laurence said *sotto voce* to Suzanne, who shrugged again.

'Old home week. Anyway, we're in this together. And you know what, Laurence? I don't give a shit any more about anything but who killed Kate. I mean that.'

Laurence put down his fork and looked at her hard.

'Well, I'm just grateful I didn't do it,' he said finally. He took his glasses off and rubbed his eyes. 'Having you on my trail'd scare the living daylights out of me.'

'Hey, guys,' Java said as she and Kevin sat down. The waitress arrived with a tray and further menus. Suzanne started picking at her eggs with less appetite than her prompt order had indicated.

'Energy juice?' the waitress said.

'That's me.' Java took the glass of orange and green-flecked sludge enthusiastically.

'That looks like one of Barbara's paintings,' I observed before I had time to wonder whether discretion was the better part of valour. But everyone grinned – even Kevin.

'They had me over to theirs last night,' I added, striking while the iron was hot. 'Barbara and Jon, I mean.'

'She's got him really well trained,' Laurence said nastily. 'Did he jump through hoops after coffee?'

'Hey,' Suzanne said, 'don't knock it. Barnes and Noble's full of self-help books on how to get your man into shape. If she put her technique down on paper she could make a fortune.'

'Barbara's much too smart for that,' Laurence countered. 'Half of her skill comes in pretending that she's just this helpless little fluffball. She wouldn't want to compromise that.'

'Iron hand in a velvet glove,' I said.

'At first it's really flattering,' Kevin volunteered unexpectedly. 'You know. "Kevin, what do *you* think of this?" "Kevin, you've got such a good eye, you're so clever about this kind of thing." But in the end you realise she's just getting you to make the decisions she wants made.'

'She's different when there aren't any guys around,' Java added. 'Or if you're not important enough for her. Do this, do that, get me Carol, I'm in a hurry. Then Carol comes down and Barbara starts cooing at her like butter wouldn't melt in her mouth. It really bugs me.'

'Shit,' Laurence said, 'we should do this more often. Gather for brunch and let off steam collectively. Very healthy for staff morale.'

'That's not why we're all here,' Suzanne reminded him curtly.

'I know that!' Laurence said, anger rising to the surface. 'Don't think I'm any less aware of it than you! Just because I'm not playing the grieving widow—'

'What's that supposed to mean?' Suzanne snapped back.

'Dairy-free zucchini and sweetcorn casserole?' the waitress said with mercifully good timing.

'Me,' Java said, raising her hand.

'So I guess the fried eggs with home fries and fried zucchini must be yours,' the waitress said, slipping the second plate in front of Kevin.

'So,' Laurence said. 'Fried food: Kevin Says Yes.'

'Yeah, you should go easy with that,' Java said. 'Every so often is OK, but not on a regular basis.'

Certainly Java looked like an advertisement for perfect nutrition. The whites of her eyes shone like pearls. She looked less unreal than she did with make-up on, and even more beautiful.

Kevin stared at her worshipfully. 'You think maybe I should get a salad too?'

Java shrugged. 'Couldn't hurt.'

'You know she used to model in Japan?' he informed us. 'She was really big over there.'

'They like girls who look mixed,' Java explained. 'You know, like my eyes are rounder, and my skin's a bit paler than if I was completely Oriental.'

'Did you model over here?' I asked.

Java shook her head. 'Too short and not white enough,' she said, matter-of-fact. 'But I didn't care that much. I always wanted to work in a gallery.'

'How did you get the job?'

'Oh, I met Stanley at a party,' Java said. 'He told me there might be a job at the gallery, so I just kept calling up till they gave it to me. I didn't have any experience or anything so I read up all I could on the artists BLT handles, you know. And I went around all the other SoHo and Chelsea galleries so I could talk about what everyone else was doing.'

'Carol was really impressed,' Suzanne said.

Java shrugged again. 'If I do something,' she said easily, 'I like to do it right.'

'You'll be a partner in ten years' time,' Laurence said.

'Hey, I wish!' But she gave him a lovely smile.

I had the sudden sharp awareness that I was being watched. Turning my head, I saw Kim and Lex standing rather hesitantly just inside the door. I waved at them, drawing everyone else's attention to their presence. They looked very morning-after. In fact, they reminded me of the boy in Snoopy pyjamas I had seen in the Ludlow. Their clothes were loose, their hair hadn't seen a brush since yesterday, and their trainers were laced up just enough to keep them on their feet.

'We can fit a couple more chairs in, can't we?' I said.

Kim and Lex came over slowly, shooting me dagger-like glances which I ignored as blandly as I could. I hadn't told them that there would be anyone else here when we had arranged to meet, and they resented it. But I had wanted to see what would happen if I threw them together with the gallery staff and got everyone talking about the murders. Something might pop up. You never knew.

'Hi,' Lex said to the general assembly, sounding as if he were arriving at a wake. Kim mumbled something and pulled up a chair.

'I didn't realise there were going to be so many people here,' she said crossly in my ear.

'It just snowballed, you know?' I said, aiming for innocent and regretting it halfway through. Kim would never be taken in by innocence from me. I should have tried hung-over instead.

'I know you!' Suzanne was saying to Lex. 'Where have I seen you before? Must have been pretty recent.'

Lex looked panic-stricken. And for some reason I had the feeling she was playing with him. It was nothing I could put my finger on, just an instinct. But then I saw her lips purse for a moment while she watched his reaction, as if she were savouring it, and my suspicions grew. Did she know that Lex had been staying at Kate's?

'This is Lex,' I explained, since the young man in question was too busy doing a startled fawn impression to speak for himself. 'Lex Thompson. And Kim—'

'Oh, right! I'm Suzanne, I work at Bergmann LaTouche. Great to meet you. I must have seen your photo in the leaflet we've been sending out,' she continued. 'You looked so familiar.'

But even while she let him off the hook, she was observing him as carefully as if he had been a lab rat. Lex sagged with relief, completely unaware of any undercurrents.

'So how long have you been over here?' Laurence asked. 'We thought you weren't due in till next Wednesday. I'm Laurence, by the way. And this is Kevin and Java. We all work at the gallery. Apart from Sam. She just finds the bodies for us.'

'Each to their own,' I said.

'You heard about that?' Java asked Lex. 'It's so terrible. And scary.'

'Java,' Suzanne said warningly.

'Well, it is,' Java retorted unanswerably. 'I mean, he's going to have to find out about it sooner or later.'

'Lex knows,' I said, cutting in. 'He's actually been here for a few days now, staying with me and some other friends.'

Lex's relief at my covering up for him was pathetic. He managed a smile at me and relaxed back in his chair for the first time that morning.

'Hey,' he said, recovering fast, 'isn't this a place where you can get stuff to eat? How does that work?'

Kevin handed him a menu. Kim was already looking at hers.

'You've been shagging, haven't you?' I muttered to Kim.

Kim stared at me. 'How d'you know?'

'My sex antennae are wobbling madly. Remember them?'

She and Lex both looked so physically relaxed that I could have bounced tennis balls off their foreheads without them noticing. Besides, there was the unmistakable nuclear-fuelled, I-had-sex-last-night glow, like the Ready Brek kids' halo.

Kim sighed. 'OK, we did it. All right?'

'Are you ready to order?'

We both started.

'Uh, yes,' Kim said, picking something more or less at random from the menu. Lex, his eyes on my margarita, ordered one to go with his brunch.

'And I'll have what he's having,' he said, pointing at Kevin's plate. 'With sausage.'

'You mean chorizo?' said the waitress politely.

'You what?'

'OK, we'll put some on for you,' she said, maintaining her cool.

'You guys don't have chorizo in London?' Laurence said disbelievingly.

'Of course we do,' I explained. 'We just don't know how to pronounce it.'

'We just drop our t's instead,' Lex said, thoroughly relaxed by now.

'Don't you mean h's?' Suzanne said.

'Nah. T's. Wha' d'you mean? Tha's ridiculous, inni'?' he illustrated.

The Americans tried this out for a few minutes. The spectacle of them mouthing away at what the Sunday papers called Estuary English was diverting, but eventually it palled, and I resorted to spooning up the pale green slush at the bottom of the margarita glass with a straw.

'So are you a friend of Lex's?' Laurence said to Kim.

'Actually, I'm a really old friend of Sam's. We knew each other at school in England.'

'You're Kim Tallboy!' Laurence exclaimed. 'I knew I'd seen you before. You must have come into the gallery for Barbara's show, right?'

'Briefly.'

'Jon's daughter?' Java said. 'Oh right, I remember when Sam said she knew you. Boy, Barbara didn't like that one little bit.'

Laurence and Suzanne turned as one to stare her down.

'What?' Java said. 'I mean, it's the truth, isn't it? We all know about it.'

'Kim doesn't,' Suzanne said.

'I bet she knows she and Barbara don't get on,' Java retorted.

'God, who elected you as the George Washington of Bergmann LaTouche?' Laurence said sourly. 'Don't you know how dangerous it is to tell the truth these days? Watch your back!'

'What, if I don't I could wind up dead? Is that what you're saying?' Java suggested.

There was a terrible silence. Laurence, more shocked than anyone else, started scratching nervously at his scalp like a monkey with nits. Stale flakes of dandruff floated down onto his grey cardigan.

'I'm really sorry, Java,' he said finally. 'It just came out.'

Java was the only one round the table who seemed unaffected.

'Sure,' she said. 'Don't sweat it.'

'I just don't get it,' Kevin said, blood rising to his blond face so that his fair eyebrows and lashes vanished into the flush of red. 'How could you even hint at a thing like that, man? With everything that's happening?'

'Hey, I said I was sorry,' Laurence snapped. He was very edgy today. Dr Sam diagnosed lack of antidepressants.

'It's fine, Kev. Honestly,' Java said cheerfully. 'It could have happened to anyone.'

'Yeah, well, it didn't.' Kevin was still pugnacious. And his facial hair was still invisible. He speared a chip and a courgette stick and shoved them into his mouth angrily. I was willing to bet that Kevin hadn't yet managed to make the beast with two backs with Java. He was irritable and tetchy in a way that suggested sexual frustration. And though she seemed to like him well enough, I wasn't sure that her feelings for him went any further than that. Unless giving him dietary hints was a sign of interest.

'Are you still seeing that guy, Java? The lawyer guy?' Suzanne asked, changing the subject. I wondered if her thoughts had been running on the same lines as mine.

'Oh, no. God. He had issues, you know?' Java put down her glass of energy juice, looking serious. 'I was like, quit dumping all this baggage on me. In life we have to carry our own.'

Even Laurence was nodding. Obviously Americans did not consider this gobbledegook. I tried desperately to memorise it for Hugo.

'Plus he was an alcoholic,' Java added. 'I really noticed it when we went away for that skiing weekend.'

'Did he go on a binge? Were you OK?' Kevin asked, concerned.

'He would sometimes drink *three glasses of wine a night*,' Java said sadly.

Lex had frozen with his margarita glass poised on its way to his mouth.

'My God,' I said. 'Three glasses of wine. Did you try to get him into AA?'

Java wasn't stupid; she knew my words were loaded, even though she was unsure with what. She looked at me warily.

'I did give him a card, yeah. When we got back to the city.'

'Did you tell him why?' I couldn't let this alone. 'I mean, did you get him to realise that he had a problem?'

'I don't know,' Java said. 'But, you know, I gave him something to think about. Like, it's got to be his choice if he gets help or not.'

Lex suddenly started choking on his food. Kevin, next to him, gave him a hefty pat on the back which caused him to splutter out what sounded suspiciously like a burst of laughter.

'I couldn't be with someone who was dependent on alcohol,' Java was continuing. 'I'm not being judgemental, but to me it's a real weakness. You know? It says, I'm needy and addictive.'

Even Kim, the born-again teetotaller, looked as if she thought this was a bit much. I shot her a glance designed to indicate that this was the beginning of the slippery slope on which she found herself. Meanwhile, Lex had caught the waitress's eye and was tapping at his margarita glass, indicating that he wanted a refill.

Behind Java's back, I held up my own as well. It was nice to have the company. At least I wasn't the only member of the group with as much willpower and self-control as John Belushi. And I had made a bet with myself that by the time I left New York Kim would be tippling again. Between Lex and me, I was sure we could manage it. I was modestly proud of my abilities as a bad influence.

CHAPTER EIGHTEEN

I had been doing Lex an injustice: apparently I was the only needy, addictive person using drink as a crutch in social situations. Lex's excuse was that he was stressed – despite having scored the night before – because he thought someone was following him.

'Well, it's not the cops,' I said reassuringly. 'They'd have hauled you in by now.'

Still, bells were ringing in my head. I remembered Lex saying this before, in Central Park. It wasn't something he was just making up now to sound interesting, or dope paranoia. And I had thought there was someone watching me when I came out of my building the other day to go to the gallery. I put this aside to think about later. My mention of the cops had reminded me of a pressing appointment he had.

I pulled out from my pocket the card Thurber had given me. 'By the way, you've got to go and talk to them. Ring them right now and get it over with.'

'What?' Lex jumped back from the card I was holding out as if it were Kryptonite and he was Superman. 'Are you mad?'

'Lex, you're going to have to sooner or later,' Kim pointed out reasonably. She yawned and stretched back her arms. 'God, I'm stiff. Maybe I should ask if I can have a game of bocci. Loosen my shoulders up a bit.' She nodded at the group of wizened and purposeful old men in caps who were playing bowls on a stretch of sand behind our bench. The game was hotly contested, but they were equally concentrated on hissing away any dog which strayed near them. I could understand that, from a dog's perspective, the sand would be pretty tempting: the grass in the park was manky at best. The bocci players didn't share this sentiment. One guy had a spare ball in his hand which he kept turning over while eyeing up every passing dog with a wistful gaze.

'Hey! You! Get that mutt outta here!' he shouted unfairly at a passing man with an exquisitely groomed little fluff of fur trotting innocently beside him.

'He is *not* a mutt,' the man retorted, theatrically wounded. 'He's a lhasa apso. Heel, Oscar!'

'Fairy,' said the frustrated bocci player.

'*Peasant*,' the man snapped back.

'Never a dull moment in Washington Square Park,' Laurence said.

Most of the dealers had already tried their luck with us, or rather Lex. Some people just attract that kind of attention. In fact he had rolled up and was now smoking happily away.

'You couldn't do this in London,' he had said. 'Not with people passing so close by.'

'Shit, that's nothing,' Kim said. 'I've seen people doing lines of coke on mirrors on their laps in clubs here.'

The kindbud hadn't helped to calm Lex down much. He was still eyeing Thurber's card as if it would take away all his superhuman powers.

'Lex, you idiot,' I said impatiently, dropping it in his lap, 'don't you realise you're off the hook?'

'You what?' He had been lying sprawled on the bench, legs splayed out, to Laurence's obvious annoyance. Lex had a physical ease, a confidence in his own attractive body, which skinny, nervous Laurence would never possess. Now he drew his legs under the bench, sitting up straight. 'Say that again?'

'You have an alibi for when Don was killed. Me. And the doorman. We can both say that as far as we know you didn't leave my building.'

'Sammy to the rescue,' Kim said cheerfully. 'Why don't you call them now, big guy? No time like the present. I'll come with you,' she offered. 'I don't have to be at work till ten.'

'Really?' Lex brightened up. 'I know I'm being a wimp. But it's not just the cops. I tell you, I'm sure someone's following me.'

'Who could it be?' I said doubtfully.

'Well, duh, the strangler,' Lex said crossly. 'I mean, why the fuck do you think I'm so worried?'

'But Lex, if the strangler's following you, what are they doing it for?' I pointed out. 'They can't be trying to frame you, because otherwise they wouldn't have killed Don when you had an alibi. And they haven't killed you yet, and there must have been plenty of opportunities.'

'The operative word being "yet",' Lex said darkly. 'That's why I want someone with me. You can't strangle two people simultaneously.'

'Maybe I should follow you,' I offered. 'See if I can spot whoever's doing it.'

'You're not taking this seriously,' Lex complained.

'It's not so bad to lighten up a bit,' Laurence said, re-entering the conversation from his own perspective. 'I just wish Suzanne could. I've never seen her like this. She thinks she's some kind of avenging angel.'

'Why wouldn't she say where she was going?' I asked him. Suzanne had left us outside the Mexican restaurant, intent on some hidden agenda of her own. Java and Kevin had peeled off too, but their attitude had spoken less of dark secrets to be tracked down than Sunday afternoon slacking.

He shrugged. 'I told you, she's obsessed with this. I'm sure she's trying to check out some theory about who killed Kate.'

'Don't you think it was the same person who killed this Don guy, then?' Kim asked him.

'Oh, I assume so. It's just – well, frankly, it's not because Don's dead that she's gone on this one-woman crusade.'

We fell silent, as if paying respect to the dead. In front of us, in the centre of the park, was a miniature amphitheatre, a sunken circle surrounded by rings of steps. In the middle sat a black guy, his face creased and lined into a rubbery mobility almost too expressive to be human. He had a big old amplifier next to him and a mike in his hand, and was holding spellbound the crowd of people sitting all around him on the steps, rapping, talking, singing the blues, taking whatever came into his head and turning it into a performance. A posse of young white kids sitting right in front of him were clapping along as he sang, yelling: 'Right on!' when he said something they particularly appreciated.

Most of them were dressed in army surplus and camouflage, mercenaries in the urban jungle who had bought big into the *Escape From New York* myth. As I glanced round the people in the amphitheatre I noticed a girl sitting on the steps with her back to us who, besides the inevitable oversized army overcoat, was wearing a knitted hat which looked oddly familiar. Maybe I'd tried it on in Urban Outfitters a few days ago. I couldn't help eyeing it up. It wasn't really me, but it might work anyway. I was becoming corrupted by New York street style.

'Right,' Lex announced nonchalantly, jumping to his feet. 'I'm off to turn myself in. You still coming with me?' he said to Kim more hesitantly.

'Sure. I mean, until I have to go to work.'

'Fine. Don't suppose you want to come too?' he said to Laurence and me.

'Yeah, right,' Laurence said nastily. 'Just how I wanted to spend my Sunday afternoon.'

Lex looked wounded. 'Sorry, mate,' he muttered, temporarily forgetting to sound American. 'I mean, it's me that's got to go and face the music.'

Laurence, abashed, was lost for words. Fishing in his pocket, he pulled out some gum, holding it out like a peace offering.

'Careful, Lex,' I said to lighten the mood. 'It's probably drugged. Rohypnol gum. He's going to drag you behind a bush and sexually abuse you.'

'Drugged *gum*?' said Lex blankly. 'I never heard of that.'

'Yeah,' Laurence said, playing along. 'I've just had one myself, actually. I always drop one when I'm out, just in case someone feels like taking advantage of me. I have to make it easy for them.' He gestured at his lanky frame self-deprecatingly. 'Come and get me, I'm semi-conscious, is basically the message I want to send.'

Kim and I were giggling by now. I took some gum and started chewing.

'God, the sky's very blue all of a sudden,' I announced.

'Oh dear, Sam's coming up on the gum. I must have got

out the wrong packet,' Laurence said, pretending to fumble in his other pocket. 'Don't worry, I've got some Wrigley's Downers somewhere . . . .'

We were laughing now, in the way that happens when the tension has been running high and everyone seizes gratefully on a funny moment as a blessed relief.

'Jesus, look at those squirrels!' Lex said, as one bounded right in front of us. They were the tamest I had ever seen, bouncing from one small square of grass to another like feathers on springs, quite unafraid of the many dogs in the park. The latter were on leads and clearly, being city dogs, were quite unused to chasing anything; they stared bemused as the squirrels ran rings around them contemptuously.

'Whoah!' Kim exclaimed, as a blader shot towards us just as a squirrel dashed across the path; there was an instant of confusion and then the girl jumped into the air, right over the happily oblivious body of the running squirrel, landing neatly on the other side with a smack of her wheels. We all clapped. She kept going, acknowledging the applause with a flip of her fingers.

'Good luck, Lex,' I said as they turned to go.

He swallowed hard, his Adam's apple bobbing.

'Yeah, right.'

'Sam!' Kim swung round. 'We'll ring you later, OK? Or why don't you come in to the bar?'

'OK. Whatever.'

'Well,' Laurence said when they had gone, stretching out his long thin limbs on the bench now that Lex was no longer there to compete with. 'The afternoon stretches in front of us like an unrolling carpet richly embroidered with possibilities.'

'You don't much like Lex, do you?' I said bluntly, noticing how much he had relaxed with the latter's exit from the scene.

Laurence looked embarrassed. 'He's got a lot of charm,' he said. 'But don't you think he's rather loud and childish?'

'If you look at it right that's all part of the charm. He's this bad little boy who women want to mother.'

'But not you.'

'Nope. I have the maternal instincts of a nanny with Münchhausens by proxy.'

'Tasteless,' Laurence said appreciatively. 'So tell me, is there something weird and suspicious about Lex being over here early?' He was horribly acute.

'Why d'you say that?' I was instantly wary.

'I just got the feeling there was more to it than he was saying.'

'I think he was embarrassed he'd been caught out in the city without having come in and said hello to everyone at the gallery,' I suggested. 'Shall we walk a bit? I'm getting stiff just sitting here.'

We stood up and started strolling across the park, heading towards the south-west corner. It hadn't distracted Laurence, though.

'Lex doesn't strike me as being that socially sensitive,' he commented witheringly. Laurence really was very like Hugo: the intellect without the sexiness. 'I still think there's something more to it.'

'When are Mel and Rob due over here?' I said, wanting to slide away from this weak point. 'Wednesday, isn't it?'

'Yup. So what are they like?'

'Well, Mel's quiet, almost withdrawn. But you get the feeling that there's loads of stuff swirling around beneath the surface. She's got this reputation for being pretty obsessive, but I haven't seen any sign of it. Mind you, I don't know her that well. Rob seems nice and easy-going. A bit boring. Lex and I are definitely the loudmouths of the group.'

'Do they drink much? I don't think BLT could take four Brits with the alcohol problems of you and Lex. Needy and addictive,' Laurence quoted winningly. 'I wanted to ask Java for some help cards for the pair of you.'

'Piss off,' I said, grinning.

We passed a group of little folding tables, each with a chess set on top and a very bored man sitting behind them.

'Chess hustlers,' Laurence said absently.

But the only table with a customer at it bore a neat handwritten sign which read: 'My name is STEVE. I am a chess teacher. I can teach you. NO GAMBLING.'

'No gambling, no drinking. The new puritans,' Laurence said, 'purged of the sins of the flesh. Plenty of 'em around.'

'Which reminds me,' I said thoughtfully. 'Talking of the sins of the flesh.'

I had got Lex to give me Leo's phone number. I wanted to go dancing tonight, and it would be a bonus if I could lubricate my energy channels with some magic powder. Tom would have shot me down in flames for that metaphor, but he wasn't here, and I hadn't said it out loud.

'Let's go and find an unvandalised phone,' I suggested. 'And then maybe we could cruise up to Urban Outfitters. There's a hat I want to try on.'

* * *

The toilets of the Angelika Film Center were the most foul I had ever seen in a long life of attending cutting-edge cinema. The queue stretched right out into the downstairs lobby, and when I finally reached the head I realised why. Two of the toilets were blocked and the door of the third wouldn't lock; it kept swinging open while the occupant was still engaged in whatever she was doing. When I finally emerged into the lobby I was feeling dazed, a sensation which the ultraviolet lighting did nothing to dispel. It was like tripping underwater, if you imagined the water bright mauve and the sea bed thick carpet; the violet slowed you down, made you dizzy, and threw in the weird white gleam of strangers' teeth and eyeballs into the bargain. I was glad to locate Laurence – impossible to miss, with the UV lights mercilessly highlighting his dandruff – and head upstairs.

'I can't believe we went to see that,' Laurence said as we pushed our way through the self-consciously arty black-clad filmgoers in the entrance lobby. They should twin this place with the Hampstead Everyman.

'It was worth it for the curiosity value alone,' I argued. 'And we laughed.'

'We certainly did.'

'That bit where they find her in the jungle—'

'Wearing mascara, and that pair of panties she'd somehow managed to weave out of plant stalks—'

'And then they take her back to civilisation and find out that apart from being Demi Moore, which you would have thought quite enough of a disability in itself, she's deaf and dumb as well.'

'My favourite bit was when she tries on the tights for the first time and starts stroking her legs in girlish wonder—'

'No, no, when she puts on the wimple and looks at herself in the mirror—'

'—and you see Brad Pitt behind her turn away sadly because he's lost her to the Carmelites—'

'Oh God, I nearly wet myself laughing.'

'Thank God we saw it here. They'd have thrown us out of a multiplex.'

'There were lots of other people laughing.'

'Not like us.'

'And the bit—' I started giggling again '—right at the end, when she sees the jungle out of her cell window, and starts talking to herself in the mirror in sign language about whether she should go back or not.'

'God knows what she'd wear for knickers, they must have thrown her plant-stalk ones away when she joined the nuns.'

'Maybe she wove herself a new pair every morning,' I suggested. 'Hygenic, with a built-in deodorant . . . . New! Jungle Chlorophyll Fragrance For All-Day Intimate Freshness!'

'Ugh, I hate the word "intimate", it's so knowing,' Laurence said.

'I have to go,' I announced. 'I said I'd meet Leo at eight.'

'Go with God,' Laurence said sourly. I hadn't actually told him I wanted to get hold of some coke, but he had a pretty good idea of why I was meeting Leo, and he didn't approve. And I doubted that he would be mollified if I said that I also intended to see if Leo had any theories about who might have killed Kate.

'I take it that means you don't want to come,' I said.

'I'd just slow you down,' Laurence said. 'You don't need the protection of skinny little me in Alphabet City. It'd be the other way around.'

'Laurence,' I said firmly, 'bitter is not attractive. Anyway, thin for boys is in at the moment. Look how tiny those men's shirts were in Urban Outfitters.'

'The printed nylon ones? Thanks a bunch. I sweat plenty as it is.'

'It's a shame about that hat,' I said wistfully. 'I could have sworn that was where I saw it.'

'Trust me,' Laurence said. 'We took a fine-tooth comb to that store. No way that hat could have escaped us.'

And on that note we parted. I was glad to have a little time on my own; there was something nagging at me, something I hadn't yet pinned down but thought I might if I had half an hour to myself. I doglegged up from Houston Street, across towards the East Village, counting the streets off with the ease of nearly a week's practice. I was meeting Leo at a coffee shop on 2nd Avenue and I was early, not having realised how close I was.

Ordering a cappuccino and an organic strawberry muffin, I sat down, still deep in thought. The coffee shop was cosy in a Fifties-meets-late-Nineties way, done up in pale blue with scarlet plastic booths at the back beyond the counter, for people who wanted to be private, and small tables in post-modernist retro Formica at the front for the rest of the world to check each other out. Everyone was keeping an eye on the new arrivals to see if they could up their cool points by knowing more people than anyone else.

A magazine rack hanging from the central pillar offered *Harpers*, *Newsweek*, and a selection of leftie papers I'd never heard of. Above them was a sign saying: 'Instant Karma #457: depriving someone of enjoying the magazine you just read by taking it with you'. A girl glided in and over to the counter in one smooth swift movement which made me blink until I realised that she was on blades. The ramps for handicapped access must have been the best news for bladers since kneepads. As so often in New York, I felt as if I were on a film set.

The guy sitting next to me had his own soundtrack playing on a Walkman, his woolly hat keeping in the earpieces. He hadn't taken off his big coat either, which was par for the course. Everyone in this town seemed to live in a perpetual hurry, needing to be in Place B even before they had sat down in Place A. It was a never-ending competition to show that they were busier than the next person.

I looked at him again and a little bubble burst inside my head. The woolly hat . . . the big coat . . . the Walkman . . . suddenly I felt extremely clever. The only trouble was I had no one to share my brilliance with. Where was Laurence when I really needed him?

'Hey,' Leo said, dropping into the other chair. He pulled it up to the table and stretched his legs out, letting his head fall to one side. 'Man, I am sleepy. I am whacked out.'

He looked even more dirty and disreputable than he had yesterday. His clothes smelt rank and his beard was well beyond designer stubble territory, reminding me of one of Tom's most heartfelt and biting poems from the facial hair sequence of his 'My Miserable So-called Holiday In India' book. In England Leo would doubtless have had a blonde, upper-class girlfriend called Camilla or Melissa who lived at the posh end of Ladbroke Grove and thought it was frightfully daring of her to be slumming it with a dirty dealer boyfriend. Though actually that type preferred black guys if possible; better to get all their shock value in one package. Then they could settle down happily with a Toby or Piers, content in the knowledge that they had had their brief moment of rebellion.

I said some of this to Leo. Though I hardly knew him, I had the instinct that this would amuse him, and it did.

'Shit, I'm in the wrong place,' he commented. 'Here everyone's majorly into money. I mean, you wouldn't get rich girls doing that kinda thing. They've already got their eyes fixed on their first marriage, the divorce, the next marriage – no time to piss around with lowlifes like me, you know?'

'This friend of mine who was in Los Angeles told me that if you chat up a girl there she asks you straight away what kind of car you drive.'

'Oh yeah. Here too. I mean, people don't drive much, but yeah, the status thing is very big. NY's better than LA, though. Here people are more real. Either they like you or they tell you to fuck off. In LA everyone's much falser. Like, they'll try to be friendly to get information and they'll stab you in the back at the same time. But they're more relaxed. In this city people are way more stressed out.'

He grinned at me.

'You don't look stressed,' I said.

'Yeah, well. I do that kundalini yoga, you know? Breath of fire.'

Long experience with guys like Leo had taught me that the best thing to do would be to let that comment go, in case he was bullshitting me. So I did.

'Hey, man, you got a cigarette for me?' said the guy at the next table, leaning over with friendly familiarity.

'Sure, man.' Leo reached in his pocket and tapped a cigarette out of a battered packet. The guy nodded his thanks and went back to his paper.

'They let you smoke in here?' I asked as Leo lit one up for himself.

'Hey, this is the East Village. The entire area's one big smoking zone.' He shoved the packet back into his pocket. 'Shall we go?'

In London, East 2nd Street would have been generously wide. After 2nd Avenue, it seemed as narrow as a Soho alleyway, and lit with the same occasional glare of ugly light – yolk-yellow or flaring red – from filthy-looking corner shops which optimistically called themselves delicatessens. Clearly the same standards of cleanliness prevailed in corner shops the world over, right down to the fruit and vegetables displayed on the sidewalk, marinating in exhaust fumes.

'We got a little way to go,' Leo said. The chain swinging from his waist knocked against his legs with every step, clinking on the metal button that fastened the huge pocket at his knee. It was practically the only sound; the streets were very quiet, and Leo was one of those men who speak only when he has something to say. Occasionally someone passing us would greet him, and once he paused briefly on a street corner to give a gangsta-style handclasp to a boy propping up a fire hydrant.

We turned onto Avenue B, heading for the Lower East Side. Steam was pouring up like smoke from the huge gratings in the centre of the road, dissolving into delicate wisps just after it reached the surface, as if it faded the further it went from the underworld. I found myself imagining that the tarmac was only a thin crust, like the earth's, and below it was something alive, blowing great gusts of cigarette smoke up through the cracks to remind us of its existence. New York was a city built for giants; it made sense that they would be down there, drawing on their cigarettes, waiting for the day they would come up from the depths and take over. Finally there would be people walking down these streets who were in proportion to them.

'This way,' Leo said laconically, ducking into an alley running down the side of a large and dilapidated building. Unusually, its fire escape was at the back: I was used by now to seeing houses disfigured by the thick tracery of Zs criss-crossing their frontages, though occasionally the fire escapes had a strange beauty of their own, like heavy white lacework. It was easy to see one of the reasons this building had been squatted. The back fire escape gave discreet access to all areas.

It didn't reach the ground. Leo had already jumped up to grasp the overhead strut of metal, and was chinning it, grabbing a foothold as he went. I followed suit, saying a silent prayer of thanks, as so often, to the person who invented Lycra miniskirts. Apart from being easy to execute gymnastics in, they were so versatile; how many outfits would take you so effortlessly from brunch to shopping to swinging around on the fire escapes of squatted buildings?

'Thought I'd need to pull you up,' Leo said, eyeing me assessingly. 'Not many girls can do that on their own. You work out?'

'Not as much as I should.'

'Good upper body strength,' he said approvingly. Everyone here was obsessed with fitness, even the druggies.

We went up four flights of rickety iron steps, along a narrow walkway, and paused while Leo undid three padlocks attached to a large and well-fitting iron door. At this height there was a breeze, dirty and polluted but nonetheless welcome, which wrapped itself round my neck and, percolating down to street level for a moment, rattled the dustbin lids in the yard behind the building, moving on immediately, restless and curious, looking for something better from the night.

The clank of chains and padlocks dropping behind me sent an involuntary shiver down my spine. The decay of these half-ruined buildings, each door as bolted and barred as a prison cell, the shapes of people flitting in and out, sleeping by day, on the move at night, was pure Edgar Allan Poe remade for the 1990s. It was easy to imagine someone walled up in one of these rooms and left to die.

Leo was opening the door, and I shook myself hard. The twisted romance of the moment was all New York, the unfamiliar sirens in the distance, the skyscrapers on the horizon. I couldn't see my imagination running equally riot about an identical squat in Hackney.

'Welcome to the jungle,' Leo said, gesturing that I should enter. 'Let's see if the electricity's working today – yeah.' He flicked a switch and a gentle light flooded the room.

There were canvases in various stages of composition hung on the walls and propped all around the room. But the walls had been painted, too, with a series of unfamiliar symbols, and they were the first thing I saw. I stared at them, assessing their power, and my hackles stayed down as I saw that the symbols remained where they were, neither reaching out to draw me in nor projecting malevolence. They weren't benign; but nor were they black magic.

Now I could look round the rest of the room. A big futon in the corner made me immediately nostalgic for my own. Nancy's mattress was like a feather bed by comparison, and every morning, half-drowned in it, I had to drag myself out of the trough dug by my own body. The far corner held a large and battered music system, stained with paint like a plasterer's radio. Behind a screen was a sink with a bucket underneath, and a toilet, both so chipped and battered that they had probably been rescued from a skip. A long trestle table against the right-hand wall was stacked with a weird assortment of paint and brushes. The room smelt, familiarly, of turps and paint and the faint cat-pee smell of dirty water.

'You must paint pretty much full-time,' I said, propping myself on the arm of the ancient sofa which faced the equally broken-down TV. Leo had rigged up a series of small lights on a dimmer strung round the walls, and the light was diffused and cosy. I felt at home here; it reminded me not only of my own studio, but all the rooms friends of mine had occupied over the years, squats or co-op houses or sub-let council flats.

He shrugged, looking almost embarrassed, as he closed the door and started re-locking the padlocks, now on the inside. 'Yeah. As much as I can afford. Though I get free paint from the hardware store down the street, when they've mixed the colours wrong, or got the wrong order – and you can pick up frames on the street often, you'd be amazed what people junk in this city. I don't really have much space to store stuff, though, mostly I'll just cut up the old ones, or paint over them, or give them away . . . .'

His tone had changed. I recognised all too well his defensiveness and insecurity, coupled with the necessarily exaggerated self-belief a struggling artist needs to keep going in the long lonely wilderness years alone with the work.

'I like these,' I said, looking closely at the one leaning against the table, almost in front of me. It was enormous but strangely delicate, thickly crusted with tiny pieces of glass, the shatterproof kind that breaks into miniature crystals. The effect reminded me of the fire escapes I had been thinking of earlier, the way some of them managed to combine a fragile beauty with a sense of their sheer heaviness. I was surprised when Leo jumped up and turned the painting away from me.

'I was looking at that!' I protested.

'Yeah, well. Whatever. I mean, you didn't come here to look at fucking paintings, did you?' he said with an unpleasant tinge creeping into his voice, already fetching a big sheet of mirror from where it was leaning behind the TV. 'Let's get down to business, OK?' he continued in the same vein. 'I'll give you a sample of the merchandise. I hate all that crap when people feel they've got to be friends with their dealer. Make nice about his paintings and shit like that.'

'God, you're defensive,' I said crossly. 'I can look at your fucking paintings if I want to.'

He was shaking a packet of coke onto a small electronic scale, but he looked up at me, his face twisted into a grimace. It was an unpleasant stare, meant to intimidate me, but it didn't. For some reason I was not at all afraid of Leo. I looked back at him coolly and after a while said:

'Are we going to do some drugs or are we just going to stare each other down all evening?'

Date Due Receipt

Library name: ROAK_65

Author: Gowdy, Barbara.
Title: Mister Sandman : a novel
Item ID: 39082096194256
Date due: 5/11/2012,23:59

Author: Henderson, Lauren.
Title: The strawberry tattoo
Item ID: 39082088408243
Date due: 5/11/2012,23:59

Borrowers Take Note: The ROPL daily overdue [illegible] been increased from [illegible] The fine for [illegible]s remains at [illegible] at www.ropl.

It broke the tension, though it didn't help his mood. He muttered something and went back to weighing me out a couple of grams.

'Here,' he said, drawing out a couple of lines onto the mirror with the skill of long practice. I bent down and hoovered one up, swallowing as I felt the chemical hit dripping down the back of my throat.

'So you're an old friend of Kim's?' Leo said as he bent to do his.

'Yeah, we go back at least ten years.'

'You English chicks all that fit?' Leo said. 'Kim can chin herself up my fire escape too.'

'She's been hitting the gym a lot since she came here,' I said, feeling the sharp bright rush of cocaine swirling through my bloodstream.

'Shit, you're telling me. You should have seen her a couple of weeks ago. Swinging on that bar like she was an Olympic gymnast. Pretty damn impressive.'

'I thought you guys hadn't seen each other for a while,' I said, surprised.

Leo was tapping off the contents of the scale into a wrap, but he shot me a glance. It was sly and knowing and sexy too, if you liked that bad-boy thing.

'That what she told you? Nah, Kim drops in every once in a while, when she gets off her shift at the bar. Four in the morning, whatever. I stay up all night.'

Surveying the room again, I noticed something that hadn't struck me before. There was no door other than the one to the fire escape. I had assumed that this was a shared house, and its occupants used the fire escape to keep any ground-floor doors and windows permanently fortified against a possible raid by the police. I hadn't realised that Leo had no contact with the rest of the building.

I asked him, and he smiled, a deliberately cynical smile.

'Hey,' he said, 'that's how we like it. None of this house-sharing shit. I have my space, they've got theirs, and that's it. Guy who lives on the top floor runs the place, collects the rent and the utilities charge. It's just like your apartment, only we don't got no doorman or elevator.'

Weirdly enough, I liked the idea of having a room like this, clinging to the side of a half-abandoned building, with a reinforced steel door padlocked against the world, high up in the air with just a steel staircase outside for access. My studio was the first permanent place of my own, and before that I had lived on the move and come to like it. That sense of rootlessness, of waking up every day unsure of where you were and where you would sleep that evening, rolled over me like a cloud of nostalgia.

Leo was staring at me curiously.

'What's up?' he asked.

'I like your room,' I said.

'Hey,' he said, less aggressively, 'so do I.'

'How do you manage to get enough light to work with?'

'I do most of my painting up on the roof,' he said. 'When the weather's good. It's a blast.'

'I bet it is.'

'You're a sculptor, right?' he said, sounding almost friendly.

I nodded. 'Big metal mobiles. You should come to the show and see them. Lex is showing too.'

He pulled a face. 'No disrespect, but I had a look at what's on at the moment, right? The wicked stepmother. Didn't exactly ring my bell.'

'The wicked stepmother?'

'That's what Kim calls her. Boy, has she got her knife into that woman. Makes her sound like Eva Braun and Cruella de Ville rolled into one.' He dropped a wrap in front of me. 'Two Gs. Like you asked for. You want to do a bit more now?' Without waiting for my answer he pulled the mirror onto his lap again. 'Yeah,' he continued. 'I tell you, if it was that Bilder woman that got whacked, I would have suspected Kim even if she was here sitting in front of me at the critical moment. You know what I'm saying? Even if I was her goddamn alibi.' He tipped out some more cocaine onto the mirror. 'So. You're the old friend who knows her from way back.' He shot me another of the Leo looks, wily, mocking and loaded with sexual innuendo.

'You should know if anyone does,' he said, almost taunting me. 'Did she do it? What do *you* think?'

CHAPTER NINETEEN

Leo was a key merchant: it was like saying OJ was guilty or Bill Clinton's girlfriends needed kneepads, one of those simple uncontestable statements so precious in a life full of doubts and uncertainties.

He waited to see if I would take the bait. I didn't. So he just grinned and said:

'I tell you, it got me wondering, though. Like, did Kim trash the show? Maybe someone put her up to it and she didn't know about Kate being killed.' His voice became serious. 'You know Kate and I were going steady for a while, right? Which was pretty unusual for me, I can tell you.'

He sectioned off two little hillocks of white powder with a razor blade and flicked them into parallel lines. 'I'm not exactly the faithful type. There's always girls coming around in the middle of the night.'

He flicked a glance at me to see if I had picked up this oblique reference to Kim. He had a streak of malice a yard long.

'But Kate was different,' he continued, bending over to do his line. 'Shit, I hate seeing myself in this fucking mirror,' he complained as he straightened up. 'Looking up my nostrils, see all my nose hair and pimples.'

'I've got a friend who uses a black mirror tile. Much more flattering.'

'That's a great idea. I'm gonna get one. Anyway. Kate. She was pretty fucking special. Did you ever meet her?'

'Just briefly. But I liked her a lot.'

'That girl broke my fucking heart,' Leo said, handing me the mirror. 'Just my luck. I fall for her because she's really got her shit together. She was so driven. I really admired her, you know? Total career woman. Majorly ambitious. And of course that turns out to be why she dumps me. Because I'm a fucking bum who lives in a pit like this, trying to be a painter.'

I passed the mirror back to him, having cleared its contents. I seemed to remember heroin use having been mentioned by Don and Suzanne, but instinct, not to mention manners, told me not to bring it up. Instead I clicked my tongue sympathetically.

'I've done all kinds of stuff, job-wise,' Leo went on. 'I mean, I'm not just this.' He gestured briefly to the mirror and the scales. 'I got this gig for a while testing cocaine for a drug abuse centre, can you believe it? They stick you in this big brain scanner and give you a shot of the stuff and you have to register how high you're getting.'

He could see I looked disbelieving. 'No, really,' he insisted. 'Then you start coming down, you get the jitters, and you tell them when you start wanting more. All the time they're monitoring your brain patterns. Nice gig, huh? And they pay you, too. I got two hundred and fifty bucks credit at a supermarket last time. Only downside is that they give you this lecture afterwards on how drugs are really dangerous. But they're just going through the motions 'cause they have to. I mean, if there weren't any drugs, they'd all be out of jobs, right?' He ran his finger over the mirror, cleaning it up. 'And I've done foot modelling.'

'You mean like hand modelling for magazines?' I said, baffled. Somehow I couldn't see Leo at a photo-session wearing white silk socks and polished shoes.

'Nah,' he said dismissively. 'Foot fetish stuff.'

I looked down at his work boots.

'Don't take this personally, but they look a normal sort of size to me. I would have thought they'd want really big ones.'

'It's mainly the width they go for,' Leo informed me. 'This guy, the photographer, was a total width queen. I'm just a 10 but I'm an E. And bony, which they like too. You can see the veins more.'

'The things you learn.'

'Weird, huh?' Leo agreed. 'You wouldn't believe the stuff these freaks do to feet. I've got my video if you want to see it.'

He got up and fished it out from the pile of other videos beside the TV. I didn't recognise Leo's feet from the teasing cover photo; it was the title which really gripped me.

'*Down And Dirty – An X-Rated Feet-ure*,' I read.

'Easiest five hundred bucks I ever earned,' Leo assured me.

'You just have to sit there, right?' I said dubiously.

'Most of the time I read a magazine,' he said. 'But then I stopped because I was getting distracted. Like, some of the stuff they do is pretty nice, and when you forget about who's doing it to you, it's not too hard to start getting off on it, you know what I'm saying? Which was pretty goddamn strange.'

A silence fell as we both contemplated this image.

'I saw you checking out my hex symbols earlier,' he said eventually. 'But I could tell you were cool with them. I got a lot of them from a book and then added my own stuff too. Sort of modified them.'

'What are they for?'

'Protection,' said Leo, very simply.

I looked again at the hexes. In my head I heard, as clearly as if it had been playing on Leo's stereo, the Massive Attack song of that name: Tracey Thorn's clear dark voice, bittersweet as smoky molasses, singing about protection.

The symbols came into focus, their strong powerful shapes seeming to float forwards as I concentrated on them. Out of the corner of my eye I saw Leo watching me: Leo, tough as nails, with his East Village squat and his three padlocks on the door, still wanting old Pennsylvania Dutch hexes round his walls to ward off evil. Oddly enough, I realised that I identified with him. Leo reminded me strangely of myself, or of someone I might have become: rootless, edgy, deliberately emphasising my dark side, refusing to connect with anyone for more than a few fleeting moments, living in a cave with a chain on the door. It was a way of life I had rejected when I'd been knocking around London, restless and unfocused but too wary, too self-protective, ever to follow that path. I was stronger than Leo. I didn't need hexes on my walls. But then, I was luckier, too. I had my own studio, my territory. I didn't need to mark it as he had his.

'You should make paintings of these,' I suggested, and as I did I knew I had said something significant. I shivered, a rush of memory and precognition swirling together through my head as I remembered Nat telling me years ago that my first sculpture, the Thing, looked like a fallen meteor. Leo would make his hex paintings, and they would be a success. I was willing to bet on it.

But, like me when Nat had made that comment, Leo only half took it in, thinking about something else.

'I offered to paint Kate's apartment, too,' he said. 'Customise something for her. I went through some books, found some stuff supposed to be specially for women, you know? But she said no.' He was staring at the hexes on the wall, but I knew that he could see Kate's face beyond them. 'I wish she'd let me do it,' he said quietly.

'She didn't die there, Leo,' I said, in an effort to console him.

He shrugged. 'It might have helped, though. You never know.' He took a long deep breath. 'It might have helped.'

We both fell silent again. I was imagining Kate's body on a bench in Central Park, waiting there, motionless, for dawn to rise and someone to find it, dew settling heavy and damp on her dark red hair. What Leo was seeing I couldn't tell. Perhaps her apartment as it would have been with his white magic in place, the walls loaded with paint.

'Protection,' Leo said. He was still staring at the hexes. 'We all need some, man,' he said slowly. 'We all fucking need some.'

* * *

Leo's room was a time capsule: the world stopped as you stepped over the threshold and the padlocks snapped shut behind you. When I emerged into the darkness of the night I felt weirdly disoriented. Though, on reflection, maybe that was the cocaine. Leo offered to see me down, but I declined, waiting on the iron walkway to hear him lock himself in again like a prisoner returning voluntarily to his cell. Or an urban guerilla monk in a futuristic film. This would make a perfect twenty-first century, Lower East Side version of a monastery.

I rang Kim from a payphone in the first hole-in-the-wall bar I found. Over the pounding drum and bass at Hookah she yelled to come over and I thought I heard her say that Lex was there too, which was exactly what I had been hoping for. I set off at once. Hookah wasn't far, and the cocaine jet-propelled my boots. I extracted my new hat from my bag and put it on, pulling it down over my brows in best homegirl style. It was horribly unflattering, but the dark helped with that. And I needed to look as anonymous as possible.

It was easier than I had been expecting. There was nowhere really to hang out opposite Hookah's frontage, just a couple of store fronts shuttered and barred so heavily the owners had probably been ram-raided a few times already. If that had caught on over here. Maybe we could add it to a list of Cool Britannia cultural exports, along with the Spice Girls and dead sharks.

Beyond the shop fronts, however, was a doorway slightly recessed from the street. It too was barred, and slumped in front of it was a human form. Not someone sleeping rough, though. The figure was huddled up bulkily in its coat, but that was all: no other insulation, not even newspaper, on a night as cold as this one. As I walked up to it, a glance darted at me out of the shadows, a brief glimmer of streetlight reflecting off two eyeballs which gleamed flat and orange for a second before the head ducked again, out of the illumination. If I had needed any further confirmation that this wasn't a street person, this was it.

I stopped in front of the huddled body. Tension radiated from it, every inch of its body willing me to go away. It was like a clockwork toy, wound up to the last turn of the key, just about to explode into action. Ignoring the danger signals, I squatted down, my eyes on a level with the orange ones.

'Mel?' I said. 'It's Sam.'

Total silence. I tried again.

'Do you want to go and get a drink or something?'

No answer. Well, that approach always worked with me. I couldn't see her eyes now. Maybe she was working on the ostrich principle: if she couldn't see me I couldn't see her.

'Mel, I'm not going to go away,' I said patiently. 'I know it's you. Look,' I added cunningly, 'I know everything Lex's been doing over the last few days. I could tell you all about it . . .'

Open Sesame. Or Arise Sesame. Mel must have been in that doorway quite a while, because she was so stiff and cramped it took her a long time to get to her feet. Finally, with the aid of the bars on the door behind her, she managed it. We stared at each other for a moment, and then I turned, heading for a bar I had passed earlier. Mel's footsteps dogged my own, walking just behind me. Maybe once you developed the habit of following someone it was hard to give it up.

* * *

The bar was a nasty-looking cod-Irish place with coloured fairy lights strung haphazardly outside its narrow frontage; through the dirty little panes of glass in the door I could see plastic booths and a fake fire. We didn't go in, though not on aesthetic grounds. Once Mel had started walking she wouldn't stop, ceaselessly patrolling a circle around Second and Fifth, with Hookah – and Lex – at its centre. Any time it looked as if we were straying too far, she brought us back again, retracing our steps as if pulled by a magnet.

'How did you know it was me?' was the first thing she said.

'I didn't know,' I admitted. 'I just guessed.' I wasn't going to tell her that at first I had thought it was Suzanne following Lex; Suzanne, who had seemed hostile to him, who was so often absent on mysterious business of her own, who had declared her intention to track down Kate's killer . . . But I felt it would just confuse Mel to demonstrate my lack of omniscience. 'Lex kept saying someone was stalking him,' I continued, 'and after a while I started to take him more seriously—'

'He knows!' Mel's voice rang out happily, cutting through my explanation. 'He knows there's someone there! That means he can sense my presence. There's a connection between us, don't you see? There's a real connection.'

I took a deep breath. It was a dark night, and despite the yellowish pools cast on the pavement by the occasional streetlight, Mel was half in shadow, hands thrust into the pockets of her coat, head ducked. Still, I was shocked by the change in her. There were dark hollows under her eyes and cheekbones; something was eating her from inside, consuming flesh she could ill afford to lose. And her eyes were too bright, as if she were feverish. I thought of the strange nervous energy of tuberculosis victims, high spots of colour on their pale cheeks, eyes burning like an Edgar Allan Poe heroine. Two references to Poe in one evening: New York was certainly showing me its darker side.

'What exactly happened between you and Lex?' I asked. 'Was it after we all went out that evening?'

Once Mel had started telling me, she couldn't stop talking. Apparently she and Lex had bumped into each other at a do the week after our meeting in the pub, got drunk and fallen into bed. A one-night stand which Mel had built up in her mind to exaggerated proportions. She recounted every banal little detail as disappointed lovers always do, turning over the tiniest sentence or action, handling it obsessively until it's worn away and grubby with use, trying to make it yield proof that they are loved after all.

'. . . so then he said he'd call me, but I didn't hear from him for three days, but then I thought, oh, he probably doesn't want to call me at home because Phil's there – that's my boyfriend—' she added casually '—so I called him, and I got his machine, so I left a message saying that Phil was out all the next day and he could ring me then, but he didn't – well, someone did and hung up, and I 1471'd it but it was a payphone, so I thought: maybe it's Lex and he's run out of money . . .'

I had half-tuned this out, listening only to see if the flow would throw up something more significant. It was appalling to hear, the familiar and terrible power one person's casual action has to throw a switch in another human being, unintentionally turning on a great explosion of emotion like water bursting through a dam.

'. . . so I got into ringing him and hanging up, he usually leaves the machine on, and if you're fast you can hang up just before it clicks on so it doesn't register someone's rung, but sometimes I'd want to hear his voice . . . then I heard he was going to New York early so I knew I had to come too.' She sounded deadly serious. 'I've got to find out what he's doing, what he wants – exactly what he wants, so I can be that for him. Once I work that out then everything will be all right, I know he likes me already, I've just got to work out what he wants and *be* it . . . .'

Perhaps it was doing her good to discharge all this sadness, pus purging itself from an open wound. I hoped so. I was still trying not to listen too hard in case Mel's story seeped into me, wrapped itself round my bones, and started eating away at me like corrosive acid.

Mel had stopped talking. She seemed to be expecting some kind of answer. I racked my brains quickly to summon up the last thing she had said.

'How did I know it was you?' I said.

She nodded.

'Well, I saw you around a couple of times. It was you who passed us outside Hookah a few nights ago, wasn't it? In a balaclava? And in Washington Square Park today I saw you sitting on the steps in front of us, in your overcoat, and your hat rang a bell. I thought I'd seen it in a shop, but I went back and looked, and it wasn't there . . . . Then I was in a coffee shop today, and a guy sitting next to me was wearing this woolly hat, pulled down over his headphones. And for some reason I remembered you wearing yours with your Walkman that time we all met up, and the pieces started fitting together.'

'Did you tell Lex?'

'No. I came to find you first. To make sure.'

'You were going to tell me what he's been doing,' Mel said intensely. She stopped walking. We were on a dark, narrow stretch of street, buildings looming over us on either side as if they were trying to meet and shut out the sliver of black sky completely. New York had a strange facility for concentrating you in the moment; perhaps it was the sense I always had here of living between inverted commas. The few cars that passed seemed miles away.

Mel was a shadowy silhouette whose expression I could not see. But I could feel her stare, utterly focused, scorching my face with its unhealthy heat. To give her too much information would be dangerous. Like the fact that Lex was seeing Kim, for instance.

'He's been hanging out,' I said, playing for time. 'He stayed over at mine one night. You were there the afternoon we came back there, weren't you? Me and Lex and my friend Kim and Leo? I sensed something when I went out later, as if someone was watching me, but I thought I was just being paranoid.'

'He's staying with her, isn't he?' Mel said suspiciously. 'And he's in the bar with her right now.'

I said easily:

'He was in a bar with me a few nights back. And he stayed over at mine.'

'I know,' said Mel, and there was something in her voice that I didn't like.

'Lex is just couch-surfing,' I said, keeping it light. 'He doesn't have anywhere to stay.'

'Now that girl's been killed,' Mel said instantly. 'He didn't tell me anything about her in London. He didn't even say he knew her.'

I wondered why Mel thought that Lex should have told her about his plans to stay with Kate.

'Everyone's running scared at the moment,' I said. 'Did you know that someone else at the gallery had been killed?'

'Lex went to the police station this afternoon,' she said, her mind still on one track only. 'That friend of yours went with him. They were in there for hours.'

'He was telling them about having stayed at Kate's flat till she was killed.'

'Well, *he* didn't do it,' she said at once.

I let a moment pass, and then said, picking my words with extreme caution:

'Do you know that because you were keeping an eye on him?' Tactfully, I had decided not to use the word 'stalking'. Mel might have thought it had negative connotations.

'He went to the cinema,' she said. 'By himself. Well—' her voice softened '—I was there too. He didn't know it, but I was there.'

'And then what did he do?'

'He bought some hash from a guy on the street. Then he went for a couple of drinks. He talked to the waitress. And then he went home.'

It was very neat; this was just what Lex had told me he had done. Sometimes when things correlate so perfectly it makes me even more suspicious.

'What did you do when he went home?' I asked. 'Did you hang around?'

'I waited,' she confirmed reluctantly. She had taken a couple of steps back and was now completely in shadow, pressed against yet another heavily barred set of windows. A light shone behind them, through the dark curtains. Each bar was as thick as my wrist. It would be like living behind the metal screens of a South London off-licence, passing the money through the grille, a sawn-off shotgun next to the cash register and a Doberman in the back room, bored and angry, battering at the plywood partition in a constant attempt to get at the customers.

Finally she said:

'I was there for a few hours. Then I went back to my hotel. But I stayed till four at least. I was waiting to see when Kate'd come back, but I was so tired by then I couldn't wait any longer.'

She said this almost defiantly, as if she were making an assertion that might be challenged. I looked at her hard, wishing I could see her face. Kate had been killed around midnight; in furnishing Lex with this alibi, Mel was giving herself one too. Her eyes gleamed in the dark, their whites the only feature I could distinguish. She looked eerie and half-mad.

'Where are you staying, Mel?' I said. 'Do you want to come back to mine? We could have a drink and talk about Lex.'

She shook her head violently.

'No,' she said. 'I don't want to talk to you about him any more. I wish I hadn't now.'

'It's good to get things out of your system every now and then,' I said. Whenever I try to sound understanding, I fail dismally, and this was no exception.

'Don't talk to me like a bloody agony aunt,' she said contemptuously. 'Or some BT ad. "It's good to talk," ' she mimicked viciously. 'Well, I don't want to talk any more. I want Lex and you're not helping me. What do you know, anyway? You could only keep him for one night, same as me. After that he went off with your friend.'

She had started to shift from one foot to the other, eager to get away from me.

'What are you going to do?' I said cautiously. I was treading on eggshells now and putting my foot down in all the wrong places. 'Are you going back to Hookah?'

'You'd like to know, wouldn't you?' she said. 'Maybe you're trying to find out what I'm doing so you can do it too. Are you?'

She didn't give me time to reply. Leaning forward, staring at me intensely, she almost spat the last two words in my face, spun round and was gone, running fast back down the street in the direction from which we had come. I could have caught up with her, but what would have been the point? If she didn't want to tell me where she was staying I couldn't follow her until I found out. She was so paranoid she would know at once if I were on her tail.

And I had to admit that I didn't want to follow her. As I watched her disappear into the shadows I felt as if a great weight had been lifted from me. Mel was infected with her obsession. A strong sense of contagion emanated from her, almost tangibly. The best comparison I could find was something from a horror film: her aura was like a fog which could wrap itself around you and eat your soul out.

CHAPTER TWENTY

I didn't want to tell anyone about Mel. No logical reason for that: it was pure superstition. Just as only the bravest of us can look hard at the worst ravages of nature, we shy away from the destruction caused by love; we press tranquillisers on the sufferer, trot out the usual clichés about time healing everything and run away as fast as we can. Love scares the shit out of most of us, and I'm no exception. In a weird, twisted way I found myself actually admiring someone who could give herself to it so completely.

So I felt oddly protective towards Mel. She might have crossed the line, but if it were kept quiet she would have much more chance of finding her way back over it again. And I would stay silent about it – as long as she hadn't garrotted anyone en route. That was my one stipulation.

In the meantime, I had work to do.

* * *

'Wonderful! It looks just wonderful!'

I basked happily in Carol's praise. This was the advantage to her being a no-bullshit kind of person; when she went overboard, it was clear that she meant it.

'Yeah, you've done a great job,' Laurence chimed in appreciatively. 'It's really clever the way it looks site-specific but doesn't have to be.'

We were in the upstairs gallery, in which the mobile hung between the two pillars, just as Don and I had envisaged it. Only a close glance would tell that the mobile had not actually crashed into the second pillar, but was resting against it; the angle at which I had rigged the supporting chains created a powerful optical illusion. I had to admit to a sneaking feeling of smugness. Any paintings hung here would have to compete hard to hold the attention. The heavy silver mass of the mobile was so charged with kinetic energy it looked as if it had smashed into the pillar just moments ago.

'Don has to take some of the credit too,' I said. 'We worked it out together.'

Mother, I cannot tell a lie. Actually this frankness was less due to my exquisite sense of honesty than to my wish to see the reaction Don's name would provoke, mentioned unexpectedly.

Carol, always in control, merely nodded briefly.

'Don is sorely missed,' she said, as if pronouncing an epitaph.

Laurence looked uncomfortable and Kevin looked sick. Which was no change in their reactions from the moment I had found the body. Suzanne, who was sitting behind her computer at the desk, didn't bat an eyelid. And Stanley, who was hovering nervously behind Carol like a satellite in danger of decompressing if it strayed too far from the mothership, flinched. I looked at him more closely. Stanley was interesting me more and more. He was as groomed as ever, but since the murders he had lost the glossy sheen which had been his signature. No longer did I associate his shine with that of a rich man's fingernails buffed to a high lustre; now it was plain old sweat and nerves.

It was definitely time to have a chat with Stanley.

'Sam, you've been a heroine to organise this all yourself,' Carol was continuing. 'I'd just like you to know how grateful we all are. Usually we do *not* expect our artists to have to install their own pieces – well, not to this extent.'

She was alluding to my having spent most of the morning up a stepladder with a drill in my hand. Nice of her to worry, but since that state was pretty much my idea of absolute happiness, she didn't need to bother.

'It was fine,' I reassured her. 'In a way I prefer doing it myself. And Kevin was a great help. Well, Laurence too, until his dust allergy started kicking in.'

A sour expression flitted across the latter's face. This was only the start for him and Kevin: now there were Lex and Rob's installations and Mel's paintings to hang. And since Mel had started her series of close-ups on the genital areas, her canvases – not to mention their subjects – were gigantic.

'Let's check out the one downstairs as well,' Carol said, heading for the stairs. 'I just know that this is going to look spectacular too.'

The second mobile didn't have the visceral, action-laden impact of the first; all it did was hang enormously in the middle of the room. But modestly I had to say I thought it did that damn well. I had really let myself go when I made it, knowing I had all the space I wanted, and I was very happy with the result, which was better, on purely aesthetic grounds, than 'Organism #2' upstairs. God, I hated the names I had to give them. Other people usually picked them for me. If it were up to me they'd just be 'Thing 14: The Return'. I could see that 'Organism #2' had a touch more intellectual credibility but I disliked it anyway.

'Organism #1' was a great silver seed pod, half-open, a series of strange silvery leaves and tendrils emerging from it like a monster in a science-fiction movie. This, again, was only how I saw it, and Carol would doubtless prefer me to keep the image strictly to myself. The catalogue notes drew comparisons which were much higher-class. The usual litany of pretentious babble, in other words. But hey, if it sold more pieces . . .

'Wow,' said Suzanne, who had followed us down. 'That's fabulous.'

This was exactly the kind of response I liked. I grinned at her.

'Isn't it just great?' Java said enthusiastically. She had been watching us as we hauled it up and most of her comments had been spot-on. Much more so than Kevin's. While a useful source of muscle, he had been a broken reed in the constructive-criticism department.

'Java was a lot of help,' I said to Carol, rendering favour for favour. 'She has an excellent eye.'

Carol smiled at Java, a brisk, acknowledging smile. 'Good. I'm glad to hear it,' she said. A neat tick had just gone in the column opposite Java's name on Carol's mental score-sheet. Five and you got a gold star; ten might even be a promotion.

I thought of my gallerist in London, Duggie, with his rounded paunch, his slightly stained waistcoats and his long-term feud with his partner in the gallery, an ex-boyfriend with whom he loved to squabble. Duggie had a series of brawny young American or Australian boyfriends. He liked them meat-fed from birth, with expensive white dentistry, like a surf god from a daytime soap. Thus he never ceased complaining about the assistants hired by Willie, his partner, who stocked the gallery with the effete aesthete type he preferred. I couldn't see Carol existing in that happy confusion for more than ten minutes: she'd walk in, sack everyone who wasn't up to scratch and energise the rest.

'OK,' Carol was saying, 'this is a great start. A really great start. This show is going to be a big success. Let's get everything else up here and play around with it a little. I have a pretty clear idea of where I want everything, but I'm open to suggestions. Laurence, Kevin, could you start bringing up the paintings first?'

The boys were dismissed. Kevin wasn't too happy but went off docilely enough. Laurence however, after shooting Carol a resentment-filled glare, slunk away, trailing bad attitude. I almost expected him to hiss like a villain in a Victorian melodrama.

'Sam, I'd just like to thank you again,' Carol said, taking my hand between both of hers and pressing it for a moment. 'You've been a real trooper. I can't tell you how much we appreciate this. Right, Stanley?'

Stanley jumped at the mention of his name, horrified that she had actually noticed his presence. Maybe he had thought that if he stood still enough he would be taken for an installation and mercifully overlooked.

'Oh yes, of course, absolutely,' he managed to burble with a sadly faint resurrection of his once oozing charm. 'Charming girl, wonderful . . . .'

Carol, favouring him with a look which indicated as clearly as a slap round the face that he should pull himself together, fast, turned back to me.

'When does everyone else get here? The other Brits?' I asked.

'Lex is here already. Well, you know that.' Carol's lips tightened a little. She was much too professional to express out loud her dislike for the whole situation, which was now generally known; once Lex had told the police that he had been staying at Kate's, he could scarcely try to keep the staff at the gallery in the dark. He had rung Carol this morning and told her. The gossip had spread at once. Carol, naturally, was furious at what she saw as Kate's act of disloyalty. Lex's behaviour had been less reprehensible, as he was not an employee of Bergmann LaTouche, but that didn't seem to have made Carol happier about it. I suspected that most of the anger which Carol was prevented from channelling Kate's way was being diverted onto Lex instead.

Stanley cleared his throat nervously. We both looked at him, expecting him to say something, but he flapped his hands to indicate that he hadn't meant to distract us. When Carol's gaze returned to me it had a distinctly long-suffering glaze to it. Stanley's weight was not inconsiderable, and he wasn't pulling a pound of it.

'And Mel and Rob are due in this afternoon,' she said. 'They're on the same flight.'

Which would mean that she would have sent a car for both of them, and thus wouldn't know that it contained only one occupant. Unless anyone bothered to tell her. I wondered if Rob knew the truth of Mel's earlier-than-anticipated visit to New York. It was quite probable. The London artist scene was small and more incestuous than Sunday lunch in Appalachia.

That solved one of my problems. Later on today I would know at least where Mel was supposed to be. I could leave it till then to work out what I thought the situation required.

'Sam, thanks again. I won't forget this,' Carol said to me, pressing my hand once again in a valedictory gesture as the boys emerged from the stairwell. An unfeasibly large painting by Mel was hoisted awkwardly between them, being much too big to fit in the lift.

'Careful with that!' she called.

I could hear Laurence's snarl quite clearly, so I assumed Carol could too. But she was too smart not to know about the discretion/valour connection. She confined herself to a raise of the eyebrows as Kevin and Laurence, puffing slightly, carried the painting over to the far wall under her supervision, propping it there. Carol went over to a bank of switches and turned up the spot-lighting till the white wall was suffused with gold, like sunlight on an Aegean village. It made a perfect background for the silver sheen of the mobile. Still, I doubted Carol's gratitude to me would extend to granting a demand that she leave that wall empty.

'OK, now hold it up,' she directed. 'I want to see how the light hits it.'

The enormous canvas rose slowly up the wall in the sweating grasp of two very pissed-off assistants who by now were as demoralised and miserable as the chained-up galley slaves in *Ben Hur*. It was mainly executed in what some hosiery and cosmetics manufacturers still unreconstructedly call flesh tones, by which they mean a pale beigey-pink. At the centre was a large and puckered dark brown area which I had no difficulty in identifying as what my Aunt Louise would have called the back bottom. But then I was already familiar – as the actress would have said to the bishop – with Mel's work.

'Which is this one?' Carol looked around for her notes.

'Over here, Carol,' Java said, coming round the desk with a plastic folder in her hand. 'It's called "Anal Mouth".'

I suppressed a terrible impulse to burst out laughing, imagining the caption to the press photo. 'Seen at the Bergmann LaTouche Gallery: Sam Jones's "Organism #1" in front of Mel Safire's "Anal Mouth".' I turned away to cover my giggles and found myself directly in front of Stanley. He was nodding his head to one side, repeatedly, in a way that I took first for a particularly neurotic tic and then realised was a request that I accompany him into the second room.

'What is it, Stanley?' I said, following him dutifully.

He wouldn't answer me until we were round the corner and out of sight, at least, of everyone else. Then he whispered, his eyes darting from side to side:

'I need to talk to you! Can we meet up in a couple of hours?'

'What's wrong with right now?'

It was a stupid question. Stanley's head started jerking, and this time it really was a nervous tic.

'No one must know!' he said frantically. 'We can't talk here!'

'Sure,' I said, by now dying to know what it was all about. 'When and where?'

'Three o'clock. The Staten Island ferry terminal. At Battery Park. Not a word to anyone!'

'I promise,' I agreed gravely.

Looking briefly relieved, his head relaxed to its normal position. Then the give-this-man-some-Prozac routine started up again.

'Quick! We must go back or they'll get suspicious!' he said, ushering me back into the main room. No one even seemed to have noticed our sixty-second absence, but Stanley stuttered something about having been showing me the facilities next door. Since it contained nothing remotely resembling a facility – unless he meant the power sockets – this was a pretty awful lie, and he compounded it by stammering unconvincingly. Stanley was the worst conspirator I had ever met.

* * *

Further proof of this was offered to me as soon as I stepped off the bus and looked around, shading my eyes against the sun. Crossing the street to the ferry terminal, I realised that to give it as a rendezvous was like telling someone to meet you at Port Authority or Bloomingdale's: there were far too many rendezvous points. Stanley wasn't outside the subway entrance. I went up the long curving concrete ramp to check out the main ticket office, but drew another blank. The massed rows of plastic seats inside were almost empty. It wouldn't have mattered if they were full to bursting. I would have been able to spot Stanley instantly from his nervous tic.

I would just have to keep circling till I found Super Spy. In the meantime I could do with a trip to the ladies' room. It was a bizarre contrast. The whole toilet area reeked of excrement, and yet the floors were wet with disinfectant whose sharp, would-be-fresh scent somehow made the smell of faeces even worse, like perfume on a rotting corpse. It was almost unbearable. I'm one of the least fastidious people I know, but though all the fixtures seemed clean enough, this was one of the few lavatories where I recoiled from touching anything without six layers of toilet paper between me and it. I had a sudden rush of sympathy for Tom. Maybe I hadn't taken all his dysentery stories seriously enough. I determined to put aside some quality time for him when I got back home.

As I came out of the toilets, the sun, streaming through the glass wall of the terminal, lit up the hall, brightening the shiny sweep of floor, exposing the dirt trodden into it by millions of commuters. Crossing the hall, I pushed open one of the glass doors, leaning on the concrete wall and looking at the water rippling into the distance, its surface beaten and teased by the wind into an endless flurry of tiny waves. London couldn't compete with this. I thought of the flat brownish waters of the Thames, and grimaced. Beyond and to my right was the Statue of Liberty, small and perfectly formed, yet provoking less of a reaction. As with so many totem landmarks, I had seen it so many times in replica that its reality was an anticlimax.

'Sam? Sam!' I looked down to see Stanley standing on the pavement below, waving up at me anxiously.

'Shall we go and sit on a bench over there?' I suggested as I came down the ramp, pointing towards the scrubby beginnings of Battery Park.

A few guided groups of tourists ambled past, but the river front was as relatively quiet as the City of London on a work-day afternoon. We found an unoccupied bench with ease. On the next one were a couple of girls flirting loudly and happily with a young man who was scuffing his trainers on the ground in the traditional shy peacocking of the mating ritual. Apart from their gold jewellery, the three of them were dressed completely in black, from their leather jackets to their hooded sweaters and the girls' high-heeled shoes. Even their faces were the colour of that expensive dark chocolate which guarantees at least seventy per cent cocoa solids. They looked smart and shiny and well-to-do, all the attributes that Stanley had so noticeably lost since I first met him. And they certainly weren't interested in eavesdropping on our conversation.

'OK, Stanley, what's going on?' I asked.

He was too nervous to beat around the bush, for which I was grateful.

'Do you – do you know where Lex Thompson is?' he said in a rush.

I was taken aback, but not so much as to blurt out that Lex would almost definitely, from this evening, be staying in the Gramercy Park Hotel, into which Carol had booked him and the others. If I pointed out that very obvious fact, Stanley might simply run off to the hotel, waiting for Lex to show up. And I wanted to find out what was up with him first.

'What do you want to see him for?' I asked inelegantly.

Stanley looked at me. He could see that I wasn't going to tell him anything until he vouchsafed some information. One hand went nervously up to smooth back his hair in the old lady-killer gesture.

'Come on, Stanley, spit it out,' I said firmly. Stanley was reminding me of someone I had met years before, who I had nicknamed Egg-Face, and had responded best to bullying. Instinct told me that this would work for Stanley too.

It did. His head started twitching again, but he began to talk. As long as I didn't watch him I wouldn't get motion sickness.

Stanley apparently needed to get in touch with Lex because he wanted to find out if Kate had told Lex anything. I expressed annoyance at the vague way he put this.

'What do you mean, *anything*? What was there to tell?'

It took ten minutes of an insistent mixture of prodding and browbeating him to elicit the information. But it was more than worth it. To my astonishment, Stanley finally confessed that Kate had been planning to set up her own gallery.

'*What*?' I exclaimed.

'She asked me if I'd back her,' he said nervously. 'It was really exciting. A new gallery, starting from scratch . . . my name on it . . . .' This was clearly very important. 'I've asked Carol about adding my name to Bergmann LaTouche, but she said it would be too complicated.' He huffed. 'After all, I am a full partner. It seems only fair.'

But I was staring at him, open-mouthed, and didn't reply. Wheels within wheels within wheels . . . . Now I could make sense of Kate's putting Lex up in her apartment. Why else would she have risked Carol's displeasure, perhaps even her job, just to do a favour for someone she hardly knew and – according to Lex – didn't want to go to bed with? Kate must have been intending to ask him if he wanted to show in her new gallery, and through him to make contacts with more young British artists.

'She'd found a space in West Chelsea, a garage building we could have converted,' Stanley was saying. 'SoHo rents are just crazy now, there's no way we could have afforded to set up there. And you can't find places for delivery trucks to park either, it's too crowded.'

This must have been parroted direct from Kate. I couldn't see Stanley concerning himself with the nuts and bolts of art consignments.

'West Chelsea's the place now for contemporary art,' Stanley was continuing. 'SoHo's getting more and more mainstream. Those are the only dealers that can afford the space. Do you know prices per square foot have gone up thirty per cent in the last two years alone?'

'That's fascinating, Stanley,' I said encouragingly, stifling a yawn. 'So were you putting up all the money for the gallery? That's got to be a pretty hefty whack, even in West Chelsea.'

Stanley shook his head. 'Kate had another backer,' he informed me. 'We were going to meet up this week—' The sun was full in our faces and his forehead was getting sweatier by the minute. 'Before – before . . .'

A group of people passed us, oohing over the silhouette of the Statue of Liberty across the water. In their baseball caps and shapeless, sexless clothes, they were indistinguishable from the down-and-out rummaging furtively in the litter bin just behind them. I focused hard on Stanley, trying to wrench him back on course.

'Did Carol suspect this was going on?' I said.

Anguish and guilt in equal measure stamped his expression.

'I don't think so. I really don't think so,' he said fervently. 'She hasn't said anything to me.'

'Stanley,' I said slowly, 'do you think it's possible that Kate might have trashed Barbara Bilder's exhibition to bring the gallery into bad repute? I mean, if Kate was trying to take clients and artists with her – and she'd certainly have wanted to do that – it might have helped to be able to point to the fact that Bergmann LaTouche was sloppy enough about security to let a show of theirs get vandalised.'

This thought had obviously never popped into Stanley's pea brain before. I was reminded of the joke that goes: 'Why do men have bigger brains than dogs? So they won't hump women's legs at cocktail parties'. Intelligence-wise, Stanley was definitely on the cusp between man and canine. He looked horrified.

'You think *Kate* did *that*?' he said, as shocked as if I'd suggested she'd had sex with donkeys and filmed it for posterity.

'I have no idea. I'm asking you,' I said, firmly but patiently.

'I – well, absolutely not,' Stanley spluttered. 'Kate was a reputable person. She would never have stooped so low.'

'Bet she was planning to copy Bergmann LaTouche's client list and persuade as many artists as possible to come with her to the new gallery,' I rejoined. 'How reputable is that?'

But I had gone too far. Stanley started muttering about my not understanding normal business practices and looking nervously at his watch.

'I take it the new gallery plan's dead in the water now, without Kate,' I said.

Stanley nodded.

'You just want to get on with life at Bergmann LaTouche and pretend this all never happened, right?'

Stanley's nodding became vehement and uncontrolled.

'So do you think someone killed Kate to stop it happening, knowing that you wouldn't go off and do it on your own?'

The agony in Stanley's expression said clearly that he had spent every waking second since hearing the news of Kate's death trying as hard as he could not to envisage this possibility.

'I don't know!' he practically wailed, his voice rising so that even the courting group on the next bench glanced over in our direction for a moment.

'You said you'd tell me where Lex Thompson is,' he begged, leaning over towards me. I crossed my arms so he couldn't clasp one of my hands in a pudgy grip. 'You said you'd tell me.'

Actually, I hadn't, but I didn't feel like pressing technicalities. I wrote Kim's number for him on a piece of paper, which he grasped as eagerly as if it were a certificate absolving him of all responsibility for Kate's murder.

'I wouldn't ring him, though, if I were you,' I advised as Stanley rose. He froze, confused.

'What do you mean?'

'I don't think Kate told him anything,' I said. 'I mean, why would she have started stirring things up till you guys at least had the premises for your new gallery? Kate wasn't a fool, by all accounts, and Lex is about as discreet as a guest on Jerry Springer. I wouldn't go giving him information he doesn't already know. He'll spill it out to everyone and then your goose really will be cooked.'

Stanley stared at me bitterly.

'You mean I told you all that for nothing?' he said, grasping the point faster than I had thought he would.

I shrugged. 'Not for nothing,' I said. 'You satisfied my curiosity.'

I gave him my best smile. It didn't seem to help much. Stanley glared at me, made an impotent flapping gesture with his hands, and finally turned, making off towards Whitehall Street. I relaxed back on the bench, arms spread wide, taking the sun.

CHAPTER TWENTY-ONE

Out on the water the breeze was glorious. I closed my eyes for a second and felt my head tilt back in the force of the wind. Beside me were three Hasidic Jews, father and sons, the latter no more than boys. Their hats were tilted back on their heads like Anne of Green Gables, and they fingered the ringlets at the side of their faces nervously, as if they'd done them round a hot poker and were worried that the wind would blow out the curl. All of us were holding onto the chain for balance, entranced by the Manhattan skyline before us, the skyscrapers glowing golden in the sun, their panes of glass reflecting the blue of the sky. We were drawing closer to the point where the Hudson and the East Rivers met, and that moment seemed intensely concentrated, as if everything were flowing powerfully together and all I had to do was gather the various strings in my hand and knot them up into one single strand of meaning.

Taking the ferry had been an impulse decision. As I walked out of the park, I had been swept up in the waves of people converging on the terminal, flooding through the gates, and I let myself be swept along with them into the ferry. Strictly utilitarian, its plastic seats were dented and beaten down by heavy use. It smelt of disinfectant and McDonald's, that peculiarly identifiable McDonald's smell that was at its height in the Big Mac special sauce: gherkins and mayonnaise and the crisp high-voltage fizzing artificiality of a cocktail of additives.

The front and back docking platforms of the ferry were the only places where you could stand in the open air. Probably I should have said prow and stern, but they seemed too grand for what was only a glorified shuttle bus. I watched the Jersey coast and the high delicate Verrazano Narrows Bridge, seeming to sway in the air currents, as we headed out to Staten Island; and when we reached it I crossed back to what was now the front and settled myself in prime position for the view back to Manhattan.

There was a sudden flurry of movement at my side. Pushing up against me were two more small boys in over-large hats. Underneath them, attached with large unsightly hairpins, they wore, rather touchingly, black crochet snoods, presumably to wedge on the hats. Three little girls shoved up behind them, wearing matching floral dresses. It was practically the Hasidic version of the Von Trapp family. Directly behind them stood the mother. She too wore a heavy frilled dress and round her bald head was wrapped a turban of equally flowered material which looked as if it had been made from curtains – the Von Trapp references were coming thick and fast by now. The poor woman was worn out by childbearing. And having to shave her head when she got married couldn't have helped on the self-esteem front.

The children were everywhere, all around me, swarming like flies. Probably there was another little one in Mama right now, adding new stretch marks to her already interesting collection and bulging out her varicose veins for good measure. I shuddered, losing all interest in anything but escaping from the boat as soon as possible. Children in any quantity give me hives. I was the first person off when we docked, practically sprinting across the road towards the payphones. Some of the small fry had actually touched me with their horrid sticky little hands while trying childishly to clamber over the rails and get themselves flattened between the metal plates of the prow and the dock. Strange how they instinctively tried to cull themselves, as if knowing there were too many of them in the world.

Kim was at home, merciful God. She answered on the second ring.

'Sam!' she said at once. 'Where are you? I've been trying to get hold of you for ages!'

'At the Staten Island ferry terminal,' I said.

'Oh, did you do the crossing? Cool! So why don't you come around right now? I've got shit-loads of stuff to tell you.'

'On my way.'

I hung up and looked around me for a taxi. Sod the subway, I needed some civilised adult company fast. Well, OK, that was an exaggeration. Civilised adult company wouldn't touch me with a bargepole. I needed Kim.

Placido Domingo greeted me as the taxi pulled away, telling me to buckle the seat belt 'because *you* are important'. Yeah, right. Placido sounded dangerously Americanised. What had happened to the European sense of irony?

It was the first time I had been to Kim's flat. Five flights of rickety narrow stairs to reach an apartment the size and shape of a pencil case, a gas ring in one corner and a shower room in the other with the grout from the tiles curling everywhere, like Revenge Of The Killer Worms.

'Isn't it great?' Kim beamed as she let me in. 'It's a good deal, too. I only pay seven hundred bucks a month.'

I remembered Laurence welcoming me to his only slightly less cramped and dilapidated pit with the same self-congratulation. This whole phenomenon baffled me: people here not only lived in shoeboxes stacked on top of each other but considered themselves lucky to get them.

'Want some tea?' she said. 'I'm just boiling the kettle.'

'Great,' I said, perking up at the thought of a restorative English cuppa after my climb.

'OK,' she said, pulling open a cupboard, 'I've got liquorice, orange zinger, raspberry buzz, lemongrass and lime, camomile flower, fennel and nettle—'

'Whoah, whoah.' I held up one hand. 'Can I just have a Cup Of Tea?'

Kim looked uncomfortable.

'You mean *tea* tea? I don't drink it any more. The tannin's really bad for you.'

'Not even one miserable teabag lurking at the back of the cupboard?' I pleaded.

Kim shook her head. 'And anyway,' she confessed, 'I don't have any milk or sugar, so I couldn't make it properly.'

'No *milk*?'

'Well, soy milk. But it wouldn't taste right.'

I put my head in my hands.

'What's *happened* to you, Kim?' I moaned. 'This city has changed you, it's sucked out your brains, you've turned into some dairy-free health nazi—'

'No, Sam, don't be that way! That's not a good way to be!' Kim said instantly.

This was an old, old catchphrase which we'd picked up from some long-lost Seventies TV programme and made our own. It was so immediately, achingly familiar that my head came up again as if it had been pulled on a wire.

'I'm still me!' she said, throwing her arms wide and doing her best cheesy winning smile.

'There's a lot less of you,' I pointed out. It was a hot day, and she was wearing a little top which was a cross between a workout bra and a cut-off T-shirt and revealed most of her honed stomach, perfectly flat apart from the light curve of her ab definition. A pair of dark grey sweatpants hung just above her hipbones, and when she turned to take the whistling kettle off the gas it was obvious that her buns were made of steel. Her skin glowed and her short hair was shiny with health and deep-pack conditioner.

'You have completely changed your body,' I said, flopping down into her inflatable pink plastic armchair.

'Years and years of work and I have to watch it like a hawk,' Kim said. 'Did you want any tea?'

'Yeah, give me that one with the buzz in it. I like the way you've done your place, by the way.'

Sunlight poured in through the single window onto the white-painted floor. The futon sofa with the fake sheepskin rug thrown over it must be the bed by night. Over it hung a canvas of a bright pink cauliflower on a white background. Like the painting of Kim's I had at home, it was from her Inappropriate Colours series. Her collection of Barbies and Sindys was lovingly arranged on a series of silver-painted shelves, and stacked next to the bed was a pile of books on bodybuilding. One of those classic modern-woman contrasts.

'Do you remember those Daisy dolls?' I said reminiscently. 'The Mary Quant ones you were always trying to find?'

'Shit, those are real collectors' items now. There was a great carrying case for the clothes, too. Red with a white and yellow plastic daisy appliquéd on the corner. But you'd never find it in the States. UK distribution only.'

Kim brought the mug of tea over to me.

'Just don't put it down on the armchair,' she warned, 'or it'll burn through and pop.'

'The thing I can't understand here,' I said, settling back in the pink plastic chair and holding my mug well away from its surfaces, 'don't get me wrong, I'm not criticising – but everyone lives in these tiny little studios. Why don't people get together and rent a big apartment to share? There'd be lots more space for the money.'

Kim sat down on the floor, cross-legged, her back to the futon, blowing on her tea to cool it.

'It'd never work,' she said. 'No one rents bigger places. Everyone's too busy to bother about sharing, they just want their own pad to crawl back to at the end of the day. Besides, people are pretty tough here. They go through friends like potato chips. They'd want to be free to discard someone who wasn't useful any more.'

'Seriously?'

'Sure. People are your weapon here, you use them to get ahead. Besides, you can just step out the door here and meet everyone you know. I can bump into people four times a day in the East Village. And then there are all the lounges. I mean, you've got all the social life you can handle right there.'

'That's how you knew Kate and Java?' I said.

'Yup. Well, Kate used to date Leo. That's how I knew her.'

There was a slight frostiness in Kim's voice as she pronounced Kate's name.

'Didn't you like her?' I said, stirring.

'Never any hiding anything from you,' Kim said. 'No, I didn't much. I thought she gave Leo a really hard time. She soured him on women. He was really into her. I always thought that was partly because she worked in a gallery, though . . . OK, maybe I'm kidding myself,' she said ruefully, catching my eye. 'But anyway, when she dumped him he got all bitter and twisted. I told him a while back I wasn't coming to see him any more 'cause he'd just drop all this misogynistic shit on me. When we met him in the park I was livid.'

'I remember.'

'But he seems to have mellowed out,' she admitted. 'Anyway, I was too busy trying to get into Lex's pants to bother with Leo for long.'

'Having fun?'

'Sure.' She grinned at me. 'I sent him off to the hotel today, though. Sort of felt I needed my own space for a while.'

'Very mature.'

'Tell me about it.'

'So what's this news you were all excited about?'

'Shit, yeah. I forgot.' Kim sat up straighter and put her tea mug down. 'You know we went to the cop shop yesterday? Well, Lex did. They kept him there for ages, it was really dull. Anyway, you'll never guess what they told him.'

She paused for dramatic effect. I shook my head dutifully.

'That guy Don who was killed? Apparently he knew who killed Kate, or who trashed the gallery, or both, and he was blackmailing whoever it was.'

'How do they know?'

'He rented a room off this friend of his, and he was late coming up with the rent. So he told this guy he was coming into money, to keep him sweet, and they got drunk together and Don let that much slip.'

'If the police told Lex that, they must be on a big fishing expedition,' I said. 'They don't have much else to go on and they're trying to stir stuff up.' I sipped my tea. 'Knowing Don, I have to say that it makes sense.' I thought back, remembering Don's air of mocking the world, the way he had so easily got under Suzanne's skin. Not to mention my own. Don was the kind of person who liked working out what made others tick, knowing their secrets. 'I can easily see him as a blackmailer. He must have been at the gallery, late in the evening, painting, and heard whoever it was come in to do the graffiti.'

'Shit, everyone's a painter in this town,' Kim said with a sigh.

'Film-maker, designer, writer, painter. All of us wannabes. Then there are the model/actress/whatevers. I call 'em the gaping MAWs.'

'Pretty good,' I said appreciatively.

'Hey, bitch, I can still turn a phrase.'

We grinned at each other.

'But it's really tough,' she went on. 'Packed onto this tiny island with everyone else trying at least as hard as you to make it .... Jesus, sometimes I wonder why I bother.'

'Well, if your stepmother managed it with those industrial-effluent paintings of hers, then you can, too.'

'My stepmother screwed her way up the ladder,' Kim said bitterly. 'You know that story, right? And when she'd got where she wanted she stole my dad away from us and rotted out his brains. It's incredible how one person can change another that much. Most of the time he's not even himself any more. He's like her zombie. God, I hate that bitch.'

She blew out her breath. 'Whoah, time to change the subject! Bitter and twisted alert! Why didn't you drop into the bar last night? I was expecting you.'

'Damn!' A sudden flash of memory hit me. I looked at Kim, deciding that I had to tell her, if no one else, about what I had been doing last night. If Mel did turn nasty – if she already had – I couldn't leave Kim in the dark about the situation; she was the person most likely to get hurt. Apart from Mel herself.

In a few words I sketched it in. Kim took the information more calmly than I had been expecting.

'Shit happens, you know?' she said. 'People send each other crazy. Sounds pretty minor league for this town.'

'Still, keep an eye out, eh? She's not all there at the moment,' I warned.

'OK. Poor thing. Lex hasn't mentioned her to me at all.'

'Well, he wouldn't, would he?' I said reasonably. 'He's not going to start telling you about all his one-night stands in the last few months.'

'No, I meant with her turning up here for the show. He might have warned me there was something. I mean, he wouldn't know she was stalking him, but if she's been making all these phone calls he must guess something's up.'

'You know men,' I said. 'Bury their heads in the sand and then complain when it gets in their eyes.'

'That is so fucking true.'

'So what's up with Lex?' I asked pruriently. 'I mean, is it serious?'

'I don't know,' she said. 'I'm just having fun at the moment. I don't think I'm ready to start seeing someone seriously. I got hurt a while back and I'm still recovering.'

I wondered if she meant Leo.

'And anyway,' she said with a wicked smile, 'I mean, Lex is good in bed, but he's not *that* good. I mean, he's not *stalker* good.'

We started giggling. This was the old Kim, in spades. The more we hung out together, the more she was coming back. I listened happily as she expanded on her theme.

'I mean, you have to be pretty damn hot to get *stalked* after just one night of luuurve. You have to be *all that*. Why, you have to be goddamn—'

'Finger lickin' good!' I chorused with her as we fell about laughing. It was another of our old catchphrases.

Kim was putting a tape into the stereo. The first chords of our favourite songs filled the air: the Pointer Sisters with 'Slow Hand'. And soon our caterwauls were flooding out through the open window into the East Village.

'If I want it ALL NIGHT—' Kim sang, pointing at me.

'He says ALL RIGHT!' I yodelled back.

'It's not a FAST GROOVE but a SLOW MOVE
On MAH MI – YI – YIND . . .'

we whooped together, sounding even more crap than early Bananarama. Probably Kim would put on early Bananarama next – Robert de Niro, talking Italian . . . . There was no way Kim and I could embarrass each other. That was the glory of it. We had already done our worst to each other and survived.

That turned out to be an exaggeration. But some things are impossible to predict. Even for Miss Marple crossed with weedkiller.

CHAPTER TWENTY-TWO

My first New York gallery opening should have been one of the best nights of my life. So of course it was an anticlimax, like seeing the Statue of Liberty. Oh right, tick that one off the list, and is there a bar anywhere round here? The best nights of your life sneak up on you when you're not expecting them and take you completely by surprise, on the day you put on your oldest, tattiest pair of underpants.

I should have known better. I did know better. Openings are always hard work. You get to be the centre of attention, but the payoff is having endless ghastly tedious conversations with people you'll never see again while fixing a bright smile on your face. I try, but after a while I lose it completely, go over to the bad side, get pissed and turn raucous. Which, ironically, is probably what the buyers prefer – some yBa bad behaviour to spice up the purchase. If there is one.

At least in a group show the burden gets spread. And you can always push off and talk to one of your fellow artists, rather than hanging round the bar alone, waiting to have the next buyer or journalist produced to be serviced with a few soundbites. Unfortunately, the camaraderie among the yBa posse had been eroded since our merry encounter in Old Street. Only Lex and Rob had arrived so far. Mel had left a message to say she'd be a little late. Carol, while annoyed by this, in the way of a teacher checking everyone was on time for the school outing, put it down to Mel's having problems deciding what to wear.

'It's easier for men, isn't it?' she said to me and Suzanne. 'It took me twenty years to decide what suited me, what would do for work, and combine the two.'

'Carol's black suits are famous,' Suzanne told me. 'She never wears anything else.' She herself was statuesque in a white knit dress which was totally unfashionable and suited her perfectly. Round her neck was her usual strand of pearls and her white-blonde hair was swept back and up, adding inches to her height.

'They're so easy,' Carol said cheerfully. 'Jil Sander is my heroine. Cost a fortune and worth every penny. I hope Mel's here soon, though,' she said sharply. I was taken aback by this swift change of tone. Carol could switch moods faster than a Morse code operator could send an SOS. 'Maybe I'll just go and ring the hotel to hurry her up.'

'Carol never, ever loses sight of what's happening to business, even when you're having a chat with her,' Suzanne said as the former clicked away. 'She can separate out the two halves of her brain.'

'Like playing games of chess simultaneously,' I suggested. 'No, like playing a game of chess and having a conversation about which colour lipstick suits you best.'

'Exactly. She's pretty amazing. I've learnt a whole lot from her.'

'How come you're not an assistant yourself?' I asked. 'If that's not being nosy. I mean, instead of working on the archives.'

'Two reasons,' Suzanne said. 'One, I get paid a decent wage for what I do. With the assistants it's more love than money. And—' she smiled at me '—love's fine, but I prefer money in the end. Besides, I don't have a great eye. I can't spot trends or know what will sell. It's a real gift and I don't have it. But Kate did.'

Her voice had lowered on the last few words. She looked round assessingly.

'OK,' she said. 'No one within earshot.'

'You're pretty smooth,' I said admiringly.

'I'm the queen of social conversation. So.' She gave me a very serious look. 'When do we do it?'

'Not for a while yet. Wait till the evening's in full swing, even winding down. I've got to do the whole public relations bit. After all, it is my opening.'

She couldn't argue with that.

Over the past few days I had become increasingly convinced that I knew who had killed Kate and Don. It was just an instinct, though: I didn't have a shred of proof. I needed an accomplice to help me get some. And Suzanne had struck me, for many reasons, as being exactly the right person to ask.

She had jumped at the chance as soon as I explained what my idea was.

'I knew it!' she said jubilantly. 'I can't believe you think it's her, too! God, I've been so frustrated not being able to talk to anyone about this.'

'I thought you suspected Lex,' I confessed. 'When you were nasty to him at brunch.'

Suzanne flushed slightly. 'Not really. But I was a little jealous that Kate hadn't told me he was staying with her. She could have trusted me. I guess he got the fallout from that. Still, I never actually thought it was him. I've been trying to dig up dirt on you-know-who.' She looked triumphant. 'Guess what – she's done this kind of thing before.'

'Strangled people?' I said incredulously. 'But surely someone would have picked up on that already?'

Suzanne tutted at my stupidity. 'Trashed paintings. I've been going back through the archives and I found this mention of something . . . so I tracked it down, I've been talking to a couple of people who knew her then, and both of them told me they were sure she'd done it. In confidence, though. I mean, there's no hard evidence.'

'That's what we need to get.'

'Just tell me what to do,' Suzanne said, her voice hardening. 'Anything. I mean that.'

She was a little disappointed when I explained what I had in mind. But it wasn't hard to talk her into it.

'Say about eight-thirty?' I suggested now. 'Sound about right?'

'OK. I'll give you the signal as soon as I've done it.'

Her eyes flickered over my shoulder. Someone was coming up behind me.

'Hey, babe!' Two strong arms enfolded me from behind and so did one of those Nineties ozone-and-fresh-grass scents which Kim always wore nowadays. Ten years ago it was Poison, the Goth perfume of choice, rich and sweet like rotting flowers. For her sixteenth birthday I stole her a nearly-full tester from Boots; it was one of her most prized possessions.

I wrapped my arms around hers and hugged them.

'Suzanne, this is Kim, an old friend of mine.'

'Hi,' Suzanne said, her high white forehead creasing. 'From the Mexican restaurant, right? You're Jon's daughter.'

'You got it. Are they coming, by the way? Him and Barbara? Me and my dad aren't great at communication these days.'

'I think so. They were certainly invited,' Suzanne said.

'That'll be fun.'

'I'm going to help with the drinks table,' Suzanne said. 'Good employee discipline.' She shot me a significant look and undulated away, the white knit dress slithering voluptuously as she moved.

'It looks wonderful, Sam,' Kim said when we were alone, leaning back and looking at the mobile. We were in the main, ground-floor gallery, 'Organism #1' hanging majestically in the centre of the room, dominating it effortlessly. It beat the crap out of Mel's 'Anal Mouth'.

'Don't you think it looks like something out of a Fifties science-fiction film?' I said. 'Pod 9 From Outer Space?'

'Totally! It's brilliant. I'm really proud of you.' She hugged me again. 'I can't believe you're here – showing in Barbara's own gallery – it's so fucking cool, like you've done it for both of us. Great frock, by the way,' she added more prosaically. 'I love this stretch velvet.'

'Betsey Johnson,' I confessed. 'I had a splurge.'

'Well, fuck it, you deserve it,' Kim said encouragingly.

' "Because I'm worth it!" ' I cooed, parodying a recent shampoo ad.

'Oi! Do I get a hug too?'

Lex bounded down the stairs and crossed the room towards us.

'Fuck Sam's monster artwork, I want to show you mine,' he said, taking Kim's hand.

'I thought she was pretty familiar with it already,' I said. 'F'nar, f'nar.'

They both pulled faces at me.

'Hang on, young lovers,' I said, as Lex started to drag her off. 'I have something for you.'

I closed my hand round Kim's free one. In it was a wrap.

'Is this what I think it is?' she said, lowering her voice a little.

'Leo's finest. Go with God. That's yours, by the way. I've got my own.'

'And talking of that, where's your boyfriend?' she said, momentarily forgetting the coke in a rush of sisterly feeling. That's what I call a true friend. 'I thought he was due in today.'

'He had to stay over in England,' I said petulantly. 'He's got a call-back for this important thing he won't tell me about. So you'll have to shag for the both of us. He's promised me a fab holiday if it comes through.'

'What if it doesn't?'

'Oh, he whines for months and I finally dump him out of boredom.'

Lex pulled Kim into the next room as eagerly as a little boy determined to show her his latest mud-pie collection. I felt hot breath on my neck and turned round to see Stanley hovering behind me nervously.

'Hi, Stanley,' I said resignedly.

'Everything I said to you was strictly in confidence,' he said in a burst of authority.

'Of course it was.' I tried to sound reassuring. As usual it was a dismal failure. I thought he was looking a little better tonight, though.

'Had some good news?' I said, more by way of making conversation than anything else. I didn't feel the need to butter Stanley up, having discounted him a long time ago as having any meaningful effect on my possible future career with Bergmann LaTouche.

'Well, yes, I have, actually,' Stanley smirked. 'I have an alibi for the time Don was killed. The evening before he was found. I had a friend to dinner and she ended up staying over.'

The smirk was of Cheshire Cat proportions now.

'It was you who actually found the body, wasn't it?' he said, twisting his pudgy fingers together and looking down at them in a way that on Peter Lorre would have been indefinably menacing but, when performed by Stanley, looked more as if he were frustrated by his inability to curl them over each other properly because of the adipose deposits around each joint. 'Some people might say that was rather strange.'

It was like being attacked by a handful of enervated sea slugs.

'No one'd say that who knew me well,' I said flippantly. 'I have a knack for stumbling across bodies.'

'What are you,' came Laurence's voice, 'Miss Marple's punk granddaughter?'

He and Jon Tallboy had just come up behind us.

'Laurence!' I said reprovingly. 'Think before you speak!'

'Casting aspersions on a maiden lady's name. I stand corrected.' He flourished a Three Musketeers' bow.

'Laurence!' I exclaimed again, taking in his appearance. 'Your suit! You've changed it!'

'I have two,' Laurence said nonchalantly. He took my hand and kissed it, waggling his eyebrows like Groucho Marx. 'One for work, one for state occasions.'

This one was darker than the other, almost charcoal, much better cut and positively clean. Laurence's day-wear version, apart from the dandruff, was worn in some places and greasy in others. Also it was that nasty light cheap-looking grey worn by men who sell kitchen suites on hire purchase.

'Sam! Great to see you again.' Jon Tallboy gave me a fatherly hug. 'And the sculptures are amazing. It really takes me back – when I think about you and Kimmy dressing up in her little room and going out to paint the town red – or black, considering what you were wearing . . . .'

Would I never live this down? But I couldn't help sharing his fond memories. I grinned back at him happily.

'You've come so far, so fast,' he was saying affectionately. I'm so proud of you.'

'Thanks, Jon.' I was very touched. 'Kim should start to paint again, too,' I added enthusiastically. 'She was so good.'

The predictable expression of discomfort flickered across her father's face.

'Mm, yes,' he said.

'She's here, you know. Lex and I invited her.'

'Oh, that's nice!' Jon said, looking as if it were anything but. On a nervous reflex, one of his long legs lifted, hovered and twisted itself behind the other one, the corduroy trouser riding up to reveal a slice of bony ankle. He looked like a confused stork.

'So,' he said lamely, after having cleared his throat. 'You're Miss Marple's granddaughter, or some such?'

Clearly he was unable to talk about Kim for more than thirty seconds at a time. Any residual fondness disappeared in a moment. I found myself despising him thoroughly.

'It's not the first body I've found,' I said coldly.

'Do you catch 'em too?' Laurence asked. 'The guilty parties?'

'Sometimes.'

Everyone thought I was joking, which was fortunate. My annoyance with Jon's total failure as a father had betrayed me into saying more than I should have done. I remembered Don calling him a dumb candyass and I endorsed that sentiment heartily.

A pair of hands closed over Jon's eyes from behind.

'Guess who?' said Kim evilly. Lex, following in her wake, gave me a coke-enhanced grin.

Jon's whole body writhed with embarrassment.

'Kim,' he said feebly.

'Yes, Daddy darling!' Kim had been hitting the toilets with a vengeance. Her eyes gleamed and she was loaded for bear. 'It's your darling daughter!' She looked around her. 'Where's stepmommie dearest? I've been *longing* to see her.'

Kim, in a bright orange Stephen Sprouse tribute minidress with cutouts at the waist, was quite fabulous enough to get away with this brattish behaviour. Stanley, of course, was goggling at the sight of her. Moving fast for a little chubster, in a flash he was by her side, slipping an arm around her waist.

'Jon! You never told me you had such a lovely daughter!' he oozed. 'You must be very, very proud of her.'

He was smiling up at Kim so hard his wide lips looked smeared across his face, his fingers edging themselves far enough around her to touch the bare skin revealed by the cutout. It was mesmerising, in a flesh-crawling kind of way. Lex's eyes were also fixed on the gradual creep of Stanley's podge-laden fingers.

'Jon?' called Barbara from across the room. Her husband spun round as if she had just lassoed him and was pulling on the rope.

'Coming, darling!' he called in an attempt to escape from our happy little group. Too late. Barbara was already heading towards us, Carol by her side.

'Mrs Kaneda's taken both the paintings she was thinking about!' she announced gleefully. 'Carol just told me! Isn't that wonderful news?'

'Oh, sweetie, I'm so pleased!' Jon hugged her.

With every endearment he lavished on Barbara, Kim's face drew in on itself as if she were sucking a lemon. She seemed scarcely aware of Stanley's fingers insinuating themselves onto her bare hipbone.

'They were the ones that were vandalised, weren't they?' Jon was saying.

'That's right,' Carol said. 'I was concerned, because frankly they haven't cleaned up a hundred per cent successfully, but Mrs Kaneda was fine about it. The notoriety, I guess.'

'Isn't that a triumph for you!' Jon said happily. 'Don't let the bastards get you down!'

'I was just congratulating your husband on having such a lovely daughter, Barbara. And she's a painter too, apparently!' Stanley put in with a blissful lack of timing and tact. 'I'd love to see your work,' he continued in oily tones to Kim. It was extraordinary that he could articulate so clearly through the two feet shoved firmly in his mouth. 'I'm sure it's fascinating.'

Kim stared at him blankly. 'Oh, yes,' she said at random, still too upset to make sense of him.

'Yeah, it's great,' Lex said, elbowing his way to Kim's unoccupied side and standing there possessively.

Barbara's round-as-a-doughnut face was as expressionless as the pastry it resembled, her eyes small and hard and icy. She flicked them up and down Kim's scarcely clad body with one razor-sharp cut of her eyelashes and then swivelled towards Jon.

'Darling, I'm terribly thirsty,' she cooed in a melting voice which went about as well with the rest of her manner as ice cream does with processed cheese slices. 'Shall we go and get something to drink?'

'Of course, sweetie,' Jon responded instantly, taking her arm.

'Bye, Kim, nice to see you again,' Barbara had the chutzpah to throw over her shoulder as they turned to go.

Kim might have been turned to stone. Even Stanley, Mr Insensitive, noticed that something was wrong and withdrew his arm from her waist.

'Kim?' Lex put his arm round her shoulders. 'Hey, fuck them, OK? Fuck them all. Come and have a drink.'

I took Kim's hand and we guided her across the room and upstairs, away from Barbara's orbit, with a brief pause at the bar for a bottle and three glasses. When it's your own show they give you a bottle all to yourself. Further perks to be noted.

'Stanley, can I have a word?' I heard Carol saying in savage tones as we left them. Stanley was about to get ripped to shreds. I wished I could be there for the explosion.

Just in front of us on the staircase was Kevin, trotting up the steel treads with a glass in each hand and – I caught a glimpse of his expression as he rounded the bend – hope in his eyes. I made a bet with myself which I duly won as we came into the upstairs gallery and he headed straight for Java, who was circulating with a bottle of her own refilling guests' glasses with a perfect waitressy manner. The idiocy of bringing a drink to someone who was busy providing them didn't strike home till he was actually proffering the glass. Then he went red, laughing nervously. Actually, embarrassment quite suited him; his blond handsomeness was too smug in repose, and the blush softened it. Not enough. Java gave him a kind rebuff, accompanied by an I'm-really-busy look which showed no promise of being improved on by time.

'He's just a bastard, Kim,' Lex was saying comfortingly as we reached a quiet corner of the room. 'Fathers are bastards. Nothing to be done about it. Here, have some bubbly.'

He put a glass in her hand and after a moment she raised it to her lips.

'I hate him,' she said after having drunk half its contents. 'Bastard.'

'There you go!'

'And she's a total bitch. Bitch, bitch, bitch. With those fucking awful ethnic sacks she wears.'

'That's the spirit!' he encouraged.

Kim emptied her glass and looked around for more. I was already unpopping the bottle of fizz.

'It looks brilliant, Sam,' she said once the second glassful had gone down. 'Your mobile. Brilliant. And so does Lex's. You're all brilliant.'

I didn't think this was the time to mention her own paintings; I sensed that it would make her maudlin. Kim needed happy thoughts right now. I cast around for one.

'That's a nice skirt,' Kim said, lightly tipsy. She was staring at a girl who had just come through the door.

'Too skinny,' Lex said, concentrating on the contents rather than the packaging. 'Scary. Nothing under there but bone.'

'I'm thin,' Kim said in a fit of self-doubt.

'You've got lots of lovely muscle,' he said, squeezing her waist at the exact place Stanley had previously been fondling. 'Feel that. Something there to get a grip on.'

The girl in the Chinese silk skirt accepted a refill from Java, and as she turned towards her I caught a glimpse of her face. I had been right when I had thought before that she had looked as if she were being consumed from inside. On fashion shoots, if the clothes don't fit properly, the stylist nips them in at the back with bulldog clips, where it won't show for the camera. Mel's skin was as tightly drawn over the bones as if it had been pulled back and held in much the same way. She was wearing a little vest which should have been snug but instead hung loose over the horizontal slats of her ribcage, baring their vulnerability. Above them her collarbones were as defined as a skeleton's.

I noticed that her eyes lacked the frightening intensity they had had a few nights ago. Instead they seemed dulled, as if there were a film stretched over them. Perhaps the immediate proximity of Lex meant that she couldn't afford to burn at high voltage, or she would explode.

'It's Mel!' said Lex, happily unaware of any undercurrents. 'Oi, Mel!' He waved at her. 'Over here!'

Mel turned. Her gaze scarcely flickered when she saw Lex. She was carefully made up, simply and effectively: mascara on her long dark lashes and lipstick the same flaming shiny red as her silk skirt. The few touches of colour threw the pallor of her lightly powdered face into relief, her eyes black against her skin, her mouth crimson as a geisha's. She looked macabre and beautiful, like a painted death mask.

'What's happened to you, then?' Lex was saying as she hesitated for a long moment and then slowly started towards us. 'You've got really skinny. What's all this? Been dieting?'

He prodded her stomach. Men like Lex, who had an easy familiarity with other people's bodies anyway, became even more physically affectionate once they'd had sex with them. It was a near-brotherly gesture. But poor Mel didn't know that. A wild flush scorched her cheekbones. I thought again of Edgar Allan Poe: his wife Virginia had died of tuberculosis, and if this was how she had looked, I could understand the strange glamour that was attributed to the illness.

'I haven't been very hungry lately,' she said, looking him straight in the eye as if neither Kim nor I existed for her.

'Well, you'd better get something down you. Eating disorders are so last year, as Kim would say.'

He hugged the latter affectionately. Mel went rigid. If I had reached out and pushed her at that moment she would have hit the ground all in one piece, like timber.

'This is Kim, by the way,' Lex said. 'She's an old friend of Sam's. Mel did that body painting you liked,' he added to Kim. 'There's another one in the next room.'

Lex was being unusually socially conscious: making introductions, giving useful information. It must be the coke.

'Shall we go and have a look?' Kim suggested. She was looking uncomfortable and I couldn't blame her.

'You go,' Mel said in a little hard voice. 'I'll wait here with Sam.'

'OK,' Lex said with unabated cheerfulness. Wrapping his arm round Kim's shoulders, he drew her across the shiny parquet and into the next room. Mel watched them go. Her body didn't move, just her eyes, swivelling as if they were made of glass and set into the plastic head of a doll. It wasn't pleasant.

'You didn't tell him, did you?' she said when he was out of sight.

'No, I didn't.'

'Why not?' For the first time this evening she stared directly at me. I wished she hadn't. It felt as if she were trying to drill into my skull and find out what I was thinking.

I shrugged, uncomfortable as I always was when caught doing someone a favour.

'No reason.'

Meeting Mel's eyes was like looking down the twin bores of a shotgun. I cracked at once under the silent interrogation.

'Call it female solidarity, OK? We've all been fools for love in our time.'

'You haven't,' she said with certainty. I felt like I was wriggling on a hook.

'Well, OK, not like that. This. You.' I flapped my hands around in a Stanleyesque way.

'Not about him,' she said as if confirming this to herself.

'Not about anyone! Look, Lex and I never went to bed, Mel. OK?'

I wanted to get this clear, not so much because I cared what she thought as my concern that Hugo might in some way hear a different version of the facts. But her gaze didn't waver. It was with tremendous relief that I saw Rob across the room, talking to Suzanne and some of her Belgian friends. The latter were unmissable: not a man under six foot three, and built to match their height. There must be growth hormone in the mussels. Why Hitler had thought the master race originated in Germany was a mystery. Beside the males of her species, even Suzanne looked small and delicate. It was quite an achievement.

All the men looked as if they had come straight from negotiating some enormous bid, trousering a hefty commission in the process. Their watches were made by Rolex and Patek Philippe, their suits Armani and Hugo Boss. The meanest of them would be more than capable of keeping Suzanne in the style to which she wished to become accustomed. How long she would endure it before dying of boredom was presumably not her principal consideration.

And mine right now was being rescued from a cross-examination by Mel. I waved Rob over as eagerly as if I were standing on the hull of a sinking boat and signalling frantically to a passing ship. Although he seemed taken aback by the warmth of my welcome, as well he might be – I barely knew him, after all – he joined us with alacrity. Staring at Belgian men's nipple areas couldn't be that confidence-building for a guy.

'Hi,' he said. 'Suzanne's been showing me round the gallery. Did you clock all those Rodriguez paintings in the back office? Really wicked.'

'The egg cup ones?'

'Egg boxes,' he corrected me. 'Yeah. Pretty powerful stuff.'

I wrinkled my nose in disbelief at this criminal misuse of words. If those things were powerful, what did you reach for to describe a Rothko? Still, I was too glad to have had my tête-à-tête with Mel broken up to start hammering Rob about the paucity of his vocabulary. I could do that any time.

'Yours look excellent,' he said generously. 'I really like the way you've hung this one.' He gestured to 'Organism #2'. 'Good stuff.'

'Oh, thanks. And your pub video's great,' I lied unctuously in return.

Rob was a video artist. He had made his name with a film of three girls sitting still for twenty minutes; his latest piece had been made by putting a hand-held camera in the middle of the table when he and a group of mates, all lads, went out drinking, and turning it every ten minutes to face a different member of the party. There were six of them, so the video lasted an hour, which was fifty-nine minutes more than I had watched of it. Below the TV screen which was showing the video on continuous loop were pinned Polaroids of each of the participants with their names signed at the bottom. Riveting stuff. It was amazing what boring crap you could get away with if you were clever enough to call yourself an artist. A film-maker with the same project wouldn't have held an audience for any longer than Rob's video had me.

'Yeah, it's all right,' he said modestly. 'Andy was pretty cool. You know, the second-to-last guy, where he says all that about Tarantino.'

Oh *God*. I pasted a smile onto my face. Even Tarantino couldn't do Tarantino any longer without sounding derivative. I mumbled some further polite words of appreciation and hoped devoutly that I would never have to watch the wretched thing all the way through.

Rob was flushed with the wine and the accolades, which meant that his skin, already subject to breakouts, looked as raw and pink as if he had just run a cheese grater over it. He was still in his dark blue denim outfit, but now one of his popcorn-bucket-sized turn-ups was much higher than the other. I had the feeling that this was some kind of hanging-with-the-homeboys, I-just-got-out-of-prison statement.

'God, it's great to be here, isn't it!' he exclaimed, raising his glass. 'New York and all that! Brilliant, eh?' Then he looked round our little group: me distracted, Mel in a voodoo trance. 'What's up with you lot?' he demanded. 'We should all be on top of the world!'

Mel stared at him without saying a word. Her expression was enough to take most of the wind out of his sails.

'Mel! Sam! Rob! You guys can't stand and chat together! You're supposed to be circulating!' Carol cried, bearing down on us.

I couldn't help relishing the irony of this.

'Stay here for now,' she said to me and Rob, speeding Mel away efficiently. I pitied the poor buyer who tried to get a few friendly words out of Catatonia Girl. 'I'll be bringing someone up to talk to you.'

I pulled a God-I-hate-this-social-shit face at Rob. Then I noticed that he was wearing one of those long Leo-type knee chains.

'Tell me something,' I said, succumbing to curiosity. 'Isn't it really difficult to keep that from getting wet when you go to the loo?'

I pointed at the chain. Rob was taken aback. Reaching down, he felt along its length. A strange, distant look flittered across his face and as he straightened up he wiped his hand discreetly along his jeans.

'Nah, no problem,' he said bluffly.

I made a mental note not to touch any part of Rob's body. Nice, for a change, to have a resolution which didn't tax my self-control to the limit.

CHAPTER TWENTY-THREE

An hour or so later I had done most of my polite conversations with potentially important people. One of Mel's paintings had been sold, for quite a lot of money, and the rest of us were trying to be pleasant about it rather than succumbing to jealous fits. It helped that we had all imbibed freely and consequently were able to take setbacks in a broad and generous spirit.

Released by Carol for the time being, I went upstairs, finding the door to the offices wedged open to allow people access to the toilets without having to tap in the entry code every time. How thoughtful. I cast a quick glance round the gallery and saw Suzanne on the far side, heading towards our target. Sensing my eyes on her, she flickered her fingers at me discreetly. I didn't have much time.

As I emerged from the loo, refreshed and ready to face the world once more, I bumped into Laurence.

'What're you doing hanging round outside the toilets?' I said reprovingly.

'Trying to perv a look through the keyhole, of course,' Laurence rejoined. He must have been hitting the sparkling wine heavily; he was much more relaxed than usual.

'Any luck?'

He shook his head disconsolately. 'These toilets are useless. You can't even see anything through the crack in the door.'

'Poor Laurence. Looking good, though,' I commented, noticing anew the sharpness of his suit. 'Did Kate help you buy that?' I asked, in one of those weird lightning strikes of inspiration I get on drugs.

'How did you know that?' he said, eyes goggling behind his glasses.

'No idea at all. But it looked like you had some help from a woman.'

The suit did wonders for Laurence, its impossibly narrow cut turning his skinniness into a virtue.

'Yeah, she did,' he said, fingering the lapel. 'I can't believe you just guessed that. I bullied her to come with me when I needed a new one. To be honest, I was kind of hoping she'd take me out and dress me up like she wanted, you know? Make me over into her fantasy.' Laurence pulled such a self-deprecating face that I couldn't help laughing. 'But there's no way I could ever have been Kate's fantasy. God. Do you ever watch *Friends*?'

'Sometimes.'

'There's this bit where they're all sitting around in Central Perk, talking about the lines you give people, and what they really mean. You know, "I'll call you" means "You will never hear from me again as long as you live", and "I think we should date other people" means "I am already, hahaha!"'

'I didn't see that one.'

'Good, then you won't have heard my punchline. Which is when Chandler says: "You're such a nice guy" means "I'm going to date black-leather-wearing alcoholics and complain about them to you".'

'That's so true,' I said, struck by the profundity of this observation.

'Tell me about it. Story of my life. I was crazy about Kate. And we'll probably never catch whoever killed her. She'll be just another number in the Manhattan yearly homicide statistics. Hell, now I want to get even drunker than I am already.'

It was time for me to get going. Suzanne would be worried. As I emerged from the offices she was talking to Carol, but I could see by the turn of her head that she was looking out for me. Her hand curled into a fist, one finger emerging to point downwards. I slipped downstairs according to plan. Everything was going fine so far. It was on the ground floor that I hit an unexpected hold-up. Rob was starting upstairs just as I came down.

'Sam!' he exclaimed. 'I was coming to look for you! Group photo! Come on!'

Rob was holding out his hand. I managed to wiggle past it

without either touching it or giving offence, I hoped. The photographer was in the far room, and all she wanted was a quick group shot. It was over in five minutes and a series of bright flashing ricochets. I made my escape at once. Still, I had lost some time. I pounded down the staircase, heading for the basement.

It felt empty without Don in the back room, stretched out on his Eaze-E-Boy, an ashtray balanced on his chest. I clicked on the light, blinking even despite the flashes that had so recently stung my eyes. The single bare bulb hanging from the ceiling was surely an affectation of Don's; hard to believe that Carol wouldn't have provided him with a proper light fitting if he'd asked for one. It glared at the centre of the room, leaving the edges weirdly shadowed. The effect was stark and unwelcoming, probably just how Don had wanted it.

The glass wall was ahead of me, the lightbulb reflecting in the panel of the sliding door that opened on the small yard. It dazzled my eyes briefly and I blinked before focusing again, my gaze pulled beyond the room to its mirror image in the dark sheet of glass hanging behind it. My brain was buzzing lightly and pleasantly from the coke. I wondered if that last line had been a mistake.

Like the rest of the gallery, this room had been thoroughly searched by the police in the aftermath of Don's death. But this was the only place that hadn't subsequently been tidied up. They must have pulled out all Don's canvases, which were racked up against the filing cabinets, facing out into the room. These were crude and garish, the canvases fashionably large, their surfaces thickly plastered with paper collages, mainly of body parts, over which were scrawled apposite commands. 'SUCK ME', 'EAT ME', 'SWALLOW ME'. Alice in Wonderland meets Hugh Hefner. Still, at least they were less pretentious than the bad drawings of women's bodies with 'WRITE MY STORY HERE' or 'THE IMAGE IS THE REALITY' scribbled along their hips. One canvas even had a single red arrow with 'READ ME' written over it pointing to a part of its model's body recently immortalised by Mel. God knew what he had expected her back bottom to have to say for itself. As an artist Don had scarcely been a great loss to the world.

I thought I heard a movement behind me and swung round fast, my instincts working overtime. Nothing, just an empty corridor. I let out my breath on a slow exhale and found my eyes tugged irresistibly towards the far wall where the room was reflected in the sliding doors. I had caught a movement there. For a second I thought someone was out in the yard, beyond the glass.

And then I realised that the person was already inside the room: hidden behind the open door, still half in shadow, but moving now, coming for me. The shape was tall and thin and seemed to sway towards me, its hands outstretched, the wire between them held out as if in offering. It walked with a terrifying lack of speed. Like a zombie from a horror film, it held me paralysed long enough for it to reach the light in the centre of the room, showing me its face. And even then I couldn't move.

My heart, which had been pounding away, had stilled itself all at once, blocked. I was reminded, in one of those crazy flashes that were exploding inside my head this evening, of an Agatha Christie novel I had read when I was small, which had always terrified me – the moment at the end when the heroine, who as a child has witnessed a murder without ever realising who the killer was, sees a family friend, a doctor, pulling on a pair of surgical gloves, and suddenly she realises how familiar the gesture is, that it was him she saw all those years ago, about to strangle his own sister . . . and when she screams he starts to come after her, climbing the stairs towards her, the rubber-gloved hands reaching for her neck . . . .

I knew this man. For most of my teenage years he had been my surrogate father figure. Unable to turn round, as if seeing him in the flesh would make it too real, I watched in the glass doors as Jon Tallboy advanced towards me from behind. The wire between his hands was reaching out towards me, his lips drawn back from his teeth in a grimace of concentration.

He didn't speak. Crazily, I was waiting for it. It seemed impossible that he would kill me without saying a word of apology or explanation. More fool me. My hesitation nearly got me strangled. I was frozen, unable to believe that he would actually go through with it in utter silence. He had the wire almost over my head before my survival instincts snapped into action, and then it was nearly too late.

I came to life in a surge of violence, throwing myself back against him as hard as I could, pushing myself clumsily off the filing cabinets to give me extra leverage. It took him completely by surprise. I heard a startled yelp behind me as we crashed back onto the floor together. We twisted as we went down, sent off-balance by the shove of my foot against the filing cabinet, and I landed heavily with my left arm wrenched up behind me from a thrust back I had given him with my elbow. It wasn't the only thing caught between us. One of the toggles of the garrotte was cutting into my shoulder-blades. I felt him desperately scrabbling to work it free. With my right hand I reached round and caught his, connecting on the two middle fingers and wrenching them back, away from the wire, so hard I heard them crack. He cried out, his arm going limp. The garrotte was useless to him now; he needed two good hands to grip it tight enough. But he thought fast. As I tried to roll off him and get to my feet, my weight came off his left arm. Immediately it closed round my neck, his upper arm digging hard into my windpipe, cutting off my breath. For a moment the tweed of his jacket scratched against my throat, and then I couldn't feel the texture any longer, only the terrible insistent pressure.

The canvas in front of me spun and blurred crazily before my eyes, Don's lurid images whirling in a riot of crimson like the blood dancing in my head. Choking, I hammered my right elbow back into Jon's ribcage, trying to reach down to his stomach and wind him too. He writhed, attempting to avoid the worst of the blows, and his contortions only made his arm grip me harder. I was nearly unconscious, gasping for breath. Perversely, I had the sudden lucid thought that if people who self-asphyxiate for pleasure had ever tried getting their kicks this way it would put them off the whole experience for good. Whether or not they put a satsuma in their mouth first.

The idiocy of this idea gave me an added charge of energy. Or maybe it was the thought of dying like a Tory MP or Michael Hutchence. My left arm was still caught behind my back, trapped under the weight of my own body, twisted painfully up as if Jon had got it in a lock. But I still had my right one. Hooking it back, I reached above my head; my fingers closed on his nose and I shoved it back as hard as I could with the palm of my hand. He threw his head from side to side as if he were a horse trying to shake off a fly, not caring how his skull bumped up and down on the floor as long as he dislodged me. The arm which wasn't throttling me pounded against my ribcage, clumsily, because of the broken fingers at the end of it, but enough to catch the air in my lungs on one long spasm which would have been a cough if I hadn't been being strangled. I thought I was going to pass out then and there.

Desperately I forced my arm still further back and my hand sank over his cheekbones and into the pits of his eye sockets, my thumb and middle finger outstretched like twin prongs. He had jammed his eyes shut to protect them, his other arm coming up now to try to beat me off, flailing at my hand like a club. But I was already sinking into the lids, shoving them against the eyeballs, down, down till I could feel the slits parting and the jelly-like texture of the balls yielding with a sudden, horrible ease as my hand slid off the shelf of bone and sank into them hard.

Jon Tallboy screamed, his head snapping back, his whole body arching away from me. The arm cutting into my throat slackened its grip momentarily and I gasped in air, my head swimming. His right arm was levered against my hand, the thumb hooking under it, dragging it away from his eyes. Finally I managed to wrench my left arm free and, closing my mind to the pain as the blood flooded back into it, I used it to drag at the fingers of his good hand, forcing them down, releasing the pressure on my windpipe.

Through the blood roaring in my ears I heard something crashing nearby, metal bouncing off metal, and what sounded like laughter. Crazily I wondered if the lack of oxygen was making me hallucinate. I grabbed at Jon's arm with both hands, gripping it like a vice, desperately dragging it from my throat, still struggling to draw breath. And then there was another crash and I heard voices.

'Ssh! Ssh!'

'Fuck, the light'sh on! Ish there shomeone here?'

'Come here, you dumbass— '

'God, you're shexy—'

'Lex – *aahh* – yeah—'

'You're a hot shexy tart—'

A bang, the scuffling of feet, Kim's giggling, the wrench of clothing. They were very close and they must be drunk as skunks because otherwise they would have noticed us already.

Jon recognised the voices at the same time as I did. Suddenly the arm I was tugging at wrenched free in one movement as his muscles slackened in shock. My lungs cramped and coughed as the pressure on my throat vanished. I was gasping, my body torn by different impulses, sucking in air and trying to roll off him all in one movement. I collapsed in a heap over to one side and managed to get up on my knees, doubled over by spasms of wheezing. When I finally got my head up I was looking at the glass again. In its reflection was a motionless tableau: Lex and Kim had slammed each other up against the door jamb and frozen there, suspended in that instant like the effect I had painstakingly worked to create for 'Organism #2' upstairs. Lex's shirt was open and ripped half-off his back, his hands up and under the bright orange skirt of Kim's dress. They would have looked as sexy as anything out of a Calvin Klein advertisement if their expressions had been the lineaments of unsatisfied desire; the only incongruity was their blank and disbelieving faces.

On the floor behind me Jon Tallboy lay unmoving. One hand was covering his eyes. After what seemed like an age, the other one started across his chest, groping slowly, painfully, two of its fingers sticking up at an impossible angle. Something fell to the ground, dislodged by the broken hand. The wooden toggle of the garrotte made a tiny hollow sound as it hit the concrete, the wire slithering after it like an unwound puppet string.

Kim caught her breath as she realised what it was. But still no one moved. It felt as if I would never stand again if I didn't get up right now. Somehow I dragged myself to my feet, using a filing cabinet for support. I bent over it, drawing in my breath slowly. It hurt every time. My throat must be badly bruised.

'What the fuck—' Lex said finally, sounding as if the words had been dragged out of him. 'This is *unreal* . . . .'

It wasn't the first time I had fought people who were trying to kill me. But always before I had had my anger to spur me on, winding me up to a point of no return. I had hurt people much worse than I had hurt Jon Tallboy. I had even killed someone I had loved. But never had I felt this weird, disbelieving lack of affect. In fighting him off I had been fuelled only by the most basic instincts of simple self-protection, and they had ebbed at once, leaving me without the usual charged-up aftermath to protect me from the knowledge of what had just happened. I felt as vulnerable as if I were missing a layer of skin.

I lifted my head now, no matter how much it hurt, and looked at Kim. She and Lex were detaching themselves from each other, slowly, almost unconsciously, as if sleepwalking. Their eyes never left the scene in front of them. In a trance she pulled down her skirt and stood there, staring at her father's body. The hand which had been fumbling for the garrotte now lay on his chest, the broken fingers protruding straight up as if he were giving some kind of signal. They were already beginning to swell around the breaks.

'Dad,' she said, her voice flat, utterly toneless, as if she were trying out for the first time a word in a language she had never heard before.

Jon Tallboy didn't answer her. He was breathing; I could see the shallow rise and fall of his chest. But apart from that he was motionless, as if the machine that moved him had broken down.

Kim's head turned towards me. She stared at me and I braced myself for the choice she was about to make between me and her father. All my emotion seemed to have drained away; I felt as empty as an upturned bucket. I tightened my grip on the filing cabinet. Against it was propped one of Don's canvases, the one that had been whirling in front of me as Jon's arm cut off the blood flow to my head. Slowly I leant down a little way and looked more closely at the big red arrow pointing to the woman's backside. Through the bright scarlet paint I could see that it was made of lined paper. And it had 'READ ME' written on it in black marker. I caught a fingernail underneath it and peeled it off. It came away all in one piece, and underneath there was writing on it. As I straightened up, Kim finally spoke.

'Your *neck*,' she said, sounding stunned. 'Your poor *neck* – oh, *Sam* . . . .'

And in a rush she was by my side, her arms around me, holding me up. I wrapped my own around her with more gratitude than I had ever imagined I could feel. Kim tightened her grip, taking my weight easily, her strong body a prop for me to lean on. I let go completely. One of Kim's hands closed over the back of my head, easing it down, resting it against her. My eyes closed and I realised that I was crying into her shoulder. Each sob caught at my bruised throat with a spasm of pain. But I couldn't stop, not for a long time, not until other people came running down the stairs and piled into the room. Not until Jon Tallboy, like a reanimated corpse, finally stirred, pulling himself up to a sitting position to slump, arms wrapped round his head, blood from his eye sockets trickling down his cheeks. Refusing to answer questions, he was stubbornly shutting out the world.

CHAPTER TWENTY-FOUR

'The so-called white man has stolen our heritage! It says so right here, people! Let me tell you how Esau, for a piece of meat—'

'FAGGOTS are pro-FANE! FAGGOTS are pro-FANE!'

The first man broke off and glared at the second. They were supposed to be a team, but they had no co-ordination. Faggot Guy seemed incapable of letting Piece of Meat Guy get on with his Bible reading. Maybe he was jealous of his colleague's outfit, a red silk military jacket, tied at the waist with a wide gold fringed lamé belt, worn over baggy blue silk trousers. On his head was a little red toque set at a fetching angle. I might have thought that Faggot Guy's interruption had been meant to make some kind of point about the campness of Piece of Meat Guy's outfit if Faggot Guy himself hadn't been dressed like an expensive biker queen, head-to-toe gold-studded black leather with a big gold medallion at his forehead like a Village People wannabe. Took one to know one.

Piece of Meat Guy adjusted his toque and started again.

'Esau, for a piece of meat—'

'LESBIANS are pro-FANE!' Faggot Guy cut in, his voice cracked with belief. 'LESBIANS are pro-FANE!'

'Aren't these Farrakhan guys the business?' Kim said to me *sotto voce*.

'Do they always talk across each other?' I asked. 'And if he's going to say faggots, why doesn't he say dykes? I mean, at least it would be logically consistent.'

A guy standing next to us hushed me disapprovingly. There was only a handful of spectators gathered on this street corner in the middle of Times Square, and most of them were unashamed kitsch-collectors like ourselves. It was just my luck to be next to the one person who was taking this seriously.

'Brothers! Sisters!' Piece of Meat Guy shouted through Faggot Guy, who was beginning to sound like a broken record. 'Listen up, now! ESAU, FOR A PIECE OF MEAT—'

Just at that moment a police car shot past, its siren going full blast, deafening everyone temporarily. We were clearly destined never to hear about Esau and what I remembered as having been a mess of pottage. Not that I fancied arguing the toss with Piece of Meat Guy, who was having a bad enough day of it already.

I stared behind him at the giant video screens at the far end of Times Square, stacked one on top of each other up the side of a building. The displays were ever-changing, an endless, unstoppable parade of advertising, the quality sharp as crystal. On the top perched an enormous cutout of a coffee cup with a constant head of steam, swirling up and away into the clouded sky with infectious enthusiasm. A perfect *Blade Runner* moment, from the luridly dressed crazies in front of us to the latest in technological displays above our heads. To my left three bands of mandarin-orange tickertape wrapped another endless stream of figures round the top corner of another building. Everything in New York moved fast and dragged you right along with it, hurrying you up so that you didn't have time to look down at your feet and see how dirty the pavements were, how poor and ragged some of the people, how scummy this area still was despite the famous musicals that were playing all down the street.

Kim and I started up Broadway, neither of us speaking much. The streets were crowded and noisy and lurid and what we had to say to each other was too private to be shouted. It was hard enough just to walk side-by-side without people elbowing one of us out of the way. As Broadway widened still further into Columbus Circle my sense of smell alone would have told me we had reached Central Park by the rich ripe scent of horse sweat and droppings. There were three carriages pulled up on the further side of the roundabout, each with a docile horse nibbling at straw, their heads ducked almost sheepishly, as if they were only snacking out of boredom because business was slow. One carriage was straight out of a fairy tale, painted white and lined in sky blue, all its trimmings picked out in the same colour. Cinderella meets My Little Pony. Even the two plastic buckets of horse feed slung beneath it were the same sky blue. A couple of pigeons fluttered down and perched on the rims of the buckets, pecking at the feed.

'I thought we could walk up to the Met,' Kim suggested as we crossed into the park. She set our path up the wide avenue. 'Have you been there yet?'

'No.'

'Good.'

Conversation tailed off. Neither of us wanted to be the first one to mention what had happened the night before last.

Jon Tallboy was in custody, having confessed to the murders of Kate and Don. I had spent most of the intervening time being drugged with super-strong painkillers and having ice packs pressed to my throat to bring down the bruising, which was spectacular. I was wearing a polo neck and would be for some while to come. At least it gave me an excuse to go shopping. I had in mind some New York-style, black high-neck little sweaters which would go in a very Emma Peel way with my leather trousers. I'd just have to make sure no one in the changing rooms saw my neck, or they'd start screaming.

I fingered it absently and winced. It felt raw. Kim noticed my gesture.

'How's the neck?' she said.

'Oh, OK. I'll just have some spectacular bruising for a while. I thought I might say I've had a sex transplant and this is from reconstructive surgery on my Adam's apple.'

She smiled, but her heart wasn't in it.

'I still can't believe it,' she said. 'I keep playing over the moment when I realised what was happening, just to convince myself it's true.' She looked at me. 'He's going to say Barbara knew nothing about the murders. Take all the blame on himself.'

My jaw dropped, which hurt my throat considerably.

'You're joking. The only reason I got myself in that mess was that we laid a trap for Barbara! How does he explain that?'

'Yeah, do you want to tell me about that, by the way?'

Kim and I hadn't had a chance to talk about this till now.

'Oh.' I shrugged. 'I was pretty sure it was Barbara. The more I thought about it, the more the financial advantage to her of the whole scandal seemed the strongest motive going. I did wonder about Carol, because of Kate's plans to leave the gallery and take so many clients with her. But the way Kate's death was tied in to the graffiti kept blocking me. I couldn't see Carol ever doing that to her own gallery. And all these little things kept confirming the Barbara theory. She was the one who rang the cops about the graffiti so it would be public and linked to Kate's death. Her sales hadn't been so good before and now they were flourishing. I wasn't sure whether she could actually have expected that result, though, till I spoke to Suzanne. She'd found out that twenty years ago, when Barbara had just started the affair with that gallery owner, the one who made her career, there was a break-in at her studio and her paintings were slashed. It looked as if it was the guy's wife who'd done it. So it was completely hushed up, but he restored and sold all the slashed paintings for her – even put the prices up and let the buyers guess as to whether the damage had been done deliberately. It was a sales ploy.'

'God, that's clever. Especially the keeping it quiet.'

'He had to. He thought it was his wife.'

'So that made you guys sure it had been Barbara.'

'Pretty much. But there wasn't any proof. So we got the idea of setting her up. Suzanne told Barbara that she'd heard from me about Kate's plan to start a new gallery with Stanley. The story was that before Kate was killed, she told me who the third investor was – trying to persuade me to come with her – and I was wondering whether to tell the police about it. I was only guessing that Barbara was the mystery investor, but it was worth a try. There was nothing to lose. Suzanne said that she could tell it hit home with Barbara, though she hid it well. So she went on to the next bit: she said I might have been exaggerating, because I'd had a lot to drink, and she'd suggested I go to have a lie-down in Don's old room.'

'Not a totally improbable story,' Kim commented.

'Always invent a lie that's as close to the truth as possible. And Suzanne did a great job. Barbara fell for it. We were hoping she would follow me down to the basement and try to strangle me. Suzanne was keeping an eye on her, without seeming to, and she would have come after Barbara if she started downstairs, as a witness. Of course Barbara talked to Jon, but Suzanne didn't make the connection. We were so sure it was Barbara . . . I was delayed because of that photograph, and by the time I got downstairs he was waiting for me.'

I looked at his daughter. 'Even when I saw him I couldn't believe it. We all underestimated Jon.'

'She planned it all,' Kim said. 'I got that much out of him last night. We went out in the yard and talked. Carol sent Kevin down as well, to keep an eye on him till the cops arrived, but I made him and Lex wait inside so they couldn't hear.' She shot a glance at me. 'I thought it might be my last chance to talk to him alone for God knows how long . . . . Anyway, he said Barbara's sales were falling badly. Then she came up with the idea of trashing her show to get publicity – only they realised they'd need the keys and the alarm code to the gallery. And Barbara knew that Kate wasn't happy at Bergmann LaTouche, so she sounded her out. Kate told her about her plans to set up a new gallery and asked Barbara to come with her.'

'She was asking everyone,' I commented drily. 'If Barbara wasn't selling she wouldn't have been much of an asset.'

'Barbara knows lots of people,' Kim pointed out. 'She could have been very useful.'

I nodded. We were passing the lake now, its surface like an old mirror which, silvered with the years, blurs and softens everything it reflects. Only the water was the misty green of oxidised copper, the trees hanging on its surface a brighter green, their edges clouding into each other like melting wax.

'So they strung Kate along,' I said.

'Barbara told her she'd come in with her as a partner.'

'But she didn't have that kind of money.'

'Barbara said she'd made some good investments and Kate believed her because she wanted to. Dad said it all spun out of control really fast. One minute he and Barbara were talking about vandalising the show and the next Kate was on board and Barbara was spinning her all these lies about investing in her gallery to get her to agree to hand over the keys and tell them the alarm code.'

I nodded. 'And then it got even more complicated, because Don was working late and saw her trash her own paintings.'

'Dad said he couldn't have brought himself to do it, poor sap. I bet she got a twisted kick out of it, too.'

'Did you read Don's note?'

Kim nodded. The red arrow I had peeled off Don's painting had turned out to be his insurance note. He had written it while waiting for Jon Tallboy to arrive with the blackmail money, then painted the back red and stuck it to his latest work-in-progress. That was typical Don: such an oblique way to do it, as if he were mocking himself for even taking that kind of precaution. The police hadn't found it, though they'd searched the whole place thoroughly: but they would never have started picking bits off the paintings. It might have stayed there for ever if I hadn't remembered last night that it was the same painting that I had seen just before I had found his body, the only one that had been turned around to face the room . . . .

The note wasn't enough to convict Barbara on its own. It said that Don had seen her trash her own paintings, then heard her ring Jon on her mobile to tell him she was coming home. 'I haven't just done the paintings,' she had said gleefully. 'I've made sure that little bloodsucker won't be able to tell anyone about our deal.' Hearing that, Don had insisted that it was Jon who came with the money.

'It was stupid of me,' I admitted. 'I knew Don could only have been killed by someone he didn't take seriously. Carol or Laurence, or Suzanne, or even Java – he knew most of them didn't like him, or he respected their intelligence, so he'd have been on his guard. And that ruled out Barbara, too. You just have to look at her to know she's capable of murder. But if Jon went in there, with a bottle of bourbon shaking in his hand because he was so scared – that part he wouldn't even need to act – and offered Don some . . . well, Don would have thought that Jon was just Barbara's errand boy, and despised him. I heard him call Jon a dumb candyass. He probably knocked back half the bourbon in one shot just to show Jon how real men drink. That was Don all over.'

'Thank God for that note,' Kim said heavily. 'Dad was trying to say he killed Kate, too. Hopefully he won't get away with it. Barbara must always have planned to kill her, to keep her mouth shut. She'd have worried that Kate would talk when she realised the promise to invest in the new gallery was a crock of shit.'

'Difficult, without implicating herself.'

'Not if she managed to get the new gallery going anyway. And she could just spread the rumour quietly. Everyone would love the story of Barbara's being that desperate.'

She took a deep breath. 'We're talking about this so rationally . . . but even if my father didn't kill Kate, there's still Don. And he tried to kill you too. *You*. I mean, you're practically my adopted sister. I still don't believe it. You know what?' Her voice hardened. 'All that fuss about Kate's tattoo? Barbara knew about it. Dad let that slip. Kate showed Barbara when she'd had it done. That's why Barbara picked Strawberry Fields. Maximise the news value.'

Her face was white and tense. There was nothing I could do. I sensed that she didn't want a hug or words of support. The last thing she needed was the kind of softness that would break her down into tears.

'That bitch,' she said viciously. 'Dad takes the rap and she could still get off scot-free, if she plea-bargains and testifies against him. Or just denies killing Kate and says Don made that part up. There's no hard evidence. Plus,' she added furiously, 'she's raking in loads of publicity. She's made for life.'

Call me superficial, but this rankled with me, too. I didn't notice the *New York Times* ringing me up and begging for an interview about my life and times. Who cared about some obscure British artist whose show had just opened? The entire media population of Manhattan was probably doorstepping Barbara right now. And she'd be pretending she loathed the attention while quietly planning how to maximise its effects.

'Thurber and Frank aren't stupid, you know,' I said in an effort to be consolatory.

'Who?'

'Those two detectives. They're pretty sharp. No way they think Jon did it all on his own. They'll nail her if they can.'

'Really?' Kim brightened.

'Jon still has to explain why Barbara went straight to him and told him what Suzanne had said, about me knowing who the third investor in Kate's gallery was. If Barbara didn't know anything about it, why would she bother to tell him?'

Kim looked more cheerful. But it was a sop I was throwing her. If Jon were determined to confess to both killings, even the most conscientious cops would settle for that. Nobody would want to complicate things when they had nice neat guilty pleas to both murders.

I thought of Jon Tallboy as I had seen him being taken away by the cops; a broken man in every sense.

'Cracked two fingers and nearly put one of his eyes out,' Thurber had said to me with a hint of approval in her flat Dalek voice. 'Nice going.'

'Brits must be tougher than I thought,' Frank chimed in.

'She's trying to say something,' Thurber observed in exactly the same way that she might have used to comment on an animal in a zoo.

I coughed and gestured for her to come closer.

'She says will she have to testify,' Laurence said, tendering me another ice pack.

Thurber flipped her hand.

'The guy's spilling his guts as we speak,' she said. 'One of those confession nuts. He Catholic?'

'Don't make her talk!' Laurence said crossly. 'Can't you see it's hurting her?'

'Take a lot more than that to hurt her. Right?' Thurber gave me a one-tough-woman-to-another twist of her lips which on another person would have been a smile. 'But yeah, unless he gets a fancy lawyer first who shuts him up, we're looking at a guilty plea. Which lets you off the hook.'

'We gotta go,' Frank said. 'Paperwork calls. Enjoy the rest of your stay in New York, Ms Jones.'

Thurber huffed out her breath. 'You crack me up,' she said to him as they moved away. 'Are you serious? Enjoy the rest of your stay in New York?'

'Courtesy is my watchword,' Frank said blandly.

'Yeah, right. And I'm Doris Day.'

★ ★ ★

We were nearly there. The grey bulk of the Metropolitan Museum loomed up at us through the trees. As we turned onto Fifth Avenue a blader shot towards me along the pavement, an Alsatian racing along beside her, its lead in her hand. At the last minute, just as it looked as if the lead was going to catch my knees and send me sprawling, she let it go and she and the dog spun off on either side of me in a neatly executed splinter movement.

'Bet she does that on purpose to freak people out,' I muttered.

It didn't break the ice. Kim hadn't said a word for the last ten minutes. A pall of gloom wrapped around her, so thick I could almost see its dark shadow. The silence fell again and hung around us as we climbed the sweep of stairs leading up to the entrance of the Met. Kim led me through the great entrance hall and down a wide corridor. We skirted a huge cafeteria that looked as if it belonged at Bloomingdale's, with its taupe walls and tasteful peach lighting to flatter ladies who lunched, and turned into a series of richly appointed galleries.

But Kim shepherded me into a lift which shot us up to the fifth floor, and as the doors opened daylight flooded in, bright and unmistakable. We were on the roof. Through the glass lobby I saw a pergola, green leaves climbing up the stone wall, shining in the sunlight like a magic garden. Out on the roof a breeze blew gently, stirring the leaves. A huge bronze statue in front of us caught the sun and shimmered in its heat as if its surface were still molten. Behind it, running all around the edge of the balcony wall, was a thick box hedge, outlined by a silver rail.

'It's the Sculpture Garden,' Kim informed me curtly as we pushed open the glass door and stepped out onto the roof. 'I come here when I'm feeling down.'

In the centre of the space was a Rodin which I recognised at once: three superbly muscled naked men, bending over, their hands clasped at knee level. They were supposed to look mournful – these were the Three Shades from Dante's *Inferno* – but no ghosts were ever that well built. Their genitals, thick and juicy, nestled in the crooks of their groins, as if they were so heavy they needed to rest, supported, for a brief moment. And their heads clustered together, touching affectionately, like their hands. It looked like they were making a pact: we three against the world.

Kim had moved past me. I watched her walk out onto the extension, whose floor was made of boards, reaching out to the Upper East Side like the prow of a liner. At its tip was a statue of a standing woman, poised on tiptoe, one hand to her face, the gleaming bronze set into relief by the skyscrapers behind us. Kim passed it and disappeared round the hedge. I went round the statue and leaned on the wall, looking at the New York skyline, as spectacular a view as the sculptures themselves. The stacked and stepped blocks and towers flowed into the distance, their pale greys and browns dazzled almost white by the sunlight, their windows flashing back the rays like signalling mirrors. And if I narrowed my eyes and stood back, the green flat-cut surface of the box hedge merged into the tree-tops of Central Park, which stretched away, thick and still and close-packed as a moss garden high above the city.

Hugo would have loved it up here. Anything to be on top of the world. If the devil had tempted him in a high place he'd have sold his soul straight away for dominion over what he saw and counted it a fair bargain. And judging by his news, he'd already made a decent start.

'It's a new drama series, BBC1, prime time,' he'd said gleefully when he rang me yesterday. 'And I, my dear, am the Leading Man. Stardom beckons. The cover of the *Radio Times* is calling me. And I probably have to go on a diet. I thought I looked rather fat on screen.'

'Hugo, you don't need to go on a bloody diet,' I said as testily as I could with the soreness of my throat.

He sighed gustily. 'Wait till you see the tape.'

'I don't care about the tape. I'm not having sex with a stick insect.'

'It would be technically difficult,' Hugo agreed. 'But you're so resourceful I'm sure you could if you put your mind to it.'

'Oh, I've got some more blonde jokes for you.'

'Just one. Then I'm going. You sound like Marlene Dietrich with a bad cold and I'm feeling guilty at torturing you like this.'

'OK. What do you do if a blonde throws a pin at you? Run like hell – she's got a grenade in her mouth!'

I couldn't help laughing, but my throat was so painful that I had to stop halfway through, croaking. Hugo swore at me for hurting myself and hung up to stop me talking further. It was his way of showing that he cared. I couldn't help missing him.

'Great asses.'

'Where?' I looked round at once.

Kim had rejoined me. She propped her back to the guard rail so she was facing onto the terrace and the Rodin sculpture. I turned round too, setting my shoulder to hers.

'Mm,' I said appreciatively, not having looked at the statues from this perspective. 'Don't they remind you of American footballers in a huddle? You know, about to throw their arms overhead, yelling something rude.'

'That'd be the only thing that'd get me watching American football,' Kim said. 'If they all played naked.'

'And looked like that.'

'Mm . . . . Do you want a drink?' I suggested. 'There's a bar over there.'

'Shit, Sam, put you down in the middle of the Gobi desert and you'd know where the nearest bar was in five minutes.'

'We all have our special skills,' I said modestly. 'I don't like to boast about mine.'

The bar was tucked into an L made by the main building, out of the wind. Still, the guy behind it was snugly clad in a watchcap and thick leather jacket. I bought a couple of glasses of red wine and we sat down on a wooden bench in the pergola. An unwieldy steel sculpture to our left, its surface scratched to resemble amateurish brushstrokes, flickered in the sunlight like a cheap hologram postcard. It had been cruel to put it next to the Rodin. I wondered if the curator had a twisted sense of humour.

'To us.' I handed Kim her plastic cup of wine and we touched them together in a toast.

'To us,' she echoed.

She didn't say a word about being a teetotaller, just took a long drink of the wine. It tasted like red ink and probably stained our tongues crimson. With my bruised throat, it hurt to swallow, but I forced myself anyway. Our silence was no longer loaded; the grief for her father was draining out of Kim as the wine went down. By the time we had finished it she was almost mellow.

'Guess what?' she said. 'Mel's boyfriend turned up last night, totally unexpectedly. Apparently he sensed something was wrong and came over from London to surprise her.'

'Takes the pressure off you and Lex.'

'Rob said he wants to try to look after her, get her to go to a shrink.'

'And an eating disorders clinic,' I added. 'What does she say?'

'Oh, she won't even see him.'

'Surprise me.'

'At least if they convince her to go, she can afford it now,' Kim said. 'Did you hear she sold three paintings already?'

'Three? I only heard about one! Bitch!'

'Maybe you should start making giant sculptures of your body parts.'

'Hey, if it sells . . .'

'Any sales on the horizon?'

'Not a one. I think Carol's going off me already.'

Kim squeezed my hand.

'Let's have another glass of wine,' she proposed by way of consolation. Kim was back, alcohol abuse and all. I hadn't envisaged it happening this way, though. Drinking to forget your father was a murderer wasn't quite the joyful return to the booze I'd hoped for. Still, compromise is an essential part of life.

I found myself staring at the Rodin men as Kim went to the bar.

'Not for us,' she said as she returned, nodding at them.

'Much too handsome to be straight,' I agreed. 'And look at the way they're holding hands. Ah well. Hey, you got a bottle! Good woman.'

'I thought we could stay up here until we're off our faces,' she proposed.

'How long till the museum closes?'

'Couple of hours.'

'Oh, *well*,' I said, relaxing back into the bench. 'No need to hurry, then.'

She filled two glasses and handed one to me.

'To us.'

'Against the world.'

Plastic knocked against plastic. Across the roof the bartender in the watchcap winked at us.

'I think he likes you.'

'Nah, he's looking at you.'

'Let's ask him which one of us he fancies.'

'Tell you what,' I suggested. 'Let's both have him.'

'Are you joking? He wouldn't last ten minutes.'

We dissolved into giggles. The bartender, mercifully unable to hear us, winked again, which made us laugh even harder. Then Kim started crying, and I hugged her for a while, and she dried her tears while I refilled our glasses.

'I've got a great idea!' Kim said as we finished that. 'Why don't we go get a tattoo each?'

'A tattoo?'

'In memory of Kate! Isn't that a great idea?' She was slurring her words a little, but she was holding up remarkably well for someone who hadn't had a drink in God knew how long. That was my Kim. 'I know someone in the East Village with this tattoo parlour – I've always meant to get one and it would be so nice to do it together . . . .'

'Now that really would be a nice present from New York for Hugo,' I said thoughtfully, my brain racing with possibilities.

So that was what we did. It was just one of those afternoons.